Tag Day

By

Jay W. Murphy

Copyright © 2013 Five Stars Publishing, LLC

Library of Congress Cataloging-in-Publication Data is available

ISBN: 978-0-9895076-1-5

Prologue:

It waits. Patient, yet persistent, lurking in the shadows camouflaged to perfection. Today, no human suspects the peril about to be wrought upon the unsuspecting child blissfully at play. The timing has been planned to perfection. Unwearied and incredibly deliberate, a sloth looks swift by comparison. Basking in delight, its target's parents were unaware that destiny had chosen their precious bundle of joy at birth. Six long years of growing, yearning to fulfill an ominous need, the assault is close at hand. The incredibly unstoppable and insatiable force will not be denied. The drive toward this moment has been marinating for years in the deep chasms of the unknown. The victim, oblivious to any foreboding, feels nothing...yet. He's been uniquely created for this menacing and sinister villain's sole purpose. The prey has been chosen and the deliberate process is only moments away from attack. The enemy of the child's chemical state will forever be altered.

Enjoy the rest of the adventure...
Found in Flame and Moonlight

ACKNOWLEDGMENTS

A team of people were involved in the making of *Three Christmases* and are mentioned below; however, any errors within the published novel, whether existing there intentionally or not, are ours alone.

Enormous appreciation goes to Kristi at Picky Editor, editor extraordinaire.

Huge thanks to Heather and Misty, our close friends and cheerleaders. Special acknowledgement and gratitude goes to Misty for bringing to light the humorous naughty in pointed punctuation.

To our social media friends, fans, supporters, readers, reviewers, and bloggers, both those we've interacted with thus far and those we look forward to meeting—we are immensely grateful for all you do. Your unending enthusiasm for reading our stories fuels our excitement to write them.

Stone, what in the world could I say here to cover the depth of my gratitude to you? Not enough. But I will say that I'm so glad we took a wild idea over pizza out one night and turned it into a labor of love and laughter. I'd shout out some of the hilarious moments to make you laugh, but I have a feeling you're already thinking about them...and smiling.

Kat...Wait, what? Is this like wedding vows? You know what you mean to me. The journey. The love. The laughter. *Squirrel!*

Chapter 1

"You can't get me unless I let you! I won't be *it* unless I wanna be *it,*" said a hustling six-year old Tony.

He was playing tag with about a dozen friends on his front lawn. The game was being played at a frenzied pace. John knew better than to try and tag Tony as it was just a foregone conclusion he'd fail. He made a half-hearted attempt and then moved on to someone he had a real chance to tag.

Tony had that little extra something allowing him quickness and speed, as well as a kind of rudimentary sixth-sense regarding his environment. If someone was about to tag him, even while he wasn't looking, he'd somehow seem to know to make the appropriate adjustment.

Knowing history was in the process of repeating itself John quickly veered away from Tony and tagged Pat on the elbow. "Pat's it!" John announced to everyone.

Pat was *it* and Tony, as well as almost everyone else, knew they could take it easy because Pat was one of the slowest kids in the neighborhood. They didn't call him Pat Mertle the Turtle for nothing. Pat wouldn't even think about going after Tony. At a safe distance Tony stood, still smiling at the efforts of Pat and the friendly taunts of the others.

Suddenly, without notice, everything went dark for Tony. It was just for a second and then he was right back watching his friends. Immediately, it happened again. Then it repeated

1

again in rapid succession. It came in waves. The sensation was that of a camera shutter out of control. To Tony, each hard slam of his eyes had the volume of a massive metal door banging shut.

Tony certainly didn't know what was going on as he stood silently absorbing this shutter shock to his eyes. It was as if a sudden urge had come upon him forcing Tony to do this. Something had built up in him and then the rapid eye blinking just...happened. Strangely enough it seemed to occur in sets of three hard blinks and a pause. The urge would build quickly again and BLINK, BLINK, BLINK. He couldn't stop it.

Then something extraordinary occurred that had never happened in the history of playing neighborhood tag. Pat tagged Tony!

"You're *it* and no tag backs till you count to five!" said Pat, shocked yet proud of his accomplishment as he rumbled away from Tony.

Brushing aside this unnatural and unwanted episode of eye blinking, the fog lifted and the surprise of him being tagged by "The Turtle" started to wear off. Being a six-year old he really wasn't sure what was stranger, the eye blinking episode or being tagged by Pat. He'd been double tagged, but he certainly didn't know to what degree. One of them would change the course of his life. Without showing the slightest hint of anger he very slowly and loudly counted to five as everyone scattered to avoid becoming the victim of Tony's tag.

Because of his speed even the older kids knew he could catch any of them at any time. Tony scanned the faces from left to right to locate his target. He of course went directly after Pat to retaliate for what he took to be a personal injustice. To Tony it just wasn't fair that he was tagged while experiencing something he couldn't explain. Not only that, but he was embarrassed he was tagged by "The Turtle."

Tony shouted, "Pat! Pat's it!"

Chapter 2

Jacquelyn and Tony James sat leisurely swaying in their glider rocker on the backyard patio of their suburban Portland, Oregon home. Everyone who participated in Tony's 31ˢᵗ birthday celebration seemed to have a very nice time. It left both of them satisfied, but completely worn out.

Surrounded by the tranquility of the warm summer evening, they took solace knowing their two precious children were sleeping safely in their cozy beds. This is their special time they can share with each other when all of life's distractions evaporate.

He put his right arm around her kissed the top of her head and wondered, *How'd I get so lucky?*

Well into their conversation the stunning brunette lifted her head from his shoulder then calmly asked the most direct and simple of questions. It had been on her mind for some time now. She just never asked as she knew it could bring unwanted emotional discomfort to him. But, the mood seemed right with the calming touch of a light whispering breeze washing over them. The bright twinkling stars above seemed to say, "Go ahead, we're aligned just right for you."

Jacquelyn finally asked, "So, when did you first realize it?"

"Realize what?"

"You know very well what I'm talking about Tony."

Tony did indeed know exactly what his beautiful wife was talking about. His attentive demeanor slowly changed from complete focused engagement to an artificial gaze upon the brightly lit sky.

Well, I guess tonight's the night, he thought, dreading the idea.

He had turned his head upwards conspiring to hide his eyes as they changed to a slightly glassy-eyed, distant look. It was his hope it appeared to her he was slowly trying to bring back a memory while star gazing. His brain began moving at the speed of light. This wasn't something he had really thought much about. Thought about? No, avoided would be a better way of putting it. Anytime he came close to wandering into this crevasse he quickly occupied his mind with something else. Even after all these years he felt even less ready to reveal the answer. He knew the origins of his unique skill. Contemplating the exact wording of her question made his logical mind rush to find an appropriate answer. *When* did he realize it?

This wasn't an area Tony wanted to excavate. Some of the emotional scars were hard to look at. However, Jacquelyn not only had seen him in action, she actually requested and received his expertise on numerous occasions. As he continued to gaze up at the stars Tony knew he'd provide her an answer. It was how he'd answer that puzzled him. Tony searched the stars looking for help.

Their relationship was already filled with a lifetime of happiness together. There were no secrets between them, but one. No questions were ever off the table and always answered with complete honesty, except if that *one* ever came along. However, this was a subject requiring him to delve deep and not skimp on any of the details. He wanted to start at the beginning. It would take him all the way back to when he was a feisty, six-year old.

As Tony James contemplated this task he tilted his head down and looked at the love in her beautiful, inviting, brown eyes. Even after years of marriage Tony still viewed Jacquelyn as his bride. Tony then decided he would much rather ease into his answer than take a cannon ball plunge into the deep end of him being a first grader. It was just a tough memory to put into words, even on this particularly peaceful evening.

Tony had never before divulged his entire story to anyone before. This included his beautiful Jacquelyn. If she had asked, he would have told her, but she never did. She was now nibbling at it. Until this moment he didn't grasp how thankful he'd been that she never asked prior to this night. Tony realized she loved him so much that she didn't want him to feel uncomfortable.

Jacquelyn's so very smart. She knew over time I'd reveal bits and pieces until almost everything was on the table. She'd then just put the pieces together like a jig-saw puzzle and, if needed, ask for the final one. Well, she's asking now, he thought.

He finally landed upon the idea of telling her about their first meeting. Well, they hadn't actually spoken or even

6

locked eyes back then, but for Tony it was when *he* met her. Jacquelyn was excited since she'd never heard his side of the story before.

Call it cliché, but Tony had fallen for Jacquelyn upon first sight at the ripe old age of nineteen. But, then again who wouldn't. Her silky, long, dark hair framed her angelic face, of which he just couldn't divert his eyes. Her five-foot-five figure was out of this world. She walked in a reserved grace with beautiful bronze legs that began at the floor and seemed to never end. But, for Tony, this wasn't just as simple as physical attraction. There was a dimension which set this goddess apart from all other earthly beings.

She exuded a compassion which penetrated and engulfed him like that of a warm fire on a cold winter's night. It was one of those moments that made him wonder if he were to look away and quickly back again would she still be there.

Is she a mirage?, he thought.

The decisive silent inundation of a feeling penetrated him. However, this time, it was as if he had been pierced by Cupid's very own arrow. This feeling warmly enveloped him at this moment and could only be verbalized into the words *incredibly compassionate* and *perfect*.

Tony purposely turned away for a short moment. Enough time to shed the extraordinary feeling that had just visited him. Upon re-focusing back to this goddess, the very same all-encompassing feeling returned with the exact same powerful words in accompaniment.

There were many other people around in the vast lobby of the office building. The tall man wearing an expensive suit projected an ambitious feeling accompanied by the word *aspiring*. A stylish woman, appearing to be in her early thirties stood alone apparently waiting as she looked at her watch for the third time. From head to toe everything was in place to perfection. Tony felt her guarded personality. Very quickly the word *secretive* stabbed at him. The delivery guy with his protective bicycle helmet awaiting a signature for the parcel he just delivered. Tony was speared with a clear feeling of deception. Immediately the word *dishonest* crossed his consciousness. He hadn't even turned around yet and he felt an open-mined person connected with the word *tolerant*.

For the longest time he only had a hypothesis where this sensor was generated. This time, seeing her, the words that pierced him were stronger than he'd ever experienced up to this point in his life.

It would be difficult to explain the unusual detail of fact, that August day, that Tony didn't actually meet Jacquelyn face to face. He experienced her overflowing compassion from a distance of at least forty feet.

Jacquelyn wasn't doing anything unusual to attract attention. But, then again, looking like her, she didn't have to do anything but exist. Heads turned as she walked to the information desk. Jacquelyn never saw him as he was at an angle that conspired to hide him from her. This was most definitely on purpose by Tony. In his mind he had a very good reason to shield himself. Hiding in plain sight became a specialty for him throughout most of his life.

Jacquelyn nodded her head at the professionally dressed woman who apparently gave her directions to her destination. Tony could read Jacquelyn's lips as she gave the helpful receptionist a thank you. She then walked toward the elevator doors. Jacquelyn calmly pressed the up button as one of the doors was three-quarters closed. It appeared she was in no hurry and very willing to wait for one of the other elevators. Suddenly, and just in time, a man's arm quickly popped out from inside the closing elevator doors closest to Jacquelyn stopping them from completing their task. The doors opened showing this man and three irritated women. It was hard to tell, but he appeared to be in his forties with a bit of a paunch sticking out from his cheap navy blue pin-striped suit. He gave her a big gawky smile and offered her to ride up as if it were his personal elevator. She got in and nodded her appreciation. The other women gave each other a quick knowing look of disdain for this man making them wait.

I bet she gets that kind of attention from guys all the time, Tony thought.

As the doors were still wide open he could see by her body language she wasn't quite as thankful as she pretended to show.

She doesn't like the attention. I like that, he thought.

Tony didn't get a read on the 'Good Samaritan'. His focus was on Jacquelyn and, for some reason, making sure she was alright. For whatever motivation, Tony felt the need to protect her. The doors slowly closed and Tony let out a sigh.

"She gone," he mumbled dejectedly.

He fought the urge to go after her and took one step forward, stopped, then watched the illuminated numerals above the elevator's lights begin to climb. *What am I thinking? She has her choice of anyone when it comes to guys*, he thought.

Chapter 3

Tapping his fingers on the steering wheel to the song on the radio Tony had drifted into his world of logic, analysis and calculations. *No way should we have lost that softball game last night. All the pieces were in place with a one run lead going into their last at-bat. We might have to move Johnson to center field and let Slater close out as pitcher. He's got better control especially under pressure*, he thought.

Tony James is a sports junkie for various reasons. For one he's a naturally gifted athlete. Another major factor is the enjoyment he gains from the mental aspect of any game. While playing, he relishes the process of strategy almost more than the game itself. He loves to find strengths, weaknesses, patterns and trends that are hidden away in another dimension whispering to anyone listening to come find them. It's as if he has a direct line to the bodiless voice in the movie "Field of Dreams". His body reacts to the physical needs of the game, while his mind seems to go into a proactive mode to find the hidden fun within the sport. Stated simply, it's a way for Tony to play a game within a game. His natural instincts, for the most part, usually keep him one or two steps ahead of his competition. Little did Tony know he had developed a core system of multi-level analysis that he trusted with his life. This strategic hyper-awareness seems to tap into his sub-conscience bringing forth a higher level of scrutiny.

No matter the sport, teammates and opponents will, on occasion, gravitate to him when seeking help to improve. Tony has a natural knack to help guide them to a higher level. When young talented athletes request his advice he always asks them one question up-front.

"Do you love to win or hate to lose?"

From his perspective, people fall into one of these two clear-cut categories. He sees ultimate success or failure wrapped up in that one simple question. For Tony there's a great distinction between the two answers.

He knows everyone prefers to win. He also knows people don't like to lose. From his philosophical perspective the difference in a person's competitive makeup comes in the degree to which they hate to lose. That is, if they actually feel that emotion. Tony hates to lose almost more than anything else. He believes by being a person who loves to win that they, by default, don't truly expect victory. If they expected success then why would there be so much love of that feeling after they win? It should have been expected.

Tony began to talk it through. "I know Sid's hatred of losing outweighs Justin's love of winning. Sid will do whatever's required not to feel the death sting of a loss. This is a dog-eat-dog world and our pitcher has to bring that mindset in crunch-time. I know Sid carries the same philosophy as I have. He's a 'hate to lose' person just like me. Justin embraces a 'love to win' belief system. I know if people have even the slightest competitive streak within, then they're either a 'love to win' or 'hate to lose' person. I'd put

12

my money on a 'hate to lose' person every time. I know this isn't limited to sports only. I believe in my heart that much of life to be a competition within our societal construct. Sid's in. Justin's out."

Tony's Smartphone phone rang out as he was pulling into the driveway. The display revealed a name that provoked his shoulders to drop.

"Why do you have to call me now? Can't you wait until I have an hour or more of windshield time?" he complained.

This client likes to gab. He wouldn't be calling if it wasn't important. Tony politely answered, parked the car in the garage then cut the engine. After the initial reason for the call was established the conversation began to meander into areas which carried no interest for Tony. He listened. However, he listened more closely for key words and inflection. Tony got out of the car and headed into the house while continuing to listen to the one-sided conversation. Hungry, he grabbed a quiet snack he could eat while listening saying "Yup" and "A-ha" on occasion as he sat down.

Tony wanted to ask this guy if he understands just how much other people's time he wastes with these types of calls. But, Tony knows he is a flawed man himself. So he continued to listen, however, paying closer attention to what wasn't being said. Trying to end the conversation by summarizing was to no avail. The caller continued. Tony put his elbow on the counter then placed his head in his hand as he closed his eyes. Other than the business aspect of the call Tony got the feeling he was listening to stories mixed with as much fiction as truth.

I wish I could see him instead of just hearing him. I'm not getting all the feedback I need, he thought.

To Tony, it isn't just about listening. Absorbing body language and posture are big keys to his natural sensory system. At an early age, Tony came to know the mouth can say anything, but the body just doesn't lie. Only the mind can produce, and attempt to present, a logical masterpiece of false facts and deception. The body, on the other hand, tells the larger story of true emotion. The mind creates the story of words. Tony doesn't count on words alone to know truth. The nuances of inflection, feelings of tone, along with the physical body combine to reveal all.

This conversation was well beyond its journey into the valley of his perception of trust. He isn't consciously trying to catch his client in a lie. Tony is automatically deciphering a relational trust quotient. Can he trust, at face value, what is being passed to him through this phone call? Based on his instantaneous assessment Tony automatically gave an immediate fail grade. Pass or fail, no grading on a curve for Tony.

Since he did fail, Tony would keep his guard up and at full alert even while bored. Normally he would extricate himself from the conversation. But, because this was a client he remained silent and continued to listen. This came so naturally to Tony.

Jacquelyn came home from work to find Tony sitting on one of the kitchen stools with his cell phone to his ear. She didn't make any noise as she figured this was likely a business call. He rolled his eyes pulled the phone from his ear and gave her the 'blah, blah, blah' hand gesture toward the phone. Finally, his client began to run out of steam and Tony took advantage to end the call as quickly as possible.

"Another adoring fan of yours?" Jacquelyn said kiddingly.

"No, another client who thinks he's the center of the universe."

Jacquelyn walked over to him as he got up from the stool. Tony had a red mark where he had rested his head in his hand while on the phone. She gave him a quick peck on the lips and a playful rub on the head.

"What was that?" asked Tony as he grabbed her at the waist before she got away.

"What was what?" she teased.

"You call that a kiss hello?"

Tony stood and pulled her to him. He cupped his right hand lightly on the back of her neck while lifting then stroking her long hair with his fingers as if they were a comb. Jacquelyn melted. Looking deep into her gorgeous brown eyes he leaned in giving her a long luscious welcome home kiss. At the end of the kiss Jacquelyn reluctantly withdrew then rested her head on his shoulder.

He slowly shifted her backward to see her face and in a playful tone said, "Now *that's* how you give a welcome home kiss." He gave her a big smile.

Hoping Tony didn't notice her trying to catch her breath; Jacquelyn turned and said, "You need a haircut."

He couldn't help but continue to smile as he said, "Really, that's all you have to say?"

Tony felt the top of his head where he could still feel Jacquelyn's touch and said, "You're probably right." Then he thought, *I think I'll put off the agony of sitting through a haircut for another week.*

"All kidding aside, how was your day?" asked Tony.

"Um...Good," she said half-heartedly after a brief pause.

"You don't sound too sure."

"I'm just tired. Chalk it up to another busy day. I wanted to make a few changes in my lesson plan for the next unit. It just took a little longer with other teachers stopping in wanting to talk."

"Who were you talking to when I got home?" she asked.

"If you hadn't noticed, I wasn't doing much of the talking."

"I did. If they only knew what lies beneath that docile exterior of yours."

"Is that a compliment or —?"

16

Jacquelyn quickly cut him off. "You know very well I meant that as a compliment. It just seems everyone that comes in contact with you winds up telling you their life story while you give them nothing. I don't know how you get away with it."

"I just love to hear other people talk, I guess. Besides I don't want to intimidate anyone by vomiting my life story," Tony said kiddingly.

"Oh, please, who are you going to intimidate? Sure, you can't hide that you're six feet tall, but if they only knew you're made of pure muscle underneath those baggy clothes of yours."

"What's wrong with what I wear?"

"Nothing except I think your hiding so as not to intimidate."

"Now why would I do that?"

"People are more at ease to provide more information than you have to give. Simple as that."

"Did you ever think I just don't like to wear tight clothes?"

"Okay. Then how about how you walk?"

"What's wrong with how I walk?"

"Your gait projects an ever so slight self-conscious attitude, but you also glide at the same time."

"I don't get it."

"You seem to try to not move as the natural athlete that you are. It just seems to me that you're trying to throw people off."

"And why would I do that?"

"To blend in with control and a zero intimidation factor so you get more information than you have to give," she replied. "See…full circle," she added.

"Jacquelyn I was just kidding around. I agree that I do think I blend in more than stick out, but I've never thought about even the slightest possibility of me being an intimidating person."

"Oh? What about on the racquetball court? You've told me stories."

"That's different," said Tony.

Jacquelyn realized she was still reacting to Tony's welcome home kiss message. She paused and said, "I'm sorry Tony. You got me flustered. You're right."

Jacquelyn hit a nerve with her control remark though. Unknown to others, self-control is one of the pillars of Tony's life that's required to help him feel somewhat normal. If he can, to some extent, control a situation his world is a much better place.

Changing the subject Tony said, "Remember, I have to attend the Portland Horizons Computer Seminar tomorrow."

"That's tomorrow?"

"Yup, CIT's the sponsor this year. They booked the ballroom at the Hilton Executive Tower downtown. I have to be there by 7:00AM. Can you take the kids to school?"

Jacquelyn knew Tony didn't care too much for these conferences. Way too much sitting around for him.

"Not a problem," she replied.

The next day Tony parked his car far enough for a good leisurely walk avoiding the parking structure. He wanted to burn some energy as well as create the opportunity to make a quick exit and avoid the heaviest traffic at the end of the day.

As he entered the hotel Tony first scouted out the perfect "release room". After checking in and clipping his clear plastic nametag to his shirt he entered and scanned the vast conference room. Without hardly any effort on his part he very quickly found the seat that would serve his purpose.

As usual he avoided sitting up front. Tony almost always sits in the back because he has to focus so hard to not physically or audibly make a mistake. He must split his concentration so he can listen to what the presenter has to say while giving his ever-present tormentor its due.

His tormentor lives within him every waking minute of every day. It forces urges of movement and vocal noises that he must suppress for his perceived need of acceptance. He calls these "mistakes" because he tries so hard to suppress and control them. But when the pressure builds to the boiling point they slip out and Tony looks at it as a mistake.

Today the majority of his more pronounced tics are on the right side of his body, including his face. It can change from day to day for a reason unknown to him. That's why today's strategy is to sit in the back on the right side of the room. His need to conceal these tics from the rest of his peers is, in his mind, vital.

Tony set his briefcase down on his chair to let others know the seat is taken. He then went out to the lobby to find breakfast. As he was eating a doughnut and holding a cup of orange juice he heard his name from a short distance.

"James!" shrieked the voice he recognized immediately.

It was his supervisor's assistant, Daryl Harwood. He didn't want to have much to do with Harwood, but made small talk to be polite. Tony knew this conference was as much about networking as it was about the consumption of information from the presenters.

However, as Harwood went on and on Tony thought, *You're such a brownnoser. If your boss stopped mid-stride your head would have to be extricated from her rear end.*

Just as quickly as Harwood was on Tony he waved to someone else releasing Tony from his obligation to listen to the blow-hard. Tony then mingled and talked shop with numerous competitors while meandering through the burgeoning crowd on his way to his seat.

About an hour into the first presentation Tony could feel his need for more focus toward his tormentor was in order. This allowed for less concentration on the information being presented. It was time as he began to feel himself making more and more mistakes. His tormentor's urging was becoming too much for him to keep chained. Tony knew if he sat there much longer a really big mistake was about to occur. It was as if a full body sneeze was about to blow.

I've got to get out of here, he thought.

It was as if a feather was moving about his skin, but he couldn't scratch without looking like a twitching fool. He certainly didn't want to try to wait until there was a scheduled break. His release room could be packed then.

Tony calmly left his seat and walked to the bathroom he had scouted earlier. Facial and shoulder tics began popping out along the way. He tried to hold on as long as humanly possible. As he entered he checked to see if anyone was around.

All clear, he thought.

He entered the stall designed for handicapped people and locked the door behind him. Tony chose it for its larger size. He let go of his vice-like focus that kept his tormentor locked in its jail cell. Like opening the floodgates of the Panama Canal the physical and verbal tics began. His tormentor was on the loose. It wasn't so much a concern, but a thought streaked through his mind that more than once he's almost passed out due to a particularly violent head tic.

The urge was so strong he was thankful he left the seminar when he did. He lifted his head up high as if looking like a huge sneeze was about to take place. Then, instead of a sneeze, he slammed his head swiftly down, chin to chest, as hard as he could to a quick stop then raised it again in rapid

21

succession. His chin at times actually hit his chest with a rather violent blow. He brought his head back up to the top then stuck his neck out and once again quickly slammed his head back down. He came dangerously close to hitting his head on the handicap rail on that one. Fortunately, on this occasion his tongue didn't get in the way resulting in a familiar bloody mess. Along with the head tic he rolled his shoulder as if he were trying to loosen it up. Tony repeated this in sets of three. He almost looks like a guitar rock star head-banging to non-existent heavy metal music. To say the least this caused him to see stars. At worst he ran the risk of literally knocking himself out. In-between sets he made a grunting sound as if he were being punched in the gut. To Tony, the severity of each episode seemed to be in relation to how long he could hold his resolve.

Tony knew once the tic release episode was over the big tic urge would subside and he could move on with his plans of hiding considerably less severe tic activity. Unfortunately, as a result for Tony, he had to go back to the seminar with a terrible headache as the consequence. Luckily it didn't last long. The urge to tic still remained, but significantly reduced for a period of time. This was a normal everyday activity for Tony. He would focus so hard to keep his tormentor at bay and win the battle. He, unfortunately and ultimately, would lose the war and succumb to the beast within.

Tony's been tormented almost his entire life. It's something completely out of his control. Sure, he can focus and control it for a while, but ultimately he must succumb to it. Some people have a tormentor that's ten times as wicked as his. They just simply can't control it no matter how hard they try. Most don't even begin since it's such a losing proposition.

His tics are involuntary, rapid, sudden movements or vocalizations that occur repeatedly in the same way. In Tony's case he can disguise the vocal tics as a sound of merely clearing his throat or a fake cough.

Tony made it through the rest of the seminar with only one more visit to release the beast. He beat the traffic and was pleased with his overall planning of his day.

When he got home Jacquelyn was just retrieving the mail. Tony gave her a big smile and a wave as he pulled into the driveway.

As he got out of the car she asked, "How was your day, Tony?"

"Different day, same stuff", he replied drolly. "Where are the kids?" he asked.

"Oh, they're playing in a world of imagination next door", replied Jacquelyn.

"And how was your day off?" he asked.

Jacquelyn pondered how she wanted to answer him. "Revealing", Jacquelyn answered in a little more excited tone.

She'd made a discovery that had the potential to change Tony's view of his world. Tony set his briefcase down then was led to the couch in front of the TV. Tony had no idea what she was up to.

Jacquelyn said, "I saw an interview today I thought you might be interested in. I recorded it for you."

"What's it about?" Tony asked.

After a pause Jacquelyn vaguely said, "Baseball."

"You know I love baseball, but let's eat first. I'm starving."

"I think you might want to see this before dinner. It's not long and the kids are still next door", said Jacquelyn in a very leading tone.

Tony knew something was up. "If you say so," he said reluctantly agreeing.

The TV was already on so Jacquelyn picked up the remote control then pressed play. An announcer came on with the sounds of cheers from a great hit into the outfield filling in the background noise.

"Hey, that's Jim Eisenreich." Tony proclaimed. "One of the most underrated hitters baseball has ever seen", he added.

After a brief bio the show got rolling and it took on a more serious tone. Jacquelyn sat back knowing what was ahead. The announcer spoke of the difficulties Eisenreich faced while out of baseball for a few years due to a medical disorder he couldn't control.

"I didn't know he left baseball for that long", said Tony.

Jacquelyn half smiled, but remained quiet and focused on the program.

Tony knew Jacquelyn all too well to know she wouldn't have gone to the trouble to record this show and ask him to watch it right away just because it was about baseball. When he heard the announcer describe Jim Eisenreich's disorder Tony felt electricity shoot up his back while sitting to Jacquelyn's right. He was mesmerized by what the commentator was describing. Unfolding Eisenreich's disorder was as if he was describing Tony! The program ended and he looked at Jacquelyn. Tony had moist eyes that he tried to hide by pinching the upper portion of his nose.

Jacquelyn gave him a big hug then cupped his face and said, "You've got some investigating to do."

Tony looked at the love of his life and said, "Thank you so much. You have no idea how much this means to me. You're truly an angel sent from heaven."

Chapter 4

Jacquelyn had left Tony with his thoughts and emotions. As she re-entered the room she saw the distance in his eyes after his third viewing of the recording. Jacquelyn stood quietly until he came back from wherever his mind had taken him.

Once she saw his eyes re-focused on the present she sat down with him and asked, "Are you okay, Tony?"

He focused his eyes back to her. "I just can't believe there's a disorder describing my tormentor as perfectly as this."

With a little investigating, and Jacquelyn's encouragement, he found a doctor nearby that dealt with this particular disorder.

Could it really be possible I'm not just weird and I have what Jim Eisenreich has? Tony pondered. *It sure is worth checking it out.*

After his quick internet investigation, Tony made an appointment for the following week and told them if an opening came up to please call and he'd be there to take it.

On the day of his appointment Tony's tics were worse than ever. He felt excitement yet stressed of thinking about a diagnosis. His twitching and clearing of his throat were off the charts while he was alone. He managed to keep them somewhat under control while around other people. But, when he was alone, well let's just say he rocked out.

Tony introduced himself to the receptionist using the time of his appointment leery of announcing his name to those in the waiting area.

"I have an 11:00 A.M. appointment with Dr. Knox."

Beverly, according to her name tag pleasantly said, "Good morning. Please fill this paperwork out and I'll let you know when the doctor's ready for you. You may have a seat anywhere you'd like."

How about I go back home and sit on my recliner, Tony thought to himself. He was nervous.

Tony completed the paperwork quickly, returned it to Beverly then sat trying to look calm. Unfortunately, inside he was as excited as a five-year old on Christmas morning. On the other hand, he felt very uncomfortable to see others there as well.

How many bricks short of a full load are they? he wondered.

"Anthony?" His first name was called and he was quietly led to the exam room.

It crossed his mind that it was very thoughtful she didn't use his last name. He was told he just needed to sit and wait for the doctor. No gown or anything was required of him. He was told to relax and "just be you."

Easier said than done, he thought.

The doctor came in and introduced himself. "Good morning, Mr. James. I'm Dr. Knox."

The moment they met, a little bird whispered to Tony...*sneaky*. "Please, call me Tony."

Dr. Knox then proceeded to ask Tony what he likes to do in his spare time. He was attempting to put Tony at ease. Tony truly did appreciate this gesture. However, Tony could feel the time for chit-chat was coming to an end. Sure enough, ground control said ignition on and the good doctor launched head first into the reason for the visit.

In a gentle tone Dr. Knox said, "For a proper diagnosis I need to see what tics you're exhibiting."

Upon hearing this, Tony felt like he was going to jump out of his chair. *What, are you nuts, Doc?* he thought.

He didn't show his true feelings to the doctor of course. He'd been specializing in concealing his tics from the rest of the world for so long that he wasn't ready for this invasion of privacy, even here.

Tony was put in the proverbial rock and a hard place. He devoted his existence to hiding in plain sight. Some of the strategies he developed were very impressive. Tony was actually, in some unusual way, proud of this. Now this doctor was asking him to unmask the tormentor and let it show its ugly face.

I don't think so, thought Tony.

In Tony's agitated state, it wouldn't have been very hard for him to comply at least to some degree. But, he did his best to continue to hide the tics. Tony doubted he'd pull it off in front of a trained professional. He figured his focus would just not be strong enough.

This is a dilemma I didn't envision. I want a diagnosis, but I don't want to have to perform like a circus monkey. I have my pride. As misplaced as it may be, I still have my pride, he thought.

Tony felt both an occasional physical and verbal tic slip out of him. He hoped he covered them up well. He tried extremely hard to hold them in and not make mistakes. He wasn't sure he could fool a professional for very long. Everything in his DNA told him he needed to try and hold back his tormentor. It's what he'd done his entire life. He really didn't know anything else. Even in this case, for some reason, he just couldn't bring himself to let his tormentor win even at the risk of a cure.

This makes no sense! he wanted to scream.

It was as if he was so hard-wired that he wouldn't put down his protective shield for anyone…even now. Down to his last fiber Tony is a true 'hate to lose' person, even at his own expense.

I don't know if I trust this guy. Why did the word sneaky come to me the moment we met?

As if right on cue Dr. Knox asked Tony, "Is this you letting go or holding back?"

Tony looked him square in the eyes and said, "I'm completely holding back."

Dr. Knox seemed to understand, but encouraged Tony to show him the full spectrum of his symptoms. The more he pushed, the more Tony automatically deepened his focus to not show him.

Dr. Knox crossed his arms and once again let Tony know, "Without seeing the full expression of your tics, I can't provide a proper diagnosis."

He kept pushing Tony. Tony stubbornly held on. The doctor changed the subject by asking about his siblings and parents.

This guy knows I can't hold out forever so he's going to wait me out. I've got to hang on. Tony doubled his focus and answered his questions. *I think I'm going to explode*, thought Tony.

Then the doctor looked at his pager, paused, and said "Excuse me, I'll be right back."

Thank you to whoever paged you!

Tony was so grateful the doctor left. This would give him the chance to let out the tics that had built up during this trying visit. As soon as the door clicked shut and he was alone, his tormentor dropped on him like a ton of bricks. His entire arsenal of physical and verbal tics was released without regard to the knowledge that someone might hear him. When done, Tony settled back into the cloth chair.

About five minutes after he'd left, Dr. Knox returned and said, "I'm very sorry about that."

He watched the doctor resume his position on his leather stool on wheels. *Boy, am I glad you left when you did. Better yet, good timing on your return,* thought Tony.

Dr. Knox asked Tony, "How often are your tics this bad?"

Tony gave a vacant stare as he wasn't sure how to answer this question. Tony then said, "I haven't been able to show them to you yet. I told you it makes me feel like an act in a freak show."

"So, you're going to be stubborn and not get a proper diagnosis and let me help you. Is that it?"

"It's just that I have a very hard time with this, even with you Doc. I've spent most of my life hiding this from everybody and here you are asking me to just step up on the stage and show you. I can't seem to do that," Tony said in a dejected tone.

"But you have shown me. The head banging, eye twitching, shoulder jabs, leg movements and throat sounds demonstrates that you have a full blown case of Tourette Syndrome."

Tony was stunned! *How in the world could he possibly know specifically what tics I have?* Then it dawned on him. Tony's eyes widened. "Oh, I get it. Does everyone with Tourette's have these basic tics? You're pretty clever, Doc."

Feeling much better and almost a little cocky Tony settled his nerves down. *Okay! I'm past the tough part of his exam. I got my reprieve.*

The first five words, "But you did show me", that had come out of Dr. Knox's mouth, uncharacteristically, didn't even register with Tony.

He thought, *Okay, now he can diagnose me without me looking like a fool in front of him.* "You have them down. Those are the tics that I have currently", Tony said in relief.

"That's not it, Tony. Do you remember the paperwork you filled out when you came in today?"

"Yeah," Tony said dismissively.

"Well, you agreed to be observed without a doctor present in this room." He let the words hang in the air like a lead balloon.

"I did?" Tony said this not so much as a real question, but thinking more like, *Oh crap!*

It didn't take a genius to figure where Dr. Knox was headed. "So you saw everything I did when you left the room?" Tony asked in a deflated tone.

"Not only saw, but heard as well," said Dr. Knox.

As Tony was sitting he bent down and put his face in his hands with elbows resting on his legs as embarrassed as he's ever been. Surprisingly, unlike many occasions, Tony didn't take this as a personal injustice.

I wasn't tricked. That was pure genius, sneaky as hell, but genius, he thought. Tony sat up straight and looked him in the eyes with a new found confidence in the doctor. *So that's what sneaky means,* Tony concluded.

"I'm very sorry that I had to resort to it, but I'm here to help you, Tony. Can you understand that?"

As if he felt the band-aid had been quickly ripped off his flesh Tony calmly said, "I understand."

"Tony", said Dr. Knox in an authoritative voice. "I have good news and bad news for you. Which would you like first?"

I hate that question, thought Tony. With just a slight hesitation Tony said "No games. Just tell me, Doc."

The doctor paused and said, "I can tell you with one hundred percent certainty you indeed have Tourette Syndrome, or Disorder if you prefer. It has no cure at this time." Tony didn't even hear the second part of the statement.

This was one of the most important sentences Tony had heard in his entire life. After all this time he now had the name of his tormentor! *Tourette's,* he thought to himself. He was actually happy for the moment.

Tony cracked a tight-lipped smile. Dr. Knox looked surprised and asked "Why the grin?"

Tony said, "After all these years I thought I was...weird. Now I have a name to attach to the torment I've endured."

Dr. Knox looked pleased then continued. "Okay then, so here's more good news. Your affliction is considered moderate and with medication we can reduce the impact of the tics you've been experiencing." Tony was in heaven hearing this. "Just so you heard me I said we can reduce, not eliminate. There is no cure. Also, just one more question. You covered up some relentless tics for approximately twenty minutes in a highly stressful environment unlike anyone I've encountered. Can you tell me how you accomplished that?"

Tony calmly and simply said "No, not really." Will power, sneaky man, and I hate to lose, especially to my newly named nemesis, thought Tony.

When he left the office, prescription in hand, Tony seemed to float as if on a cloud. He now possessed the knowledge that he was not, after all, a little weird and he had his tormentor's name. It was no longer an unidentified source. Its name is Tourette's.

"I have a real disorder. Now I can hunt it and try to kill it."

That became Tony's focus. Tony's first act as a newly diagnosed Tourette's patient was to drive straight to the pharmacy to get his prescription filled. He decided to go to the drive-up window because he felt embarrassed getting this particular prescription. Tony didn't want to be around other people as they called him when his antipsychotic medication prescription was ready. The sanctuary of his car was just fine with him. If he went inside he imagined he would hear the pharmacist loudly call *Tony James? Do you have any questions taking your crazy pills, Mr. James?*

He put the piece of paper in the tray and waited for the attendant to extract and process it. Tony answered the mandatory questions of verifying the correct spelling of his name, address and then confirmed his phone number.

34

This medication is going to take away the one thing that made me feel different from everyone else since I was a little kid. This could change my life. It also means I'm now on a serious medication that puts me in the category of officially being treated as more than a little weird. Well, being better out-weighs the latter, he thought.

The doctor had told him there's no single drug of choice when it came to limiting Tourette's symptoms. A very careful matching and monitoring of multiple medications to the specific needs for each individual patient is critical in treating this disorder.

I really hope that this will be the one drug that will do the trick, thought Tony.

Dr. Knox told Tony he was starting him out on Haloperidol also known as Haldol. If required, he'd prescribe an additional appropriate medication to take with this first one. He also told Tony Haldol is the go-to drug of choice as this had been proven to reduce the urge to tic physically and vocally. However, as with any powerful medication, there are side effects.

At the moment I'm not concerned in the least with the side effects. I can't imagine anything being as all-encompassing to my life as my tormentor has proven to be. I just want to get to the healing, he thought.

As Tony waited in the car he envisioned being able to sit quietly without the urge to move a muscle. This was his vision of heaven. A voice through the outside speaker blared out to him.

"Mr. James, this will take one hour to fill. Can you come back and pick it up then?"

Tony was very disappointed, but didn't show it. He understood then looked at his watch.

"No problem. I'll be back in an hour."

"Thank you, Mr. James" boomed the voice through the speaker.

Tony was happy he didn't hear, *Hey, weird man, come back later and we'll give you your happy pills.* As he drove off he looked at the dashboard clock, confirming the time, and would be back precisely in one hour.

Tony went home and found that Jacquelyn wasn't there so he headed straight for his personal computer. He needed to find out more about this complicated and so-called incurable disorder via the internet. As he read from various websites he found that Tourette's is genetically passed on through DNA.

Hmm, I didn't catch Tourette's, I inherited it. This means I can't give it to anyone else except through lineage. Well, the kids seem just fine so far, he thought.

He continued on his exploration and found its symptoms include both multiple motor and one or more vocal tics present at some time although not necessarily simultaneously.

Tony verified that a diagnosis of Tourette's contains the occurrence of tics many times a day, usually in bouts, nearly happening every day or intermittently throughout a span of more than one year. Also, there are periodic changes in the number, frequency, type and location of the tics. There's a waxing and waning of their severity. Symptoms can sometimes completely disappear for weeks or even months at a time.

"Well, in my case the urge to tic is constantly present unless I'm sleeping," he mumbled.

All of the information contained on the websites confirmed onset occurs before the age of 18. The term, "involuntary", used to describe Tourette's tics can sometimes be confusing since it's known that some people do have a little control over their symptoms. What's not recognized is this control, which can be exercised anywhere from seconds to hours at a time, merely postpones more severe outbursts of tics later in the day.

"Hmm, just like I experience every day."

Tics are experienced as irresistible and, just as the urge to sneeze, eventually must be expressed. People with Tourette Syndrome often seek a secluded spot to release their symptoms after delaying some of them for a short period in school or at work. However, people who have a more severe case cannot stop them at all. Typically, tics increase as a result of tension or stress, and decrease with relaxation or when focusing on an absorbing task.

Tony thought, *At least they completely disappear while I'm sleeping.*

As he finished reading he concluded the bottom line is this isn't a psychological disorder, but a circuitry problem.

When it comes to the brain everything is chemically based, he contemplated. This put him at ease. *Many people who haven't been diagnosed with Tourette's may think they may just have a nervous disposition or are a little bit weird*, he thought.

Unfortunately, even Tony's own personal family physician said the urges and tics are, "Just part of your personality." Tony knew, deep down, this just couldn't be the case. He was in his early twenties when he was told this. Tony now knows it's very important for anyone who exhibits traits of Tourette's to seek out a specialist as early as possible. He found out that general practitioners, God bless them, don't have all the answers.

Growing up, Tony didn't know he had an actual disorder with a name. His symptoms were a mystery that kept him off balance and on the defense. So, the more he controlled his world, the better it made him feel. The better this makes him feel, the less stress he has to deal with. Stress is such a contributing factor when it comes to Tony's level of physical and vocal tics. Luckily for Tony, his moderate case of Tourette's affords him the ability to suppress, but not eliminate, the urges this tormentor throws his way. Also, fortunately for Tony, he's developed an advanced focus to suppress the discomforting urges to tic for a period of time.

I feel so sorry for the people who have a severe case of Tourette's. They have no chance to hide their embarrassing tics, he thought.

One aspect of severe cases of Tourette's that surprised Tony is called Coprolalia. This is what the world sees through the filtered lens of television reporting. He found Coprolalia is involuntary swearing and inappropriate comments. It is, unfortunately, the characteristic most associated with Tourette's cases because of sensationalized journalism.

What a shame when a media outlet decides to feature Tourette's they don't provide the full spectrum from mild to severe. There are hundreds of thousands of people who aren't represented when they choose to focus solely on the most severe cases, thought Tony.

After Tony successfully holds off many of the physical and vocal tics, they always come out a short time later. They don't just trickle out, but they attack with a vengeance. Tony can usually control the worst of it while engaging with others, knowing an impending tic tsunami will crash into him later.

An hour passed and Tony picked up his prescription then returned home with the promise of a new future.

Ah, living a better life through chemistry. I'm not taking my first dose until Jacquelyn and I are together. I want to discuss the possible side effects so if I don't notice them she'll be there to monitor me, Tony thought.

Because Haldol is an antipsychotic medication it certainly had an intimidation factor for Tony even before he took the first capsule.

I want these tics to go away, but I'm really nervous about taking something so strong, Tony thought. He was so thankful Jacquelyn was going to be home soon.

While he waited Tony read the warning of side effects which was stapled to the pharmacy bag. It was very sobering. However, Tony also knew every medication, even antibiotics, came with severe side effects warnings. He figured this was the legal profession at its best.

"Okay, Haldol's function is to interfere with the neurotransmitters in the brain. I remember reading online that these neurotransmitters are chemical messengers that nerves manufacture and then release to communicate with each other. So, Tourette's is simply the misfiring of these neurotransmitters sending out messages to tic. Haldol is designed to block the miscommunication of chemicals, thus, reducing or preventing tics. This seems simple enough," he said to himself.

The first side effect Tony noticed was death. *Isn't it always? These lawyers sure do cover themselves,* he thought.

The second one he took note of was something called extra pyramidal effects. This was described as sudden, often jerky, involuntary motions of the head, neck, arms, eyes or body.

"What is this? A how to get Tourette's medication," Tony nervously joked to himself.

He continued reading. Dizziness, hyperactivity, tiredness and nausea may accompany the taking of this medication.

So far it sounds like a lot of fun, Tony sarcastically thought.

A condition called orthostatic hypotension may occur in the first week or two.

"Pretty fancy way of saying you could get dizzy getting up from lying on the couch because of a sudden drop in blood pressure," he said.

After Tony read this information he was still ready, but even more nervous about taking the medication. He reminded himself he'd stop if it interfered with his so-called "normal" daily life.

"I so want to be free from the tentacles of Tourette's." He did, however, remember his doctor told him he'd have to be weaned off this medication over time if needed.

Tony heard a car pull into the driveway. Jacquelyn and the kids are home. He put the bottle away and greeted them at the door.

As they entered he gave Jacquelyn a kiss and said to Sam and Nick "About time you guys got home. Where'd you go, to a movie?"

With quick hugs the kids headed straight for their toys and games. "How was your day?" he asked Jacquelyn as he helped her off with her coat.

"Some of my students are so bright I think I'm going to move more quickly than I anticipated," she said pointedly.

"That's a good thing, right?"

"It is, but it means extra work for me." "Anything new with you today?" she asked.

41

"I had my doctor's appointment", Tony said flatly.

Jacquelyn's eyes opened wide then kiddingly said, "I completely forgot." Then in her normal compassionate tone she asked, "How'd it go?"

Tony filled her in and left the best two pieces of news for last. "Well, I was diagnosed with Tourette's just like Jim Eisenreich. I got a prescription."

"That's great news! Well, you know what I mean…that you have something and you can be cured."

"Not exactly," said Tony.

"What do you mean?" Jacquelyn asked.

"Well, Tourette's doesn't have a cure yet. But, Dr. Knox gave me a prescription and said my urge to tic will be reduced."

"When can you get your prescription?"

"I already had it filled."

"Do you feel a difference yet?" Jacquelyn asked eagerly.

"I was waiting for you to come home before I took it. There are some side effects I wanted to make sure you knew about. I thought you could help me out if I don't notice one of them."

Jacquelyn reached up and with one hand squeezed his chin and lovingly said, "Smart man. I knew I married you for a reason." She pulled toward him for a quick kiss. Jacquelyn understood how big this news was for Tony.

Later that evening, after the kids were tucked in bed, Tony got the prescription bottle and information out for Jacquelyn to look over.

"These side effects sound worse than what you already have!" she exclaimed.

"You know how they have to cover their rear ends legally. I did some research on the internet and the FDA didn't originally allow this drug in the United States until changes were made in the late 1960's. Dr. Knox wants me to start out with a low dosage and increase each week. I'm supposed to call him three weeks from now and give him an update."

Jacquelyn asked a few more questions about Tony's appointment then said, "No time like the present. I think it's time you trust the doctor."

Tony opened the plastic childproof prescription bottle and said, "Here's the first bullet to try to kill the beast within."

He was disappointed he didn't feel any different after the first week. Tony asked Jacquelyn if she noticed any changes in him.

Tuned into Tony's mood she kiddingly said, "Well, we can rule out death as a side effect."

She gave him a big smile. Jacquelyn reminded him that this isn't a sprint, but rather like a marathon. As usual, she said exactly what Tony needed to hear. He could relate to a sporting event.

Following Dr. Knox's instructions Tony adjusted to the next higher dosage. By the end of the week Tony began to think he felt a little different, but wasn't sure. He carried on as usual. That night he went to bed a little early as he was tired from a busy week.

The next day he raised the dosage once again for the upcoming week. By Wednesday he began to really feel the effects of the medication. Tony felt as if he were moving in slow motion. He was so tired all the time. It was as if he could nod off and fall asleep at any given moment. However, the urge to tic had been greatly reduced. This was big news. He just hoped he could stay awake to tell Jacquelyn later that evening.

After dinner and working together cleaning up in the kitchen Tony asked, "Jacquelyn, have you noticed any changes in my tic level yet?"

"As a matter of fact I have. They've really been cut back."

"Have you noticed anything else?" he asked.

"You just seem like…a quieter, slower version of you," she replied thoughtfully.

"I feel like a zombie! Every time I blink I'm not sure my eyelids are going to open back up again. Dr. Knox did say this drug has an accumulating effect. I think I've hit a point that's too much for me."

"You're due to call him on Friday aren't you?"

"Yeah, but I'm calling him tomorrow morning. I can't stand feeling like I'm walking around in a fog. I feel like my personality is slowly being taken from me."

"You shouldn't visit any clients tomorrow. Take an office day Tony."

"That might not be such a bad idea," he replied slowly and softly.

The next day Tony woke up, rolled over to check his alarm clock and realized he slept through it. Jacquelyn had gotten the kids ready and out the door without him hearing a sound. Tony's body clock was something he could always count on, but not today. The last time he slept until 12:30 P.M. were weekends in college.

Tony slowly got out of bed and headed for the shower. He stood letting the water cascade over him for fifteen minutes then realized he should get going.

I never stand in the shower that long, he thought. Ever so slowly he toweled off, shaved then dressed.

"I feel like I'm moving like a turtle in a rabbit's race."

He had cereal for what was now lunch then made a phone call to Dr. Knox's office. The pleasant voice on the other end of the line told him the doctor will call him back.

Tony said, "Okay, No problem."

He waited on the couch with both phones, home and cell, nearby then dozed off once again. Far off in the distance he heard a faint sound. Before he realized it was the home phone, the noise had stopped. Tony looked at the missed call on caller ID and figured it was Dr. Knox's office. After shaking the cobwebs from his slumber he re-dialed the last number that came in.

To Tony's surprise Dr. Knox answered. "Doctor, this is Tony James, did you just try calling?"

"I did. I was just about to call your cell phone. How are you doing?"

Tony explained how the day had gone thus far.

"It sounds as if that dosage is too strong for you Tony. Did you feel the urge to tic with the previous dosage?"

"Yes, there was no change until I hit this level."

"And your tics have been reduced now?"

"Yeah, but I feel like I'm the lead zombie in a slow motion movie. I'm just not myself. I haven't told Jacquelyn, but I'm a little scared to drive because I'm so sleepy from the medication."

"We need to have you go back to the previous level and add one other medication."

"Add another one?" Tony asked in a stunned tone. He knew he was told this was a possibility but it still caught him by surprise.

"This is part of a very normal process to find the right combination and dosages. I'm ordering a prescription of Pimozide for you. Did we discuss what this medication does?"

46

"Sorry Doc, but I don't remember."

"That's okay. It's my job as your physician to make sure you understand how each piece of the puzzle fits. Look at Pimozide as a very close relative to Haloperidol. It does basically the same thing using a different chemical. What I'm attempting to do is create the right balance between the two medications. It's similar to mixing paint. A little blue combined with red produces just the right shade of purple. Once again I'll start you out on a very low dosage and each week increase as needed. Remember, for now; go back to last week's Haldol dosage. We'll introduce Pimozide beginning tonight just before you go to bed."

"Will this take care of the sleepy feeling I am experiencing?" asked Tony.

"It should in time, but there are no definitive answers here. We're taking one logical step at a time to find the right combinations with the proper doses to help you out. I'll call your prescription in immediately so you can begin tonight."

"Okay, thanks Doc."

"Call me in one week, or earlier, if you have any questions."

"Will do," said Tony.

He picked up his new prescription via the drive-thru. Once again, Tony went over everything with Jacquelyn and took his first dose of Pimozide that evening at bedtime.

One week went by and there seemed to be no adverse effects for Tony. However, he was still so tired. Tony called

Dr. Knox to fill him in and he bumped up his dosage of Pimozide.

Tony forced his way through the week, but now felt just as sleepy as when he was taking the higher dose of Haldol. This combination was working, but the drowsy issue was going to have to be resolved in the long run.

The third week being on this combination of medications did in fact reduce Tony's urge to tic in a big way. However, his personality was changing from very vibrant to that of a dull lapdog. Tony became frustrated, but enjoyed a minimal urge to tic.

One night, at 3:05 A.M., from out of nowhere, Tony found himself in bed in a panic. He was laying on his back yelling "NO, NO, NO!"

Jacquelyn woke quickly and saw Tony with arms up and palms of his hands facing the ceiling as if trying to stop something.

"Tony you're having a nightmare!" Jacquelyn said urgently.

"No, get out of the room! The spiders are coming down!" exclaimed Tony.

She grabbed Tony by his left arm then realized he wasn't sleeping. He was hallucinating. Quickly Jacquelyn quieted her tone and spoke to Tony to try to help him through this. She had no training with hallucinations and was completely taken off guard. Thankfully, she's a quick thinker.

"Tony, are you sleeping or awake?"

"Just get out of the room!" shouted Tony.

Jacquelyn repeated her question, but this time grabbing him by his shoulders and forcing him to look into her eyes.

"I'm awake! Get out of here before they drop down on you!"

Jacquelyn quietly and slowly let Tony know she didn't see any spiders so therefore they don't exist. He closed his eyes. She grabbed his face and forced him to look at her.

"Do you hear me Tony"? He didn't respond. The fear in his eyes remained.

In a more forceful tone she asked, "Can you hear me Tony?"

His view was forced to locate Jacquelyn's face. With a realization in his eyes he asked in desperation, "You really don't see the spiders?"

"No, Tony, there aren't any spiders. You're hallucinating," she said firmly and calmly.

After a very long pause Tony wiped the sweat from his forehead and shakily said, "Holy crap, this stuff is worse than having Tourette's! I'm done with it!"

Once the episode was over and Tony calmed down he got out of bed and called Dr. Knox's direct line he'd obtained from caller ID. He left a message to have him call as soon as the message was picked up and that it was extremely important.

Since Tony didn't dare try to go back to sleep, he was pretty tired. He didn't want to take the chance of falling asleep and thus possibly encouraging another hallucination. *I'm never going through that again! I don't care what Dr. Knox has to do to get me off these meds,* he thought.

Dr. Knox called back within ten minutes after getting to his office. "Hi Tony, this is Dr. Knox. You called?"

"Thanks for getting back to me so quickly Doc. I had a hallucination earlier this morning." Tony went on to describe the episode.

"Were you sleeping and sure it wasn't a nightmare?" asked Dr. Knox.

"I'm positive and so is Jacquelyn." Tony replied.

"Well, it sounds like we need to make an adjustment to —" Tony cut him off.

"Doc, I'm done with these meds. Tell me how to wean off of them."

"Hold on Tony, give them a chance."

Tony had made up his mind and disregarded the last statement. "I didn't take anything this morning. Is that okay?"

"It is, but —" Tony cut him off once again.

"Just tell me what I need to know to safely wean myself off this stuff."

"I wish I could change your mind Tony."

It's my mind and if I don't want to change it then it's not going to change, Tony thought defiantly. "It's not just that I'm freaked out about a hallucination Dr. Knox. I'm tired of feeling like someone I'm not. Believe it or not, Doc, since I've been on your medication cocktail I actually have missed my old self...tics and all."

Dr. Knox told Tony he was making a mistake, but had no reply other than to instruct Tony on the procedure to eliminate the medications. "It will take about thirty days to completely purge from your system. If you go any faster you run a high risk of severe side effects."

I'll follow your instructions to a tee then I'll add one more of my own. Your phone number goes in the garbage, he thought.

Tony ended the call by pleasantly saying "Okay, thanks for trying Doc." He didn't mean it.

Within the next two weeks Jacquelyn said, "You seem to be getting back to your normal level of energy Tony."

"I feel so much better. I can't wait until I can put this cluster of an experiment behind me." At least I tried. It's too bad. I had such high hopes that I was on my way to a normal life. Well, back to the drawing board. There has to be something that'll work. I'm not giving up." he declared.

By the time Tony's thirty days was complete he was indeed back to his normal abnormal self. He actually appreciated how much he missed himself. *Aside from my Tormentor I actually like myself. Not including Jacquelyn and the kids, I think I'm my own best friend.   Hmm, I wonder why I'm still calling it my Tormentor.   It has a name,* he thought.

Chapter 5

Tony learned at an early age that people like to hear themselves talk. In particular, they like to talk about themselves. At one point he was so curious why that he even went to the extent to find out what the most used word is in the English language. He found the answer to be "the." However, not surprisingly, rounding out the top ten is the word "I".

We sure do like to talk about ourselves a lot, he thought.

When engaging in conversation Tony usually makes sure his inquiries are of a personal or pinpointed nature. It's his way of putting people at ease while automatic internal calculations and conclusions are made. To what degree are they a personal threat to his emotional need to keep his secret safe and sound?

His way of communicating is not by accident, but rather by an all-consuming strategic design of emotional self-preservation. Tony knows that if he's doing the talking then all eyes are on him. Even if he's conversing with just one other person he, at times, feels there are two more eyeballs on him placing him on alert. It depends on his assessment of that person at the time. His newly named tormentor has always required a frequent release from the focused prison sentence Tony forces it into on a daily basis. Tony watches very closely and always looks directly into the eyes of the people with whom he speaks. He found out, for some odd reason, many people aren't one-hundred percent comfortable with this type of close attention. As Tony converses he's always looking for an opening whether natural or manufactured. Fortunately, he realized, when people speak there's always a point when they'd shift their eyes away from his if only for the briefest of moments. When they'd do this Tony takes advantage and unlocks the door of his confined tormentor quickly then re-seals it for relief even just for that short-lived moment. The release of a very quick small tic gives Tony the manageability to continue on with a secret focus which goes on behind the scenes of his side of the conversation.

Tony has lots of acquaintances. Most people call these friends. Tony doesn't have a lot of what he considers the true definition of close friends. To him a close friend is someone he can tell anything to without hesitation or judgment. Trust, for Tony, doesn't come easy. For the longest time he felt he didn't have that one really close friend with whom he could confide. It wasn't that they weren't around. It was due to Tony's protection of his self-imposed code of silence. Jacquelyn is his soul mate and that's really all he needs. However, even with Jacquelyn, talking about his tormentor rubs against his life's experience and self-imposed view of himself.

A pleasant outgoing personality is part of his DNA. Tony figures he inherited this from his mother, Mary. He loves to meet new people. He's also very comfortable making new "friends". Regrettably, Tony really thinks of them as close acquaintances. If Tony were to create a close friendship scale from one to ten, nobody other than Jacquelyn, would climb above a six. However, from their perspective, most of them feel much closer to a ten than Tony's reality. They just don't know to what extent how lop-sided their relationship really is. Tony lets them in just so far. He has his perceived dark secret to preserve after all. Tony learned a lot watching his mother as he was growing up. Mary always said hello to just about everyone she saw. Her warm greetings came across in such a way that it appeared to Tony she knew each person extremely well. Tony's interactions are very close to the same. He must have learned this though the process of osmosis. He absorbed it like a sponge. Tony also, unknowingly, practiced the underlying code from the movie "The Godfather"; "Keep your friends close and your enemies closer." Tony wanted to stray far from this code, but never really did. He just needed to keep his secret safe.

If Tony lived in Spain he may have been considered a communicator's matador. His goal was never to get gored. He didn't always succeed. However, there was no conversation topic, or question, he couldn't side step if the need would arise. When questions become too personal, that's when deflection becomes his communication tool of choice. He lets people in just so far then very gently slides out of the way before they get too close to even get a whiff of his secret. Due to years of practice, he does this so automatically and seamlessly that no one feels slighted in the least. As a matter of fact they feel closer to him because he winds up appearing to listen to what's on their mind so intently. It's not that Tony doesn't want close friends. His overriding promise to himself as a six-year old took root and blossomed into a way of making it through each day. Tony enjoys people and is not a loner by any stretch of the imagination. He loves to socialize.

He just always has his antennae up and chooses his friends and social events carefully.   In other words, he has enough confidence to wing it.

Chapter 6

After enduring a prolonged Oregon winter, both he and Jacquelyn are looking forward to their trip, just the two of them. No commitments or kids. Tony knew Portland's airport flew to many countries now, but for most people it isn't widely known to be the hub of international travel. They both are excited with the travel deal they found on the internet.

While they waited for their flight to be announced for boarding Tony got up from his seat next to Jacquelyn to throw his empty popcorn bag in the garbage can. As he approached the receptacle he noticed a man about his own age with an "S" shaped scar on his chin seated nearby. The man was oddly sitting stiff-backed staring straight ahead without blinking.

I wish I could do that, Tony thought.

He focused his attention on this individual without anyone taking notice. As Tony approached he purposely un-crumpled the popcorn paper loudly then re-balled it up again. Just as Tony had hoped the man appeared to come out of his trance and glanced at what was creating such a racket. He looked directly at what Tony was holding in his hands. He looked up and made very quick eye contact with Tony and then right back to staring straight ahead.

Tony quickly licked the remaining salt from his fingers then threw the garbage away as he barely glanced at the man. A dreadfully strong feeling came over Tony. A feeling so strong that he swore the man actually told him to be extremely afraid of him. Of course this didn't literally happen. This message was delivered to him just like so many others. The word *killer* penetrated Tony's mind. With a quick second glance back at him he saw the man was back into his trance-like state.

Tony turned away then walked back to sit with Jacquelyn. As he sat, he focused his attention, but not his eyes, on this scar-faced man. That terrible feeling hung over him. Tony's nerves caused him to bounce his right leg up and down quickly as he sat. He made a decision. Tony would rather be safe than sorry.

He turned to Jacquelyn and said, "I need to use the men's room before he gets on the plane."

"Before who gets on the plane?" she asked.

"I meant before I get on the plane," Tony corrected his slip-up.

She calmly said, "Make it quick we should be boarding shortly."

"I won't be long," Tony said reassuringly. He got up and started toward the men's room. As soon as he was out of Jacquelyn's line of sight he circled around to head in the opposite direction. Tony knew exactly what he needed to do at this very moment. He had to find a US Air Marshall. He also needed to make sure he kept his focus and not appear nervous in the process. A guy twitching like crazy is not the best endorsement for instilling confidence.

Quickly surveying the airport security staff, Tony found his target. His intuition told him upon first sight that the woman, who appeared to be in her mid-forties, had a hard shell on the outside but a very soft heart inside.

Get past her hard shell first and fast, he strategized.

Tucking his shirt in, with shoulders back, chest and chin out he gave his stride an exaggerated almost military purpose then stopped the TSA agent.

Extremely busy she became very annoyed at first when she heard a stern, "Excuse me," declaration from Tony.

She was disgruntled because, to her surprise, this phrase appeared to be directed towards her. She was used to dolling out the directions around here. The tone of this voice she just heard was going to take her away from her job and she wasn't about to let a traveler address her like that. She was used to this being asked as a question, but not in a declarative statement. Little did she know this interruption was going to help her do her job better than she could ever imagine.

I certainly can't tell her I'm just a passenger.

So, he prepared and put on his most authoritative, serious face then leaned in quietly, yet calmly and spoke into her left ear.

He assertively said, "Ayesha, I believe we have a security breach."

Ayesha looked surprised that this pushy man called her by her first name. However, using first names only was one part of the protocol for onsite security. Total luck on Tony's part. Tony simply took advantage of hearing her name from a co-worker. He only saw her last name on her TSA security ID badge dangling on her blazer as he approached. He'd made sure she didn't see him glance at her ID prior to eye contact. Tony recognized he was spot on with the first part of his assessment of her...*hard shell*.

After the TSA agent almost popped a gasket, she recovered and asked in a demanding tone, "Do I know you?"

"You should. I see you every day." Lifting his eyes, Tony gave a very quick glance at one of the many security cameras built into the structure of the ceiling. "All you really need to know is what I just said and I'm not going to repeat it," Tony firmly replied.

Ayesha looked at Tony with skepticism. Tony focused so as not to tic or that would be the end of this conversation. The last thing he needed was for her to bring in her supervisor for fear he'd be detained and the man with the scar gets on the plane with Jacquelyn and the other travelers.

Before she could jump into standard operating procedure mode, Tony forcefully said, "Direct me to the A-M nearest gate 46A with as much discretion as you can muster." Tony threw in the letters for Air Marshall to aid in helping make him seem more legit.

Ayesha's change of demeanor showed that she accepted him as one of the security personnel who remained nameless and usually faceless. She briefly glanced at one of the security cameras mounted up in the ceiling. She then jumped at his order never even questioning why someone this high up would need to ask her for this information. It just didn't register. *Thank God,* he thought. Tony was extremely relieved as he had concerns about those very same cameras.

As was her duty, she knew each Air Marshall and their designated positions that were within her specific area of responsibility. Her harsh demeanor changed and she proceeded to pretend to engage Tony as a traveler in giving him directions to a destination in the airport. This was protocol if approached by an "S.O". That's what she thought Tony's position was, a high ranking Security Official. She had never seen one outside of training before. They're the eye in the sky, otherwise known as Big Brother behind cameras.

With her right index finger, arm extended, she provided some directions to the airport executive business lounge in a voice loud enough so other people could hear. Tony nodded his head. Then, looking like a dinosaur with one short arm, she quickly pointed from chest high and close to her body.

Ayesha said in a very quiet tone, "Mr. David Clark is wearing a Yankee's baseball cap and he has a carry-on bag which is to always be in his possession. I think you know what's in it. The bag has emblems on each side that reads "Uptown Stanton Mall."

Tony gave her a slightly puzzled look. She looked at him as if doubt had begun to enter her mind about his authority.

Tony quickly recovered and sternly said, "You must verify."

He then held his breathe. She began to answer and his normal consumption of air returned to his lungs once she began speaking.

"The first letter of each word is red then white and finally blue. They're large and very bold letters. You can't miss them."

"Did you say Uptown Stanton Mall?" Tony asked as if confirmation was protocol.

"Yes, *USM*...United States Marshall", she said in a deliberate and almost condescending tone.

Tony said, "Thank you, Ayesha. Your supervisor will be made aware of your willingness to go above and beyond the call of duty."

Immediately after saying this he turned and rolled his eyes and thought, *What an idiot I am. That sounded like it came right out of a crappy movie.*

Tony then made a bee-line to locate Mr. Clark, grabbing his jacket he had stashed on his way to the TSA agent. As he approached his gate he scanned the area where Ayesha said he'd be located. Tony really wasn't looking for a person. Rather, he was looking for a Yankee's cap and the USM bag. At first he couldn't locate his target and he was under a time constraint. Boarding could begin at any moment.

Then, he stood still and thought to himself, *If I were a US Air Marshall where would be the best location to see everything and everyone in the gate area?*

The two of them locked eyes and Tony gave a quick tilt of his head for Mr. Clark to follow him. Tony got up and the US Marshall casually followed about 30 seconds later.

Tony waited in a secluded area, newspaper up, for them to talk.

In a hushed tone, "How'd you know I'm a Marshall and how in the hell do you know my name?" demanded Clark.

"Long story and we're short on time," Tony said.

"Give me the whole story or I'll arrest you here and now. What's your name?" he demanded.

"James," Tony said misleadingly. "I'm so thankful you're here, Dave."

"Cut the bull. I've got a job to do!" scolded Clark.

"Well, this is just going to piss you off then," Tony said with a glare. "We're all in danger."

"From what?" Clark asked.

Tony lowered the newspaper slightly and described the man near the garbage can.

"What about him?" Clark asked with piercing eyes. "Do you know him?" he asked before Tony could answer the first question.

"All I can tell you is I think he's a danger to everyone in this area and if he gets on that plane there's no telling what might happen," Tony stated.

"What evidence do you have?" Clark asked slightly softening his tone.

Now it was Tony's turn to take control of the conversation. Tony took a stab.

"You've had your eye on him for awhile. It doesn't take a brain surgeon to figure that something's up," said Tony.

"How the hell could you know that? I don't make mistakes when I am tailing a person of interest. Are you ex-military too?" questioned Clark.

"At least we're on the same page now. What's your plan to keep him from harming everyone?" asked Tony.

"That's none of your business. What's your name again?"

"I already told you, it's James."

"Go back to where you came from Jimbo and let me do my job," demanded Clark.

Tony folded and dropped the newspaper in the garbage next to him, threw his jacket back on and thought about heading for the nearest stall to release a few tics before returning to Jacquelyn.

There's not enough time. Jacquelyn's got to be wondering what's taking me so long, he thought. He made his way back to his seat next to her.

"You were gone awhile," Jacquelyn said as she looked up from her book.

"When nature calls..." said Tony not finishing his sentence.

Jacquelyn went back to reading her book. Tony was relieved at this, but stressed about getting on a plane with the man with the scar. He tried to conceal his tics the best he could. The amount of stress he felt was pushing him to the limit. If there was ever a time he could use an empty room it was now.

I should have hit the bathroom stall, he thought.

He settled for crossing his right arm and placing his left hand on his chin. Very quickly he twitched his chin and neck while rubbing his whiskers for cover.

The gate attendant's voice came over the sound system and notified the passengers boarding would begin within a few minutes. The sound in the gate area came to life with passengers preparing themselves to board.

Tony looked for Clark, but couldn't find him. He wasn't back in his regular seat.

"Now boarding all priority miles members," said the gate attendant over the loud speakers.

"That's us," Jacquelyn said excitedly.

As Tony got up, the man next to the garbage can was clearly still there but looked as if he had broken his trance. Tony's urge to release tics was almost at its breaking point.

He began to say "Jacquelyn, I don't think we should —." He stopped when he heard multiple loud growling noises.

Tony stood up and was amazed at what he saw. There were two huge German Sheppard dogs on top of the man with the scar. He saw Dave Clark handcuffing him while a police officer appeared to be reading him his rights from a card in her hand. The noise from the passenger's reactions rose to a thunderously high level. Tony took advantage of the distraction to release the build-up.

Jacquelyn and Tony stood watching the man being arrested. Dave Clark stood up, flashing his badge and said, "Everyone remain calm. Everything is under control. "This man has had too much to drink and is in violation of travel safety. Please go ahead and enjoy your flight, there's no danger whatsoever."

Clark then scanned the area for Tony and finally found him. He gave him a nod.

Jacquelyn asked, "Did he just nod at you?"

As Jacquelyn asked this, Tony looked behind him, turned back, and replied, "Must have been someone back there. Ever since the 9/11 attacks I think these guys work in pairs, don't they?"

Tony stood in line to have his ticket scanned and asked, "What was that all about."

The attendant said, "We get some passengers who just don't like to fly and have a little too much pre-flight liquid anti-anxiety medication."

Tony gave a quick look back at the man in handcuffs and thought to himself with an internal half grin, *Tag. You're it.*

Chapter 7

Tony opened one eye to see a slice of the early sunrise piercing through a crack in the shades of their hotel suite welcoming him to his Punta Cana vacation. He slid out of bed without waking Jacquelyn which is no small feat.

Normally she'd wake up to the sound of a cricket, he thought.

He quickly slipped on a pair of shorts and an Air Force tee shirt and sauntered to the lobby. Tony used a resort computer and went online to find out if any news outlets reported yesterday's incident. Sure enough it made the front page of The Portland Tribune and a buried story in USA Today. The headlines were exactly the same: "Suspected Terrorist Plot Foiled."

"Terrorist plot?" he said to himself.

He paused to clear his mind after he clicked off. With a chin tic, throat clearing, shoulder roll and a sigh, Tony let out a deep breath and went about enjoying his long awaited vacation with his beautiful Jacquelyn.

Both of them were in harmony when it came to vacations. Neither of them liked to plan ahead when it came to daily activities. Each preferred to greet the day and then decide to do whatever felt right at the time.

"I didn't even hear you get up," said a sleepy Jacquelyn.

"I wanted to check the place out and get a newspaper. I brought you a coffee." Tony felt a little ashamed for the small white lie, but he did in fact check the place out.

"So where's the paper?"

Thinking quickly Tony said, "I guess I got so caught up with the place I forgot." Then he asked, "Do you want me to go get one?"

"No, I just feel like getting ready and then have breakfast. Thanks for the coffee. How about you? What are you up for today?" asked Jacquelyn.

"Anything as long as I'm here with you," he said as he threw himself on the bed landing on his back. He lifted his head and gave Jacquelyn a kiss on the lips.

"You are just too smooth," she said playfully.

"Can you believe we're alone and have the opportunity to do nothing but lay on the beach and read?" asked Tony.

"Let's make a pact," declared Jacquelyn. "All conversation topics are on the table, as always, except one while we're here."

"And which one would that be?" Tony asked already knowing her answer.

"No talking about the kids," she said with a devilish expression.

"That's a deal," said Tony in total agreement.

He knew Jacquelyn all too well. There was no way she could go more than an hour before Sam and Nick were brought up in conversation.

"Which restaurant do you want to eat at for breakfast?" asked Tony as he stared into Jacquelyn's big brown eyes.

Like a wrestler she wrapped her arms around Tony, flipped him over and said, "Breakfast can wait a little while."

This is going to be a great vacation, thought Tony.

Chapter 8

Tony and Jacquelyn have two wonderful rambunctious children, Samantha and Nickolas. Sam, at the ripe old age of eight, is a bright, talkative bundle of joy with a great imagination. She used to play for hours with any toy or nothing at all. When she was younger one of her favorite things to play was what she called "Family." Usually, it just so happened, her play family was comprised of a mommy, daddy, big sister and a little brother. It amazed both Tony and Jacquelyn that she played for hours at this and the family figures were TOOTHBRUSHES. Tony still shakes his head when he thinks of the toys he, Jacquelyn and others have given her over the years. All they really needed was a set of four tooth brushes and she was good to go. What an imagination.

Little Nick is a non-stop, full speed ahead, six-year old boy with places to go and things to do. At the end of the day it's not unusual to find Nick curled up in a cozy corner fast asleep from his busy day. He apparently has a mischievous schedule to keep and it seems to just wipe him out. Nick adores his big sister. That's why he follows the little brother rulebook and drives her crazy. All he really wants is to be with her. To describe Nick's personality is as easy as looking up the word mischievous in the dictionary. His picture will surely be there.

This typical close knit family lives in a well-groomed home in the growing suburbs of Portland, Oregon. Jacquelyn chose to work part-time as a teacher until Nick was ready to move up to the next grade. Now she's back to full-time. Tony and Jacquelyn feel strongly about raising Sam and Nick instead of outsourcing these duties to daycare. Jacquelyn sacrificed a lot by staying home with the kids before they were both ready for full days of school. Tony hopes they remember her sacrifice someday. He is in awe of how Jacquelyn, with a 4.0 GPA in grad school, seamlessly has her finger on the pulse of the kids' needs. She's the glue of his wonderful little family unit.

Tony's job sometimes takes him on the road overnight, but not too often. Working for the largest computer consulting firm in the United States has its perks. His office is in his home. His responsibilities range from reconfiguring multidimensional servers for Fortune 500 companies, the United States government, troubleshooting international bank security interfaces and everything in between. In short, he's a troubleshooting expert with a hefty dash of sales responsibilities thrown in for good measure. He enjoys working with most people however he feels that sometimes they can be a real pain in his butt. Tony really prefers to work alone, but as jobs go, he's satisfied.

The pay is decent, but he really hates having to answer to a boss. He frequently reminds himself he can put up with a lot of crap as long as he can go home to his family. They are his sanctuary.

Tony fully admits working as an "Information Technology Sales Engineer" actually is as boring as it sounds, but very necessary. Tony isn't into titles, but he really doesn't like his all that much. He doesn't feel like an engineer. It's his job to solve the client's computing issues then, upon success, sell them one of the many technology packages CIT offers.

One would think having Tourette's would discourage a person from even considering getting into anything that remotely resembles a sales career. But, Tony never looked at sales as selling something. He looks at it as problem solving.

Over many years he had to re-learn how to get away from the theory of selling that was drilled into him to be successful. And he is very successful. If there's such a thing as a natural born sales person Tony is one. Why anyone would tamper with his natural instincts was foolish. However, companies have their way of doing things and that's just the way it goes. Tony is ultra-competitive so a sales position is a good fit because it's easy to keep score. He either wins or loses. As you already know he hates to lose. It still is, of course, with great irony that Tony places himself in the stress-filled sales arena. Fortunately, with his approach, there's less emphasis on sales than problem-solving. Once he's done completing his task for the client Tony then seamlessly moves to the sales aspect of his job. His transition is so natural he makes it easy for the client to agree.

Tony, however, does not come across in the manner as many engineers do. He thinks engineer-speak is like Latin without the personality. In his mind's eye many, but of course not all, engineers are very intelligent people who can put people on the moon, but don't know their butt cheeks from their elbows when it comes to social interaction. Nevertheless, his job provides for his family in a manner which they're all comfortable and he has a full grasp of his anatomy.

It's as if he can't help it. He is extremely adept at learning someone's life story within just minutes of meeting them. His questions are like darts as he consumes the information candidly provided. Answering questions with more questions is second nature to him. It's amazing how much he knows about others while they really know very little about him at all. They just think they do and they really like him. Who wouldn't be partial to a person who takes such deep interest in them? Half the time Tony is only really trying to get through the conversation without any mistakes. He does care, but only to a certain point. If it makes them happy, it's just frosting on the cake. Tony extracts what he deems important to remember and deletes the rest from his mind. He has enough going on in his brain than to load it up with what he considers inconsequential information.

Because his job allows him the freedom to work from his office in his home he's the go-to computer guy in the neighborhood. Almost everyone in the neighborhood has asked him for computer help from time to time. The reason is obvious. It's not unusual for them to drop their computer off for Tony to repair. They trust him not to go snooping around their personal files. His character shines through.

Chapter 9

Tony and Jacquelyn got back from the white sands of Punta Cana and they're celebration of their dream anniversary, two years late. One of the few perks that come with Tony's job is he can keep and use any and all frequent flyer miles he racks up...hence the reason for the delay in their trip. Tony and Jacquelyn both tan easily and look healthy and bronzed from their sun-worshiping getaway.

As Tony unpacked the car in the driveway, one of his neighbors from down the street drove by with a little honk of their horn. Tony was busy unpacking the car and only turned halfway providing a friendly wave.

I haven't a clue who you are, but hello anyway, he thought.

Jacquelyn called to him from the front porch. "Are we ready to pick up the kids? I can't wait to see them!"

"I just need to take care of the backseat and we're all set. It should take only few minutes," Tony called out.

He took a personal oath that he wouldn't look at his work issued Smartphone until he and Jacquelyn picked up Sam and Nick and then spent good quality time with them. So now it was on to Grandma and Grandpa's to pick up the kids.

"I'll drive. You drove home from the airport," offered Jacquelyn.

She was more than happy to do this even though she was tired as well. Their love seemed to come from a place only angles can touch. They're a match made in heaven. Sure they have their disagreements, but it's always very civil and productive. Just like with any couple, frustrations can sometimes run high. Happily, they agree way more than they disagree. Each looks out for the other.

"You look tired," said Jacquelyn.

"You look great," Tony quipped looking at his bronzed beauty. "Since you're driving there I'll drive home. Is that a deal?" asked Tony.

"That's a deal," said Jacquelyn.

Tony put his hand out to shake on it, but Jacquelyn just gave him a smile and said, "What are you, in the fourth grade?" They both smiled.

As they turned onto the tree lined road to Jacquelyn's parent's house they saw a gaggle of kids playing in the front yard. The freshly budding trees and flowers created a beautiful back-drop. Jacquelyn pulled the car over well before they were detected.

"What are you doing?" asked Tony.

"I want to watch the kids play," replied Jacquelyn.

From Tony's vantage point in the passenger seat he could see the kids playing and also be able to take in the view of his bride. Jacquelyn's freshly tanned face exuded the joy she was experiencing as she cracked open her window to add to her sensory system of hearing the children at play. They both sat in silence and listened to the sounds of the game going on at her parent's front yard. Her serene, angelic smile showed just how much love Jacquelyn has for Sam and Nick. Tony watched her and smiled with a tender feeling of love in his heart. He knew he was the luckiest man on earth.

Tony then turned his attention to the kids. He picked out Sam and saw a wide grin on her face. She was having a great time. He had a little tougher time finding Nick. Tony scanned the entire front yard, but couldn't see him. Then in a flash Nick came into view running behind a chubby, but older neighbor boy, Jason. Nick had the expression of a determined world class sprinter on his face. Jason looked like he saw a ghost. Apparently Nick was *it*. The tag was made and all the kids seemed to slow down to a moderate pace. They knew Jason would have a hard time catching many of the other kids so this gave them a chance to catch their breath.

As Tony watched with Jacquelyn from the car his world seemed to begin to disappear. He felt his past tugging at him once again. Just the sight of Sam, Nick and the other kids playing tag transported him back to that fateful day. This time the colors and smells were even more vivid. The last thing he remembered was his name being called out once again from the fog.

Off in the distance the playful child's voice transitioned into Jacquelyn's. "Tony...Tony...Tony." As he came out of his childhood memory he was, just for a second, surprised he was sitting in the car.

"Are you okay?" asked Jacquelyn.

She didn't know if there were long term side effects from the Haldol and Pimozide which had caused his terrible hallucination.

Coming out of his haze he said, "What? Oh…yeah, just waxing nostalgic I guess."

"Were you —?" Jacquelyn began.

"Yup, back to tag day," he said.

"Were you hallucinating?"

"No," Tony said emphatically.

"So, tag day, that's what you call it?"

"Yeah, pretty lame huh?" he said sheepishly.

"No not at all. That's clever, actually. I never knew, but it fits because of the double meaning," she said.

They both sat for another minute in silence watching the game.

"I love to see our kids at play. Even tag, I guess," said Tony.

"I'm sorry Tony. I never should've put you in this position," Jacquelyn said compassionately.

Tony just smiled and let her know she did absolutely nothing wrong and he's better off that this memory exists.

"I love watching Sam and Nick when they don't know it. They're such good kids," he said.

"You're right. Thankfully they take after me when it comes to manners," Jacquelyn said with a wry smile.

"Okay, we should probably go get them now," Tony said with a smirk. "Do you think Nick wiped your mom out?" he asked.

"I think she'll sleep for the next three days," answered Jacquelyn slowly. "But I'm sure she had lots of fun along the way", she added.

Jacquelyn thought about asking Tony about details from tag day. She decided to let it go, for now. She started the car and then honked the horn as they approached the driveway. The honk was just as much an arrival announcement as it was for safety.

"Mom and Dad are here!" shouted Sam to Nick.

She and her little brother came running with arms open and big smiles on their faces.

"What'd you bring us?" exclaimed Sam.

"First, I have a great big hug for both of you," said Jacquelyn.

Nick jumped into Tony's waiting arms.

"Dad, do you wanna play with us?" he exclaimed.

Just before he answered, his mother-in-law stepped out with a big welcoming smile.

"Let me talk with Grandma first then I'll be out to play," said Tony.

Nick jumped down after kisses from Jacquelyn and shouted to the gang, "I'm back in!"

After Jacquelyn's welcome home Sam was next to hop up and get a big hug and kiss from Tony.

"Did you take care of your little brother while we were gone?" asked Tony with his forehead pressed to Sam's.

"No, that was Grandma and Grandpa's job," she retorted.

Popping up she asked, "What'd you bring me?"

"Great to see you too," needled Tony. "I see you've just been moping around without us haven't you?" Tony said this as he gazed upon the yard full of smiling and laughing children.

Using two syllables Sam said, "Dad."

Tony whispered into Sam's ear, "Just one quick question Miss Samantha. Did you or Nick need to use "boogers" while we were gone?"

Sam giggled. The kids chose the word boogers as their secret alarm word. They were to use it if they found themselves in some need of help, but couldn't say so, especially over the phone.

After listening she shook her head and said, "Nope."

"Good, go ahead and get back to your game and we might have something for you later. Is that fair?" asked Tony.

"Okay," said Sam and off she went.

Tony went over and gave his mother-in-law, Angela, a big hug.

"They take care of you okay?" asked Tony.

Angela smiled and said, "We had a great time together."

This warmed his heart. Tony adores Angela. He always fell silent anytime one of his friends or co-workers told a "mother-in-law" joke. It always fell flat for him. He knew he had the best in-laws of anyone he knew. Michael, his father-in-law, was at work at the moment. They would catch up with him later. Tony and Michael loved to be outside and just talk. Tony knew how comfortable his relationship was with Michael based on the fact that if there was a period of lingering silence during one of their conversations it was just fine. Neither of them felt uncomfortable about it. They were more friends than in-laws. Tony thought he was the luckiest son-in-law in the world.

That night, well after the kids were tucked snuggly in their beds, Jacquelyn groaned that her spring break vacation was officially over.

"It's so hard to face the reality of work tomorrow," she said.

Tony said, "I suddenly feel as if the air has been let out of my balloon. I wonder how many other people feel about looking towards a Monday full of work. But, at least we get to sleep in the comfort of our own bed. Good night, Jacquelyn. I love you."

"I love you too."

For some reason Tony awoke at 2:15 A.M. and couldn't get back to sleep. After fifteen minutes he got out of bed making sure he didn't disturb Jacquelyn.

Almost every single day since the appearance of his tormentor, upon waking, the first thing that greeted him was a tic. Even before he opened his eyes. He learned that single tic put him on notice he wasn't going back to sleep for awhile. It was time to let the tormentor out so it could play. Sometimes Tony thought of Tourette's as a train rolling down the track. Every time it starts it only picks up steam. At an early age Tony tried to fight it, but soon realized it was to no avail. Once awake he was going to stay that way until he was drop dead tired.

Walking quietly down the hall he was hoping not to see the small, red, blinking light on his desk intruding upon the darkness. He had placed his company-issued Smartphone in the charger, on silent, and left it at home while he was away on vacation. He wanted a real vacation from the temptation of checking his email or messages while gone.

Knowing he was going to be awake for awhile he felt the need to try and get a head start on the day regarding the items awaiting his attention. At first he saw nothing as he approached the desk. Tony knew this couldn't be true. He rubbed his eyes then saw the little red blinking beacon of reality showing its ugly face.

Now my vacation's over, he thought.

Tony closed the door, turned on a small light and picked up the phone. He saw he had ninety-two emails, twenty-one missed calls and seven new voice messages. The voice messages could wait until later. He didn't want to hear anyone's voice from his world of work just yet.

Tony swiftly pressed a sequence of letters and numbers to unlock the screen and began thumbing through his email. He was thrilled.

Almost all of this is junk, he thought.

Since he knew he'd be up for awhile, Tony decided to be productive. He turned on his office computer. He accessed and devoured the bulk of his email. He flagged the few that required action.

A couple of hours later Tony headed back to bed with the knowledge he could attempt to sleep without the thought of any immediate responsibility to his job. However, try as he might, he just couldn't get back to sleep. His tormentor was fully awake and still wanted more amusement.

This wasn't out of the ordinary for Tony. Normally when he went to sleep he'd get at least seven hours straight. But, if his sleep was interrupted for any reason he would be up for hours. It wasn't that he had too much on his mind, but his tormentor just wouldn't let up on him once awake. Ultimately he'd slip into slumber and then eventually welcome the day, albeit, exhausted. The greeting wasn't necessarily a sweet one as he would wake to another day of Tourette's. He had no choice but to plow through and get on with what was required of him.

As a school teacher Jacquelyn's alarm would go off first at 5:25 A.M. After a couple of five minute snooze taps to the alarm she'd be up and ready to begin her day.

Tony was fortunate his commute could be measured in feet rather than miles. He was one-hundred percent in control of his schedule so he had the luxury of being able to lie in bed until 5:45 A.M. Tony hardly ever heard Jacquelyn's first alarm. He did, however, awake almost every day at precisely 5:30 A.M. He set his alarm for 5:35 A.M. but rarely required it. Tony's normal routine was to get up, change into sweat pants, then go directly to his office and begin his work day initiating and responding to email.

After that he'd hit the shower and be ready to greet the rest of the world. One of his favorite things in the morning ritual with Jacquelyn was their kiss goodbye. She always looked so beautiful and put together. Every morning they'd wish each other a good day and everyday Jacquelyn would apologize for getting lip gloss on Tony's lips. He loves this routine. After Jacquelyn was out the door he got the kids ready and took them to school.

Now it was time for him to get down to sustained work. He dreaded getting back into the grind. But, it paid the bills and helped provide for the lifestyle he and Jacquelyn now enjoyed with Sam and Nick.

As he sat down at his desk he let out a sigh. After going through the flagged emails he moved on to the voice messages.

"I left a very specific out of office recording. Apparently it didn't deter these idiots from accepting that a vacation meant I was *GONE*," he mumbled at the phone.

He returned the calls to make sure they were contacted and taken care of by customer service in his absence, which he confirmed they were. So, this waste of time turned out to be just a show of him being conscientious.

I guess that's not such a bad thing, he thought.

He did, however, remind each of them that when he's gone they are in the hands of very dedicated and capable people. Tony was merely trying to get his point across not to leave a message when his outgoing message clearly states he will not have access to messages until he returns.

Call me then, he thought as he scowled.

Since there were no emergencies it was time for him to prioritize. Tony quickly decided on priority number one. He swiveled in his chair and turned the TV on to ESPN to catch up on the world of sports. Priority number two was to work on a firewall protection project at his desk as he listened to Sports Center.

His mind wandered and he began to think about his getaway with Jacquelyn and how wonderful it was. Tony then pictured all the kids playing on the front lawn at Angela and Michael's house. Slowly he began to recall more specifics of what his memory was while in the car with Jacquelyn as they watched the kids play tag.

Chapter 10

After his first contact with his tormentor, little Tony went through the rest of the summer experiencing the ferocious eye blinking off and on. It would last for a week then go away for a day or two. Early on, when it took its brief hiatus, he got his hopes up that it was gone forever, but somehow it always returned. When it did return it seemed to little Tony that it came back much stronger than before.

During one of his eye blinking bouts he made a grunting sound along with it. While they walked on the sidewalk his best friend Ted Barker asked, "What was that?"

Tony thought quickly and proclaimed, "I just swallowed a bug!"

He went so far as to pretend to try and spit it out. They both laughed. There was no reason other than embarrassment for Tony to lie to Ted. However, this seemed to pacify his best pal and made Tony feel almost normal.

They both proceeded to try to run on the sidewalk as fast as the cars passing them by on the street.

"Here comes one!" shouted Barker.

Tony left him in the dust. Of course in little Tony's imagination he kept up with the vehicle for a short time.

He turned to Barker and said, "If you were any slower my grandma could beat you…and she's about a hundred!"

It just wasn't part of Tony's nature to cut the people he cared about any slack when competing. This may have been a trait he picked up from playing with his older brothers and sisters. They were all very competitive. They never took it easy on him just for being the youngest in the family.

The street lights were now coming on earlier at night as summer was coming to a close. Little Tony was about to begin first grade. He was excited and, of course, a little frightened at the same time. His eye blinking and grunting had not only stayed with him through the remainder of the summer, but it had increased in both harshness and frequency as the school year loomed. As far as he could tell relief from the unusual combination now seemed to come only when he slept.

Tony's parents never asked him to stop. It was as if they didn't even notice. As a matter of fact they never said anything about it, at least not to him. Tony took his cue from them and didn't bring it up either. He may have misinterpreted this to mean it should never be spoken about. However, when Tony began constantly clearing his throat he was taken to see the family doctor.

Tony's mother, Mary, was a nurse for a few years in Memphis, Tennessee prior to meeting and marrying Ned. She figured little Tony had a sinus infection or allergies that were the cause of his throat clearing.

So off he went to see the doctor. Dr. Evad inspected Tony's eyes, ears, throat and lungs looking for a reason for the reported throat clearing. Just like a toothache that suddenly goes away when seeing the dentist, so too did Tony's throat clearing retreat into the abyss. This of course was through the work of extreme focus by little Tony. He also tried to keep his eye blinking to a bare minimum. He fought the urges with everything he had during the appointment. Tony was set on not being, in his mind, weird during the appointment.

"Well, Mary. Your son is as healthy as any first-grader I've seen."

Upon hearing this little Tony asked, "Mom, can I use the bathroom?"

"Certainly," she said giving him a nod and a smile.

Tony jumped off the paper covered bed and bee-lined to the bathroom leaving his mom to take care of whatever mom's do after a doctor's appointment. Tony quickly shut the door and began releasing a flurry of tics. He flushed the toilet and ran some water while he had a blinking and throat clearing storm like he never experienced previously.

When he came out of the bathroom Mary asked, "Are you all right Tony? Your eyes are all red."

In an upbeat tone he said, "Yeah, I'm fine. Let's get going so I can play baseball with the guys at the park."

One week prior to school starting Tony began tapping his right hip with his right elbow. It was a movement that kind of looked like he was hitching up his pants. For some reason Tony did this tapping in sets of three, and often.

If one were to closely observe the combination of blinking, throat clearing and tapping it seemed as if Tony had a systematic base melody going through his mind. At the time, he always had the urge to blink, clear his throat then tap his hip, in that order.

Tony also had a proclivity to the number three. While playing little league baseball and his turn at bat, he'd walk from the dugout to home plate with two goals in mind. He needed to get there in a particular number of steps and get on base.

He counted his steps meticulously. However, it wasn't your normal internal count. Tony counted one, two, three, one, two, three, etc. He was internally driven to land on number three when arriving at home plate. If he were about to finish on numbers one or two he would stutter-step to make sure he arrived on number three. Somehow this made him feel better, but he didn't know why. He could feel the restlessness well up if he was coming close to not making it on number three. No one ever knew this and he didn't think it was in his best interest to tell. Besides, many of the professional baseball players he watched had their little idiosyncrasies at the plate. Tony figured this was one of his. Now it's called Obsessive Compulsive Disorder or better known as OCD. In Tony's case it's a first cousin of his tormentor.

Tony didn't know what was happening to him, but he did know when it began. In Tony's visualization of that summer day he pictures a dark shadowy long-armed menace emerging from beneath the ground from behind and ominously reaching out. He was being tagged by Tourette's as he stood and watched his friends. He didn't know he'd been tagged to be *it* for the rest of his life. It doesn't seem fair that a child should have to bear this burden. At the time, however, he couldn't foresee the gift it would bring to him in the future.

Chapter 11

Tony found working with computers very therapeutic. It takes focus and this appears to keep his urge to tic at a minimum for some reason. This solitary task seems to please him even though he views himself to be a people person. Well, maybe a people person with a slight handicap. He enjoys his alone time just as much as he loves being around others. It provides a good sense of balance.

Tony remembers how he fought his way through multiple CIT interviews with extreme focus. Being hired by the largest computer consulting company in the country and being able to remain in the Portland area was tremendously rewarding. He slowly started to make a name for himself by taking on all levels of tasks. One day he would help in customer service and the next he would be troubleshooting computer virus prevention.

Driving over the Ross Island Bridge he headed for his favorite Starbuck's on SW Market Street. There were coffee shops much closer, but the extra few miles didn't bother him. Traffic was always light on weekends and he was looking forward to some quiet time. Unknown to him his big break came on this routine Sunday morning while using his laptop at his old college days' coffee shop. Tony didn't drink coffee, but he loved the wonderful aroma that engulfed him as he walked through the doorway. He ordered and paid for a small black coffee, which he knew he wasn't going to drink.

The cost of admission, he thought.

He grabbed the sports section of a complimentary newspaper on his way to his corner seat. Tony didn't really read the paper because he figured it was just full of old news. Like so many others, he preferred to get his up-to-the-minute news online.

Tony specifically positioned himself in the corner to have a complete view of the entire coffee shop without anyone behind him. He also liked the reflection of the windows that offered more lines of sight. He didn't purposefully think of where he was going to sit, but this of course was how automatic he'd become to protect himself. If he felt a significant urge to tic he simply would use his newspaper as cover. He mastered hiding the small tics with simple techniques that looked like normal movements. Coughing or clearing his throat took care of his verbal tics. He'd even pretend to need to stretch sometimes if he had shoulder tics. He looked as if he were just unwinding a little. At least he thought so.

As he read the sports section of the online version of the Portland Tribune newspaper he felt a presence that, for some reason, brought his antennae up. He lifted his eyes from his computer screen and saw through the reflection of the window next to him a very upscale older woman just entering the café.

Tony instantly got a feeling that whispered *double-edged sword* to him. He had no idea what this meant, logged it into his memory bank, then went back to reading his article.

Hmm, they think the Seahawks look to be a playoff contender this year. Great news, but they say that every year and break my heart, he thought.

About fifteen minutes later Tony glanced at the fashionable older woman as she was using her laptop. It wasn't an unusual site to see clientele with their computers as this establishment enticed new customers by advertising free Wi-Fi. With her forehead and eyebrows bunched up in apparent bewilderment she sat back and exhaled rather loudly. Tony watched her turn to see if other computer users were online. She looked back at her laptop and seemed quite discouraged over her computer troubles. An idea popped into Tony's head.

It's not a bad idea to help people out and, at the same time, advertise for the company I work for, he thought.

He also was curious about what *double-edged sword* meant, so Tony raised his newspaper and released a flurry of tics then walked over and introduced himself.

"Please excuse the interruption. My name is Tony James and I couldn't help but notice you're having trouble with your computer. I work for CIT."

"Hello Mr. James, I'm Ms. Shelton. You are correct. I am having difficulty getting online for some reason. What company did you say you work for?" she asked.

"It's called Computer Information Technologies or, CIT. We're the largest computing consulting company in the United States," Tony said proudly. "I can try to help you, but I don't want to intrude."

94

Audrey looked at Tony and said, "Intrude away. I'm not getting anywhere with this thing and I have an extremely important meeting to prepare for tomorrow. I guess this is my lucky day," she exclaimed.

Tony sat down next to her and found she required a downloadable patch for her internet browser to access the essential data program.

"Don't I need to be on the internet to get the patch?" asked Audrey.

"Normally you do, but I can find a way around it," said Tony. *Points for knowing that*, Tony thought.

He went back over to his corner seat and took out a thumb drive and inserted it into his computer and downloaded the patch. He then went back over to Ms. Shelton and, with her permission, plugged the thumb drive into her laptop and uploaded the file. After numerous lightening fast keystrokes, the file was installed.

"Well Ms. Shelton, you should be all set."

His instinct told him to call her Ms. Shelton. He usually uses everyone's first name. He once gave racquetball lessons to the head of one of the largest companies in the United States. He specifically was told to call his new pupil Mr. Warner.

As soon as he saw him he said, "Hi Phil, I'm Tony. It's a pleasure to meet you." He gave a slight little nod to Andrew's stuffed shirt assistant who accompanied him.

"See if you can get on the internet now," said Tony.

With a double click on her browser icon she was in business. "Thank you so much Mr. James."

"Please, call me Tony."

"All right, Tony, thank you for your kindness, and you may call me Audrey. Have you a moment to sit?" asked Audrey.

Tony was very comfortable with this request so he said, "Absolutely, but just for a few minutes. I don't want to take up too much of your time."

"How long have you worked for this computer company Tony?"

"Not real long, but long enough," he said vaguely.

Let her direct the conversation, his instincts told him. Normally he would jump right in and begin asking questions and deflecting the ones that came his way. *There's something interesting here,* he thought.

"What is it you do besides help perfect strangers in a coffee shop?" she asked.

Tony gave a small chuckle.

"I'm temporarily in an annual re-training program at our corporate headquarters during the week. Normally I work out of my office in my home helping clients, and potential new clients, with their computer needs."

"What do you mean *supposed* to be?" asked Audrey.

"Well, I already know the job inside and out so I've been freelancing on various floors doing whatever's needed instead of attending the boring classroom sessions."

"Aren't you missing out on important information by skipping them?" she asked.

Before he could answer she quickly asked, "How do you know what's needed if, as you said, you've not been there real long?"

Tony noticed a small change in her demeanor. I hit some kind of a hot button with that answer for some reason. I'll answer her bluntly and see what reaction I get, he thought.

"Well, Audrey, I hop on the elevator and pick a number that feels right and go to that floor. Every few days I try to first go to a higher numbered floor. My temporary cubical is on the second floor. You know, the higher the number the bigger the big shots. I then find the closest person in charge and let them know I'm there to fix it," said Tony.

"Are you saying because you're on the second floor that your company doesn't think much of you?" she asked.

"No, I don't think that at all. It's just temporary. As I said my real office is in my home."

"So, that's it?" she asked.

"That's what?" he asked a little confused.

"You just find the person in charge without hesitation?" she clarified.

"That's it," Tony replied succinctly.

She paused in a manner as if sizing him up. She broke her silence and said, "What an adventurous, confidant, clever and sneaky young man."

Ouch, she said sneaky, that's not good, thought Tony.

"But, I love it! I think your company is very lucky to have you as an employee Tony."

I know a backhanded compliment when I hear one, he thought.

Does your boss know?"

"No, a very nice person but she's, let's say, isn't the brightest bulb in the box."

"Do you think they have misplaced you within your company? That is if you actually do fix whatever you show up to fix."

You might not be as bright as I originally thought. Why would I just show up to fix something if I didn't have the confidence to actually do so, he thought.

"Oh, I always find a way to get the job done," smiled Tony. "I always find a way."

Tony noticed Audrey had tapped the touch pad on her computer twice now to keep it from going into sleep mode. This was his key to remove himself from the conversation.

"I know you didn't come in here just to talk to me so I'll let you get back to work," Tony said. What Tony really wanted to say was, *I see you want to get to work and I have to go tic now, so goodbye.*

"If it weren't for you I wouldn't be able to get anything done. Thank you once again Tony James, and it has been a pleasure meeting you."

"Likewise, I hope we run into each other again someday."

"It's a small world. That's always a possibility Tony. You have a good day."

"You do the same Ms. Shelton."

Tony went back to his seat and picked up the newspaper and released some of the tics that had piled up since sitting down with Ms. Audrey Shelton.

Chapter 12

Being the youngest of five children, Tony grew up fighting hard to set himself apart from his two big brothers and two sisters. Much of the time he did this with humor and hustle. He couldn't tell a story joke with an accurate punch line to save his life. On the other hand, he'd been blessed with a lightning quick wit that provided endless laughs. Banter became his verbal playground.

He grew up in a home full of love and laughter. Because of the closeness of his family he was surrounded by love. He was given a solid foundation in the important personal characteristics of life.

His mother, Mary, was a stay at home mom. Her listening skills were impeccable. Seldom did she interrupt. It appeared she had a deft ability to make a connection on a very personal level with almost everyone she came into contact. She could massage nearly any situation with her nimble communication and personality traits. People frequently went from total disagreement to complete and happy agreement with her. She did this without even the hint of argument. Mary looked the part, but wasn't an athletic individual by any means. Nevertheless, she had the strongest, yet most unassuming mental toughness of anyone in the family. For example, when she went for dental work she would never accept pain killing Novocain. She just focused and blocked out the bad stuff.

Tony's humble father worked hard on his way up becoming a Regional UPS manager with a big work ethic and an even bigger heart. His involvement in coaching athletics at almost every level provided him the satisfaction missing from the daily grind. At his core he's very shy, but gets along with people extremely well. There are many things Ned James wanted in life, but nothing even comes close to his relationship with his soul mate, Mary. It's as if the angels in heaven held a meeting and paired them together.

He is the king of role models to Tony and his siblings when it comes to what marriage is suppose to look like. He doesn't need to talk the talk. He walks the walk. One of Ned's blessings to his children is that in his heart of hearts he's a natural born teacher. This extends well past athletics and into the core of life itself. Ned prides himself as a disciplinarian. However, Tony always saw through this façade and quickly realized his bark only covered up the lack of a flesh penetrating bite.

Some kids idols are movie stars, rock stars or sports figures. Very few kids idolize their parents, including Tony. He respects them. Tony believes his view of his parents is exactly what it should be. It's the result of how he was raised.

Tony's early childhood idol was his oldest brother Gary, who is almost nine years his senior. Popular with friends, good at sports and when they were kids he treated Tony like most big brothers do. He pushed Tony around when others were near, but he became the best friend any little brother could possibly have when they were alone together. Tony wanted to be just like him. They had many similar personality traits as well as the look-alike factor. Of the five siblings Gary and Tony were definitely cut from the same physical genetics pool.

Henry is the second oldest of Tony's brothers, as well as, his position on the James' sibling family tree. He has a blend of personality traits from both Ned and Mary. When Mary and Ned went out and Gary wasn't around, which was often, Henry became the de-facto parent in charge. He took good care of Tony.

Little Tony always appreciated that Henry walked at his pace. This was one thing his father had never conquered. Ned walked at Ned's pace and little Tony would just have to keep up.

As they walked, Henry always had a guiding hand on the back of Tony's neck. It wasn't meant to be controlling, but to create a connection between brothers. Henry was a good athlete at some sports. He didn't have that "it" factor when it came to athletic ability. Henry's athleticism required him to think his way around opponents rather than beat them physically. Tony took early notice of this interesting fact and soaked in as much as he could from his big brother.

His oldest sister Olivia was very popular in high school. She was a cheerleader and a 4.0 student. She never really excelled at sports, but played tennis well enough to give many players a run for their money.

She didn't have that desire to destroy her opponents. No, Olivia is just too nice to do that to anyone. In fact, she's so nice she had a hard time saying no to her friends. One day she had gotten out her last piece of gum and began to unwrap it. One of her friends asked if she could have a stick. Olivia gave it to her, but really wanted it for herself. It was her last one, but she just couldn't bring herself to deny her friend. She desperately wanted to say no, but she couldn't let down a friend. So, she went without. Saying no was so very difficult for Tony's oldest sister.

Olivia is the third oldest of the James family siblings. When it came to Tony she took the responsibility like that of a second mom. Not that one was needed. But, that was just Olivia. There seemed to be a stronger sense of responsibility for her when it came to Tony. It must have been because he was the youngest. She saw how his brothers picked on him.

Maggie, being just three years older than Tony, was more of a playmate and target for Tony. Maggie's sense of responsibility and following the rules gave Tony buckets full of teasing ammo. Of course that's what little brothers do. It's in the rule book.

On one particular sunny summer day little Tony and Maggie each purchased some candy at a neighborhood store.

"I got an extra dime in change!" announced Tony once out on the sidewalk.

"You have to take that back into them and give it back. It's not right for you to keep it," ordered Maggie.

With Tony being younger he decided that he would obey his big sister and gave the money back. He went back in by himself.

When he returned Maggie asked, "Now don't you feel better?"

"No, I feel the same," said Tony as he skipped away in a teasing manner.

Maggie quizzed him all the way home and even asked to see his pockets turned inside out. She didn't believe he actually gave the dime back. He had given it back, but this was the kind of fun little Tony had at Maggie's expense. Tony had not only read, but memorized the little brother rule book. Maggie might say he wrote a chapter or two.

When Maggie grew up and was in high school she became a top ranked player in the state of Oregon in women's tennis. She was a true tactician and practiced very hard with her dad. When they were little Tony would always go to the park with Maggie and their dad for her practice sessions. He would beat the ball against a giant wooden board which carried a white stripe across it representing the top of the tennis net. As he banged the ball against the wall he'd listen to his big sister's lesson as closely as possible.

It hadn't surfaced to his conscious level yet, but when he was focused at hitting the ball, and listening to his sister's lesson, he was tic free. No wonder he wanted to go every time she had a lesson. At times Maggie had some frustrations about a particular part of the game that just wasn't going the way Ned wanted. To her credit she would argue her case, but it usually ended the practice session and they would then have to go home. It was the same every time.

"Tony, let's go. Get in the car. We're done for the day!" Ned would shout.

This was his way of telling Maggie he was displeased, as her coach, and the lesson was over. He never told her why as she fumed for hours. Tony knew at such a young age that this was, of course, a tactic and part of the lesson. His dad was trying to toughen her up.

Chapter 13

It took a full two weeks for Jacquelyn and Tony to get used to facing Monday mornings again. They seemed to come around too quickly as Tony again hit the snooze alarm twice before rolling himself out of bed. Jacquelyn was already up and getting ready for another full day of teaching. They looked at each other and didn't have to say a word. Both of them were still having a hard time getting the ball rolling up hill after such a wonderful vacation. Today, Jacquelyn wanted to take the kids to school.

Instead of working out of his home Tony drove to CIT's corporate headquarters in a mental haze. He entered the building then took the elevator to the second floor. He checked his watch and the digital readout showed it to be 7:56 A.M. As he stepped off the elevator he headed straight for his mailbox and picked up the three envelopes and a small package that were waiting for him.

Tony proceeded to his temporarily assigned desk and reviewed the barren surroundings. As he sat down he took a closer look at his mail. All three envelopes were garbage and discarded immediately. Next up was to open the box. Tony read the label and to his surprise it was from the office of human resources.

He carefully opened the package and removed its contents. *This is strange,* Tony thought. It was a coffee mug. *I already have a company mug and two more at home*, he reflected. At second glance he realized it wasn't a CIT mug but rather a Starbuck's mug. The typed note-card inside read:

Thanks for your help, Mr. James. I will see you at 4:00 P.M. today in my office on the 33rd floor. I'm guessing you haven't made it up to this level yet. There is a problem to be fixed.

Best regards,

Audrey Shelton

Audrey Shelton, President and CEO

Computer Information Technologies Corporation

Tony almost accidently knocked the mug off his desk as he read the note.

"I can't believe the one person I told of my extracurricular activities at CIT was the president of the whole company! What kind of an idiot does that?!" He paused lifting his head from the note then said, "I'm being fired, I just know it." As his eyes came back to focus on his surroundings he saw a few heads had turned his way. "What are you looking at? Get back to work," he said without regard to hurting anyone's feelings.

His mind raced to find a safety net. He called Jacquelyn's cell phone, but got her voice mail. He didn't leave a message. *What to do*? The stress at the moment was enormous for Tony. The proverbial light bulb suddenly went on over his head.

I sure hope the office supply room is unoccupied right now, he thought.

As he entered the room he said good morning to a young woman just leaving. She struggled with the door due to the many items she was carrying. Tony held the door for her. He entered, looked around pretending to locate an item, and to his relief found he was alone. He then locked the door behind him. After the torrential release of tics in the supply room Tony decided to try deep breathing before he left the confines of this sanitarium. By the time he unlocked and opened the door he was ready to get back to his desk and settle into a normal day.

Normal...how can today be normal? I'm sure I'm going to be fired, he continued thinking.

Tony made a conscious decision he was going to strap himself to his desk. He wasn't leaving his floor unless there was a fire.

Hey, maybe pull the fire alarm about 3:50 P.M. and I'm home free! What am I, eight years old? Take it like a man. I guess now I know what the double-edged sword feeling means. But, somehow, that just doesn't seem right. It didn't come across like that to me at the time, he thought.

Chapter 14

Years earlier there was one specific occasion which became the impetus for little Tony to put the nail in the coffin of feeling that he needed to try to hide his involuntary movements and sounds. This singular occasion changed Tony's entire view of his world. More precisely, he felt the tectonic shift of how the world viewed him.

Guests were over and the entire family was together for an enjoyable time talking and laughing in the living room. One of the James' family rules was none of the young children were allowed to eat in any room except the kitchen. Big brother Gary cemented that rule years before when he spilled a cherry drink on the carpet while watching TV. So, pre-first grade Tony and his sister Maggie, ate their popsicles while sitting on the linoleum kitchen floor at the entrance to the living room.

Tony's parents made sure none of their children ever felt left out so Tony and Maggie happily joined the conversation as they licked their icy treats. Little Tony's tongue and mouth were a carbon copy color of his red cherry Popsicle. He took joy out of being able to be with his family and have a treat at the same time.

Then it happened.

His mother, Mary, was telling a story and currently the center of attention. While enjoying his treat Tony looked up to find his oldest sister, Olivia, staring at him from the other side of the room. When their eyes finally met she did something that set Tony on a path to permanently try to hide his involuntary movements and sounds for the rest of his life. Once she knew Tony had locked onto her eyes she very precisely mimicked the hard blinking and hip tapping that Tony was experiencing. He was so surprised and embarrassed he stopped mid-lick to absorb this surreal moment. No one else noticed.

Still stunned, Tony continued to look at Olivia while she did it again! He couldn't believe that his big sister, whom he loves so much, was making fun of him! Olivia had always looked out for Tony. This made no sense to him!

The conversation in the room became muffled background noise as Tony sat and focused his young mind to force himself to stop his unwanted movements. He succeeded for a short time, but then a flurry of quick repetitions enveloped him. All he could think to do was to get up and go outside to sit alone on the cement porch. He didn't need the pressure of his sister staring and making fun of him.

Feeling betrayed by his own loving big sister was THE wake-up call that moved Tony to impose strict adherence to a code he would live by for the rest of his life.

He thought, *HIDE THIS FROM EVERYONE*!

Olivia only meant to help little Tony. Her heart was in the right place as she thought he could control these unusual movements. She was only trying to help him become aware of what he was doing. She succeeded.

At that moment Tony had no idea how he was going to hide his tics, but he knew he had to try.

If Olivia will make fun of me, what about everyone else, he questioned. Rolling through his young mind was the thought, Mom and Dad never said anything to me.

After sitting on the porch a few minutes he got up, threw what was remaining of his melting icy treat into the bushes and ran up the street as fast as he could. His destination was anywhere but home. Tears streamed down his determined face.

He found himself breaking his parents rule by crossing the street without asking them. Not only did he cross the street, but he ran full steam to the park on the North side of town. The inviting array of playground contraptions was always a special place where his mom took him after things like a dentist appointment. He also loved the dog park area since they had no pets of their own. In another section of the park the atmosphere was that of a carnival complete with live caged animals and a small version of a steam train to ride. What little boy wouldn't want to immerse himself in this world of fun especially after being slammed by a humiliating two-by-four over the head?

Little Tony wasn't at an age in which he could really capture and process what he was experiencing. All he knew was that he needed to get away and be by himself. He became more aware of his tics than ever before. On any other given day he would have no qualms about asking another little boy to play on the teeter-totter with him. However, as of this day he viewed himself differently. He became hyper-aware of his tics and, when possible, of who was watching him. His big sister parted his shroud.

Cloudy words gnawed at him, "Pay no attention to the little boy behind the curtain."

Chapter 15

He sits at his temporary CIT desk and can feel the ache of each minute passing as if they were hours. This situation is one of the few times he has felt stricken with fear not caused by his tormentor. Tony's core personality isn't a fearful one. As a matter of fact it's quite the contrary. He enjoys taking risks. When he and a group of co-workers went skiing Tony was the only one to head directly up to the black diamond trail just for pure excitement. The problem for Tony is that he has to rely heavily on a filter because of Tourette's so he always chooses his adventures with it in mind. However, everyone has fears and one of Tony's is disappointing Jacquelyn. Getting fired would certainly be a disappointment to her and cause a major bruise to his ego. The more Tony thought about how it would make Jacquelyn feel his emotions began to shift him into a melancholy mood. He, for some reason, wound up thinking back to when they met each other. This time it wasn't just Tony meeting her from a distance. It was when they actually met each other.

They physically met at JJ Floyd's Athletic Club and got to know each other on a very casual basis. The club catered to all levels of fitness buffs, as well as having a well rounded social calendar. Tony normally would play his racquetball league match then hang around outside the glass court to socialize with fellow players. This was his element. He rarely went upstairs to the beautiful glass encased bar that overlooked the courts. He knew he'd have to work too hard suppressing his tics. There were just too many people around for him to get away with hiding them in plain sight for very long.

However, on this particular evening he glanced up from the court and noticed the very same stunning goddess from the office building! She was by herself, watching his match from the upstairs bar behind the thick glass. His heart rate was already high from running around the court like a mad man. Seeing her again raced it into the red zone! His stomach did a double flip. He was glad his match was almost over. Tony poured it on and disposed of his opponent as quickly as possible. He didn't want this opportunity to pass him by.

Tony wasted no time hanging out with his fellow players. He showered quickly and headed upstairs to see if she was still there. The first place he looked was where she'd been watching. No luck. As he moved through the crowd he continually scanned for her as he said hello to just about everyone. Because of Tony's racquetball success, just about everyone in the place knew him.

His heart was beating fast, but then began to slow. He no longer saw the angelic woman he so longingly wanted to meet. Tony slowly moved into the middle of the bar and did a 360 degree move once again without luck. With a heavy sigh and slight slump of his shoulders he began to turn and head for the exit behind him. As he did so he bumped into the future Mrs. James.

After a stuttering start, Tony introduced himself and they wound up finding a semi-private place to sit and talk. As it turned out she was interested in taking racquetball lessons. She had never played before and wanted to learn. She knew nothing about Tony and his racquetball success. Tony gave lessons all the time. They set up a day and time and were set. Tony was in heaven!

About a week later Tony was on one of the courts with a glass back wall teaching a group lesson. A gentle knock at the door came about five minutes after he'd begun. He excused himself, opened the door and there she was.

Jacquelyn said, "Did you forget something?"

Tony was basically incoherent.

"We have a lesson on court four and it started five minutes ago," she said politely staring deeply into his eyes.

After a quick apology that he must have mistakenly double booked himself she said, "That's alright. I'm sure they won't mind rescheduling."

He loved that she wasn't a wet dishrag. She was willing to stand up for herself.

Tony quickly said, "Head back to court four and I'll be right there."

He re-entered the court and told the group his scheduling situation then provided them specific drills to work on during their hour. The men in the group didn't blame him as they had caught the lovely vision when she originally tapped on the court door. With their blessing he then hustled on over to court four with an extra spring in his step.

Tony was mostly used to giving private lessons to the up and coming future stars. He rarely wanted to give a lesson to teach beginners about the basic rules. He loved getting to know the people, but teaching the rudimentary aspects of the game bored him. It was most definitely atypical with his new pupil. He didn't mind at all.

To his surprise Jacquelyn wanted to book another lesson for the following week. He figured he'd blown it by being incapable of keeping their first lesson appointment. But, they really hit it off both on and off the court. After each lesson they spent some time talking about a wide variety of topics. They got to know each other pretty well after awhile.

He really wanted to ask her out on a date, but his self-protection mode kicked in once again. Tony was enjoying his time with her and he didn't want it to stop. He figured once she said no then the lessons would likely end and that would close the door. She'd be out of his life. Tony just simply felt he was so completely out of her league. To his surprise, it wasn't Tony who asked Jacquelyn out, but rather the other way around.

Once alone he questioned aloud, "Of all the guys on earth, why does she want to go out with me?"

He loved it, but still felt completely unworthy.

Chapter 16

Saturday finally arrived. Tony's first date with Jacquelyn. Tony awoke extra early. As he opened one eye he reached out to illuminate the time on the clock next to his bed.

"Seriously? 4:58 A.M.?," he groaned.

Try as he might he wasn't getting back to sleep. As he slowly came to life he became energized thinking about his first date with Jacquelyn. Conversely, he began thinking about his tormentor intruding just at the wrong time.

When was there ever a right time, he thought.

The evening plan was just a simple traditional dinner and a movie. It seems backwards, but he knew he could handle the dinner with ease. Covering facial tics using his napkin and coughing or clearing his throat almost always proved successful for his vocal and facial tics.

However, sitting still through a two hour movie began to consume his thought process. Tony felt a little unsettled just thinking about it. His leg tics were bound to bring notice. He knew he would seem nervous and fidgety to Jacquelyn.

What a turn-on, he thought.

Tony so wanted to impress her, but knew he could only do so much about his tics. After turning himself inside and out he determined he only had so much control and it would have to be enough.

Tony then reminded himself of the feeling brought to him regarding Jacquelyn...*compassion*. This in itself helped him. He was going to do his best and be himself at the same time.

I don't know how to be anyone else so I might as well just be the person I am, he thought.

The lack of complete control just made things worse as stress kept building through the day. He went for an extended run then lifted weights at the club. His knees swelled from pounding the pavement, but it was worth the resulting lower stress level. Evening was upon him and finally time for Tony to pick Jacquelyn up. Standing at her front door, flowers in hand, he peered through the glass portion as she came into sight. At first his mind went totally blank.

She is absolutely stunning, he then thought. Of all the women in the world he couldn't think of going out with anyone but her. *What the heck is wrong with her that she wants to go out with me? Maybe I've done a better job of hiding these tics than I thought. Don't tempt fate*, he reminded himself as she opened the door.

They went to an upscale restaurant for dinner knowing full well the bill would put a dent in his monthly budget. There was never a lull in conversation. Both Jacquelyn and Tony were having a great time.

Prior to leaving the restaurant Tony excused himself to use the men's room. He didn't need it for its natural intended purpose. Tony felt much better after the moderately needed tic release. After dinner they headed off to the theater for their movie, conversing the entire way. As they entered and chose their seats Tony could feel his tic level building. Nobody could tell, not even Jacquelyn. He had forced himself to be a master of disguise. However, he couldn't wait for the lights to go down so he wasn't conspicuous in relieving some of the tics without the worry of notice. He made sure he bought popcorn just in case he needed to clear his throat of that one kernel which seemed to always get stuck.

I'm sure it's in the movie rule book, he jokingly thought.

The movie began and Tony was enjoying himself with Jacquelyn sitting beside him so much that he made a critical error. For most people it's no big deal. However, for Tony, this was a gargantuan mistake. Tony put his right arm around Jacquelyn.

The dilemma wasn't that she didn't like this. Quite the contrary. She leaned his way. The issue was, now that his arm was around her, he couldn't take it back. That would just be rude. Tony certainly wasn't going to be discourteous. Not to Jacquelyn.

The big issue was the longer his arm was around her the more he had to try and not allow his right shoulder to tic. Minutes seemed like hours. He just couldn't hold on any longer. His tormentor broke through and Tony began moving his shoulder in an up, down then backward motion. But, that wasn't all. He did this in repetitions of three.

Tony knew Jacquelyn had to be wondering what the heck was going on.

Turning to him she finally politely whispered, "Is there something wrong?"

119

Tony was embarrassed, but with the lights so low she apparently didn't notice.

"I, uh, worked out today and my shoulder doesn't feel so good in this position," Tony whispered back.

He felt guilty for making up such a story, but he couldn't imagine telling her the truth. Jacquelyn gently took his arm and helped him place it on the armrest between them.

Thank God. She is so sweet! "Sorry," he said.

Then to his surprise she placed her head against his shoulder and interlocked their fingers. Tony absolutely loved this except he was going to have the same problem with his tormentor if he wasn't allowed to move the immovable arm and fingers. This was how his tormentor loved to play. Fortunately Jacquelyn moved with the action of the movie providing minor room for tic relief.

After taking Jacquelyn home he drove away thinking, *I really like her. I can't wait to see her again. She's perfect.*

He just couldn't stop thinking about her.

Chapter 17

Still sitting at his temporary desk at CIT, Tony checked the setting on his digital alarm wrist watch. He had set it for 3:45 P.M. so he'd be on time for his meeting with Audrey. He really didn't need to because today after lunch he checked the time about every five minutes anyway. It was finally time to head to the elevator. He packed up his few personal belongings. Just two pictures of Jacquelyn and the kids from his temporary desk and put them into his briefcase. Tony didn't want to suffer the humiliation of a security guard escort from his desk, then out the front doors.

Tony felt at home riding the elevator, even with the camera in the upper right corner peering down at him. He took note that he never did press number thirty-two in all his previous brief adventures. He also noticed number thirty-three didn't exist. He rode straight to the top and the elevator provided the proverbial ding of destination then the doors opened. He got out and a man wearing a blue blazer with a security patch on his pocket glared at him.

"You lost?" he asked sternly.

Even in his frame of mind he couldn't help but think, *Amateur intimidation tactics are so lame.* Tony raised his left arm out in front of him to pretend to look at his watch. In his line of sight he could catch a glimpse of the big man's ID badge.

"Actually, I'm right on time Paul, but thanks for asking."

Thanks for not having a first name like Richard. It would have been a stab in the dark based on the number of nicknames derived from it. *Hardly anybody ever named Richard goes by Richard*, Tony thought. He saw the subtle change of Paul's relaxed body language. *Try to intimidate me will you*, he thought sarcastically.

"I've got a 4:00 P.M. meeting with Audrey, Paul," he said nonchalantly.

That's right Paul. I called her by her first name because I belong here. I also know your name because, well, I'm just sneaky... but that's beside the point. And another thing, if I'm getting fired I still want you to think I've got one over on you, he thought to himself.

Tony always found it a bit amusing that he could manage the mood of some people. Paul's body language changed once again. This time it was to that of a more deferential posture. Paul checked Audrey's guest schedule for the day on his computer. As Paul turned away Tony raised his left hand to his chin as if to scratch it...tic, tic.

"Right this way Mr.?"

"James, Tony James." *Now I just sound like I'm in a Bond movie*, he thought.

This was just a test question by Paul. Tony had his ID badge in his shirt pocket so Paul couldn't identify him. This was completely accidental. Out of habit Tony was used to putting his ID badge in his pocket when on the elevator moving from floor to floor. Paul then grabbed his huge ring of keys which were attached to a retractable wire on his belt. He located the one that unlocked the only elevator that led to the thirty-third floor.

Tony stepped in to his right, pressed the lone button available to go up, took one step to his left and said, "Thanks Paul, see you when I'm done."

"Have a good meeting Mr. James," he replied.

Now there's a change of attitude. If he only knew I was about to be fired.

"Thanks," Tony said with poise.

Tony knew he was on camera once again so he tried to force his tics into solitary confinement. As the elevator began to move he bent down to dust off his right shoe to conceal a triple tic he couldn't keep at bay. The short ride up one floor allowed him enough time to get his game face on.

If she's going to fire me I'm going out with a bang. I'll let her know exactly what's on my mind, no holding back. I was just trying to help the old bag. Why did I open my big mouth anyway, he questioned knowing he brought this on himself.

The elevator door opened and Tony expected an opulent receiving area. He figured Audrey's assistant would talk to him in a dismissive manner then wait too long while she made him sweat. He figured this was in the big shot handbook somewhere. As he stepped over the elevator threshold he was taken aback. He was instantly in her office. There was no assistant, no outer waiting area, just her big spacious office. Two sides provided a fantastic view for miles.

She sat with her back toward him looking out the window over the city while talking on the phone.

I wonder why she waited this long to decide to fire me?, he thought. Tony snuck in a few quick tics while pretending to re-arrange the contents of his briefcase. *Now I'm ready, so let's focus*, he thought.

As he entered her office a little further he got a double feeling about being there. His visual attention was on Audrey, but the same feeling came to him about her as it was in the coffee shop. It certainly didn't feel threatening.

He very quietly said, "Okay, this is confusing. Why am I now getting two feelings? It's not the same as Audrey's *double-edged sword* feeling. This other one is, he paused... *calculating*, but I don't think it has anything to do with her."

Audrey finished her call and swiveled her chair to greet Tony. She stood up and sweetly said, "Welcome, Tony. Don't be afraid, come in and have a chair right here." She pointed to the very cushy seat in front of her mahogany desk.

Tony didn't expect such an enthusiastic greeting. *She must be one of those head honchos that likes to kill with kindness before she bats people around. Well, I'm not in the mood. I'm not up for cat and mouse....especially since I'm the mouse.*

"Hello Ms. Shelton," said Tony in a business-like tone.

"What's with the Ms. Shelton? "Did you forget my first name?"

"Of course not I just thought —"

124

"Just because we're at work doesn't mean we can't be on a first name basis. Especially in my office," she declared.

Tony decided to pounce while he had the chance. "I think that was a pretty lousy way to go about setting me up today."

"What are you talking about?"

The features on her face turned sour, yet sincere. Tony sensed he better change directions quickly based on his consumption of auto-feedback from Audrey. It wasn't just her words or body language that Tony picked up on.

Something is wrong with this picture, he thought.

Tony continued, but did a 180, "You send me a Starbucks mug and make me wait until the end of the day to let me thank you?" he retorted.

Ah, she's smiling again. Feedback confirmed. *I'm not busted...yet*. Tony lightly scratched his forehead removing a tiny bead of sweat.

Audrey was saying something to Tony, but he had focused elsewhere. *Calculating* was a word that seem to whisper to him from somewhere within the confines of this office. But, where was it coming from?

Then he heard Audrey ask, "Did you bring your new mug? I have fresh coffee," she said with a hint of excitement in her voice.

"No I'm sorry I didn't," Tony said in a disappointed tone.

He'd thrown it away earlier in the day out of spite.

"Well I think I can remedy that. How do you prefer your coffee?" asked Audrey.

Tony was trying to decipher the mixed messages he was receiving. Not only was he focusing on Audrey, but he had to hold the urge to tic from Tourette's, while trying to figure out this *calculating* message he was receiving.

"I have a confession, Audrey," he blurted.

She stopped dead still.

"I don't drink coffee. I only buy a cup because I use the coffee shop to get some alone time and they have free Wi-Fi."

Audrey quickly unfroze at Tony's proclamation.

"Alone from what?" asked Audrey.

"Don't get me wrong, but when you have young kids at home you just don't get much peace and quiet on weekends."

"I completely understand. My children are grown and have been on their own for a long time. But, I do remember those days," she said.

"Here's your coffee."

"But I don't —"

She cut him off and said, "Just like the coffee shop then…right?"

"Right," Tony said uncomfortably.

"May I ask you a question Audrey?"

"Of course you may."

"Why didn't you tell me you're the CEO of CIT when we met at Starbuck's?"

"I'm sorry about that Tony. Seeing you proudly represent this company to a perfect stranger on a Sunday morning made me want to know more about you. If I had revealed myself I wouldn't have met the real you would I?"

Tony paused for a moment then said, "No, probably not."

Audrey sat back down and said, "Let's get down to business then, shall we?"

"All right," he vacantly replied as he sat across from her.

"I've read your file, which includes your background check. You are exactly the type of person I've been looking for. CIT needs someone who is very likable, helpful, ambitious, adventurous and willing to break a few rules for the greater good every now and then."

"Audrey I was just trying to —"

She held up her hand to stop him. "I meant that as a compliment Tony. I have thousands of employees and I can count on one hand the number of them who actually think for themselves. I now count you in that minority."

Tony's instinct told him to say very little from this point forward.

"Thanks," he replied.

I'm still getting that vibe, but it's not from Audrey.

"So, here's what I'd like to offer you," she said.

"Offer me?" he asked. *I thought you were going to fire me*, he then thought.

She laid a red folder in front of Tony to open. In it was a new job description, while keeping his same Information Technology Sales Engineer title. He was being asked to become an "ambassador" for CIT.

This is a promotion without a title change. I don't get it, but I'm just fine with it as long as it pays more, he thought.

"What do you think Tony?"

"Will you explain it to me?" Tony asked.

"Your generosity, personality and skill set are a perfect fit to be our representative at functions throughout our global reach," she said proudly.

"Global?" Tony repeated timidly.

"Don't worry, Tony, you won't be traveling away from your family that much."

"That much" could mean anything, he thought.

"As a matter of fact one of the perks is your family can accompany you often."

"How much travel is involved?" Tony asked.

"You would be overnight every now and then."

Still vague, he thought, but didn't push it.

Her phone rang and she excused herself to take the call after looking at caller ID. Tony quickly looked the document over and then re-focused on the nagging feeling he was receiving. He bent over to pick up the pen he *accidently* dropped...blink, blink, blink. He just couldn't pinpoint its genesis. Tony took in a few breaths to try and clear his head. He then looked to his left as if to admire the décor of Audrey's office. Tony was, however, beginning to hone in on this feeling. His ability, at least this time, was like a torpedo moving through water and correcting course quickly and automatically. For some unknown reason, after sweeping half the room, he came back to a white framed full length wall mirror. He stared at it with a vice-like focus.

Bingo! That's where it's coming from.

Tony stared at it as if he were trying to bore his sight right through the thing like Superman. Audrey was finishing up with her conversation so Tony went back to the folder he was holding.

"So what do you think Tony?"

"I think this is a very nice opportunity."

"Did you notice the rather large bump in pay?"

"I did," he said. *Not really. I was busy,* he thought.

"Do I still work from home or do you want me here at CIT?"

"Where you work from doesn't change. Take the documents home. They explain everything in detail," she said as she began to stand.

Tony felt he had no choice but to stand as well.

129

"Okay then, go home, talk to your bride and let me know your answer by Friday."

Your bride...how thorough was this background check? he wondered.

Tony stood, shook hands with Audrey then stole another glance at the mirror as he turned and left the room.

Tony entered the elevator, exiting one floor below.

"Have a nice evening, Paul."

"You do the same, Mr. James."

Paul logged the time Tony left the boss' office. Tony then rode the regular elevator to his temporary second story office floor. He returned his few personal items then headed to his car to go home.

As he walked through the parking lot he reviewed the meeting with Audrey. However, he was way more interested in why he picked up on an additional feeling that was apparently being generated from that mirror.

How can an inanimate object possibly grab my attention like that?

Tony got into his car and was delighted to be out of site. To Tony, his car was just about as good as any empty supply room he could find. After making sure he was alone he unlocked the jail cell and let the Tourette's flood gates open. Upon the major tics quickly settling down, Tony waited about a minute before putting the car in gear. He had to do this to let the stars fade from his eyes due to the ferocious triple head tics. He was happy he didn't hit the top of the steering wheel this time.

"Wow, this was one stressful day. Am I glad it's over," he told himself.

Chapter 18

After establishing his code, little Tony moved along in grade school and continued to develop a hyper-awareness of his surroundings. His unusual movements and throat noises now bothered him so much he began the task of trying to suppress these urges by means of mental focus and physical tactics with even greater vigor. He used simple tactics shielding facial tics by pretending to scratch an itch.

As if he were tired, he'd purposely rub his eyes as camouflage. This was, of course, a way to mask the hard eye-blinking tic. While in class he'd feel the urge to touch his elbow to his hip. Nonchalantly he'd stretch his arms down, shake them a little, and put them back up on his desk. On the way up he'd swipe his elbow to his hip without any notice. Sometimes he'd deliberately drop his pencil to meet the terms of his tormentor's demands as he hid a tic while leaning over. Each time he desperately hoped no one had noticed.

The throat noises were a little more troublesome to hide. He'd conveniently cup his fist to his mouth and cough. At the end of the cough he then immediately "cleared his throat" followed by an internal purring cat sound that only he could hear, but mostly feel.

His approach seemed to work. None of his classmates treated him any differently. However, Tony couldn't completely control the urges by focus alone so he knew classmates must have seen and heard something. He masked them enough not to be confronted with a barrage of name calling which he so desperately was trying to avoid. He very much just wanted to fit in.

Contrary to popular belief, Tony found hardly anyone really likes long term, direct eye-to-eye contact. It made people somewhat uncomfortable. This enlightening fact had been a huge discovery that Tony took full advantage. This aided him tremendously in all one-on-one encounters. During these briefest of moments he allowed the release of, what he hoped to be, a stealth tic. If he wasn't able to let out a few quick tics, he found his tormentor would force him to double or triple the urge to move and make sounds at some point shortly thereafter.

He was well liked by most and competed in all manner of activities and sports. It appeared his tactical maneuvers were winners. Not understanding why he was being tormented was the hardest part for little Tony to comprehend.

The single most difficult task he encountered was that of splitting his focus between what his teachers were saying, taking notes, knowing his surroundings, feeling urges coming and his tactical maneuvering. His brain was being split up into little compartments. By the end of the day he was wiped out!

He wondered why he was under attack every waking minute of every day, but didn't dare complain. It wasn't about being brave. He was just trying to cope and didn't want anyone to know his secret. His single simple goal was not to become the mutant of the school.

To Tony, recess and sports became something much more than being able to go out and play with friends. It was a time to release the beast! The urge to blink really hard, touch his hip with his elbow, make throat clearing sounds and more were just so much easier to hide with all the activities going on outside.

No matter what the game, or how old the kids, Tony was usually in the middle of it and as tenacious as anyone. He developed the ability to seamlessly incorporate the wide variety of tics into almost any physical activity. Running games and contact sports were his refuge. Tony would rather be *it* playing tag so he could run around even more.

As Tony moved into the higher grade levels his tormentor stepped it up and became even more aggressive. Every night he prayed that he would wake up the next day and he'd be back to normal. It was not to be. Just as all days previous, the first thing to welcome him was a physical and verbal tic. *Well, maybe tomorrow,* Tony thought.

Long gone were the days of just a few impulsive movements and a single sound. No, he wasn't getting off that easy. His tormentor created a new level of full volcanic body movements and the urge to make new multiple sounds. Amazingly Tony developed the focus and tactical skills to use as needed. His techniques and focus grew exponentially with this new level of activity. Unfortunately, he felt he always had to be on the lookout for anyone who might target him in a mocking way. He was fortunate however, that he was a "jock." At that stage in life, athletic skills and a decent personality usually were a cure for being picked upon.

Tony wasn't so sure he was getting away scot-free. But, at least he wasn't ridiculed directly to his face. With his attention to eye movement, masking tactics and mental focus, Tony continued to minimize the repercussions from his fellow classmates. At least it appeared to him he was succeeding.

Sadly for Tony there was a real downside to hiding his tormentor's efforts. At some point during the day he had to be by himself and allow a release of the pent up movements and sounds. He'd find a secluded spot. The tics would be released at a furious pace, then subside when the stockpile was diminished. At times Tony gave himself pretty bad headaches due to such severe head jerk movements during this release period. But, this process somehow did provide him room to maneuver through the remainder of the day until the stockpile filled up again. It became a way of coping on a daily basis. He couldn't hold back all tics, but it was his goal to minimize them. Tony wouldn't have such ferocious tic bouts if he didn't fight to hold them back for lengthy periods.

Sports became an ever increasing stabilizer in Tony's life. He didn't know it at the time, but the more he physically exerted himself the less severe his tormentor's demands were of him. In basketball he could play any position except center. In baseball he pitched, played shortstop and hit clean-up. In football he was the running back. Tony loved to play all sports, but something about football was special to him. Even though he was nowhere near the biggest guy on the team, he relished the challenge and the camaraderie of his teammates.

In football practice, Coach Gubbs used a one-on-one drill, at which Tony excelled. This was highly unusual because

135

everyone on the team hated this drill, including Tony at first. The exercise was to teach the ball carrier and the tackler at the same time. Its secondary purpose was to toughen the players by running head-on collisions. It was about technique, courage, heart and overcoming fear. For Tony it became a way to release a rage that resided deep within him.

Tony's coach instructed two teammates to lie on their backs, on the ground, with the top of their helmets pointing toward each other, approximately ten yards apart. Eyes looking skyward. At the sound of the whistle each player would get up as quickly as possible. Whoever found the ball, which had been quietly placed closest to him, became the runner. The goal was to pick up the ball and run in a perfectly straight line and NOT get tackled. The other participant's goal was of course to tackle the runner.

Neither player could stray from a straight line. If anyone violated this rule then a severe chewing out and additional distance running was in store at the end of practice. This drill was like watching two trains at full speed barreling down at each other on the same track. In a macabre way it was fun to watch, but hell to be a participant. Many parents thought the drill was way over the top. However, Coach Gubbs was not on the school teaching staff and therefore, apparently, not held to the same high principles of conduct.

The first time Tony took his place on the ground he was just as nervous as the rest of his teammates who had gone before him. While Tony waited in line he watched the violent collisions of his teammates. Fear struck everyone on the team. Tony's thought process began to show its benefits. As Tony got into position he became extremely focused. He was thinking ahead. Since his central role on the team was that of a running back he logically figured he would most likely be the runner. However, he did play defense as well.

The whistle blew and sure enough the ball was his. Tony quickly picked it up and ran as fast as his legs would carry him directly at his would-be tackler. He was on a mission to deliver a violent blow rather than take one like all the previous runners. While he was lying on his back, in anticipation of the whistle, Tony experienced a unique feeling. Unfortunately he didn't have time to figure it out. He had picked up the ball and proceeded to literally run over his opponent with a collision fit for two cars on a tight two lane highway.

Initially Tony gave no thought to the pre-whistle feeling, but rather the pleasure of release he felt from his successful run. However, as coach Gubbs reamed out his would-be tackler, Tony began to realize something had happened to him. Just like when he was six, he found himself once again standing alone on the grass in a state of trying to sort out what had just occurred. It wasn't the run itself he was pondering, but what had been triggered just prior to the whistle.

As Tony stood, deep in thought and still holding the football, a distant roar finally pierced his thoughtful haze. It was coach Gubbs ordering Tony back to the starting position from which he'd just come. He snapped out of it and caught the end of his coach's rant. Coach removed Tony's victim, Eddie Velker, and was telling everyone to watch Dan Smith and *his* tackling technique.

"Smith will show you how it's done!" he said in a loud menacing tone to the rest of the team.

Dan Smith was the biggest and roughest kid on the team. If you ever knew someone from the wrong side of the tracks then you have a good idea what Dan is like. No one wanted to be paired against him as the runner or tackler. As a tackler he'd take your head off if it was within the rules. Unfortunately for the runners who went up against him the rules of engagement didn't exist in Dan's mind. Many times it was the same with coach Gubbs.

With a grin he usually just yelled, "That a boy Smitty! Next."

Tony felt a slow burn building as he took the lack of respect from his coach not even mentioning his successful run. To Tony this was a personal insult. He made a great run and blew through his opponent like a tackling dummy. Tony felt rage at the injustice. But, Coach Gubbs gave no credit. All he cared about was that Dan Smith was going to show everyone how to take out a ball carrier. It seemed Tony was just a uniform to his coach at the moment and apparently just a fluke mismatched victory.

As Tony jogged to get into position he was slowed by another feeling that he took in like a dry sponge seeking water. It happened as he passed Dan Smith, the supposed perfect tackling machine. Smith was exuding fear. He was scared! *Does everyone see this?*, Tony wondered.

Tony looked at his teammates to see if they were seeing the same thing. Obviously they weren't because they were stepping back away from him as if he were a dead man walking. Tony then realized he didn't see Smith's fear, but he actually *felt* it.

How could this possibly be?, Tony confusingly thought.

Tony didn't have much time to question it. He knew, however, this was information he could, and would use. With his already irritated mindset over his coach's blatant bias toward Smith's tackling prowess and his team-mates lack of support, Tony was determined to run this guy over like a Mack truck! The whistle blew and as expected Tony obliterated him and laid him on his back. Coach Gubbs was so red in the face he grabbed Smith's facemask and screamed at him to take Tony out.

They ran the drill two more times with the same results. Tony knew he'd be successful, because he could actually feel Smith's fear growing every time he put him on his back. Tony only grew stronger as Smith grew weaker and more fearful.

Coach Gubbs finally gave Tony the recognition he deserved by slapping him on the helmet and holding him out of end of practice laps. As a matter of fact, the following week coach Gubbs invited a few of his friends to come and watch Tony perform in the one-on-one drill against the entire starting defensive line up, one at a time.

Tony learned something huge through this experience. He not only had the heart to take on the tough guys, but somehow, he could actually feel an emotion being emitted from other people. It was the first time he really accepted, and believed, this fact.

Chapter 19

Sam heard the car first and yelled, "Dad's home!"

As soon as he walked in the door he was greeted by his two munchkins. He picked them both up, one in each arm, and proclaimed, "I'm making dinner tonight."

Sam and Nick shouted out "Yay" in unison.

Tony smiled at Jacquelyn as she knew exactly what this meant.

"What take-out place are you calling tonight," she asked with a grin.

Pretending as if in deep thought he paused then said, "I'm in the mood for 555-9000."

"What's that Daddy?" asked Sam.

"That is the number for pizza!" he exclaimed.

Once again another unified "Yay" from the kids as they hopped down and ran off. Jacquelyn smiled as she rolled her eyes.

"You have to be one of the best cooks I've ever met," she said sarcastically.

"I just have magic fingers," he retorted wiggling his digits.

"Someday you're going to have to learn how to make something other than pancakes and spaghetti," Jacquelyn said in a fun-filled needling tone.

Later that evening, after getting the kids to bed, Tony and Jacquelyn sat in the living room and talked about the events of their respective days. Jacquelyn was frustrated that one of her student's parents didn't understand how to read the online grading system.

"I had to call her and she just kept complaining about the grades I was giving her son."

Tony listened intently as he loved this part of the day. This is when they could connect, vent or just plain ole' shoot the breeze.

"I must have told her at least three times that I don't *give* grades. Students *earn* them. I tried to explain that he's earning a B+ overall, but she just wouldn't listen to me. All she wanted to hear was that her son would get an A. So, I finally asked what grade *she* taught."

"Why'd you ask that?" Tony questioned.

"She apparently thought she knew way more than me so I decided to give her a little rope." Jacquelyn replied.

This ought to be great, Tony thought. "You gave her enough rope to hang herself, didn't you?" he said with a grin.

"I would never do that and you know it, Tony. All I did was let her come to the realization that I'm the teacher and she's not. Her son achieves not receives. My point was to open her mind to the fact that I know what I'm doing and she doesn't have a clue. Actually I didn't say that last part out loud, but I wanted to! Once we finally cleared the clutter it was a piece of cake. She just needed to be put in her place and listen instead of running off at the mouth. I slowly went through the online program with her and the proverbial light bulb finally glowed brightly."

"Did you have a lot of problem parents today?"

"No, that was really the only one," she said.

"Why is it we humans seem to be hardwired to focus on the one percent of negative aspects rather than the ninety-nine percent positive?" asked Tony.

"When you figure that out I'll help you write a book," retorted Jacquelyn.

Jacquelyn then asked, "Any fun facts you want to share with me from your day today?"

"As a matter of fact I do. "Remember the older lady I told you about at Starbucks from over the weekend?"

"The one you helped with her computer?"

"That's her. Well, I received a package from her today."

"What, she dropped off cookies or something?"

"She dropped something off all right."

"Didn't you get a strange feeling from her?"

"Yeah, it was double-edged sword."

"Don't tell me she seems like a nice old lady, but she's really a stalker?!"

"No, it's nothing like that at all," he said.

Tony went on to explain the contents of the box along with the memo.

"I saw I missed your call, but I was teaching at the time. You didn't leave a message so I figured it wasn't real important."

"Actually just hearing your voice on your outgoing message helped me out."

He went on and told her about the appointment with Audrey and the promotion he was offered.

"You travel a few days a month now. How much more travel would you have?"

"I'm not sure. It's spelled out somewhere in these documents." He handed the red folder to her.

Jacquelyn flipped a few pages and said, "Congratulations Mr. Ambassador."

"Yes, well, I'll only be representing one country at this time, but soon I'll rule the world!" he said in his most serious yet sarcastic voice.

"This is really great news Tony!"

"It is, but I don't know if I'm going to accept it."

"No, I mean the raise. The really great news is the raise! We can use the extra money," she said with a twinkle in her eyes.

"Very funny," said Tony.

"Why wouldn't you jump at this opportunity?"

Tony hesitated then said, "It sounds really weird Jacquelyn."

"Well, let me hear it and maybe I can help out."

Tony explained the two feelings he got in Audrey's office. He then sheepishly explained the fact he pinpointed where the additional one originated.

"It was coming from a full length mirror, Jacquelyn." He paused then added, "I know; weird huh?"

"You've never mentioned to me that you could get a feeling from an object before."

"I never have and I don't believe I did today."

"What do you mean?" she asked.

"This is going to sound crazy so hear me out on my, so-called, logic."

"So far I don't see any logic Tony," said Jacquelyn.

"Humor me then," he quipped.

"I don't always get a feeling from everyone I meet."

"Right," said Jacquelyn with a nod.

"I've gotten a feeling from a person in the area even though I couldn't see them," he admitted.

"Okay," she said listening intently.

"What if I was picking something up from the other side of the wall?"

With eyebrows furrowed she asked, "Has that ever happened before?"

"It has. Please don't laugh because I can only explain it in terms of something like 'The Force', you know, from Star Wars."

Jacquelyn reacted by pursing her lips a bit, but kept an open mind. She knew exactly what Tony was saying and she knew him so well that this wouldn't be beyond the realm of possibilities. She saw the pain it took him to tell her, so she knew this was really bothering him.

To lighten the mood she said in a terrible Yoda imitation, "So, a Luke Skywalker moment you had?"

Tony looked at her and began to grin.

"Is this your way of saying you bought a light saber," she followed up jokingly.

"Come on Jacquelyn I'm being serious. You know I don't like to talk about this stuff."

"I'm sorry Tony, I was just playing around," she said in a very sincere tone. "Do you think you could have been wrong about this Ms. Shelton?"

Jacquelyn knew better since, to her knowledge, Tony was never wrong when he got a feeling about a person. She just wanted to cover all bases.

"Not a chance. The feeling I got at Starbucks and seeing her again in her office were identical. No, this was a completely different and separate feeling. Do you remember about three months before Tom Franklin's car accident I asked you if he was sick?"

Tom was Jacquelyn's best friend's husband. He and Tony had become very good friends as well. Tom didn't make it.

Jacquelyn shifted uncomfortably and replied quietly, "I remember."

Tony took note of the change in her demeanor. This was still a fresh wound for her. Tony treaded lightly.

"I'm really sorry to bring this up, but it kind of illustrates my point. We both took solace that when he was called to heaven so suddenly that we leaned heavily on my feeling that he was seriously ill and therefore didn't suffer from a prolonged illness."

"Oh, I see what you're saying," Jacquelyn said in an almost relieved tone.

She had quickly made the connection, but didn't want to dwell on this emotional topic so she got right back on track.

"Is there another office right next to Ms. Shelton's?" Maybe you were picking something up from the person working next to her," Jacquelyn countered logically.

"No, there wouldn't be room enough except maybe for a closet and I didn't see a door or doorknob. There was just the mirror attached to the wall."

"Well if only you and she were in the office then what's your gut telling you?"

"That's just it Jacquelyn. I can't seem to put my finger on this one. That's never happened to me before," Tony said in a deflated tone.

"Sometimes it's best to sleep on things and the picture is much better in the morning," she said.

"You're right. We're both tired and I'm sure things will look different tomorrow."

They started to clean up after Sam and Nick. "Remember, we have Sam's concert tomorrow night."

"That's right, I almost forgot. Is this the one at the University with the college orchestra?"

"It is," she said.

"That should be fun. How about we leave the rest of this for the morning?"

Jacquelyn offered her right arm to Tony as she dropped one of Nick's toys and said, "Go ahead and twist my arm."

They were off hand-in-hand looking forward to a good night's slumber.

Chapter 20

While in high school Tony was, at first, a little freaked out at the revelation of actually being able to feel what someone else was privately emitting out into the vastness of the universe. He questioned it greatly.

Am I some kind of receiver, he wondered.

As time passed he became more and more aware of this phenomenon constantly reoccurring. He no longer could reject it as just some freak accident or something he thought maybe he just made up.

Tony went through the autumn season and began to compare his uncontrollable movements and sounds. He had found they were much worse when he wasn't involved in playing football. The extreme focus he put into practicing and playing the game somehow aided in the diminishment of his unwanted urge to move and make sounds.

He also began to realize he enjoyed football for additional reasons. Wearing a helmet aided him in the concealment of his uncontrollable eye blinking episodes. The hip pads allowed him to *adjust* them as needed without any odd looks from anyone. Because this sport is, as Vince Lombardi once called it, "a collision sport," there were always noises to cover his verbal tics. Tony also realized the embryonic thought that extreme physical exercise might be reducing his need to tic. He just wasn't sure and he let it go for the time being.

As time went on, Tony developed a new variety of unwanted uncontrollable movements and sounds. His entire body became his tormentor's amusement park and Tony was on the gigantic roller coaster. Unfortunately for Tony, this ride never stopped until closing hours. Only when asleep did Tony get the chance to step off the ride.

There were times his uncontrollable movements and need to make sounds would lessen for a few days. They never completely went away, but anything less than normal was a great relief. Tony didn't question why this was the case. He was just so thankful for any short-lived reprieve. He was always disappointed when they returned to full force. One thing he began to count on was they would be back as strong as ever. He reminded himself to enjoy the short vacation while it lasted.

One day in high school Tony was so disengaged from his teacher's lesson as he sat at his desk in the back of the room. He set about counting how many different movement combinations his tormentor had recently conjured up for him. It was an astonishing thirty-four! It included almost every imaginable body part. Granted not all of these were severe movements and sounds, but they were nevertheless, for the most part, uncontrollable and distracting. Upon contemplation Tony began to see the combined compound movements and sounds as almost rhythmic in their chaotic nature.

Tony took note and realized that at its worst he seemed to have to move and make a sound at least fifty seconds out of every minute. He was shocked this calculated to over fifty minutes out of every waking hour of every day! Some days

149

were better than others, but even if they were cut in half it was, to put it mildly, a major distraction and the beginning of a unique thought process.

As Tony began to think about what he was going through, he decided to make sure of one thing. Whatever these cards that were dealt to him, they were still just cards. In a nutshell his identity wasn't wrapped up in these unusual movements and sounds. This was something that was part of him, but didn't define him. However, there was no denying it still dominated and affected his thought process and direction in almost everything he did. It was still something he felt the need to hide. His code was rock solid.

Tony had begun to think of seasons in different terms. Not spring, summer, fall and winter. He started to think baseball, football, and basketball seasons. He immersed himself in such sports for the intense love of competition. Tony also loved that he *felt* an edge over his competition. Sports seemed to give Tony a reprieve from his tormentor. Maybe it was the other way around. Tony didn't know. He immersed himself even further in his secret code he swore an oath to sitting on the back porch all those years ago. He would continue to try to hide these tics from everyone.

Tony began watering the seed of thought that the combination of physical expenditure through sports, combined with extreme mental focus, could possibly make the unwanted urges of movement and sounds subside. This could be huge for Tony. It could mean a victory of epic proportions for him even with the smallest of positive outcomes. He began to think there might be something he could actually do to lessen his tormentor's edge.

Chapter 21

The next evening Samantha was so excited. Jacquelyn bought her a new dress and styled her hair.

Tony picked up her hairbrush as if it were a microphone and asked, "So what time is your solo, Ms. James?"

Like so many times before Sam stretched the word dad into two syllables followed by a tilt of her head. "Dad, I don't have a solo and you know it."

"Oh, that's right you're letting your classmates sing with you this year. I forgot," Tony kidded.

He kissed her on her head and said, "Just remember, this is for fun."

Tony knew both his children had very competitive streaks in them and he wanted to make sure he kept Sam grounded for her performance.

As they arrived at the auditorium Tony pulled up to the front entrance to let Jacquelyn and Sam out.

"Nick and I will park the car. Do you have your cell phone with you?" Tony asked.

"Let me check. Yeah, I do," replied Jacquelyn.

Kiddingly Tony retorted, "I was talking to Sam."

He knew just how to help his little girl stay loose before her performance. Samantha giggled as she looked at her mom. Jacquelyn gave her and Tony a warm smile back.

As soon as the passenger doors were shut Tony looked at Nick in the back seat and asked, "Do you want to drive?"

Nick laughed and said, "Only if we can go to McDonald's."

"Well your sister would be awfully upset if you didn't hear her sing so I better stay behind the wheel for now."

"Okay Dad," Nick said gleefully.

With the car parked and Nick in hand they entered the university auditorium. Tony was handed a program for which he politely thanked the completely bored high school student.

He picked Nick up and asked him, "Do you see Mommy?"

Neither of them did so Tony called her on her cell.

As she answered she said, "I'm backstage helping the children."

"Okay, Nick and I will find seats."

As Tony set Nick down he automatically processed where the best seat would be for him based on his current tics. He happened to pick up a "winking" tic recently for some reason. It was predominantly on the left side of his face. So, Tony chose to sit on the aisle on the right about midway back of the auditorium. He knew he could use the armrest with his elbow then use his hand to cover this particular tic. He also calculated that the first quarter of the rows would be lit by the stage. Sitting further back he could hide in plain sight with very subdued lighting once the performance began. All this automatic calculating was done instantaneously.

Tony called Jacquelyn once again and let her know where he and Nick were settled in so she could easily find them when she was done helping out.

He let Nick burn off some energy by allowing him to run up to the first row and then back a few times. Jacquelyn finally arrived to their seats with just a hint of a frown and holding Nick's hand.

She said firmly but politely, "Now you go ahead and sit right there and stay still."

At first Tony thought, *You could say that to me, but no way could I comply.*

"Why'd you let him run up and down the aisle?"

"You can thank me later," replied Tony.

Jacquelyn wasn't amused. She'd just come from helping out amidst chaos backstage. The full house sounded like a thread of thunder for what seemed like an eternity. Finally the house lights flashed and all the guests settled in and the noise level quieted.

Then one of Tony's favorite parts of any performance like this finally arrived. Of course seeing his daughter was the highlight, but he had a secret secondary favorite. The lights were lowered. He knew everyone's eyes would take a short period of time to adjust. This gave Tony the chance to release a few quick tics without anyone taking notice. Not that he loved to tic, but he was thankful for this small reprieve.

The children came on stage to a thunderous round of applause. Tony took this opportunity and pretended to scratch his left cheek for yet another quick tic release. He knew all eyes were on the kids so he was safe. He cleared his throat a few times before the applause died out.

Sam looked very cute and performed each song with her classmates with ease. After a handful of songs they rearranged themselves to make a complete half circle. The orchestra began warming up with what sounded like a Beatles song played backwards.

The conductor raised her wand and the mish-mash of sound was replaced with the beautiful sound of classical music. It engulfed the auditorium like a big hug. Tony let out a few quick tic releases during the song while Jacquelyn appeared to be enjoying every note. Nick was quietly playing with one of his cars Jacquelyn allowed him to bring to keep him busy knowing he'd be bored.

At the end of the musical composition everyone clapped. As they applauded Tony continued his usual quick release of tics which he blended in with the clapping. He then turned to Jacquelyn and gave a nod for her to look at Nick. He was playing quietly. She looked back at Tony and raised her eyebrows as if to say *let's hope it stays this way.*

From the very first note of the next composition, which was introduced as a composition by Mozart, something strange happened to Tony. It was as if he entered a zone he did not want to leave. During the instrumental Jacquelyn slightly leaned over to Tony to garner his attention, but he just sat there staring straight ahead.

She finally whispered, "Are you Okay?"

Tony didn't answer her.

"Tony," Jacquelyn very quietly implored.

He still didn't answer.

"What's going on?" she asked with a little despair in her voice.

This time Tony slightly held up his hand which had been resting on his right thigh. He raised his index finger letting her know everything was just fine and he would be with her in a minute. He continued staring straight ahead.

I don't know what's going on, but this is fantastic! So this is what it's like to not have Tourette's. Just take it in and enjoy. Don't move or I'll jinx it, he thought.

The music came to an end and so did the incredible stillness that had overtaken Tony. Then just as if the world had shifted back to its proper order he unfortunately had the urge to tic once again.

He leaned over to Jacquelyn during the applause and told her that during the musical serenade something good happened. Jacquelyn stopped clapping and leaned back with her eyebrows up then smiled. Neither one of them understood what had just happened, but this wasn't the time or place to discuss the matter.

Tony enjoyed the rest of the concert, but only connected with the zone he had found during that one particular Mozart composition. He began to think, *Maybe there's no cure, but there sure as heck has to be a way to improve the level of tics. I just experienced it!*

On the drive home the four of them picked up some ice cream to celebrate. Both Jacquelyn and Tony peppered Sam with questions about her experience on stage. Nick even chimed in with his own questions. Most important of all she had the time of her life.

Late into the evening Tony and Jacquelyn sat in the living room once again to review their day. Jacquelyn was particularly interested in what was going on with Tony when he waved her off during the concert.

"I'm so sorry about that Jacquelyn and I owe you an explanation. Do you remember the second instrumental the orchestra played?"

"Yes, that's when something was going on and you didn't want to be disturbed."

"Well I don't know what happened to me, but I didn't want to move because I was free from all urges to tic during the entire song."

"You're kidding!" she exclaimed.

"No, I felt so free. Not to mention stunned! I was savoring every second so that's why I didn't answer you."

"So all of a sudden you were Tourette's free?" she asked in an excited tone.

157

"I was," Tony replied.

"You experienced this through the whole song?"

"Yes," Tony replied as if it just surprised and snuck up on him again. "Then, just as if a stopwatch began once again, so did the urge to tic as soon as it ended."

"Do you think it had something to do with the rhythm of the music?"

"It definitely had something to do with that instrumental or that particular arrangement."

Ever the teacher Jacquelyn said, "You know, I remember reading about Mozart and the repetitive notes he used while composing."

She shot up and got her laptop computer. Once online she placed the words *Mozart Tourette's* into the search engine. Tony was sitting across from her and was watching her reaction.

"You won't believe this Tony! Come here and look at this," she said excitedly. "There are over fifteen thousand two-hundred results that came back from just that one search."

She turned the computer slightly so Tony could get a better view. Then she clicked on the third link since it seemed to have the most pertinent information in the subtext.

Jacquelyn began to read aloud to Tony then said with her voice rising with excitement at the end, "It says here that Mozart was described as having Tourette's Disorder."

"But how could they know that since Tourette's didn't have a name until after he died?" Tony asked.

Jacquelyn was already reading ahead. She could read faster than anyone Tony ever knew.

"Right here, they took historical documents and based on the descriptions of his facial tics and vocal sounds the medical profession diagnosed him with Tourette's posthumously."

I guess that's what happens when you're that famous, Tony thought as his left eye ticked with a double wink.

This was followed up with a clearing of his throat and a quick right shoulder roll. He was thrilled with this new information.

"This one claims he composed music that may have fit certain criteria to alleviate his symptoms," Jacquelyn said excitedly.

"Really? How so?" asked Tony.

"Apparently some of his music wasn't just relaxing, but so complex it created a difference in the nerve center of the brain. Colleges have done medical studies on the subject."

In an exasperated tone Tony said, "I wonder why Dr. Knox didn't provide me with *this* information. It would've been nice to know that there was some hope to lessen my symptoms *without* medication."

"Not all doctors, but many, think only of medication and not alternative methods of treating their patients. Don't hold it against him Tony. I think his heart was in the right place," she said lifting her big brown eyes to meet his.

"I know he was trying to help, but he was ineffective," said Tony.

Jacquelyn reminded Tony by saying, "Tourette's is just a chemical imbalance. Obviously he was trying to create a chemical balance."

Trying to create a zombie, Tony thought.

"Tony, do you have the program sheet from the concert tonight?" Jacquelyn asked.

Tony got up and opened the closet door. He reached into his coat pocket and nabbed the program. As he handed it to her he sat back down with Jacquelyn at the computer.

"I want to know the name of the composition the orchestra played that had such an effect on you. Here it is. It's called Mozart's Symphony Number Forty, First Movement. According to this website Mozart's music contains a mixture of chaos and control," she said.

"Boy, if that isn't putting Tourette's to music I don't know what is!" Tony exclaimed.

Jacquelyn continued, "It says his music runs off in chaotic directions, but then he always brings it back under control."

"Hmm, I wonder if life imitates art or the other way around in this case. Do you really think there's something to his music?" asked Tony skeptically.

160

"Why not? You experienced something very unusual tonight, right? Music can have a great effect on our mood therefore, it affects the brain. The brain is definitely made of chemicals. It adds up," said Jacquelyn the teacher.

Tony became very intrigued with the idea that somehow Mozart's music may be in sync with the chemical and circuitry processes of the brain.

Chapter 22

Because Tony had been so extremely active during one of his growth spurts as a teenager he developed Osgood Slaughter Disease. This is a painful inflammation of the patellar tendon where the knee meets the top of the tibia or shinbone. It's caused by physical stress on the tendon that attaches the muscle at the front of the thigh to the tibia. The powerful quadriceps muscles pull on the attachment point of the patellar, or better known as the knee-cap, tendons during intense activities.

This intrusive disease encroached upon every sport Tony loved to play. It was particularly painful, in both knees, while playing basketball. Lateral movements weren't a problem for him, but any jumping and he was in serious pain.

Tony was a good point guard on the junior varsity basketball team. He tried out for the varsity team his sophomore year. There really wasn't a true try out for Tony. Unknowingly to him, he was pegged to be the backup point guard even before the first practice. This was the case for just about every position on the team. Each player chosen was pre-determined to fill an impending void by the graduation of a senior. It was a fairly well kept secret to the young men trying to make the team.

As practices began the coach went through the normal weeding out of the students who were not already silently recruited and had a slot waiting for them. No student knew if they were chosen or not, so everyone had to push hard. These practices were extremely physical. Tony really didn't mind, but his knees were beginning to scream at him.

On one particular evening after practice Tony went home and said hello to his sister, Olivia, who was watching TV in the living room. He was walking gingerly and lowered himself down into a cushy chair without using his legs. He placed both hands on the arms of the chair and eased on down with a grimace on his face.

Olivia certainly took notice and asked in a concerned tone, "Are you okay Tony?"

He surprisingly said, "No." It wasn't like him to complain.

"What's wrong?" she asked.

"My knees are killing me. I don't know if I can make it through another practice."

"Let me take a look," said Olivia in a concerned tone.

Tony rolled up his sweat pants and to her surprise Tony's knees were swollen to the size of grapefruits.

"Tony, you have to tell Mom and Dad. You can't keep this up or you'll really mess up your knees!"

Tony replied, "I'll tell Mom, but I'm not telling Dad."

Wasting no time Olivia went to find Mary. The only consolation in this was his dad wasn't home at the time.

After examination Mary asked in her usual calm and soothing voice, "Is this happening after every practice Tony?"

"Yes," he said.

Olivia was back with two bags of frozen vegetables to place on Tony's knees.

"What are you thinking of doing?" asked Mary in a leading tone. "This is not going to end well. The doctor said so when you were diagnosed when you were thirteen years old. I know how important this is for you, but after all it's just basketball," she added.

Tony's mom didn't know to what depth he loved to compete and play on the team. However, she was right and nothing he could do would correct his knees except to stop playing basketball. This was a real blow to Tony. The reprieve he got from his tormentor through physical exhaustion and the exhilaration of competition was being ripped from his stern grip. This was one more thing out of his control.

He thought of his dad who'd been extremely proud to show the picture of his son from the local paper as being part of the team. Tony and his dad had bonded even tighter than usual because of this. It was going to be hard to tell him he couldn't take it anymore. He asked his sister and mom to promise not to say anything to him. Tony wanted to be the one to break the news.

After pretending to be at practice and still on the team for almost two full weeks Tony knew time was running out and he had to break the news to his dad. Olivia and his mom were beginning to put the pressure on him. Neither one wanted to be part of a lie. Tony couldn't blame either of them.

The conversation was a blur, but what Tony took away from it was the disappointment on his dad's face and in his tone. It almost seemed as if his dad was the one who couldn't continue. This hurt Tony deeply because he thought his dad would sympathize with him and the physical pain he put up with due to the condition of his knees. It wasn't to be. His dad looked more defeated than Tony felt. Tony would remember this look and feeling for the rest of his life. He knew deep down his dad always had his best interests at heart. But, like most teenagers, Tony was conflicted from letting his dad down and rebelling to the point of wanting to be a thorn in his side every step they took together from that point forward.

Tony pretty much went into a shell for the entire basketball season. Without competition, extreme physical activity and teammates, Tony felt he lost his identity at school. High school can be a very cruel place for those who fall from grace. It didn't matter why Tony couldn't be on the team. He just wasn't. In his mind he became just one of many hundreds in his school without positive distinction.

At first Tony still hung out with his basketball buddies at school, but slowly began to feel very left out. What were normal conversations before were now forced as he wasn't up on the inside jokes. After awhile Tony began to take a few ribbings the wrong way. He'd become so self-aware of his urges and tics that he became tremendously diligent in his focus. He felt around every corner and expanded his peripheral vision to monitor his "who's looking at me" radar.

Tony wasn't shy and he certainly wasn't the worst looking guy in high school. However, because of the ever

165

exhausting focus he put into hiding his sounds and tics he never dated much. He had dates, but not as many as he would have liked. The experience of one-on-one conversation with a girl was just something Tony decided he'd try to ignore. It was too bad, but he didn't go to prom or any of the dances because of his tormentor. The stress of occasions such as these would create a tsunami-sized urge to tic.

So, he began going to the local YMCA and found an outlet for his competitive side of his personality. He played pool, table tennis and shot hoops without any jumping. He won a lot of games of HORSE. He enjoyed watching a good match of handball and racquetball as well.

By the middle of the basketball season he'd stopped going to the high school games. He decided that if he couldn't be on the court he didn't want to be in the bleachers. He abruptly severed what was left of his withering ties with his friends and former teammates.

He thought he was going to have a tough time, but to Tony's surprise he was eventually okay with this. He began to view his former friends in a new light. His evaluation of them was that they were pure walking egos. Tony had thought he hung around with them because they were real friends and not just because they were former teammates.

As he thought about it he realized he had placed himself in a position to be respected by means of association. They were popular so he joined the club. This of course is what the reality of the high school social agenda has always been about and, unfortunately, likely will continue to be. He thought if he had to stand on his own, the results of his tormentor would define him and place him as the odd shaped peg trying to fit into the square hole.

So as he spent his time at the "Y" he'd watch his dad and older brothers, Gary and Henry, play racquetball. As it should have been, Gary was the best player in the family. Henry was a very close second. His dad taught them both. Tony had actually started to play at the age of thirteen in addition to his other many sports activities.

The few times Tony had played previously, he found he really wasn't that good. He kept up with most of his opponents due to his natural quickness, speed, hustle and a determination not to lose. The only technique he knew was from listening in on Maggie's tennis lessons with their dad years earlier.

As he watched the guys he decided to give competitive racquetball a real run for its money. It seemed to be right up his alley. The physical requirements, he figured, were quickness, speed and endurance. Tony knew he had plenty of all three.

Tony had to first make sure his knees could take the rigorous movement the sport demanded. To his surprise he had zero negative effects. There was no jumping in the game of racquetball, so he was very excited to join his dad and brothers in learning the game, and also to compete with them.

His sister, Maggie, had to stop playing tennis due to an automobile accident that almost killed her. After a lengthy hospital stay she needed physical rehab on a daily basis just to

167

get back to normal everyday living. Competitive tennis was no longer in her future due to the idiot that blew through a stop sign. Tony understood the pain Maggie was going through, having her love of tennis taken from her.

So, late one evening, Tony asked his dad if he would teach him the game of racquetball. Tony's dad tried to hide it, but his eyes lit up like the Fourth of July fireworks. Tony's mom gave him a sweet smile that implied how proud she was of him for asking.

"Of course I will. But, before you can really play we're going to have to get rid of that ugly tennis swing of yours. You're starting with a big handicap," Ned stressed.

Then he asked Tony, "How good do you want to be?"

Tony already knew this answer. He'd been around his dad and brothers and sisters when they talked about competing in tournaments. There was such excitement in their voices. Tony wanted to be a part of that.

Staring directly into his dad's eyes Tony said unequivocally, "The best in the family."

The fact was that the older James brothers, Gary and Henry, just happened to be ranked as the top two players in the entire state. So, when Tony gave his answer he wasn't just saying he wanted to be a good player. He was saying he wanted to be better than the best in the entire state of Oregon.

His father eyed Tony closely and said, "I'll get us a court for tomorrow night. Just remember we're going to have to get rid of that ugly swing of yours. You're starting in a very big hole because of it."

Tony's dad already had the beginnings of his teaching plan worked out. Ned had a template based on the success of Tony's older brothers. This made Tony feel like he just embarked on a journey with the perfect guide. Tony didn't know it but, his first hurdle was making it through something akin to boot camp.

Once out of ear shot from Tony Ned said to Mary, "The first thing I have to do is break him down. He's like a young race horse."

Mary asked, "Is that why you kept on him about his tennis swing?"

Ned replied, "Not just his swing, but his attitude."

Later that evening Tony's big brothers razzed him about trying to be the best in the state. More importantly they weren't the least concerned about him coming even close to being third best in their family.

"Dad's going to pummel you every time you play him. And don't even think about wasting our time playing with us," said Gary.

"He's just going to teach me. I'm not going to play him," said Tony.

Gary and Henry began to laugh hysterically. Only they knew the rigors that were ahead for Tony. That is, if he lasted. When they were up and comers their dad didn't give one inch when they played. Playing him was one aspect of his teaching. They said they had to earn every point they got and that was the only way he played. This was, of course, by design.

Now as for teaching sessions, that was a much different story. You couldn't find a more natural teacher than Ned James. He went beyond the physical game and developed his prized students into players who could utilize strategy and play with heart. Later that evening Mary privately asked Ned his thoughts about Tony's answer to his question.

"So what do you think about Tony's answer?" she asked.

"What answer?" asked Ned.

"You know, the one about his goal of being the best in the family." She didn't say this in a surprising tone because she always encouraged her children to go for the gold in everything as long as it made them happy.

"I wasn't surprised," said Ned still reading his newspaper.

Mary raised an eyebrow in surprise.

"Tony's cocky. He does have all the physical tools to be great. The one question I have is will he have the patience to see this through? It's going to be very difficult to change that ugly swing and *then* start from scratch," he said. "Not to mention, will he quit like he did basketball?" Ned bristled.

"Now Ned you know Tony had to give it up," retorted Mary. "Besides, if he didn't, he physically wouldn't have been in the position to ask you to help him with racquetball now would he?" Mary continued.

Ned didn't reply. It was clear he hadn't gotten over Tony quitting basketball. However, Mary had a very good point.

Make lemonade out of lemons, thought Ned.

Tony's mom always knew exactly what to say, when to say it and most importantly *how* to say it. She was responsible for Tony's dad to be happy to give him all the guidance he required.

Ned had always envisioned himself proudly looking on at the weekly high school basketball games as Tony torched the opposing team with pinpoint passes and a stifling aggressive defense. As a high school basketball player himself, he had the misfortune of coming down with a rebound only to find a knee in his back. He never forgave his opponent for that "career" ending injury. This isn't to say he would've made a professional career out of basketball.

To his credit Ned tried every sport he could and found that he not only enjoyed them, but excelled at many. It was the reason he became a very well rounded player in just about every one of them. He was particularly good with any racket sport and golf. But, to this day, none of his sons were going to fill his void as a top notch basketball player. Tony had been his last and best hope.

Ned had a knack for teaching due to his high intelligence, patient personality and his experience with so many sports. In his day he was a good athlete, but not a great one. His skill level required him to hustle and really learn the nuances of each sport and his role within it. This helped close the gap between the physical and mental aspect of becoming a winner.

He began to think about Tony's exceptional physical abilities and then set his priorities. First was attitude. Ned was going to make sure Tony knew he was the boss, end of story.

Tony had a very different attitude than his brothers and sisters when it came to dealing with authority. Many times Tony would aggressively challenge adults rather than politely keep quiet like his other children. He seemed to carry some kind of chip on his shoulder. He'd question rather than accept a statement as fact.

It seemed to Ned that if he could help Tony channel this properly he might just have a diamond in the rough on his hands. This type of attitude could definitely be a big asset. Tony wouldn't be afraid to take on the big boys. He had occasionally seen an edge to Tony only a parent would pick up on. Tony wasn't overt in this. But, knowing him as well as any parent knows their child Ned knew this could become a well honed weapon in Tony's arsenal.

Ned began working with Tony and did in fact get rid of that awful tennis swing. It took some time, but his pupil worked hard. It didn't take Tony very long to make quantum leaps in his newly chosen sport. Ned could envision him not only reaching his goal, but doing it much sooner than later. One evening while Ned and Mary went out for a bite to eat the subject turned to their youngest child.

"Tony's very excited about his racquetball game, Ned," said Mary.

"Really, what's he saying about it?"

172

"Just that he can't stop thinking about becoming the best in the family," replied Mary.

"Well, he has a ways to go but —" Ned didn't finish his thought.

Prompting, Mary asked, "But what?

Ned adjusted in his seat and leaned in closer to Mary.

"Racquetball isn't the biggest sport in the world, but I think our young Tony has the potential to be one of the top players."

He let the words hang in the air. Mary knew this was extremely high praise coming from Ned. Never in all their years together did he speak so glowingly about Tony. Gary…yes…Tony…seldom.

"You mean he could actually be number one in the state?" Mary asked.

"Not just the state Mary…ANYWHERE!" said Ned excitedly yet in a hushed tone.

Mary sat back and smiled at the pride from her soul mate. Ned had an eye for talent and an even greater understanding of what characteristics one required to become a champion. Mary couldn't recall him saying anything close to this about any of their children with regard to any sport.

As Mary prepared meals in the kitchen she had listened to Tony intently almost on a daily basis as to how he was trying to do different things with his backhand, forehand and every other aspect of his game. It was as if she was his sounding board so he could hear himself think out loud. Mary encouraged it even though she didn't understand everything he said.

Mary was so surprised when Tony began talking about how he was going to first go about beating his dad. That would be what Tony called his first notch on his win list. Then she listened to him describe an entirely different strategy to defeat his brother Henry. It was so full of detail that she couldn't keep up. Already in the works, he also had a template to beat the reigning state champion, his brother Gary. Tony said the details would come later after he possessed certain skills and experience he still lacked.

Mary explained all of this in as much detail to Ned as she could remember.

"He said all that?" asked a surprised Ned.

"Yes and he was very excited, and as you just heard, very detailed about his plans."

"Well then, we better start making room for a few more trophies in the house. If there's one thing I know about Tony, after being on the court with him as much as I have, is he'll go to any length to accomplish that goal."

Mary raised both eyebrows.

"Remember when I had my doubts that Tony would stick with it?" asked Ned.

"I do," said Mary.

"Well a few months ago we were on the court. I was trying to teach him about how to be mentally tough. He looked at me and flat out said, "You have no idea what real mental toughness is Dad." At the time I was taken aback. I didn't know where that came from. At first I was angry that this snot-nosed kid would say something like that to me. But, after putting him through his paces, in double time mind you, all he did was challenge me for more. Now that takes mental toughness!" said Ned excitedly.

Ned had no idea why Tony would proclaim any knowledge about being mentally tough.

Chapter 23

Since the night of Sam's concert Tony couldn't get that feeling of freedom from Tourette's out of his head. He desperately wanted to be able to replicate the lack of urge to tic. So, over the next few weeks Tony listened to more classical music than ever in his entire life.

I have to admit this is very calming, but I'm still not getting into that zone like I was on concert night, he thought. Maybe I have to be really focused and not behind the steering wheel when I listen.

So, one day, Tony set out to create a quiet setting at home when Jacquelyn and the kids were out. After turning off all phones he laid back in his favorite recliner, pressed play on the surround sound remote and attempted to relive the experience he enjoyed at the auditorium. He let Mozart's Symphony Number 40 – 1st Movement wash over him like a cascading waterfall. Almost without notice time seemed to slip by as he listened. At the end he pressed pause and evaluated the experience.

Well, that put me at ease that's for sure. I think my tics were less than normal, but I'm not positive, he thought.

Then Tony remembered something he'd read in a relaxation book. Take a few deep breathes in through the nose and out through the mouth. He pressed replay on the remote and began once again, this time while doing the breathing exercise.

The music had just finished one more time. Tony felt a quick jolt and shook his head rapidly. Because of this he thought, *Did I just have a major head tic?* He then realized that he'd just returned from falling into the filtered cracks of being fully awake and partially asleep.

Whoa! That was great! I only remember having just a few very minor tics and I know I was definitely not asleep! He readjusted himself in the chair and used the same breathing and music combination, but this time without success. *I think I'm too hyped up, but I know it worked*!

It was as if a lightning bolt hit Tony.

These chemicals in my brain that cause the tics can be corralled at least a little. I might not be able to be cured, but I'm certainly going try everything in my power to minimize the urges that Tourette's dishes out, he thought.

He told Jacquelyn of his little experiment over breakfast the next morning. Tony made coffee for Jacquelyn. He didn't make coffee very often, but when he did boy did it taste bad.

"Thanks for the coffee Tony," Jacquelyn said without the slightest hint of complaint.

She got up and added as much milk and sugar in her cup of coffee to drown out the awful taste. She did this overtly so Tony would see what she was doing. Her usual was taking it black, at least in the morning. She appreciated the effort, but really wished he'd get the hint.

As she sat back down Tony said without looking, "I know I make lousy coffee, but you deserve it. Wait, that didn't come out right!"

They both had a good chuckle at his expense.

Jacquelyn said, "Your radar sure is set on high alert this morning." *Coffee mission accomplished*, she thought.

"I have a question for you Tony," she continued. "Are there other times you can think of that you got totally lost in something and the urge to tic went away and didn't come back with a double dose?"

As if a light bulb dimmer dial switch had been slowly turned up, Tony excitedly said, "Yeah, now that I think about it. Back in college, during my time on the pro racquetball tour, in a tough match I felt tic-free. Those were the days. That's when the sport was so popular they almost succeeded in getting it into the Olympics."

"You can reminisce another time. What I'm interested in are the times when you were playing on glass stadium courts in front of tons of people."

"Once the match got going and the adrenalin kicked in...yeah."

"Hmm, maybe we're on to something here Tony. Can you remember the last time that occurred?" she questioned.

He paused then asked, "Do you remember the State Doubles tournament a couple months ago?"

Jacquelyn always went to watch Tony play in his local tournaments. She really only enjoyed watching Tony play singles as well as doubles, but only with Gary as his partner. However, when she had to wait around for Tony's next match she really would have rather been elsewhere. Fortunately for her Tony didn't play as many tournaments like when he was younger. There are age group divisions, but he has no interest in them.

"Sure, that's the tournament when your brother blew out his elbow in the finals. I remember thinking you were going to have to forfeit and before I knew it you were back on the court. That was the match Gary had to get out of the way of the ball because he couldn't even lift his racquet. You took on both players right?"

"That's the one," he confirmed.

Tony had fond memories of certain matches he had played. This particular doubles match stuck out. Playing younger opponents, early in the first game of the finals, Gary hit a forehand and suddenly had severe pain in his right elbow. He couldn't even finish the point. Like Tony, Gary's right handed. A maximum twenty minute injury timeout was called by the referee.

Gary was bent over writhing in pain on the court. Tony knew his big brother better than anyone and figured he didn't want people to bother him at a time like this.

We get twenty minutes for an injury, Tony thought.

So, he left his brother to deal with the pain on his own and exited the glass stadium court to re-hydrate with water.

To some this may have looked odd that he didn't even say a word to Gary, but Tony didn't care. He knew Gary and knew that it was best for the team.

As he walked to the water cooler he looked back and saw their opponents feign concern over Gary's chances of returning. Everyone else thought they were being good sports, but Tony knew better.

Give me a break, he thought as he watched them. They just want to know how bad it is, he thought.

Tony heard comments from people in the crowd that they couldn't believe the match was over and new champions will be crowned. Tony silently thought they may be right in their assessment. However, Tony didn't know the extent of Gary's injury yet. Very shortly there-after from a short distance he heard his name coming from his partner.

"Tony we need to talk," Gary calmly demanded while holding his arm against his stomach at a ninety degree angle.

"How bad is it?" Tony asked.

"Let's go to the locker room for some privacy."

Since theirs was the last match of the tournament the locker room was empty. Tony didn't want to hear Gary say he was sorry. It wasn't necessary. Injuries happen and they're a team.

Once in the locker room Gary said, "It's real bad."

Tony began, "We'll, just have to —" Gary quickly cut Tony off.

"I have a couple of questions for you."

In a prolonged and quizzical tone Tony said, "Okay."

"If you were playing singles could you beat Hailey?"

Tony envisioned the tough physical player on the court that had been playing the right side then said point-blank, "Sure, I beat him in the State Singles Tourney."

Gary already knew this then said, "Good, now what about Jansen on the left?"

Without taking his eyes off of Gary he knew where this was headed.

"No problem," said Tony.

"Do you think you could beat them at the same time?"

Tony remembered their two opponents glancing at each other and smiling before they pretended to check on Gary. *They think we're going to quit. No time like the present to wipe the smug smiles off their faces*, Tony thought.

Tony answered emphatically, "Absolutely."

"Good, then here's what we have to do…"

Little did Tony know, but Gary had some experience with a situation like this. Many years ago Gary and their dad were playing in a doubles tournament. Then Gary's partner, Ned, twisted his knee, but they somehow finished the match. However, they were unsuccessful.

Gary laid out a game plan that entailed him staying out of the way and letting Tony go to town and take every ball no matter where it was on the court. Gary wrapped his arm as tightly as possible. As they walked back onto the court Gary announced he could continue. The crowd erupted in a huge roar.

A calm focus came upon Tony as he knew it was going to be up to him to play two against one. Even before he left the locker room he'd gone through the strengths and weaknesses in both of his opponent's games. He was ready.

They don't know what's about to hit them, Tony thought.

Tony could feel the unleashing of an ice-like killer instinct from within as he remembered the arrogant smiles his opponent's had on their faces just a short time earlier. They still had an air of cockiness about them that almost put Tony over the edge. Tony then felt like he was experiencing the calm eye of the storm. He was so ready to deal out justice.

Hailey and Jansen had the serve and, just as predicted, drilled it toward Gary who was still positioned to receive the serve on the right. As the ball came toward him Gary ducked out of the way and Tony covered for him with a ferocious forehand that stunned their opponents as well as the crowd. He anticipated and moved so quickly from his position on the left side of the court almost the instant the serve was struck. Even at his age Tony still hit the ball as hard as anyone in the country and this was one of his hardest. The fans were so loud it was difficult to hear anything. Gary leaned in to speak into Tony's right ear. It looked to everyone to be a strategic point being offered.

Gary said, "I think they got the message Tony!" Then he added, "I'm glad I'm on your side!"

From that point on Gary ducked, dove and weaved while Tony hunted down every ball and obliterated their opponents. He was in a zone and so was Gary. They fed off each other. It was as if they'd prepared for and practiced this exact scenario. To watch the James brothers was like watching ballet with racquets. Their movements were so intuitive of each other. At times it looked as if Tony was going to take Gary's head off with the swing of his racquet. But, they were both so confident in each other that they never gave it a thought.

Tony wasn't surprised they'd won. However, he was just a little disappointed that it was over. *I wish this could've lasted forever*, he thought. He was so exhausted that Tourette's gave him a break for a little while.

After taking another sip of her coffee Jacquelyn asked, "So, was it because you were so focused, mad or exhausted?"

"Well I —" Jacquelyn cut him off wanting to add perspective.

"Try to remember that you were on the glass stadium court in front of hundreds of people in a stressful situation and I didn't notice any twitching at all."

Hmm, not everyone can catch me when I'm that focused, not even Jacquelyn. But, then again maybe I didn't tic. I can't remember, he thought.

"So you're asking if my Tourette's vacation was a focus issue, an emotional state or purely physical exhaustion."

183

"Right," she quickly replied with a gleam in her eyes.

She's thinks she's onto something and I hope she's right whatever it might be.

"Well, let me take it one at a time," he said as if talking to no one.

"I had to focus more than normal due to the unique circumstances of the match. I admit I was infuriated because they were pretending to be sympathetic to Gary and I knew they only cared about winning by forfeit. I was completely exhausted after the match because, well, that's obvious." After a brief pause he said, "If I had to give one answer it would be…all three."

"That wasn't the question. Besides, you were the one who relished the thought to take them both on by yourself," said Jacquelyn. She followed that up with, "You told me you were so angry over the injustice."

I know, but this is hard to talk about, Tony thought.

"Let's take the first one…focus", said Jacquelyn.

Tony said, "I don't remember trying to hide my tics at all when play started again."

"So, you had no urge to tic?"

"No, I guess not. But, then again I was in a different state of mind," Tony said in a slow surprised tone.

Deep in thought Jacquelyn said, "That's interesting."

Then she asked, "Do you think being as angry as you were had anything to do with the tic drought?"

"Actually, I think that fed right back into what I was focusing on."

"Which was what exactly?"

"I was so mad that I saw only what I could control to satisfy my anger."

"Specifically?"

"The ball," Tony replied with a shrug of his shoulders as if to say *what else*.

"Did the ball represent anything to you?"

Okay, Dr. Freud, Tony thought.

"Maybe because I could control the ball I felt like some kind of energy was being emitted from within. It sounds stupid, but I was in a comfort zone. If that makes any sense?"

Jacquelyn said, "It makes perfect sense. You were at ease with yourself in a highly competitive situation. You didn't care what others thought. My guess is you hardly even noticed anyone else. This would have been extremely stressful for most people, but you seemed to flourish within it. You've practiced so hard for so many years that you had total confidence in your playing ability. You allowed yourself to react to what you practiced. Maybe that's why the tics were gone and you played so well. Maybe you let your mind go blank kind of like when you listened to Mozart."

"But I was calculating at least three shots ahead. That's no different than what I always do when I play. Physically I don't play at the pro level anymore, but my strategy is still there."

"Okay, so maybe your emotional state had nothing to do with it then," said Jacquelyn.

I'm not buying that line. She knows stress is a major player when it comes to Tourette's. But she's really onto something so let's keep going.

"What about how exhausted you were? Have you ever taken notice of the level of tics when you felt like that before?" she asked.

Tony looked at Jacquelyn. She might as well have been a ghost since he seemed to be peering right through her. Jacquelyn could see Tony was trying to recall something so she remained quiet.

"You know what? Just thinking about it for a moment I believe my tics are actually reduced greatly after a very emotional, mentally focused and highly physical workout. I never took the time to notice those three aspects as a collective package before you brought it up," Tony said in a surprised tone.

"When you lift weights do you feel like the urge to tic is lessened?"

Tony gave that some thought and replied, "Maybe just a little, but not until I'm done."

"What about when you do cardio?"

Again, Tony let the question hang in the air and once again replied with the same answer.

"You know what Jacquelyn? I think you're definitely onto something."

Jacquelyn reached across the breakfast table and joined her left hand with his right. They locked fingers. Tony looked into her big brown eyes and gave her hand three small squeezes. It was one of their little rituals. It's a way of saying, *I Love You.* One light squeeze for each word. Jacquelyn responded with the appropriate four little hand squeezes of her own. *I Love You Too.*

Chapter 24

Tony's priorities for the summer were to make money and focus on climbing the ranks as a professional racquetball player. He spent at least six hours nightly practicing racquetball skills.

By the end of June his dad declared, "You either go to college this fall or it's time to move out."

Tony's initial instinct was to say his goodbyes right then and there. However, after thinking it through, he bit his tongue and decided to attend Portland State University.

Because of his passion for competing in racquetball he really didn't have his whole heart into his studies. He felt forced into college given the alternative of moving out at age eighteen. Tony really had no choice without the prospects of a real living wage to sustain him. He resented this greatly. He'd much rather be on the court practicing his skills for the game he loves. Tony had enough of sitting in a classroom and splitting his focus nine ways from Sunday.

Each of his siblings had either already graduated or were on their way to doing so. Tony knew this was the expectation in the James family. He'd had enough of the classroom. Just the thought of another four years of confinement made him want to scream.

At the time Tony didn't believe that a degree would increase his chances at reaching his goals. Tony had tunnel vision with regard to racquetball. He of course came to his senses, but not necessarily right away. After Tony's first semester he found himself on academic probation. The letter he received had something to do with needing to actually take the exams for the classes he signed up for.

What a novel idea, he thought while suppressing a grin.

Tony had the choice of packing his bags and taking his chances on the pro tour. Or, he could stay in school and try to do both. He buckled down second semester and pulled himself out of the hole he'd dug for himself. Tony really didn't enjoy college life because it took time away from his passion for playing the pro tour events.

When he began the first semester of his freshman year he had decided to look at it as a new beginning. He figured it had to be better than high school. He was wrong. Tony gravitated to making racquetball his priority rather than his classes.

At the end of second semester Tony signed up for a summer course to bring his college grade point average up to get off of probation. He always did well in science and decided try to get back on track in this area. It was just his opinion, and he didn't know the reason why, but the professors who taught during summer didn't seem to be of the same quality as those during the regular school year. But, then again he didn't realize this until his summer class began. He wasn't in this particular class enough his first semester. During the retaking of his class he had a very rude awakening. He thought high school was tough to maneuver. He quickly found that life after high school can be much crueler.

Tony thought he'd been dealing with his tics rather well as of late. He spent so much energy on the court and working out that he didn't make the connection that physical exhaustion seemed to have lessened his tics to a great degree. However, Tony decided to really buckle down and still enjoy the summer weather, since it was so short lived in Portland, Oregon. He also had a big test coming and he wanted to be well prepared. Unknowingly his tics became very disruptive, making it difficult for him to focus while in class as well as while studying on his own. He got through it, but not without being scarred emotionally.

In class Professor Belman would, on occasion, ask Tony numerous questions reviewing the text being studied. Even if his answer was correct the professor would find something wrong with it. He also had a different tone when addressing Tony than his other students. It appeared he just didn't like him. The feeling had become quite mutual.

Time had come for the final exam. Tony was tremendously confident he had prepared well. He unfortunately felt the pressure to get an "A" or "B," which hadn't helped with his urge to tic in class. He had to be extra vigilant due to this professor's treatment of him.

As he began the hour long exam he started to feel very comfortable as he answered the questions with a high degree of confidence. Tony zipped along at a pretty good clip. He was finally moving to the last question. He turned to the last page and it hit him like a ton of bricks.

Tony read question number forty and sat completely frozen in his desk. Staring at the words he first felt flushed with embarrassment. Then a burning rage began to swell somewhere deep down.

He reread the question:

40. What is the main cause of earthquakes and why?

A. Excessive heat generated from the earth's core

B. Tectonic plate shifts

C. Volcanic activity causing fissures

D. James' twitches

He couldn't believe his eyes. *How could Professor Belman do this to me! That S.O. B.! After all my efforts trying to hide my tics this jackass puts it in black and white for the world to see*! Tony silently screamed. Code broken.

Tony scanned the classroom and saw some students who apparently had completed the exam. The rule was that when finished you were free to go. This meant that those who'd gotten to number forty were sticking around on purpose. He saw their silent laughing eyes. He felt sick to his stomach. He knew they were hanging around just waiting until Tony got to the question. Tony was always fine as long as someone was laughing with him, but in no way could he tolerate them laughing at him. He tried too hard his entire tormented life not to be the butt of this kind of joke. He expected this stuff in middle and high school, but not in college. However, these college students were absolutely giddy when they realized Tony read number forty. It was so obvious. For once in his life Tony was completely ashamed and didn't know how to respond. His quick wit and fast thinking on the fly completely evaporated. He looked back down at his paper...tic, tic, tic.

Then Tony lifted his head and turned his gaze upon Professor Belman. What he saw was a scheming little man's black beady eyes staring directly back at him, hands clasped under his chin. He had a slimy grin on his face. The professor said absolutely nothing and yet his eyes said everything at the same time.

How could he be so cruel? Tony thought.

Tony felt his rage escalating from a very dark place within. He was no stranger to confrontation. There were times in his life that he'd been the instigator of aggression. He stared at Belman for what seemed an eternity. Tony began to see him in a different light. No longer did he see him as a professor. Now Tony saw a poor pathetic small-minded excuse of a man. Then his initial wave of emotion regained strength. He looked down at the test in his hand. Shame quickly was replaced by rage. That shift in emotions played like a movie and he saw himself doing the unthinkable to Professor Belman. After all, Tony the athlete could easily snap Belman the professor, in half. He paused for what seemed an eternity then took a deep breath. Tony put the paper back on his desk, circled and wrote the correct answer to complete the test. He wasn't leaving it unanswered as this was his way to lift himself above the scheming man that did this to him. Walking toward Professor Belman he sensed that some of his fellow students were waiting for this moment. Would Tony punch him out or just ream him out? Either way they couldn't wait for the show. They also knew they were in no position to stop him.

As Tony approached, the professor rolled his chair back from his desk and braced for what may be coming his way. As Tony strode toward him he was burning a hole in Belman with a violent glare as he approached. He paused. Tony, never removing his eyes from Belman then just laid his paper on the top of the pile. He turned and walked at his normal pace out of the room ignoring everyone. For those students who thought this would be fun got the silent message not to screw with Tony. With his jaw set and eyes looking forward he strode out of the classroom riding on rage.

I'm not giving him or any of them the satisfaction of a reaction from me! Keep to the code, Tony thought defiantly.

This, to date, was the most embarrassing moment of his young life. He got into his car and drove to Firewood Lake Park. Tony just sat in his car staring at nothing but the serene surroundings of the placid green water. He felt defeated. All the hard work he put into his strategies he developed to hide his tics seemed to have been obliterated in an instant. The one thing he didn't do was ask why he must endure the musings of his tormentor. He wasn't being noble. It just didn't occur to him because he was so furious. That would likely come later. Right now he needed a release.

Time to take this out on a little round ball, he thought. He went to the "Y" and got his aggression out with one of the best racquetball practice sessions he ever had.

This incident became low hanging fruit that had been produced from his code. Tony never breathed a word to anyone about this. It was just too humiliating for him. For awhile Tony would think where he would've ended up if he allowed his true emotions to carry out the destruction of Professor Belman.

A month passed and Tony was at a crossroads with regard to continuing his quest for a college degree. He faced the reality of life and decided he would finish what he started. Tony didn't graduate with honors, but he did walk across the stage with a degree in computer science. He now knew getting his degree was tremendously important to his future. However, bubbling just under the surface Tony was thinking of the past. He wanted to stick it to the Professor Belmans of the world. He figured he wasn't the only victim of humiliation from someone like him.

Chapter 25

As the months went by Tony began paying much more attention to the waxing and waning of his motor and verbal tics. He'd become so intrigued by Jacquelyn's idea that outside variables may indeed have an effect on the intensity of his urge to tic.

The first task on his hit list was the effect stress had on him in correlation to the level of tics. On a daily basis he went through a process of determining his tics on a scale from one to ten. Ten was of course the harshest, while one he considered very minor.

As he completed the mandatory retraining time at corporate headquarters he was now once again working from home. This was the first stressor that he noticed made a big difference in lowering his urge to tic. He didn't have to deal with traffic, office politics or constantly being concerned that someone would catch him twitching. Nobody was ever looking over his shoulder while working from home.

One of the things he realized he'd taken for granted was the solitude of windshield time in the quiet countryside between appointments. Most of all he relished the full authority over his schedule. This allowed him to succeed at solving his client's problems then get in the car, by himself, and let out the demon within as needed. Just knowing this in itself was a comfort to him. The fact that he could use the excuse of getting a part out of the car gave him the much needed boost to try to hold the tics in a little longer. Sometimes he'd actually go to the car, but most times he found an unused conference room or bathroom to release them without notice.

Tony started a computerized activity log to see if there was a definitive correlation between the level of exercise and his tics. As Tony began to see the obvious positive trend he increased the number of workouts in his exercise program. He figured if he worked out more often then he'd see even greater results on the spreadsheet. However, this wasn't the case. He clearly found the amount of physical activity didn't really make as much of a difference as he thought it would. It helped, but not to the degree he was counting on.

One early Saturday morning, before anyone else in the house was awake, Tony comfortably nestled himself into his favorite recliner in the family room. He turned on his computer and looked at the data he'd collected thus far. He focused on certain days that his tics were rated much lower than the others. Since he was keeping this data on his laptop spreadsheet he figured it should've been easy to see a trend popping out at him. He looked at each day, but didn't see anything that jumped off the screen to provide a significant answer.

Feeling a little frustrated Tony closed the computer and went to the kitchen to make some breakfast. As he got up he felt the strain in his oblique muscles due to the intense workout he had last evening. It was as if a light bulb went on over his head.

I can't believe I didn't even notice that my tics are at a really low level this morning, he thought.

He opened the cabinet and reached high for a bowl. The stretch felt good. As he did so he realized he may have overlooked something in his data input. After grabbing the bowl he set it down on the counter and rubbed his right side.

I'm actually really sore from my workout last night. What'd I do that was different, he wondered.

He replayed the workout in his mind and realized that he pushed himself with extreme focus and emotion.

"Why'd I do that?" he questioned.

His answer came quickly. *Because the Northwest Regional Singles Tournament is coming up next month. I stepped up the intensity because of the Northwest Regional*, he thought.

Though Tony was a little older he was still in great shape. His younger opponents still had lots to learn therefore making him a continued force on the court.

Tony had a theory that each tournament was really over before it began. He felt if he did everything to prepare that it was just a matter of letting those three days pass by knowing all he could do was enough. He was confident that all he could do was enough to become the champion.

Tony knew if he was in better condition than the other contestants he'd have one less obstacle to overcome to achieve success. He looked at the game of racquetball as being comprised of three elements. They include the physical, mental and emotional aspects to the game. Tony knew if he was in his best physical condition possible then his sole focus could be on strategy and playing with heart.

Tony left the kitchen and went back to his data. He filtered through the spreadsheet to pick out particular days that ranked as very good regarding his tics. As he stared at the screen he had one question.

What do these low level tic days have in common?

Tony opened up his personal calendar, which he also kept on his computer. He noted very specific information regarding his racquetball preparation. Tony utilized another file filter and pulled up the dates of what he considered important tournaments. Tony then digitally merged the two creating a graph overlap effect.

"Well, I'll be," he quietly said to himself.

He moved closer to the screen and declared, "That might be it!"

After reading his accompanying notes he said, "With an impending important tournament, the more intense and focused my workouts became."

He sat back then he cautiously thought, *Maybe it's the intensity AND visualization while working out that makes the biggest difference in the reduction of tics.* He leaned forward to take in the data with a more narrowed scrutiny. Tony thought, *I bet I'm burning off so much stress that there's a definite carryover.* He then looked closely at the state final doubles match he and Jacquelyn had talked about.

"Bingo!" he confirmed. Tony sat back with the data staring at him. *I've found hope,* he thought.

He heard Jacquelyn getting up and closed his computer to welcome her to the weekend. Tony decided he'd wait to share his discovery with her until he had a chance to really put it to the test.

"Coffee…I need coffee," Jacquelyn said quietly barely looking at her husband.

Tony filled his bowl of cereal and they both enjoyed a quiet breakfast together, that is, until the kids got up.

Chapter 26

After an enjoyable weekend with Jacquelyn and the kids, Tony got up early Monday morning to begin his work week. As always he started with his email. He felt it to be very important to communicate with his clients as early as possible.

When Tony logged on he wasn't surprised he already had a few new emails in his inbox. He figured he'd likely be able to quickly delete them as they were usually weekend auto-gens. Tony thought automatically generated emails were such a waste of everyone's time. They were mostly company newsletters or articles with very little valuable information. Four had been sent over the weekend. Most people don't know they can schedule an email to send on its own at a predetermined day and time. Some use this method to make the sender look like they're working late or on the weekend. Tony knows better.

Someone's justifying their job, he thought.

He could easily find out who the senders were, but decided it wasn't worth the trouble. Tony opened each and just as quickly deleted them.

As he was composing a follow up email to one of his clients he had worked with last week, the bottom right corner of his screen provided him a fade in glimpse to a new incoming message. Tony always found this annoying ghost unnecessary by letting him know that a new email just arrived. He tries to not look at them when they appear. He fails almost every time. Tony doesn't like to be interrupted by anything when he gets on a roll.

He completed it, sent it off and waited for the program to automatically return to the home email page to deal with what was newly awaiting him in his inbox. To his surprise it was from Audrey Shelton. He'd never before received an email this early in the morning from her. He noticed the subject line was very ambiguous. It read; *Company Business*.

"That could mean anything," Tony grumbled.

He read the very short message. **Good morning, Tony. Meet me at the Portland International Airport Executive Lounge at 9:00 A.M. today**.

"Well, good morning to you, too," Tony said to the screen sarcastically.

He hit reply and then wrote, *Good Morning, Audrey. How was your weekend?* He waited for her to reply, but one never came.

"I guess that's an order then," he said to no one. In his best Steve Martin impression he then said, "Well, excuse me!"

Tony thought Audrey's request was odd, but at least she didn't ask him to pack a suitcase. After the normal James family weekday rituals of getting ready, Tony drove to the airport. On his way he couldn't help but think back to his most recent visit.

Oh, how I wish Jacquelyn and I were headed back to Punta Cana, he thought.

201

Just before he entered the parking structure he stopped, rolled down his window and pulled the ticket out of the electronic guard box. The railroad style arm raised and he drove in to park the car. Once inside the airport he realized he didn't know where the executive lounge was located. He found the information kiosk. It was on the other side of the terminal.

As he walked he took note of the business people eating their one-handed breakfast food while reading the paper and working their cell phones.

I wonder where Audrey's flying today, he thought.

He was thankful he didn't have to go through security. He was also grateful he didn't have to endure the insanity of weekly air travel for business.

As he looked into the weary travelers' dead eyes he thought, *These people look miserable. I guess when you're the head honcho you get to tell your employees where to go and when to be there. This better be important or I just might have to tell her where to go*, he mused.

Tony found the door with the elegant plaque that told the world to stay out because there are important people in here and you're not one of them. He looked for a way in, but only found an electronic key-swipe like you see in hotels.

Nobody's around so how am I supposed to get in there?

Just as he finished that thought he saw a determined businessman making a beeline in his direction. Tony pretended to be getting his keycard out as the businessman

202

quickly opened the door. Without a word, Tony nodded good morning and followed right behind him.

It was as if he'd entered a completely different world from the rest of the airport. Beautiful stonework surrounded an impressive waterfall on the left. The inviting spaciousness of beautifully arranged leather chairs fully equipped with matching ottomans on the right. In the middle was a jolly and entertaining chef hard at work creating made-to-order omelets. Toward the back was an enclave of enclosed cubicles for what Tony presumed to be private meeting space. To his surprise nobody came up to him and asked to see any identification. That is until he felt a light tap on his right shoulder.

"Sir, do you realize we don't let your kind in here?"

At least that's what Tony imagined he heard.

What was actually said was, "Sir, may I take your breakfast order?"

"No, but thank you very much Oliver," Tony said in a confident tone.

Thank God for nametags.

Tony walked confidently to the leather chairs and picked up a newspaper along the way. He didn't see Audrey yet, but he was early. As he raised his newspaper he inspected the room.

These people aren't snobs, they're just lucky to have companies that pay for their membership to this hangout, he realized.

While scanning left to right he was getting *feelings* from just about each person. With everyone he focused upon, he received a feeling with a word as if he could see into their souls. *She's needy. He's a prick. He's afraid. She's dishonest. He's confident. She's sincere. He's a backstabber. He's calculating. She's bossy. She's...wait a minute!* He did a double-take.

Tony shifted his eyes back to his newspaper, and readjusted it so the edge of the paper and his right hand were positioned perfectly so he could focus his right eye on a rather trim man with salt and pepper wavy hair. He was wearing a navy blue suit with a white shirt and dull tie. A matching fedora rested on the chair next to him. He focused extremely hard on this man.

What are the odds of this feeling of "calculating" would come to me about this man here and from Audrey's office?

Just then the door opened to the lounge and everyone kept going about their business except Mr. Calculating. He was the only one to look up to see who entered. It was as if he was anticipating seeing someone he knew. Then with an almost imperceptible shift in his eyes he very quickly glanced at Tony while readjusting in his chair.

Tony didn't make a move. He did however continue to pretend to read the paper. He shielded his eyes from Mr. Calculating so well there was no way he could've seen Tony looking at him. Tony's stress level was inching upward... tic, tic, tic.

"Good morning Tony," she said in an over-enthusiastic tone.

Tony recognized that voice and after two more very quick facial tics he lowered his newspaper and said, "Well, good morning *again*, Audrey." Tony stood to cordially greet her.

"What do you mean good morning again?" she asked.

"In our email correspondence about 5:40 A.M., remember?" Tony asked looking for confirmation.

"What *are* you talking about, Tony?"

"You sent me an email asking me to meet you here." *Actually you ordered me to be here,* he thought. "We said our first good morning then," he followed up.

"Tony, I haven't even looked at my email yet today. You must be thinking of someone else."

"Are you telling me you didn't send me an email this morning to meet you here at 9:00 A.M.?"

"Like I said Tony I haven't seen any emails today. I had planned on doing them here before my flight to Washington, D.C."

In a hurried tenor Tony said, "Wait, wait, wait…I can show you right here the email you sent and my reply from my Smartphone. It syncs all my mail from my desktop program. Look, they're right here."

Tony had pulled out his Smartphone and entered his password. Then he pressed the envelope shaped icon and showed Audrey the emails that came in and what he sent out.

"I don't see an email from me Tony," Audrey said with a confused look.

Tony turned the Smartphone a little more toward himself for a better view.

"But it's right —," he broke off his statement.

There was no record of an email from Audrey to Tony. As a matter of fact he didn't even see his reply.

"That's odd. Maybe it's just not syncing properly for some reason," he said.

"Well, don't worry about it Tony. I'm sure there's a perfectly good explanation for it. After all, you are a computer expert," she said with a sweet smile. "Since you're here, Tony, will you join me for breakfast?"

"That sounds like a great idea. I could eat again."

"You go ahead and order me a Denver omelet while I head back to one of the private conference rooms. Order whatever you want it's on me. Tell them to put it on CIT's tab."

Tony put the order in with the jolly chef and walked back to sit with Audrey. She had her email up and running.

As Tony sat down she had anticipated what he was going to ask. She turned her laptop toward him and said, "Go ahead check your email account. I know you want to."

Tony proceeded to log on. The emails weren't there.

"You don't look well Tony."

"The emails we sent each other this morning, they're not here."

"I told you, that's because I didn't send you one," Audrey said emphatically.

"But I replied to you so mine should be here," Tony said in frustration.

After he and Audrey consumed their breakfasts they chatted for awhile. Tony pretended to be in a happier mood, but during breakfast he picked up that strong *calculating* feeling coming to him once again. It was the exact same feeling as when he was in Audrey's office and about forty five minutes ago with regards to Mr. Drab-Tie.

Tony purposely said in a little louder voice, "Have you ever had the feeling of being watched, Audrey?"

"That's an odd question Tony. Where did that come from?"

You answered my question with a question, Tony quickly realized.

He simply quipped a little louder, "You know what I mean."

"Not really, Tony. Do you mean all the surveillance cameras these days?"

Tony gave Audrey a resounding no to her question and stayed on course at an abnormally higher decibel.

Audrey asked, "Have you had that feeling, Tony?"

Once again in a little more vocal voice he said, "I have and as a matter of fact I have that feeling RIGHT NOW!"

Audrey stared at Tony with a curious look. Just a few seconds after Tony spoke, Mr. Drab-Tie exited from the meeting room right next to Tony and Audrey. Since the rooms were constructed of nothing more than thin dry wall they weren't completely private as advertised. Tony watched a man in a dark blue suit wearing a tilted fedora hat quickly walk out of the room next door and out of sight. Tony never got a view of his face, but knew it was him.

How can this possibly be? Mr. Drab-Tie had to be listening in on our conversation. This is the strangest thing. He projected exactly the same feeling as the mirror in Audrey's office...calculating.

Audrey just sat and stared at Tony.

"I'll be right back Audrey," Tony said without waiting for a reply.

He got up and walked into the main lounge area. He looked for the man in the blue suit, but he was no longer sitting in the seat he had previously occupied. Tony did a 360 degree turn, but still didn't see him. Baffled, Tony figured he was long gone. Tony pinched the bridge of his nose with his middle finger and thumb as if he had a headache. He didn't. This was just a cover up to hide the triple hard eye blinking tics.

Same guy, thought Tony. He then strode back to Audrey.

"Do you know him or something?" asked Audrey.

"I was just about to ask you the same thing," retorted Tony.

"Why would I know him," she quipped.

Audrey quickly looked at her watch. "Oh my, look at the time. I must be getting to my gate. It sure was a great surprise and a treat to see you here Tony. We'll have to have this type of coincidence again soon," she said as she gathered her belongings.

She'd already turned her computer off.

"Yeah, what a coincidence that I'd show up at a place I've never been to nor have ever had a reason to be," Tony said in an accusatory tone. He quickly recovered and said cheerfully, "You have a good flight Audrey."

Tony walked a fine line with his last comments as they came out somewhat biting.

Audrey appeared to let it slide and said, "Let me know if you find anything out regarding those emails. But, don't spend too much time on it. You're time is very valuable to the company."

"I'll get to the bottom of it quickly if I pursue it at all," Tony said shrugging his shoulders. "You have a nice time in Washington."

"Thank you, Tony."

Chapter 27

Instead of going back home Tony decided to go directly to corporate headquarters. He didn't relish the thought, but that's where the computer servers were located. He needed an answer about the emails that vanished into thin air.

Awhile back, in the middle of a sleepless night, Tony's friend, Jack, sent an inappropriate joke to what he thought was his "friends" contact list. Instead it went to the entire company. He called Tony, freaking out thinking he'd be fired. Tony went in and made the email disappear via their server. If anyone knew about the mishap they would've been able to trace the email even though Tony eliminated it. One thing most people don't know about an email is there's always a shadow left behind. However, if you don't know about the original, the shadow is like looking for a needle in a haystack the size of Jupiter. Jack was forever grateful and, to his credit, Tony never said a word to anyone.

Fortunately, Tony once again knew exactly what he was looking for regarding the email exchange to and from Audrey this morning. It took Tony all of about fifteen minutes to be able to resurrect the shadows. What bothered him most was there were only shadows to find. This meant someone did in fact eliminate the original transmissions. Someone sent the email to him, but it was impossible to locate the originator. He knew nailing this down could take an incredible amount of time without the guarantee of success. He decided he'd have to work on this puzzle another day if he felt the need. For now he was satisfied that he verified something wasn't on the up and up.

Well, since my schedule for the day is shot, I think I'll catch a solid workout at lunchtime then work from home.

After his workout he went on the racquetball court to practice his backhand. He made sure he pushed himself as hard as possible physically, as well as with focus and visualization. It was his endeavor to continue his quest to verify that more than just intensity of the workout really is a key to reducing his urge to tic.

When he got home he went directly to his personal laptop computer. He had crafted additional columns to his ever growing spreadsheet. He entitled the columns **Work-Out Intensity 1-10, Focus** and finally **Emotional**. He decided as he ended each workout he would be sure to rate each category. "1" was dogging it and "10" was crushing it. He knew this one today was a "10" based on how hard he pushed himself and the imagination utilized. It pleased him to place that number in his new columns.

I hope I can work out like this from here on out based on how I feel right now, he thought.

His urge to tic wasn't completely gone, but greatly reduced. He knew this could make all the difference in the world for him. Tony had definitely found a few extremely important factors for him to reduce the urge to tic through exercise. The first important factor was of course consistent exercise. Secondly, but just as important, was the intensity of the workout had to be at a very high level. Thirdly, he had to be exceptionally focused. Last, but not least, an emotional content level had to be present.

Tony had read many articles on the internet about exercise changing the body's chemistry. All this involved lower cholesterol, blood pressure and the like. Of more interest to him were the articles about the changes in the chemistry of the brain through consistent exercise. One article in particular spoke of the change in serotonin levels with the connection to exercise. He learned serotonin is a chemical produced by the body that enables brain cells and other nervous system cells to communicate with each another.

One very important factor was for Tony to use sports imagery while he worked out. It was as simple as mentally placing himself on a stadium court against a specific opponent. He let his imagination take him where he needed to go.

Tony found a few magic bullets of sorts. But, there had to be more and Tony was dead set on finding all he could about what could chip away at the symptoms of Tourette's. He was determined to fight and tame his tormentor.

Tony thought about following Audrey to see if in fact she really had a flight, but decided against it. At the time his tic level was up and he just didn't have the will to hold on much longer. He would've had to go through security and thought he certainly would be profiled as a nervous traveler. He got the feeling Audrey may have known Mr. Calculating.

It wasn't like her to not know that someone was right next to us listening to what we were talking about without asking me to lower my voice. It was very strange how she dodged the question if she knew him. She didn't even mention how loud I was talking. That's just not the Audrey I've come to know. Something's up...tic, tic, tic.

Chapter 28

Audrey quickly located her usual first row aisle seat in first class. Once settled and in the air she awaited the announcement that boomed over the awful speaker system green-lighting all electronics. She booted up her computer and went directly to work.

Her flight attendant, Vicky, painted a beautiful picture of their breakfast offerings in a bubbly southern-bell accent. Audrey succinctly explained she had already eaten and politely declined.

"If y'all change your mind you let me know," she replied. Vicky continued on to the other first class flyers. Audrey paid little attention and already had gone back to work.

As the food cart rolled out it stopped just behind Audrey's seat.

"Excuse me here's your orange juice," Vicky said.

"I didn't order anything, remember?" replied Audrey.

"Oh, I'm so sorry I must've gotten you mixed up with someone else." She continued on with her deliveries then returned to Audrey with cart in tow.

In a hushed voice and big pleading doe eyes Vicky said, "I'm very sorry to bother you again, but this will just go to waste unless you'd like it. It seems I've made a mistake and I just hate to throw it away."

Audrey noticed a more seasoned flight attendant watching which she presumed to be higher up on the airline corporate ladder. She didn't want this young lady to stress out over a cup of juice while her boss was watching. She also didn't like the glare she was giving Vicky either.

Audrey flipped open the tabletop from the vacant seat next to her and took the cup with the napkin. Vicky was most pleased as she thanked her then pulled her cart up to the bulkhead. Audrey was slightly annoyed, but didn't show it.

After working for a while she absent-mindedly reached over to have a sip of juice. As she picked up the cup, the napkin stuck to the bottom. She pulled it off and proceeded to quench her thirst. She was now appreciative for the error. It hit the spot. Audrey set the cup back in the holder then placed the napkin on the tray next to it. She began to turn back to her computer then did a double-take back to the napkin. There was something written in black ink on the bottom of it.

Audrey carefully picked it up using her left thumb and index finger handling it as if it were radioactive. It read: **We have a car waiting for you when you deplane**. She re-read it a second time and then looked around at the other first class passengers for any sign of the person for whom this was intended. Audrey knew it wasn't for her since she'd made pick up arrangements with Ryan O'Connor.

Ryan O'Connor is second in command at CIT. He had been her dearly departed husband's closest confidante for many years. O'Connor traveled out of Portland two days prior to her flight to make sure everything was set up for her visit.

Audrey never really clicked with O'Connor in the early days. He just wasn't her cup of tea. There was something that bothered her about his friendship with her husband. However, a close professional relationship had grown between them over time. After all these years Audrey viewed him as a CIT colleague rather than a close friend.

O'Connor's chronological age made no difference to him or anyone with whom he came in contact. At age sixty two he looked and moved as if he were twenty years younger. His energy level and gregarious manner was something to behold. O'Connor was not only responsible for keeping CIT alive through the lean years, but due to his efforts he set it on a course to thrive.

Many years ago was a very down period for CIT. O'Connor put together a business plan to go after government contracts. Her husband approved it without even mentioning it to her for months. O'Connor's success hinged upon creating long-term and lasting relationships. He brought relational selling to a whole new level within their industry. O'Connor filed for a lobbyist license then began acting like one. Elaborate hunting, fishing and tropical paradise trips became normal business activates for O'Connor. This didn't sit well with Audrey. Once she learned of the marketing plan she had recommended that her husband, President and CEO at the time, deny O'Connor from doing any further business with the government in this way, especially in Washington, DC. All Audrey saw was a den of thieves and she wanted her husband to have nothing to do with the scoundrels.

She was proven wrong as O'Connor made inroads into the lofty political stratosphere that would benefit their struggling company. After her husband's unexpected death, of which she does not speak, Audrey was unexpectedly voted in as President and CEO instead of O'Connor. Audrey counted on O'Connor heavily at the beginning. However, he was distant and in some instances downright evasive as she dug into the books.

Eventually they hit their stride and his daily mentoring became the foundation with which they built CIT into the giant it is today. He took care of sales and she took care of the rest. Ryan O'Connor became the fuel in CIT's engine. Audrey had surprisingly been voted in as Chairman of the Board instead of O'Connor. O'Connor thought he should have become CEO, but never once did he complain while working with Audrey. After he was passed over he began spending even more time in Washington D.C. than usual.

As the older flight attendant started to walk her way Audrey asked, "Excuse me, but do you know who ordered this orange juice?"

"Is there a problem?"

She said, "No" and repeated the question.

"I believe Vicky served you, is that right?"

Already frustrated with her she said, "Yes, may I speak with her?"

"We're one person short on this flight so she's taking care of the coach passengers at the moment."

This explains your grumpy demeanor. Maybe you should pitch in and help her, Audrey thought.

"May I be of assistance?"

It's about time, she thought.

Holding up the cup she said, "Well, I actually didn't order the juice so I was wondering who did."

"When Vicky comes back up we'll ask her."

"Thanks for your assistance," Audrey said semi-sarcastically.

Audrey went back to her computer and never saw Vicky again. The plane landed at Reagan National about ninety minutes later and still, no Vicky. She didn't even show for the obligatory "Buh-bye now" farewell ritual that permeates all airlines which Saturday Night Live made infamous. Audrey decided it was just a simple mistake as she trudged up the tunnel to the gate area.

She emerged from the opened breezeway doors and entered the gate area looking at the multitude of mostly men in dark suits holding up signs. Normally she never gave them a thought, but because of that napkin she figured she might see her name on one of them. As she passed by, looking to her left, there was not a single Audrey Shelton or CIT sign in the group. This solidified her conclusion that indeed a simple mistake had been made.

O'Connor was waiting for her at the baggage claim area, carousel number four. She saw him first. He was talking with a man dressed in a gray suit, but facing away from her.

O'Connor's face peaked over the man's shoulder and then gave her his big signature smile.

"Welcome Audrey! How was your trip?"

Before Audrey could manage to spit out her answer Ryan O'Connor was already introducing the man in the suit.

"Audrey Shelton this is Don Williams."

Mr. Williams turned and Audrey stopped far short of what would be considered normal socially acceptable spacing.

He took an extra step toward her and said in a calm monotone voice, "Pleasure to see you, Ms. Shelton."

O'Connor then said in his gregarious tone, "Don works for the Department of Information Technologies or DIT for short."

"It is a pleasure, Mr. Williams," Audrey said cautiously.

"Please, call me Don."

"Okay, it's a pleasure *Don*. Have we met before? You look very familiar," Audrey said in an ill-at-ease tone.

"If we have met before then this is a double pleasure," Don said choosing his words carefully.

Audrey saw that O'Connor already picked up her luggage from the carousel. She thanked him.

"Don said he has a car waiting for us."

Audrey snapped her head around to look at Don then back to O'Connor.

"What did you just say?"

"I said Don has a car waiting for you," O'Connor replied enthusiastically. "As a courtesy of the fine work CIT has done for the government he insisted that he provide transportation to his office. Isn't that nice of him?"

Audrey answered with a very quizzical look at Don and said, "Yes, unusually nice. However, I'd rather drop my things at the hotel first and meet up with you later. Is that all right with both of you?" It wasn't really a question but rather a statement.

"That's no problem, is it Don?" O'Connor confirmed to his new best friend.

"No problem at all. I'll send a car to pick you up at 11:30 A.M. Lunch will be on me," said Don.

"I'm staying at my usual hotel," said O'Connor. "At what restaurant shall I meet you?" he quickly asked.

"Is Chico's on State all right?"

"I'll see you both there," O'Connor said cheerfully.

After checking in, Audrey entered her hotel room placing the do-not-disturb sign on the outside door handle, then closed it and quickly slammed the deadbolt and secured the chain. She leaned her back against the door.

"Why would he take the chance of exposure to O'Connor?" she asked herself in a hushed voice.

Chapter 29

Back at home Tony went to work on his pile of OSR's. These are Off Site Repairs he does on a daily basis. CIT's customer service electronically sends Tony a case they couldn't bring to a complete and satisfactory resolution. He then contacts the client and remotely works through his computer by accessing the client's computer utilizing one of CIT's specialized programs. He does so with the client's permission of course. To Tony this is one of the best parts of his job. He can stay at home and meet someone new while looking like a hero when successful. It's a perfect scenario for him. If his tics are bad nobody is around to judge. Also, if his verbal tics were a little more moderate than usual he'd simply tell the client he was placing him or her on hold. At this point he'd quickly let a few tics out and return to the call. If someone were to question him he'd say he needed to sneeze and didn't want to be impolite. This seldom happened as Tony's verbal tics weren't usually too severe.

When he completes an OSR Tony puts a checkmark next to his latest priority in his daily planner. He loves to place a checkmark next to a completed task on his to-do list. It gives him a subconscious tiny little rush that his day was going as planned and provides a feeling of control and achievement.

Tony had completed most of the OSRs and decided to take a short break before finishing. Sitting back and clasping his hands behind his head as he put his feet up on his desk Tony took in the clean organized look of his surroundings.

His desk was completely clear of everything but the essential tools of his occupation. Even those were lined up neatly.

Hmm...I think I've become somewhat of an organizational freak, he thought.

As he thought about it some more he slowly came to the realization that it provided him comfort. It was the kind of comfort that gave him a sense of being in control. This reduced his stress level considerably.

I never thought about that before, he thought.

He kept very still, which is unusual for Tony, until he realized that, at least for him, being well organized brought him a sense of peace.

That means when I was so disorganized before it was a cause of stress. Stress feeds my tormentor. Disorganization Stress...Who knew? That's one that I need to add to the spreadsheet, he thought.

"Reducing stress by being organized is another natural way to reduce my urge to tic," he declared aloud.

One silent stressor that gave Tony trouble for much of his life was he didn't have a system to keep himself organized. His life changed after he attended a Franklin Covey workshop. However, before ever meeting Jacquelyn, Tony was one of the most unorganized people on earth. Others would call and leave messages that went unreturned. For some reason Tony sometimes allowed these multiple messages to escalate to the point of creating ill feelings toward him until he returned the call. Tony then had to apologize for his tardiness. It wasn't that he tried to avoid anyone, but sometimes he just let it go on too long because in his view, it was nonessential to his life's priorities. He didn't mean to do this consciously, but at the time Tony really felt he had better things to do. He also tried the sticky note method, but wound up with hundreds of notes all over the place. Just looking at them stressed him out more than ever.

Years earlier Tony's desk would have looked like a bomb hit it. He could've cared less. All he cared about was racquetball. He dreamed about it. His focus was so strong that simply returning a phone call wasn't in his realm of thinking. His organizational skills were, to say the least, non-existent. Tony hadn't had any real training yet. Of course he didn't care unless it came to his racquetball game. When it came to that he made practice charts and created a world of organized success. He measured every aspect in an orderly manner.

When Tony practiced racquetball he never took into consideration his opponent unless, of course, that was the focal point of what he decided the session was about. If Tony had a big tournament he'd refine certain aspects of his game to match who he figured would be his toughest opponents. As was his natural tendency, he remained in his world of strategic calculations regardless of the part of his game he practiced. He measured his improvement based on his criteria and nobody else's. After all, if he was going to be the best player he could possibly become it was going to be on his terms. Tony knew world class athletes possessed unique individual physical abilities. His goal was not to play like anyone else.

Nobody else had his genetic make-up. He knew his strengths and weaknesses better than anyone. Only he could put the hard work in and become the best he could be.

At an early age Tony saw an emerging pattern as a young player. He saw most of his competition practicing what they were already good at. This made no sense to Tony.

Let them have their little ego sessions. If it strokes their ego, but allows me to win the tournament, then I'm okay with that, he thought.

As a youngster Tony always went to tournaments to watch the best players. He observed them in a unique way. All other spectators watched "eyes on the ball" style. As they looked at the ball careening around the court young Tony's head stayed in one place. He watched one player rather than focusing on the ball, absorbing nuances as he studied players rather than watch a match like everyone else.

Due to Tony's passion to improve, and logical mind, he practiced shots he previously noted required improvement. He didn't just get on the court and play to his strengths like almost everyone else. Tony actually played a game within the game as he charted areas of focused improvement. Because of his willingness to practice what he deemed to be a deficiency Tony lost scores of practice matches to inferior players. Both Tony and his practice partner left the court feeling like winners. However, his playing partner looked at it as he'd won due to the final score. Technically he was right, but Tony was just fine with that. He accomplished his goal.

Tony used practice matches shrewdly by creating situations that would take advantage of almost every aspect of his game. Often times he'd play a match with his goal being only to keep the rally alive. He never ended the rally on purpose. Tony would get to every shot and return it to the center of the court. The point of this was physical conditioning and to learn how to win if his accuracy was flawed. The other guys seemed to just play to win that particular match.

You go right ahead and win the battle while I prepare to win the war, thought Tony.

Once again he found a secondary level of focus he so desperately needed, but was oblivious to the extra benefits that came his way. When it came to sports Tony rejected the old adage that practice makes perfect. He preferred Vince Lombardi's philosophy..."*Perfect* practice makes perfect."

Contrary to many others, Tony always made sure he got in high-quality matches against top players he might face in an upcoming tournament. These players were thrilled to play the top ranked player and rightfully tried to use it to their advantage. Tony had an exceptional talent to gear up for a major tournament. He knew about a player that rarely ever lost a practice match. It wasn't that he only competed against players below his level. This guy was just that good. Mike Spencer played the game with God given physical talent. He's also very mentally tough, but most of all, he plays with heart. Spencer was Tony's secret weapon. He'd make sure the last match before the tournament began was with him. Tony considered Spencer to be the third best player in the state and easily in the top ten of the Northwest Region.

However, Spencer remained unranked and just didn't play tournaments for personal reasons. Tony gave him the nickname Stealth. It was as if no one else saw what Tony saw in him. He just went unnoticed. Whomever Spencer played always wound up absolutely frustrated by this "non-ranked" player. They always came off the court and felt Spencer played out of his mind and they were just a little off that particular day. These players were so caught up in their own little worlds that they never truly watched him play. Like everyone else they too only watched the ball when Spencer played. If they only focused on him and took note of the copious abilities he possessed. Tony was enormously glad they didn't. Stealth was *his* secret weapon.

Tony perfected so many different game styles that he never allowed any one of them to see his real game plan in a practice match. In tournament play Tony could mix in as many as seven styles of play in a matter of minutes keeping his opponents off balance and frustrated. His opponents might beat him in a practice match, but rarely in a tournament. Outwardly, Tony played the part of a humble winner and politely shook his opponent's hand after each match was over.

He'd say, "You seemed a little off your game today. I'm lucky I caught you when I did."

This was just another way for Tony to mentally work on them until the very end. Underneath Tony really thought, *You have no idea what just hit you but go ahead and think you played poorly. I know what I just did to you, and that's all that matters.*

Because of Tony's multi-level thought process he'd sometimes pretend to have a problem in a particular area of his game during practice matches against other highly ranked players. This was just his way of planting a false seed if they were to meet in an upcoming competition. This type of conviction swiftly vaulted Tony into the top twenty players in the world.

And so it went with Tony. He practiced and played the games within the game at every possible moment. Some athletes are so physically gifted they don't consciously think about the mental aspects of the game. Tony is most definitely gifted, but he also takes full advantage of peering around every corner as he tactically out-thinks his competition. It's like the old saying *"When the going gets tough, the tough get going."* In Tony's case he probably already found a way around it before it got tough. He saw it coming.

Tony returned to his daily planner and saw the only two unchecked boxes on his OSR priority list. He completed those and headed off to pick up the kids from school so Jacquelyn could catch a break and head straight home.

Chapter 30

The black SUV pulled up to the curb and stopped directly next to Audrey Shelton. She stepped back. As the dark tinted passenger window rolled down it revealed a smiling Don Williams at the wheel. He summoned Audrey in with a wave of his hand.

As she got in she asked, "What's with the spook mobile?"

Don disregarded her comment and said, "I called Ryan and told him we can't make it for lunch."

"Why would you do that?"

"I sent a computer geek over to have lunch with him," said Don.

"I'll ask you again. Why?"

"So you and I can meet in private," he responded.

Audrey knew this day was coming and she thought she had a very good idea as to why. She knew at some point she'd have to pay for the decisions she made years ago.

"Is this about a certain employee of mine?"

"You know it is Audrey."

"So, this is about T —?"

He quickly cut her off. "No names Audrey. You know the rules. Let's just say CIT's newest ambassador," he quickly said.

Audrey is protective of all her employees, but she had become especially protective of Tony. She felt badly about how she dodged his question at the airport. But, it had to be done. It was part of the agreement. The last thing she wanted was to put Tony in harm's way. Whatever Don had in mind, she knew there was the possibility that it wasn't going to be a joyride.

After what seemed to be an eternity of silence Audrey asked, "Well Don, where's our meeting place this time?"

"We're almost there," Don said impassively. A minute later Audrey looked out her passenger window then scanned out through the windshield.

"This isn't a DIT property," Audrey proclaimed.

"No, it's not."

He pulled up to the first guard barrier and provided his government issued ID badge. The young soldier only glanced at it while holding what appeared to look like a small portable copier.

"Place your hand on the pad sir," ordered the soldier.

Don was at the ready and placed his left hand on what was a small portable scanning device. The blue light started at the tips of his fingers then slowly ran the length of the sixteen inch unit.

"Welcome Mr. Williams. Is this your guest, Ms. Shelton?"

"Yes," Don said in a monotone voice.

"Please roll down your window, Ma'am."

This was a command not a request. Audrey was ready with her government issued ID. As Audrey pressed down on the window button another soldier had already appeared on her side of the SUV.

She began to hand the young soldier her ID, but he said, "That won't be necessary, Ma'am."

She then followed the same procedure as Don except she used her right hand. Once complete Don rolled up the windows and continued to their destination.

"How do they know I'm really me?"

"You are, aren't you?" Don kiddingly said in a forced anxious tone.

"You know what I mean. They didn't even want to look at my government identification badge."

"They don't need to…thanks to you. Besides, you know better than anyone. ID badges can be faked as easily as a library card."

"What do you mean thanks to me?" questioned Audrey.

"Do you remember that document identification program your company created for DIT two years ago? Well, we made a few changes in the program and you just experienced the results."

"But, that was just a simple —" Don cut her off.

"This program contains all federal government employee information. This includes your handprints. You do remember providing this years ago don't you?"

"Yes, but it *is* pretty Big Brother stuff don't you think?"

"You've been part of Big Brother as long as I've known you, Audrey. If it's all right with you I don't see an upside discussing government secrets out here in a car."

Audrey just looked at Don as he drove the SUV into the number ninety nine parking space. Inside, after another security stop, Don asked Audrey if she'd like a cup of coffee.

Audrey said sarcastically, "Are you sure I have clearance?"

Don went along with the sarcasm and said, "I think you qualify, but drink it at your own risk."

"Okay, I could use a cup. What is this place?"

"Once we're in my office I'll fill you in completely. Its sound proof and screened for listening devices daily," said Don.

"You have an office here?" Audrey asked in an astonished tone.

To Audrey's eye she thought the building could be a corporate headquarters for any of the top fifty Fortune 500 companies. The enormity of the lobby and artwork alone screamed money.

Now I know where my tax money is going, she thought.

Audrey particularly liked the colorful Calder mobile hanging from the thirty-five foot ceiling entry.

With coffee in hand they rode the elevator up in silence. As they exited the elevator Don said, "To your right. My office is the last one on the left."

"I hope you have lunch ready," Audrey needled as she watched Don place his right thumb on the small scanner pad next to his door.

He then asked her to look the other way while he entered his alpha-numeric security code.

Chapter 31

Tony called Jacquelyn and let her know he'd pick Sam and Nick up from school. She was grateful since she was having a rough day teaching.

"Do you want me to pick something up for dinner?" asked Tony.

Jacquelyn exhaled then said, "That's the second best idea I've heard all day."

"Oh? What was the first?"

"That you're picking up the kids."

They both could hear the other smile through the phone connection. It made Tony feel good.

"That rough of a day?" he asked.

"I'll fill you in when I get home," answered Jacquelyn.

Tony picked the kids up and asked them what they wanted for dinner. In unison they once again shouted "pizza!"

"Okay, broccoli and asparagus pizza it is," Tony deadpanned.

"No way, I want pepperoni," pleaded Sam.

"So do I," Nick chimed in.

"Okay, I'll make you guys a deal. If you get your homework done before dinner we'll get pepperoni pizza. Do we have a deal?"

"It's a deal," said Sam.

"I didn't hear you Nick?"

Dejectedly he replied, "I have reading that's going to take forever."

"So are you saying you can't get it done before dinner?"

In a small methodical voice he said, "I don't think so."

After a pause Tony declared, "For your honesty we'll still get pepperoni pizza."

Little Nick and Sam's faces turned their frowns upside down and shouted, "YAY!"

When they got home the kids had a very light snack and got right to their homework. "Let me know if either of you need help," said Tony.

Both Tony and Jacquelyn made sure at least one of them was always available when homework was in process. Tony went into the living room to relax as the kids worked at the kitchen table. Jacquelyn finally arrived home at 4:55 P.M.

After a welcome home kiss Tony asked, "Why so late today?"

"Do you remember I told you of the student I've been working extra hard with to help bring her work into line with expectations?"

When talking about Jacquelyn's students she never used their names and Tony respects her for that. She is always protective of the student-teacher relationship. This protection encompassed everyone, even Tony.

"It frustrates me to no end when a student just doesn't try. I'd rather they try and completely fail than not even put forth the effort. That is unless a student has special needs of course."

Jacquelyn's compassion for those who touch her life is so immense it raises her stress level in a compounding manner if things aren't right. She has a difficult time turning her brain off from matters such as these. Tony usually waits to listen to her day rather than start the conversation about his. He knows it helps Jacquelyn and Tony wants to hear about what's important to her. Knowing Jacquelyn as Tony does, this became a very important ritual. Helping Jacquelyn vent a little is every bit as important to Tony as it is for her.

After Jacquelyn was finished she asked how Tony's day went. He told her about his meeting at the airport with Audrey.

"Why'd she ask you to meet her there?"

"Well, that's where this gets kind of interesting," said Tony.

He quickly went through the entire day. Tony even told her about the removal of the emails he uncovered.

"Why would someone remove emails?" she asked.

"That's what I was wondering. They have to know that I can locate any and all documents on our servers," he said.

"So you think this was intentional?"

"Yes, I do," Tony said emphatically.

235

"But why would anyone mess around with something like that given your background with information technology?"

"I think the more interesting question is *who* messed around with it," Tony replied.

"Do you have a theory?" asked Jacquelyn.

Tony told her about the man in the airport executive lounge and then how Audrey acted when he busted the guy for eavesdropping on their conversation.

"Are you sure it wasn't just your imagination?" she asked. "Please tell me you didn't go after him," Jacquelyn followed up in a concerned tone.

"You would've been proud of me. I started to, but lost him without even leaving the lounge area so I let it go."

In a relieved tone and a single head nod she said, "Smart move. So who do you think this guy is?" she asked.

"You wouldn't believe me if I told you."

"Let me be the judge of that. What's the worst that could happen? I'll just laugh at you," she kiddingly added.

"In all my life I've never gotten the same exact feeling from more than one person. For some reason they're always different. The chance of me having the same *calculating* feeling that I had in Audrey's office is very, very slim. I have never ever gotten the same feeling about two different people before"…tic, tic, tic. Just recounting the story seemed to cause Tony duress.

236

"You don't think he was somehow in or around her office do you?"

"That's exactly what I'm proposing, Jacquelyn."

"But you said you got the feeling from a mirror."

"No, I said the feeling came from the direction of the mirror. There's a big difference," he corrected.

"So, what's your theory about the link between the two?"

"Only that first, both feelings are real. Second, I got the exact same feeling from this guy at the executive lounge well before Audrey arrived. Third, he seemed to have some sort of interest in me as I spied on him from behind the newspaper waiting for Audrey."

Jacquelyn jumped in and said, "Don't you think there's the possibility he saw you and, therefore, was wondering to himself why the heck you were spying on him?"

Tony quickly responded, "Not a chance. I left no room for error." He continued, "And finally, I could swear he was waiting for Audrey."

He explained that this man was the only one to react as if waiting for someone each time the executive lounge door opened.

"Maybe he was," said Jacquelyn playing devil's advocate.

"Jacquelyn, he quietly and purposely slipped into the private meeting room next to ours from the back and listened to our conversation. And the cherry on top was when I called him on it he took off like a scared rabbit."

"How do you know he entered from the back of the room?"

"I was facing the front entry. I know my surroundings and he didn't just walk into the front entrance to that room"…tic, tic, tic.

"Another odd thing was when he left the lounge. It was as if he were trying to hide his face."

"What do you mean?"

"He tilted his hat to hide his face as he bolted. And when I asked Audrey if she knew him she acted…odd. It was as if she knew something, but had to leave right away."

"Okay, so why would this man want anything to do with you?" asked Jacquelyn.

"I have no idea," answered Tony.

"It could have been a coincidence or maybe a competitor who recognized Audrey," said Jacquelyn.

Samantha came running into the living room and announced she was done with her homework.

"Let's take a look," said Jacquelyn.

"I'll check on Nick," said Tony.

He gave Sam a quick rub on the top of her head as he got up.

"How goes the reading Nick?"

"Okay, I guess," he said not completely convincing his dad.

"What's the book about?" asked Tony.

"A fox and a goofy lion who are friends, but everybody looks at them weird."

"Hmm, sounds like your mom and I," Tony mumbled.

"What?"

"Nothing. How many pages do you have left?" Nick flipped the pages then held up four fingers.

"I'd like to hear about these two. Would you mind reading the rest to me?"

"Okay."

"Hang on just one second Nick."

Tony went into the living room and gave the international call sign, pinkie and thumb to the ear and mouth, for Jacquelyn to order the pizza. By the time Nick would be done the pizza would be on its way.

After dinner the kids played while Jacquelyn and Tony cleaned up.

"Well there's one good thing to ordering out. Cleaning up is a breeze!" said Jacquelyn.

A while later Tony began experiencing more tics than he had since he'd been home. He went down to the basement to let out some high octane tics. Tony used a towel to muffle the vocal tics.

"What's the deal with this?" he quietly asked himself.

Both Jacquelyn and Tony had changed into comfortable jeans and were now on the couch watching a favorite show they recorded days ago. Tony hit pause on the remote control.

This was emotionally hard for Tony, but he asked Jacquelyn, "Do you think pizza could cause me to tic more?"

"I don't know. Why do you ask?"

"Ever since I had that pizza I've had the urge to tic almost non-stop." He didn't tell her about his trip to the basement.

"I don't —" Jacquelyn stopped abruptly. "Did you have the same tic level all day?"

"No, it was pretty much up and down, but not to this level. Why?" he asked.

"Think about it and follow along. You had a pretty stressful day, right?"

"Yes I did"...tic, tic, tic.

"We both now know that stress is a major contributor when it comes to Tourette's."

"Yes it is"...tic, tic, tic. For some reason Tony was having a really hard time holding the tics back due to their extraordinary strength.

"Prior to these tics beginning in the last hour or so, were you more or less stressed than at the peak of your stress level today?"

"I'm less stressed, but moving up on the charts just talking about it."

"But I'm really only interested in the time just prior to them coming on strong this evening," said Jacquelyn.

"Okay, I was definitely less stressed prior to eating dinner."

"So what changed?"

"My clothes," Tony said sarcastically.

"Come on, Tony, this is an opportunity to possibly find something else that causes an increase in the symptoms of Tourette's."

Tony did have a propensity to make jokes when he really became uncomfortable talking about this particular subject.

"I ate pizza with you and the kids. That's all I can think of," Tony said in a disappointed tone.

"Did you have anything just before pizza?"

"No, just four pages of Nick reading to me."

It was as if a great big light bulb went on over Jacquelyn's head. "What did you have to drink with your pizza?"

"I had soda like you and the kids."

"We have three kinds of soda. We have Coke, Pepsi and Mountain Dew. "Which did you have?"

"I had Mountain Dew."

"If I know you, you probably had plenty, right?"

"Sure, a pizza dinner isn't complete without the accompaniment of the proper drink," Tony said with a grin...tic, tic, tic.

"Tony, what are the ingredients in Mountain Dew?"

Tony got up and read the label.

"It says here the main ingredients are carbonated water, high fructose corn syrup, citric acid, caffeine and sugar."

"So, how much do you want to bet one, or some, of those ingredients has caused your tic outburst?" Jacquelyn asked rhetorically.

With eyes wide Tony excitedly said, "I bet you're right. Four of these are STIMULANTS! What an idiot. Why didn't I think of this before! Everything I put in my mouth is chemical. My brain has a chemical glitch. Jacquelyn you're brilliant!"

He leaned over to her and put his hands on her shoulders and said "You, my dear, are in the wrong business. I don't know if you should be a doctor, detective or a trial attorney. Thank you so much!"

He gave her a big kiss and an even bigger bear hug.

Chapter 32

"You've moved up in the world, Don."

"This is home. Well, at least for work," he said. These days Don Williams spent more hours in his office than home.

Standing at the windows Audrey was absorbing the expansive view of the perfectly beautiful, cloudless sky.

"How did you snag this office?"

"Well, it's a long story."

"Then just the short version," retorted Audrey.

"It's as simple as having the right skill set and knowing the right people at the right time," he said succinctly.

"At another time I'm going to have to hear the whole story because that was the vaguest, clichéd and shortest version you could have possibly given," Audrey said with interest piqued.

"I'd like to take more credit, but it really was just a right place right time thing," Don said, averting his eyes. "Please, let's have a seat. Can I get you anything?"

As Audrey sat down in the chair facing the one Don would occupy she simply said, "Yes, you owe me lunch, thank you."

After finishing the catered meal they moved into the conference area of his office. Don took his place after Audrey at the completely cleared off table between them. He then set a sealed red file folder in front of him. Audrey has made so many trips into the Washington, DC culture that she knew this was the time to clam up. She was the invitee. Don pulled out an official document from the folder and gently slid it over to Audrey.

"For the record, do you remember signing this Audrey?" It was a non-disclosure agreement she knew to be air-tight.

He really must have something interesting, she thought.

"Of course I do," she replied.

After a quick once over she went ahead with standard operating procedure and signed and dated it just as she does anytime she has an official meeting with anyone from Langley. She still wondered about the genesis of the nickname "The Company" most insiders referred to when speaking of the Central Intelligence Agency.

"Thanks Audrey. Now let me begin to tell you why you're here," Don said as he leaned in, putting his elbows on his thighs with hands clasped together.

Without the hint of ego Don said, "I am no longer directly tied to the Department of Information Technologies. But, it's still my cover."

Audrey raised an eyebrow.

"You're looking at the Director of SSD."

"What's SSD?" asked Audrey.

"It's short for Savant Syndrome Division, which crosses the landscape of Homeland Security and yet, still CIA. The science behind it is fascinating," Don explained.

Audrey gave him a very skeptical look.

"That's quite a balancing act. Which do you report to?" she asked.

Undaunted, as if not even hearing her question, Don continued, "A few years back I was working with one of our computer hackers that we hire on an as-needed basis. As you know, sometimes to get the highest level of expertise we have to outsource, as in the case of CIT. The amazing thing was what this person did in eight hours that our entire team couldn't accomplish in eight months. It dawned on me this person must be a genius. Boy was I wrong! After looking at the below average results of the IQ test I realized I had to look at this from another perspective. For some reason this person just has the knack to hack."

Audrey wanted to comment on the poetry, but decided to politely listen. She knew this was leading somewhere important or she wouldn't be here.

"So I got our best people to investigate and sure enough there's a substantive science to this. Usually very unique and specific abilities are found in people who are suffering from autism. However, though very rare, our scientists discovered there are documented cases of non-autistic people doing the most amazing things. You ever see the movie "Rain Man"?"

"Sure, who hasn't?" said Audrey.

"Well picture Dustin Hoffman's character without any type of autism. Now there's a force of nature!" Don said excitedly. "Unfortunately there are so few people with a special ability who can, on a daily basis, function in the world normally. We literally have to go out and try to find these people. We tried advertising to hire, but that was an ugly mess," Don said making a sour face. "Remember, we're not talking about just talented folks here. We're talking true special abilities."

"You sound like you've read too many comic books."

"It is amazing how some of this stuff almost borders on comic book hero type abilities. Don't get me wrong. I'm not talking Spiderman or Wonder Woman here. But, what some of these folks can do…you can't even imagine. I've become a fan of what many call fringe science because I'm seeing the results on a daily basis."

Audrey continued her placid demeanor wondering exactly where this was leading.

"Now, for obvious reasons, I can't divulge to you who this person is or how the savant-like hacking ability had been acquired. This person literally could hack into anything that contains a computer chip. During our testing of this ability he, or she, even hacked our satellites during a lunch break. They're the secret ones *no one* is supposed to know about." Don had become exceptionally animated.

"Anyway, my point is that Savant Syndrome is real and the government is tapping these resources to protect and defend the United States of America," Don said in a very patriotic tone.

Audrey got the picture and wanted to know specifically what this had to do with her and CIT. "May I ask why you are telling me all this?"

Don stood up and began to pace in front of the windows as if he were searching for the right words. He thought this through and decided to play upon Audrey's past and natural curiosity.

"Because you're involved in this to a degree you're not yet aware," Don said, leading Audrey.

"How can I be involved when this is the first I'm hearing of it," Audrey said incredulously.

This was just the response Don was looking for. It gave him the green light to continue. Don went on explaining more assets his Savant Syndrome Division cultivated in greater detail. He then explained he wants to integrate his savant assets to work together. His vision is to take full advantage of the specific abilities each may bring to the table in live operational roles to protect and defend the interests of the United States of America.

"At times these assets might not even know they're working a mission with another savant asset. It all depends on what specific talents, or abilities, are required to get the job done."

He finally got Audrey to the point of complete curiosity as to why he was telling her all of this.

"Don, you and I go back a ways, but if you don't get to the point I'm getting up, thanking you for the lovely lunch, then heading back home."

Don was extremely satisfied that she said this since the entire conversation was of course being recorded. He was now completely protected within "The Company."

"Audrey, do you know of anyone who has shown to have a special ability?"

She deflected the question and said, "I know lots of very intelligent people, but I wouldn't say they have the type of special abilities you've just described."

Don asked, "Have you ever met someone who could be put in a large group of people and pick out a terrorist without even a hint that foul play was a possibility?"

"I can't say that I have," responded Audrey.

"Let me take that one step further," said Don. "What if I were to tell you that a person saved not only his life, but one hundred seventy-four people including his very own bride?"

Don let his question hang in the air.

Trying not to show a response, Audrey was dumbstruck when Don used the word bride instead of wife. She remained quiet, but slightly lifting her eyebrow told Don she was now completely on track. Don allowed for her to respond, but Audrey said nothing. He moved on.

"There's something I want to show you."

He picked up the remote control and the fifty inch HD plasma television screen came to life with a bright blue color. Audrey swiveled her chair for a better view. Don pressed one more button and the screen went black for a few seconds. Audrey then recognized the image that appeared was an airport gate area. She then recognized which one.

"This is the Portland International Airport," said Don, confirming her thoughts.

Don then let the video speak for itself. Audrey quickly recognized Tony and Jacquelyn. The camera remained stationary without zooming in on anything or anyone in particular. She watched Tony get up and throw some paper away then head back to sit with Jacquelyn.

"Let's finally get to the point of this Don," she said impatiently.

Don knew better than to string her along too far. As the video looped back Don pressed pause at the point when Tony crumpled his popcorn wrapper.

"Did you catch what your employee did?"

"Yes, he amazingly threw his garbage in the correct receptacle. He has an amazing ability. It's why we hired him," she said in a tone dripping with sarcasm.

"Please, take another look in enhanced slow motion."

Audrey acted as if she were being put out as she obliged with his request. Don began with a narrative.

"Notice at this point Mr. Anthony James already had the paper crumpled up."

"He prefers to be called Tony," Audrey stated.

Don continued, "Now at this point he slows down as he takes a quick look at *that* man right *there*." He circled Tony's eyes with his red laser pointer.

"Tony quickly un-crumpled the paper then apparently made enough noise to garner the attention of this man. It's just a quick glance."

Don moved the video forward with continuing commentary of each and every important detail including Tony's interaction with the TSA agent and Air Marshal. Due to security being beefed up after 9/11 the cameras have the ability to follow any individual's every move. In this case Tony James. The video's last thirty seconds flashed headlines from various newspapers hailing the U.S. Air Marshal from preventing a terrorist attack and saving lives.

Upon completion Don asked, "So, what do you think?"

"I remember reading the articles. What you just showed me was completely different than what was reported. Though, I'm not surprised."

"Audrey, as you just saw, Tony James somehow knew that man with the scar meant harm to everyone who was going to board the aircraft."

"But, how could he possibly —" her voice broke off.

She knew when Don Williams began investigating someone he never let go until the job was complete. He had to have more. She also knew a detailed report was required to have been filed by Homeland Security and Don certainly had accessed that information.

After further discussion Don asked Audrey to think back to her meeting with Tony in her office. The one in which she asked him to become the company "Ambassador."

"Is this why O'Connor pushed so hard to move Tony into that position?"

"That's exactly right." Don waited for the lights to come on in Audrey's head.

"Does that mean what I think this means?"

"Yes, Audrey. O'Connor was contacted and asked to get you to offer him the position."

"So O'Connor already knows what I just found out?"

"No, that's not the case. O'Connor doesn't know anything. I asked Walker at DIT to contact O'Connor on a purely technological point and the rest fell into place. O'Connor just guided you to the proper decision."

"You piss ant! Why didn't you just come directly to me?"

"Because we needed to set up a first "live round" test for your Mr. James," said Don.

"Test. What test?"

"Prior to your meeting with Tony I had placed one of my men in that little crawl space behind your mirror on the north wall. We had the glass replaced so my asset could monitor Tony."

At this point Audrey was beyond furious. Don expected her reaction. She knew all too well what the CIA was capable of doing. Audrey had been working with them for many years.

"What was the point of that?" she asked sternly.

"Strictly to observe and report what we thought of as a potential asset."

"You guys sure know how to waste time and money," Audrey said, red with anger.

"It wasn't a waste of time or money, Audrey. "Here, judge for yourself," Don said to her as he held up the television remote once again.

"You've got to be kidding me! You recorded our private meeting?"

"Just sit back and watch. I won't say a thing. Judge this on the facts," Don said with a slight nod toward the screen.

Throughout the video, complete with impeccable sound, Audrey had asked Don to stop and rewind at six key points. When the video was complete Audrey very quietly said, "How could he know someone was behind the mirror? I didn't hear a camera whirring or anything. Do you think Tony did?"

"Impossible, we used the latest in digital recording devices that makes no sound. And just for the record we couldn't tip you off because we needed this to be a clean test," said Don.

Audrey knew exactly what he meant. "Do you think maybe he was just looking at himself?" Audrey asked in an almost pleading tone.

Don rewound the recording a little and pressed play. He first pressed the slow motion button and then pressed pause. In full high definition was a view of Tony looking squarely at the mirror from an angle that he, Tony, certainly could not see his reflection.

"Does that answer your question, Audrey?"

"So you're telling me my employee, Tony James, has some kind of a sixth sense?"

"That's almost correct. Our scientists like to use the word ability and remember not the comic book definition. Currently our hypothesis is that we think Tony James can accurately make a correct instant assessment about his surroundings and people, but we aren't exactly sure how."

Audrey got out of her chair and did her own pacing. Don was happy to stay seated and wait. Suddenly Audrey piped up.

"So you *think*, but don't *know*?"

"That's right Audrey. We have the incident at the airport. We have the oddity at your office and the meeting at the airport executive lounge."

Don didn't reveal that he also obtained Tony's health records.

A light bulb went on. "So, you guys sent the email. That's why you sent one of your agents to the executive lounge at the airport," she surmised.

"We needed to know more about Mr. James and his capabilities. We, scratch that, I need to know if he falls into the category of having Savant Syndrome. Quite frankly, if he does, he'd be of great value to serve his country."

Audrey, now convinced of the possibility asked, "Okay. Where do we go from here?"

Don was very happy to hear Audrey say *we*.

"Our need is to field test him in his position as CIT's ambassador."

"What does that entail?" Audrey asked cautiously.

"It's quite simple. You send Tony on a trip out here to the next Information Technology Seminar. While he's here, we'll funnel him into a blind field test to explore his potential as a CIA slash SSD asset under my command."

"And what happens after that?" asked Audrey.

"It really depends if he passes or fails. If he fails he'll be left to his simple life in Oregon. However, if he passes, we will approach him in a nonconventional way."

"What do you mean nonconventional?"

"I'll assign the appropriate handler for him to see how he responds under pressure. If he passes then we'll bring him in for a battery of clinical tests. We've been doing this for some time now and matching the right handler with the potential asset is critical. On the surface it appears Tony James is not someone we could only give part of an assignment to without him quickly deciphering the untold details. I don't think anyone can fool him easily."

You can say that again, thought Audrey.

On one level this all sounded very businesslike and straight-forward. On another level Audrey was having a hard time grappling with how she had been manipulated. She let the latter go. Audrey began to think like "The Company" person she has always been.

"So what do you need me to do?"

"Just get him here to Washington and we'll take care of the rest."

Chapter 33

After the revelation that one or more of the ingredients in the soda he drank the night before had caused an incredible increase in tics, Tony decided to open up his Excel spreadsheet, and include an additional column labeled STIMULANTS. Under a separate tab he made a list of the foods he normally eats including small incidentals such as gum and mints. He went so far as to identify them as regular or sugar free. He made quite a large list from memory.

Tony's next task was to research the ingredients of each using the vast resources from the internet. He started with what made sense to him…breakfast. His first targets were frozen waffles, syrup, butter and orange juice. However, Tony quickly realized he needed to learn a little bit about reading food labels before he looked up any of their ingredients.

He discovered the ingredients listed on the package are in the order of most to least amount. The target was to find those foods that contained sugar and caffeine in larger amounts. To his amazement he was blown away that sugar went undercover.

It has so many different aliases, he realized.

He began reading the list then gave up due to its length. Tony's mind was spinning from the revelation. Questions began to roll.

How would anyone know that barley malt is really sugar? It sounds like a grain, which should be good for you, he thought scratching his head.

Tony, noticing the obvious, saw that everything ending in "ose" is really sugar. After a little more scrutiny he also found that most so-called "low sugar" products really don't contain sugar. In its place on the label is something that ends in "itol" which is really sugar alcohol. Tony was angered yet pleased he found this dirty little nutritional secret about our government allowing loopholes for the few who are in the know.

What's next? Our water regulates our life expectancy?

Tony decided whatever he was going to eat or drink he would have a complete understanding of the effects regarding his urge to tic.

From this day forward I'm going to take as much sugar out of my diet as possible. I need to know to what extent this makes a difference in tic intensity, if any, he declared to himself.

Tony didn't discard any food or drinks that were already in the house because of Jacquelyn and the kids. This was his challenge not theirs. He'd rely on will power to undergo this trial.

After two days of thoroughly looking at everything Tony wanted to eat or drink, he became extremely frustrated due to the amount of sugar in most foods. He carried in his pocket a printed list of all the names of sugar he'd come across. When he looked for something to consume he cross-referenced it to the food label. He also checked to see where on the food label the ingredient landed. If it was one of the major ingredients listed early, then Tony knew if he ate or drank it, he would likely pay the price with major tic action.

Upon the completion of a two week trial he was amazed at the decreased level of tic activity. Tony felt he was zeroing in on his target...Tourette's. He went from rating his tics a ten, based on the pizza and soda dinner, to some of his lowest scores yet. His cravings for sugar were still very high, but his will power and the promise of a daily lessened urge to tic were slowly overcoming this obstacle.

What bothered, and at the same time, bolstered Tony, is what he referred to as "The Food Police."

For some reason people care about what others eat, he thought.

It seemed everywhere he went someone was offering him a piece of birthday cake or a piece of chocolate. He understood and appreciated it, but politely declined every time.

He became very accustomed to hearing, "Of all the people I know, you're not on a diet...are you?"

For most of his life he's tried to hide his tics from everyone. He certainly wasn't about to tell them the truth. He just went along with letting them think he was dieting. Tony was amazed at the pressure certain people placed on making him feel guilty turning down freshly baked chocolate chip cookies.

At one point he thought, *It's not like I'm not telling you to go jump off a cliff. I'm just politely declining to eat a cookie that's full of sugar if it's all right with you*!

If it weren't for Tony's contrarian personality trait, he likely would have caved. However, once Tony makes up his mind, and anyone pushes, he stands like a rock.

In this case, he thought, *This is one of the toughest things I've ever had to do.*

With a complete month under his belt Tony became as sugar free as possible. The cravings stopped and he discovered the benefits beyond lessening the urge to tic. Not that he needed to, but he actually dropped a couple of pounds and felt great. Tony's taste buds changed as he enjoyed the natural sugar found in a variety of fruits. He tested so many items. For instance, one hundred percent orange juice was okay. Next he would do sugar tests with side-by-side juices on different days. Within an hour after drinking the juice he'd either have a greater urge to tic or not. If Tony did, then he knew that product had some kind of sugar that bothered him too much so he eliminated it from his diet. After awhile Tony became an expert at knowing the sugar content in the food and drinks he consumed. It was as if he found a coat of armor he could use to help protect him from his tormentor. The next target on his journey would be caffeine. Will he find more in the shadows hidden by the enemy of his chemical state?

Chapter 34

As Tony was driving Sam and Nick to school he heard the special ringtone that let him know Audrey was calling. Since he had the kids in the car he decided to let it go to voicemail. The sound of a large drip of water signaled to him she left a message. He'd listen to it after the kids were out of the car.

Tony stopped to drop Sam off first and gave her a kiss on her forehead. "Have fun today Sam."

Sam saw one of her friends and quickly unbuckled to catch up with her. Tony was happy to see Stephanies's face light up when she saw Sam.

Apparently there's nothing better than to be able to walk into school with a friend, he thought.

Nick was in the back seat. "Well Nick, do you want to come up front or stay where you are?"

"I'll stay here," he said with a sleepy voice.

"Are you sure? You can drive if you want," Tony said as flat-toned as possible. Nick seemed tired and didn't even react to the joke. "Okay, let's get you over to school and you drive next time," Tony said eyeing Nick in the rear view mirror.

Both schools were on the same campus so it was only a minute before little Nick was off and running with his backpack flopping from side-to-side. Tony watched as two of Nick's friends quickly found him. He noticed Nick seemed to draw friends to him quicker than flies to a barbeque. Tony smiled. You'd be hard pressed to find a father more proud of both his children.

Tony decided to return Audrey's call when he got back to his office in his home. She answered on the third ring.

"Hi, Audrey, it's Tony. I got your message to give you a call," he said.

"I can always count on you to return my call within a short period of time Tony. I like that", she said with a smile he could hear through the phone.

Tony detected something else in her tone that seemed somewhat off. "You're still the boss aren't you?"

"Last time I looked I was."

"Then Audrey, you get preferential treatment. You sign my check."

"This is true. But, you wouldn't believe how many people who work at CIT seem to be afraid to call me back right away."

"That's understandable," said Tony.

"Why do you say that?"

"Most people get a call from the head honcho in a major corporation and think in terms of black and white."

"I don't have a racist bone in my body!" exclaimed Audrey.

"That's not what I meant. What I was trying to say was that they identify only two options in their mind. The first is that they're getting a call for something they perceive as bad and a distant second is that it's for something good."

"I never looked at it that way before, but you're probably right. When I do make calls it's usually to dish out extra work or crack the whip. I need to make a note to call employees more often just to see how things are going. How did you get so wise to human behavior, Tony?"

"Just an observation I guess."

Audrey was now paying much more attention to the subject of Tony's "observations".

In typical Tony fashion, he quickly forced the reason for the conversation asking, "So, what bad news do you have for me this morning?"

He asked this totally flat-toned. His question didn't drip with even a hint of sarcasm, but just let it flow naturally. From Tony's perspective Audrey seemed to enjoy his needling.

"Are you familiar with —? Wait a minute!" Audrey began to chuckle. She grinned then said, "You almost had me."

"I'm just having a little fun Audrey."

I never really noticed how disarming he can be, she thought. With added emphasis on her next four words Audrey asked, "As I was saying, are you familiar with the annual ITCC?"

"Sounds like someone practiced their ABC's this morning."

Audrey once again took notice of his ease of communication, but gave a smile with a slight exhale as she did so.

"You mean the International Technology Commission Convention?" asked Tony.

"That's the one and apparently you are familiar."

"You think with all that brain power they could come up with a better name. And, yes, while in college I drove from Portland to New York when they had it there."

"Well, as CIT's new ambassador, we need you to represent us at this year's convention."

"When and where is it this year, Audrey?"

"It's next week in Washington, D.C."

"Wow, that's short notice, Audrey. I thought you said this kind of thing wouldn't happen."

"I know Tony. I'm really sorry. I had originally planned on attending myself, but my travel schedule has been a little hectic as of late. And, just for the record, I never said it wouldn't *ever* happen."

Audrey closed her eyes and the meeting in Director Don Williams' office quickly flashed through her mind. She was struggling with her decision to put Tony in a position that carried the possibility of ultimately leading him into a hazardous future. Audrey's curiosity with regard to Tony possibly having a unique ability ultimately trumped her concerns. Audrey thought back to the day she met him. After connecting the dots she realized how intuitive Tony truly is. She then made her decision based on the facts knowing he could pass, fail or turn them down. Audrey knew Don wouldn't put him in harm's way during a test. The odds were heavily on her side.

"Are you okay with me talking with Jacquelyn before I commit to this?" he asked.

"I wouldn't have it any other way", said Audrey. She knew Tony was going. *It's just a formality checking in with her*, she thought.

After he hung up the phone with Audrey Tony placed his call to Jacquelyn on her classroom phone. Fortunately her class hadn't begun just yet. He explained the situation. She understood, but didn't like it that he'd be gone on such short notice. Tony then called Audrey back. This time the call didn't go directly to Audrey as she was on her phone. CIT's central receptionist asked who was calling then placed him on hold until Audrey answered.

"That was quick, Tony," she said without saying hello.

Tony confirmed he would be going to Washington, DC.

"I'll send your itinerary via email right away."

Tony thanked Audrey and just as he ended the call his computer notified him of a new email.

That was really quick, he thought.

He opened the email Audrey sent and saw only attachments. She didn't bother to write anything.

That's not like her. She must be in a big hurry, he thought.

His travel and lodging itinerary was first. He opened it then saved this to his hard drive. As Tony did so he began to wonder why he felt something was off when talking to Audrey this morning. On a whim Tony very quickly looked at when the itinerary was originally created.

"Two days ago!" he said out loud.

With just a couple more clicks of the mouse, using a special program very few people know about, he saw that the email attachments didn't originate from CIT. They once again came from the Washington, DC area. He pinged the server that would help him find out the origin of the document, but the IP address came back reading 000.00.000.0.

All zeros? Every computer has an Internet Protocol Address! That's how the internet works. This is really strange, he thought.

He tried a few more times with the same result then mumbled, "This definitely didn't originate from CIT."

He thought about calling Audrey back, but a faint voice inside told him to hold off. Tony's world included a good dose of questioning the nuances that occur in everyday life. He knew it had something to do with overcompensating due to his lack of control over Tourette's.

Chapter 35

Tony found himself alone in the kitchen while Jacquelyn and the kids were visiting Grandma and Grandpa. He decided now would be a good time to do a little research on caffeine. This was the last ingredient on his list from his pizza night tic storm over a month ago.

He rubbed his hands together and said, fumbling his words out loud, "I'm going to start…where? I know caffeine is a stimulant, but other than that, I have no idea what caffeine is or where it comes from."

Once again he headed straight to his laptop. A simple internet search, entering the words "what is caffeine" supplied him with over 6,450,000 possible results.

"Well, I think I'm going to have a good handle on this subject shortly based on that number alone!" he said.

Tony began his journey into the world of caffeine. He learned it's as addictive as cocaine. Pure caffeine is plant based. It stimulates any central nervous system that ingests it. In nature, caffeine serves as a form of pest control for certain plants. These include cocoa trees, where chocolate is derived, coffee shrubs and tea trees. The caffeine causes insects and pests to collapse from the effects of a period of over-stimulation.

"Wow, this could be the biggest culprit of all the ingredients I've researched so far!" he exclaimed.

Caffeine on the source plant is considered a psychoactive drug. "Okay, what's that mean?"

He quickly found that it's any drug or chemical that crosses the blood-brain barrier.

"Hmm, what's the blood-brain barrier?" he questioned.

Tony found that it's a protective barrier, like a moat with the drawbridge almost always permanently in the up position. It keeps the brain as stable as possible by preventing dangerous substances from entering.

"Okay, so caffeine can cross the blood-brain barrier," he stated audibly to help keep him on track.

Caffeine acts primarily on the central nervous system. However, it hasn't been designated as a controlled substance so its use in coffee, tea and soda isn't illegal.

"Well, I guess money talks and you know what walks!" Tony said aloud to himself.

When removed from the source plant and reduced to its most natural state, it forms a white powder. *So this is why manufacturers of soda can easily add it to their drink selections.*

Continuing to talk to himself he said, "Wow, they basically dilute the powdered caffeine with sugar and the end result is a tasty, addictive, bubbly drink! I wish I knew that all these years! I'm off anything that has caffeine in it including all soda and chocolate."

Tony knew he had the willpower to tackle this just like he did with eliminating as much processed sugar from his diet as humanly possible.

Chocolate, that's going to be a tough one, he thought.

That night Tony was very tired and fell asleep quickly just after 11:00 P.M. Unfortunately, for some unknown reason, he woke up at 1:15 A.M. Tourette's never woke him up. It was always something else. He lay in bed surrounded by nothing but darkness and his ever present tics greeting him in the wee hours of the morning. He knew this scenario all too well. He was not going to be allowed to go back to sleep for a while. Tony was becoming seriously angry because even with everything he was doing to reduce his tormentor's hold on him, it just wasn't enough. Angry, but focused, he quietly slipped out of bed and headed downstairs so as not to awaken Jacquelyn. Sam and Nick could sleep through a tornado.

Before rolling onto the living room sofa he punched the cushion in frustration. Talking quietly to himself, Tony said, "What else can I possibly do to stop these stupid tics? I've gone to the doctor. I exercise to exhaustion. I watch my sugar intake. For what, so I can still wake up in the middle of the night and then be at the mercy of a chemical imbalance. I don't think so! There's got to be someone out there that has an answer for me."

He sprung from his fetal position on the couch and grabbed his laptop computer. More focused, he exclaimed, "This is the information age and I'm finding an answer. I'm finding THE expert that can get me to the point of feeling normal!"

With a quickly renewed attitude and purpose he said in a deep comic book hero voice, "To the internet and beyond!"

Feeling better about taking action he sat back in contemplation while his computer booted up. *There has to be a doctor in the Northwest that's an expert on Tourette's. They can't all be out east.*

As the World Wide Web came to life he sat up with his right hand poised over the computer touch pad. His ESPN home page came up and he quickly went to his favorite search engine's home page. Tony didn't waste a single key stroke. He quickly typed: ***Tourette's Specialist Portland, Oregon Area.***

Within one-third of a second 2,290,000 results appeared. As Tony waded through the first couple of pages he found a very promising one. It was a doctor located in Tacoma. As he read every word on each page of the website he began to realize this just might be the person he's looking for. *This doctor is farther away than anticipated, but very promising.* Tony then went back and clicked on each link within the pages he just read. The more information Tony consumed the more he thought this may possibly be the specialist to help him.

Now I just need to get in to see her as quickly as possible! After I take the kids to school I'm immediately driving the two hours and taking a chance to see Dr. Dillon without an appointment, he thought.

It was now after 4:00 A.M. and Tony stretched with a big yawn. He closed his laptop after printing out Dr. Dillon's address and phone number. He quietly went back upstairs, gently climbed into bed and successfully fell asleep until his alarm went off at 5:35 A.M. As Jacquelyn and Tony said good morning to each other she asked him if he slept well.

Slightly side-stepping the real answer he said, "I could use more," with no further comment.

After a yawn Jacquelyn said, "I slept like a rock."

As expected, Tony's body clock was temporarily out of order. They went about their morning routine getting ready for the day ahead. Tony was exhausted, but put on a show that he was ready for the challenges ahead. He was riding on just a few hours of sleep and didn't want Jacquelyn to know. Tony felt guilt dripping from his pores. He justified it as not wanting to worry her because of all the driving that was ahead for him today.

As soon as he dropped the kids at school he quickly went home to shower. Tony was on his way to try and see Dr. Dillon without an appointment.

Shoot first and ask questions later. I have to do this, he thought.

He'd tell Jacquelyn everything when they both were home for the evening and the kids were asleep.

Tony knew cold calling a doctor was one of the dumbest things anyone could possibly attempt. The guardian at the gate, the receptionist, was trained to keep unwanted people out so the professionals could do their jobs. But, for some inexplicable reason, anytime he saw a sign that said, "Keep Out", it seemed to read to him "Welcome Tony James." Tony was either that curious or that defiant. He isn't sure why he always has this reaction.

For income during college Tony worked selling copy machines. He'd been successfully trained to make cold calls. It was drilled into him that success in this industry was measured in ratios. How many business doors did you call upon? How many times did you get to see the decision maker? He was taught to make sure he was dealing with the MAN. This acronym meant Money, Authority and Need. Tony thought it was likely made up in the 1950's, as it seemed sexist to him. In today's world the MAN is male or female. His wish was for Dr. Dillon to be the Tourette's version of the MAN. He placed his hopes that the good doctor was the person who has the Knowledge, Experience and Desire to help him.

Tony thought, *That would be KED not MAN...whatever.*

One of the many ratios taught to him was number of attempts to actual successful product demonstrations. And, of course, ultimately how many demos to machines were sold? In this case, he needed to have a ratio of one-to-one, end of story. Not a lot of wiggle room.

Tony had thought he'd begun to build some pretty thick skin concerning rejection, but cold calling day after day created armor. After awhile he became pretty much impervious to initial rejection. This combined with his

271

competitive spirit, and a burning desire to deal a blow to his tormentor created a man on a mission.

While working as a copier sales person he always reminded himself that somebody got up out of their bed, showered, went to work and had no plans of purchasing a copier that day. It was his job to find them and create the overwhelming desire for one.

Tony realized very quickly it was more about *effective* cold calling than just the numbers as he was taught. Once again the old adage of practice makes perfect didn't sit well with him. After being tossed out of the nicest businesses for two solid weeks Tony began to refine what he saw and thought was a trend in the making.

To be sure, he decided to enter a large group medical office waiting area and just observe. Sales people came and went. He took notes. Less than a handful of cold callers actually met with the decision maker. He noticed most came in and asked for the office manager.

They were met with the automatic response of, "Do you have an appointment?"

To which ninety-nine percent said, "No, but —." They were, to say the least, unsuccessful.

Tony then took note of the successful cold callers and how they approached the receptionist. To his surprise none of them asked a single question. Rather, they gave a command.

"Good morning, please let Margret know that Andy is here, thank you."

Andy didn't linger. He quickly turned, sat down and began to write on his notepad he had quickly taken from his briefcase. Margret came out to him and apologized for not remembering their appointment. Of course Andy didn't have an appointment. He was successful.

I wonder how he knew to ask for Margret?, thought Tony.

He went through the same exercise in the afternoon at a large law firm. Here he witnessed the same approaches. It was very apparent to Tony that receptionists are either trained to defend or have a protection gene that kicks in at the necessary time.

The next day Tony had refined his approach to the point of not just going for the office manager of the law firm. He went for one of the partners. He figured they made the final money decisions anyway. Tony stopped at the door with the names of the partners on it. He chose the third name down, Attorney William Johnson. Tony was just drawn to the number three. He also figured the top guy likely wouldn't have anything to do with purchasing office equipment. Tony opened the door and walked in with a stride that told the receptionist he meant business.

Before she could say a word he said, "Please let Bill know that Tony James is here and give him my apology."

He then looked at his watch indicating his tardiness. He followed up with an authoritative, "Thank you."

Tony immediately turned and sat down, reaching for anything in his briefcase while avoiding eye contact, but looking serious.

The receptionist pressed a button and said, "Mr. Johnson, Tony James is now here."

Partial relief came to Tony. However, it appeared the receptionist was listening to Mr. Johnson likely saying, "Who?"

The receptionist covered her headset microphone with her hand and said, "Excuse me Mr. James, but where are you from?"

Without hesitation Tony said, "Portland, thanks," then looked away.

Once again he added the "thanks" to punctuate the end of their conversation. Tony figured she didn't ask what company he was with or anything specific so he answered her question and told her where he was from. Before he knew it, he was rushed into Mr. Johnson's office and getting a huge apology from him for not remembering their appointment! Tony became very successful with the nuances of cold calling after that experience. No one was safe. He reminded himself *perfect* practice makes perfect.

On his drive to Tacoma Tony thought about how many questions the receptionist would want to ask. He brushed up on his cold calling skills instead of listening to the radio. As he arrived he was pleasantly surprised and yet a sinking feeling overcame him.

Why didn't I just make an appointment and wait a few weeks?

Steeling his resolve he answered himself out loud, "Because I can always do that if I don't succeed today."

He remembered a saying from his former copier sales manager that bolstered his confidence. "A no remains a no unless you try."

When he arrived he saw the one story building fanning out in six directions like spokes on a wheel. Tony's past experience told him there should only be one main reception area to get through. He gathered his nearly empty briefcase, placed it on his lap and stayed in his car ready to pounce at a moment's notice.

Tony waited and observed for what he perceived to be just the right female employee heading to the main entrance. Her ID badge was dangling on a cord from her neck. Tony strode quickly, yet with confidence, and made sure he got to the door first. Like a perfect gentleman he said hello and opened the door for her. She thanked him. He started up a quick conversation about the beautiful day. Tony had positioned himself to her right after going through the foyer. This way he could see the receptionist's area to his left. At the same time he continued his chitchat as the employee held her badge to the small gray security box. The green light appeared and she opened the door. He made sure he had his CIT badge cupped in hand showing only the white back of the plastic. Once again, being the gentleman that he is, he held this door open as well. He pretended to hold his badge to the box and entered. When Tony heard the door close he knew he was in. Tony began searching his briefcase pretending to have forgotten something and said goodbye to the very helpful employee. He fumbled with his briefcase while tics were released for a few seconds. Then once she was out of sight he began to walk with a false outward confidence as if he owned the place. Tony now was definitely in on his terms.

He took note that in about eighty feet he was about to run into a hub style workstation. This is where multiple doctors use two or three people to aid them in scheduling and calling patients. In other words, another gate keeper he needed to get past. The last thing Tony wanted was to be stopped at this point. He'd come so far to get turned away now.

Stay focused and keep your eye on the ball Tony, he thought to himself.

It didn't go unnoticed that each door he passed had each doctor's name on them. The letters behind their names looked like Nick's alphabet cereal. Some of the doors were open while others were closed.

As Tony slowly approached the first open one he got a *stubborn* feeling about the occupant. It didn't mean this person was bad, but just not right for his particular purpose. He quickly skipped it and moved on. Tony stopped short of the next open office door and received a *lonely* feeling about the occupant inside. He didn't know if there was more than one person inside, but decided to take the risk. As he peeked in he saw a nicely dressed older gentleman with a gray beard sitting at his desk.

Jackpot, thought Tony.

He quickly glanced at the name on the door. Pretending to step into the wrong office, Tony lifted his head from his notepad.

In an apologetic voice Tony said, "Oh, excuse me. I'm so sorry Dr. Willis."

"That's okay. How may I be of help to you?"

"I so easily get turned around in this place. I've been in such a hurry this morning I thought this was Dr. Dillon's office. Please excuse me."

Prior to entering, Tony had grabbed what appeared to look like an empty inter-office mail envelope. It's the kind with the string that wraps around the button to keep the contents secure. He looked like a man on a mission to deliver its contents to Dr. Dillon.

"That's alright. It happens to me on occasion."

Sensing Dr. Willis was not only lonely, but obviously a very generous man, Tony asked, "So I don't waste any more time, will you please point me in the right direction?"

"I certainly will. Straight down the hall and take a right at the work station. She has the second to last office on the left flank."

"Thank you, Dr. Willis, and once again, I'm so sorry to have bothered you."

"No bother at all. I would have had my door closed if I required privacy."

Believing this could turn into a long conversation, Tony extricated himself by saying, "Well, you have a good day."

With the hint of a disappointed tone Dr. Willis said, "You do the same young man," then turned back to his desk. Tony felt guilty for using him.

Once again Tony was thankful he thought to bring his briefcase to look like he belongs. As he approached the workstation he pretended to be searching his briefcase for a particular file as he increased his pace forcing himself to not look up as he passed. Tony took a brief glance at his watch as if running late. He hoped he gave the appearance of someone who belongs. Relieved, Tony succeeded in passing the workstation without even a single hello. He knew using the inter-office delivery plan wouldn't work here since this is where deliveries are likely deposited.

Tony continued down the hallway and began to count the doors from the other end. His target destination was in sight, and open, with light shining into the hallway. His heart began to beat faster.

Then he thought, *What if the doctor's not in there? What if she just stepped out for a moment?*

Slowing his pace, Tony performed a deep cleansing breath. He then listened as he heard a drawer open then close. The words *forgiving* and *unconventional* were delivered to him regarding whoever was in the office. Tony politely knocked with one knuckle on the half-opened door as he entered cautiously.

Dr. Dillon was at her desk just like Dr. Willis. With a pen in her right hand she looked up without much surprise. "Hello, may I help you?"

It seems like they're used to people dropping in unexpectedly around here. Thank you. I'm so grateful for you placing a picture of yourself on the website. Thank you for that as well, thought Tony.

Dr. Dillon looked a little older than her online picture. She appeared to be in her mid-sixties, as opposed to early fifties. She obviously colored her short straight hair and did so very tastefully. Her sharply angled build beguiled her welcoming eyes.

May I help you? Just the question I wanted to hear from the person I want to hear it from, he thought.

Tony was about to introduce himself. However, she quickly followed up with, "Are you a new patient?"

Instead of answering her question he said, "I have Tourette's Dr. Dillon, and I think you're my best hope."

During his drive to Tacoma Tony thought about what he'd say if he was lucky enough to actually speak to Dr. Dillon. He saw he hit his mark based on her slight change of body language. As Dr. Dillon stood she extended her welcoming hand. Tony shook it. She didn't try to put a power squeeze into the handshake. It was just right.

"My 11:00 A.M. didn't show so I have a few minutes before lunch."

This was both exhilarating and frightening at the same time for Tony.

I pray to God that I don't have to perform like a monkey, he thought.

With a sweep of her arm she said, "Please sit wherever you feel comfortable."

Now that he was in Dr. Dillon's office Tony considered a couple of odd questions. *Does the choice of seat have meaning? Does everything I say or do have an underlying deep significance that a psychiatrist feeds upon?*

Tony quickly decided to sit on the front edge of the middle cushion of the couch across from two other optional chairs. Dr. Dillon took the chair on the right across from him. As she began to settle in Tony looked at his surroundings. He was in what looked like a separate mini lounge area of her office.

Much better digs than Dr. Willis, he decided.

It reminded him of a smaller version of a hotel suite. Tony quickly thought about all the movies and television shows that featured the "shrink's couch." He chose the middle cushion because it seemed to him to be the most neutral. He sat forward on the edge of the couch. The purpose of this was to convey the message that he wasn't' planning to stay long. Of course he planned to stay as long as possible, but hoped this sent the right message. He was silent until he saw Dr. Dillon was comfortably settled into her chair. Tony hoped he looked relaxed because inside he was tied up in a ball of nerves.

"So, explain to me why you're here."

"Actually, I stopped by to make an appointment," Tony said.

This was one of the scenarios he ran through his mind if in fact the opportunity to actually meet the good doctor was presented.

"As I said I have some time right now."

Elated, Tony began slowly. "Okay, I guess the best place to begin is to tell you I've been treated by Dr. Knox in Portland."

Surprisingly she jumped in and said, "I'm familiar with Dr. Knox."

Is that good or bad, Tony wondered. "I hope he's not your best friend because he's not real high on my list," Tony blurted.

"No, he's purely a professional acquaintance. "Why do you say that?"

"He put me on a couple of medications that gave me some problems."

Very sincerely Dr. Dillon said, "I'm sorry to hear that. What medications?"

"The first was Haldol and then Pimozide."

"Those are common to start with. What problems are you having with them?"

"We can use past tense on that subject Dr. Dillon. I just couldn't take them anymore. They made my personality into that of a potato with a side order of hallucinations. I won't be seeing Dr. Knox again," Tony said flatly. After saying this he hoped his bluntness wouldn't be a cause for concern.

Dr. Dillon caught Tony staring at her notepad and said, "You don't mind I'm taking notes do you? My memory just isn't what it used to be."

Tony thought, *What a crock. Her memory is probably better than ninety-nine percent of the card counters in Vegas. But, I do appreciate the gesture.* "No not at all. Take all the notes you want," he quickly said.

He told her his story hitting the pertinent information from age six to present. Tony figured he might as well give her everything on the highlight reel. He laid it all on the line except the issue with his college professor. That was a subject for another day.

Dr. Dillon did not disappoint when it came to her listening skills. She continued to take notes as Tony vomited the Cliff Notes version about his tag day tormentor. When he was done she asked a few follow up questions to certain points, mainly to confirm or clarify.

Surprisingly she said, "I can see you're holding your tics in and the throat clearing is obvious." Tony was stunned. She added, "I know we just met, but you don't have to pretend you don't have Tourette's. It's as plain as day to me."

Tony wasn't sure how to react to this, but then thought, *Thank you Jesus! You really are an expert.*

"I need to ask you some family history questions. Do you mind?"

How could I mind after barging in here without an appointment? "Shoot," said Tony.

During the routine questions Tony was surprised she hit upon something that had come up during his appointment with Dr. Knox.

"Does anyone else in your family exhibit similar symptoms?"

The only person he could think of was his dad. He said, "I don't know if this falls into the same category, but my dad has a little habit of hitching up his pants."

"I'm not sure what you mean. Will you show me?"

Tony stood and used his right elbow to adjust his belt upward. Then he rolled his right shoulder forward and quickly stretched his neck sticking his chin out then back. He repeated this in succession then sat back down.

Hmm, I didn't feel like a total dolt...just a regular dolt, he thought.

"Are those the exact movements?"

"No, I added the shoulder roll and neck stretch. I couldn't help it," he said sheepishly.

"That's okay, so everything but the shoulder and neck stretching?"

"Right."

"Earlier you said nobody else in your family exhibited tics?"

Tony nodded affirmatively. "I guess I didn't see this as a tic, but more of a habit. It appeared to me he was emulating his sports hero, Jack Nicklaus."

It didn't take him very long to figure out what she was thinking. "Are you saying my dad did that because of Tourette's?!" he exclaimed.

"No, not at all, unless he had some kind of verbal tic you noticed."

Tony sat quietly thinking about his dad. "Doctor, I can't remember a single time in my dad's life he showed any sign of a verbal tic."

"What you demonstrated is a definite sign, but without a verbal component it would not be Tourette's. It could be a mild tic disorder, but definitely not Tourette's. However, it does uncover the origin of your case of Tourette Syndrome."

Tony sat up a little straighter.

"I'd say your father likely carried the Tourette's gene which was then obviously passed on to you."

Tony sat silently thinking about the love he has for his dad. He also thought about how much he butts heads with him more than his brothers and sisters. *Was this a coincidence or nature,* he wondered.

Noticing Tony was deep in thought Dr. Dillon stayed silent for just a short time. She made a logical, but incorrect assumption then broke the silence by saying, "Tony, you can't blame your father for you having Tourette's."

Tony's eyes came back into focus and said in a very sharp tone, "Why not?"

"Because, your father was the victim of only carrying the gene responsible for Tourette's," she answered. "He was given no choice as it was purely handed down to him through DNA."

"But if he —"

"I said he *carried* the gene, but he didn't have Tourette's. It's also very likely he had no idea. He exhibited a minor tic disorder for a period of time, but he certainly did not willingly give you Tourette's."

"But if my dad had the gene and passed it along to me then he was saddled with the gene by my grandparents, right?"

"Yes, that's likely correct."

"So, let me ask you this doctor. Out of five kids in the family why am I the only one to have, unfortunately, hit the Tourette's gene lottery?"

"Maybe you aren't."

"Well, none of my brothers or sisters has it."

"When you say *it* what do you mean?"

"I mean Tourette's," Tony said almost incredulously.

"Tony, there's a big difference in carrying the gene and the expression of Tourette's. We have not yet identified the

285

exact gene that, for lack of a better statement, causes Tourette's to exhibit. However, we're getting closer," she said in an encouraging tone.

"So you're saying my dad could have passed the gene to my siblings, but just not the super sized version?"

"That's one way of putting it. Look at it this way Tony. You have Tourette's with the exhibition of physical and verbal tics while nobody else in your family displays such behavior. At this point in our research we don't have an answer as to why one sibling may fully reveal tics while another doesn't. We have scientists working around the clock trying to figure this out. Let's focus on what we can do about making your life better." Dr. Dillon saw she got through to Tony as his facial expression almost screamed, *You're absolutely right!*

"So Dr. Dillon, what can I do to make my life better?"

She said with a twinkle in her eyes, "Make an appointment and we'll discuss a plan of attack."

"Isn't there something you can do for me now?"

She went over to her desk and pulled out a pamphlet. As she got up she said, "Here's some information for a medication called Klonopin. I've seen great results in other patients with mild to moderate Tourette's."

Tony took the information and asked, "Is treating Tourette's with chemicals the only way to reduce the urge to tic?" Tony thought about asking if she had any patient bring up success with diet or exercise. He chose not to at the moment. Might have been pushing it.

"As of today Tony, but who knows what tomorrow will bring? New findings are happening all the time. Remember the physical attributes of Tourette's is completely circuitry, or chemically based, so it makes sense to combat it by using chemicals."

"So, besides death, what are the side effects of this medication?"

Dr. Dillon smiled and simply said, "The possibility of feeling tired."

"What else?"

"That's it, nothing of significance."

"Will this turn me into a zombie like the others?"

"No, we'll start slowly with a very low dosage and build to a point that you'll tell me when the amount is right for you. I promise you won't have side-effects like you did with the previous medications you have taken."

Tony had been at the ready to say no thanks to another zombie drug, but for some reason she made him feel safe. After their fruitful time together Dr. Dillon asked for the required paperwork she needed to have Tony sign.

Tony felt guilty, but stayed the course. "As I had mentioned earlier, Dr. Dillon, I came here to schedule an appointment with you." He held his breathe not knowing what kind of reaction to expect from her.

In what seemed to be the longest ten seconds of his life, he was the object of her wide eyed placid stare.

She's going to call security. I just know it and wouldn't blame her, he thought.

Then with the slightest of ease her lips very slowly began to purse with the corners moving in a slightly upward direction. Seconds seemed like minutes. He wasn't sure what she was thinking, but he now thought he had a fifty percent chance of not being thrown into the arms of building security.

Still maintaining her professional tone she began, "You drove approximately two hours to see me. As you've stated, you obviously didn't have an appointment. Out of curiosity, how did you get past security at the main reception area?"

Without hesitation Tony said, "I just walked in looking like I knew what I was doing."

"But, this place is a maze without directions. My office isn't the easiest to find. Certainly it took some time for you to locate me. Didn't anyone wonder why you were wandering the halls?"

Tony answered honestly. "I stopped in and spoke with Dr. Willis and he helped me."

In a surprised tone she asked, "How do you know Dr. Willis?" She put her hands up in a stop position. "Wait a minute. You just waltzed into Dr. Willis' office and asked how to find me?"

Tony knew he was in hot water with Dr. Dillon and didn't want the temperature to get turned up even further. So, he of course skipped the part about the feeling he got before he met

Dr. Willis and said, "He was more than willing to help me out."

Emphasizing the last two words, Dr. Dillon replied, "I'm going to have to have a talk with our friend Dr. Willis. We don't have a directory or map because all pertinent information is provided at the receptionist's desk for our privacy and the privacy of our patients."

Tony felt the scolding train leaving the station.

Dr. Dillon continued, "I believe you really did come here to schedule an appointment."

Tony felt relief, but guilt as well.

"However, I don't think for one moment that was your first intention. That was your fallback plan. May I ask you a question?"

Tony raised his eyebrows and nodded a submissive yes. He was in no position to deny her.

"Do you own a phone?"

I'm totally busted! I know where this is going, he thought.

"We both know nobody drives two hours to *make an appointment*." She used air quotes at the end of her statement.

Something inside Tony kicked into gear. He was tired and fed up with the rules. Tony also knew he was about to be taken down. He was going down swinging, though.

"Dr. Dillon I've lived with Tourette's since I was six years old. I wasn't diagnosed until just recently. I was so grateful to know I actually had something with a name at first. The euphoria of just knowing it has a name wore off rather quickly. I had my expectations built up to considerably reduce these tics by Dr. Knox and his psycho drugs. Oh, how wrong I was. But, I have to tell you, being without hope is the worst disorder anyone could possibly have. That's what's happened to me. Then I found you. You're my new hope."

Tony read Dr. Dillon's face and knew he shouldn't say anything further. He shut up. *Sometimes a good defense is a good offense*, he thought.

Without a word Dr. Dillon turned and walked to her desk.

This is it. She's calling security, he thought.

Instead of reaching for the phone she opened her right desk file drawer and pulled out two separate sheets of paper. Walking back to Tony she said in a very calm and friendly tone, "Fill these out and hand them to the receptionist at the hub down the hall. Her name is Jill."

She looked him directly in his eyes and said, "This session was a consultation. The next one will be our first official one. I'll see you next week."

Tony began, "I'm very sorry that —"

"Remember, this is your consultation visit"

Tony was so grateful he wasn't sure how to respond.

Dr. Dillon softened the mood and said, "I'm glad all my patients don't have the guts and brains to take on the medical establishment like you Mr. James. My schedule would be a mess! I know you'll be a patient I can count upon to do whatever's necessary to try to be free from the chemical chains that confine you. Now fill these out and let's get together next week."

Almost in shock Tony uncharacteristically stood, for one of the few times in his life, without a quick comeback response. He just stared at Dr. Dillon. Finally, catching his wits he said almost inaudibly and mumbled, "She really is forgiving and unconventional."

Dr. Dillon looked at him with a confused look. "What did you just say?"

Tony was caught off guard. He didn't think he had said that out loud. The only person he's ever revealed his ability to is Jacquelyn. That wasn't about to change now.

You'd think I'm truly crazy if I answered your question Doc, he thought. "I said you're forgiving and I'm so thankful," he lied.

Tony wasn't sure she bought it, but she let it go.

Before Tony got in his car for the drive home he checked his messages and was relieved that no emergencies had arisen for work. He was especially thankful Jacquelyn hadn't tried to reach him. Tony felt proud of what he accomplished today. However, he also felt a tinge of guilt for not telling her.

While Tony drove home he noticed the air was that much sweeter and life was looking up. He convinced himself Jacquelyn wouldn't have that big of a problem with him not telling her about his little adventure beforehand. Then again, he didn't tell her, and he always kept her in the loop as to what his itinerary was for the day, especially when traveling this far. It's just part of the respect and courtesy they show each other.

He turned into the driveway and pressed the button to open the garage door. Tony pulled his car in and then entered the empty house. He went right to work using the internet to research the medication Dr. Dillon had provided him in the pamphlet.

Klonopin's generic version is Clonazepam. It's in a class of medications called benzodiazepines. The main purposes are to control seizures and relieve panic attacks. It works by decreasing abnormal electrical activity in the brain.

Perfect, but what about the side effects, he thought.

He said to himself, "The side effects are much less, but the same legal department must also work for the pharmaceutical company who manufactures Haldol and Pimozide. However, it also sounds like it's easier to get off this medication than the others if it fails to do the job."

Hmm, this is interesting. With this medication a person can be adjusted up or down in a quick three day period. So Dr. Dillon will likely start me out low and move me up every three days until she and I think we hit the right dosage, he thought.

"Okay, I'm up for this," he decided.

Because of Tony's clandestine adventure he was backed up with work. He tried to catch up as quickly as possible by eliminating the personal chit chat with his clients. His alarm on his watch went off and it was time to pick Sam and Nick up at school. He'd have to complete some of this work late tonight.

Later that evening, Tony told Jacquelyn about his adventure to see Dr. Dillon.

"You did *what*?"

"I went to see Dr. Dillon in Tacoma today," Tony repeated in a flat tone.

"You didn't tell me you had a new doctor or an appointment. Or that it was in Tacoma!" said a surprised Jacquelyn.

"Well, I didn't sleep much last night," Tony regretted saying as soon as he heard his own words.

"Wait, you said you slept like a rock."

"No, Jacquelyn, *you* said *you* slept like a rock. I vividly remember saying *I could use more*," Tony said a little aggressively.

"Okay, but —" she stopped. Jacquelyn realized she wasn't looking at the big picture. "Did you have another night of not getting back to sleep?"

"Yeah, and this time, for some reason, it really frustrated me. So, I came down here and decided to take action." Tony left out the part about being curled up on the couch like a big baby. He told Jacquelyn about the research he did and how he found Dr. Dillon.

"How did you get an appointment so fast?"

293

"Well, that's the interesting part," Tony said sheepishly.

He explained everything in detail. Tony could tell Jacquelyn wasn't sure if she should be angry or proud of him. Once again she came through and decided to just love him exactly the way God made him.

"I have one question for you Tony. How are you going to make your doctor's appointment when you're supposed to be in Washington, D.C. next week?"

"Oh, crap! I totally forgot when I made the appointment!"

"Well, you don't have to leave until Tuesday afternoon, maybe you can get squeezed in on Monday," Jacquelyn suggested.

"I'll email Dr. Dillon and Jill right now and maybe they can work something out."

The following morning began much like the previous day except for one thing. Jacquelyn specifically asked if he slept all night. Tony confirmed that he did. She looked at him and he swore on his life he was telling her the truth. She playfully threw a pillow at him as they made the bed together.

"Okay, I'm just making sure you didn't run off across the state line in the middle of the night," she kiddingly said.

After getting back from taking the kids to school, Tony checked his personal email. He was surprised to see a new one from Dr. Dillon. It read that he was to call her. She provided him with her direct line. Tony didn't hesitate.

"Dr. Dillon," she said in a sing-song tone after picking up the phone.

"Doctor, this is Tony James."

"Good morning Tony. How are you today?"

"Well, thanks. I'm so sorry about —"

"No need to apologize Tony. Go with the flow. Life happens."

Tony knew when to listen and when to fill the silence. This was definitely a time to listen.

"Tony, I've placed a request for your records to be transferred to me electronically from Dr. Knox. I'll have them later this morning. I'll review them and then call you back. Is that okay?"

"I have no problem with that," said Tony. "But, what about a possibility of moving my appointment up to Monday due to a scheduling conflict?"

"Well, based on our meeting yesterday and since you live so far away, I believe once I review Dr. Knox's records I'll have enough to write up a simple action plan for you."

"Are you saying I wouldn't need to drive to your office?"

"That's exactly what I'm saying. Give me until about 10:30 A.M. and call me back."

"Okay, Doctor, and thanks!"

Tony's watch alarm went off at 10:25 A.M. He was in the middle of an Off Site Repair. He hurried the process along and said he'd call the client back. Tony then placed his call to Dr. Dillon.

Dr. Dillon answered in exactly the same manner as she did earlier. She and Tony quickly went through their phone etiquette pleasantries. The good doctor then got down to business.

"After reviewing the records from Dr. Knox and my own from yesterday's consultation, I have a very good handle on what you require to lessen your urge to tic."

Tony stayed silent and listened.

"According to Dr. Knox you have all the facts about Tourette's. You understand there is no cure. However, after the negative results from the medications he put you on it appeared you gave up. Yet, you showed up at my office determined to reduce your tics. Is that accurate?"

"It is."

"Did you read the information regarding Klonopin?"

"Yes, I also did some research online."

"And what do you think?"

Tony deflected the subject back to clarify the question and asked, "About what?"

"About trying the medication."

"If you think it'll help then I'm willing to give it a fair shot."

"All right then Tony. I'm going to have Jill call in a prescription to the pharmacy you listed on the forms you filled out. We'll start at one milligram twice daily for the first three days. After the third day please call me with any results or concerns. If an adjustment, up or down, is required then we'll make the decision together."

"That sounds good. I like the team approach you're taking Doctor."

"Well, from here on out, we are a team. Check with your pharmacy this afternoon and take your first dose at bedtime. Its optimum you take one in the morning and one at bedtime. Try to take each about the same time daily. If you somehow accidently miss taking the morning dose for more than two hours then wait until your bedtime dose. The same goes for the bedtime dose except, of course, wait until morning. Do you have any questions?"

"Yes. Are you sure this medication isn't going to make me into some kind of zombie?"

"I'm sure. You and I will make certain that doesn't happen. The most you may possibly feel is a calming effect which aids in a lesser urge to tic. Because we're dealing with Tourette's, however, I'd be surprised if you even experience this."

"That sounds great Doctor. Thank you."

That afternoon, satisfied after reading up on the side effects, Tony called the pharmacy and confirmed his prescription was ready. He picked it up. When Jacquelyn came home and the time was right he filled her in regarding his conversation with Dr. Dillon.

"You'd hate to have a problem taking a new medication while in Washington D. C.," she said.

"Good point. I did think of that. Normally I'd agree with you, but I've done my homework on this one."

"You seem pretty sure Tony."

"I am."

"Well, I know you and if you feel this is right then I totally support you," she said.

"Thanks. I know I don't have to tell you how much that means to me. I'll start tonight."

Chapter 36

It felt like a lifetime had passed since Tony had been to the International Technology Commission Convention. He found it intriguing back then. Tony hoped he could find new cutting edge information this time, but figured it likely to be a snooze fest. Most of the truly important work wouldn't be discussed or on display. But, it was his job to network and learn what he could. Most of all it was important people knew that CIT was represented. Those companies who were of significance that didn't show were conspicuous by their absence.

Tony was a little anxious and his tics seemed to be the same as usual. *I'm really glad I made the decision to begin the new medication from Dr. Dillon, but nothing yet*, he thought.

He did agree with Jacquelyn that being away from home wasn't the best time to begin messing around with his body chemistry. But, he didn't want to wait.

He loves to visit the nation's capitol. Tony appreciates the history and the vibe the district provides. After checking into his hotel he made a beeline to the conference center before everything begins the following morning. His sole purpose is to scout for possible private tic release locations. Tony had decided he wasn't going to move his dosage up while away from home. So, he felt the need to find a private place within the center, since it was likely he'd need to make a

299

visit to fulfill the release the requirements of his tormentor. He wasn't totally satisfied with what he found. There would be so many people from all over the world and there just wasn't a suitable place that would provide the kind of privacy he'd require. A little disappointed, he sauntered back to his hotel room.

Tony's home away from home this trip is the JW Marriott Hotel located on Pennsylvania Avenue. He called Jacquelyn to let her know he was safely checked in and she could reach him on his cell if needed. He spoke to the kids then organized his clothes and briefcase for the following day. The next morning he remembered Audrey had notified him that the breakfast prior to the opening event was always jam packed. She wasn't kidding.

"Don't these computer geeks ever pass up a free meal?" Tony asked himself.

Tony looked upon this as a rich environment for networking opportunities. He was sadly mistaken. With so many foreign languages spoken he felt as if he'd accidently gone to a United Nations Convention. He already had breakfast at the hotel so he had time to pick out a seat in the large auditorium where the main speakers would begin. The breakout sessions throughout the day were being held in the smaller ballrooms.

As he sat waiting for the opening remarks he made small talk with a few Americans. They each had been coming to the convention for years and were already bored. All they could talk about was sightseeing. After listening to the opening speakers Tony perused his schedule. The morning could be interesting. However, after that, he'd already heard the next two convention speakers at similar venues and knew they would bore him to tears. He thought about the conference veterans who were taking advantage of going out and seeing the sights. So he bailed on the remainder of the afternoon schedule.

Audrey won't mind, he thought convincing himself.

Rather than eat in the convention hall he went back to the hotel to their restaurant for a leisurely meal for one. Once finished, he went up to his room to drop off his briefcase. He opened the door and found a pamphlet had been slipped under, lying on the floor.

What have we here?, he wondered.

The brochure supplied him with information for a tour of The White House.

I didn't know they'd started the tours again since stopping them after 9/11, he thought. He figured everyone staying at the hotel received one. He'd be wrong.

That'd be fun, I've never seen the inside before, he thought.

Now in the cavernous lobby Tony handed the pamphlet to the concierge. He asked Michael, the name on his bronze colored hotel badge, if he could arrange a tour of The White House for him yet today. Almost imperceptibly, Michael rolled his eyes do to the implausibly short time frame Tony gave him. Tony handed him the brochure.

As a formality he said, "Let me check the computer for you."

Tony quickly found Michael to have a talk-it-through type personality.

As Michael engaged his computer he said in a much quieter voice, "All I need to do is get into this part of the program, click here, press enter and...there we go."

Surprised, he looked back up to Tony and said, "You must know some pretty powerful people."

"Why do you say that?"

"You have a VIP designation."

"And what does that mean?"

"Exactly, I like your attitude Mr. James." Michael had mistaken Tony's question as a dismissive statement.

"Michael, can you tell me who set that up for me?"

"It only informs me of your designation nothing more. So, I guess this is your lucky day Mr. James. I can book you in for the 3:00 P.M. tour this afternoon!"

Audrey must have some pretty good connections, thought Tony.

"Great, set me up," Tony said with a smile.

"All you need to do is complete this form and make sure you provide the appropriate identification," said Michael.

Tony slipped him a ten dollar bill for his efforts. Michael acted out his part by saying it wasn't necessary, but at the same time pocketing the money in record time. With the White House just around the corner Tony decided to relax on a park bench and do some people watching on this warm sunny and pleasant afternoon.

He arrived at the White House at 2:50 P.M. and stood in line with the other tourists excited to see this historic center of power that housed the president of our great nation. Since he was alone and had no one to talk with Tony began to count how many people were on this particular tour. He started with number one, who appeared to be a mother and her three grade school age children, on a personal field trip, at the front of the line. Numbers five through ten in line was a group of six "Q-tips." Ever since he'd first visited Florida Tony had a habit of calling the all white haired elderly people by this little nickname. It appeared to Tony, based on how well they got along with each other, that they have been friends their entire lives. He thought it was great how well they got along.

By the time Tony arrived at number twenty-two he was struck with a sickening feeling. This time the words that penetrated him so strongly were *impending doom*. The man wearing a long London Fog style raincoat appeared to be alone. Tony took his mind off of him because he found himself staring just a little too long. He tried to continue the count, but to no avail. He was very much pre-occupied with this man. Tony purposely looked all around, not only to take everything in, but to catch a few more glimpses of number twenty-two.

At exactly 3:00 P.M. everyone was led into a small reception area that doubled as a viewing theater. The tour leader was a very attractive and outgoing young woman in her late twenties with a gold colored name tag. It read *"Elizabeth - White House Tour Guide."* Elizabeth joyfully welcomed everyone and announced since the president was traveling today tour guests might have the pleasure of a rare glimpse of the oval office from the hallway.

Something bothered Tony. For some reason Tony got a unique feeling from Elizabeth. It was *actress*.

He thought, *Maybe she's working here for now until her big break comes along. There's something about her that's slightly a little...off.*

Tony kept his peripheral vision on Mr. Twenty-two. The strong feeling he experienced outside took on an even greater value now that he was confined with him. This made Tony split his focus between the tour guide and Mr. Twenty-two, while fending off the urge to tic. His stress level continued to elevate as he felt the weight of a "stockpile" he knew would have to be released soon. This was inevitable and there was nothing he could do about it. His tormentor wouldn't let him off the hook for too long.

This was supposed to be fun, he thought.

Tony took note of the number of cameras pointed at the tour group. He wondered how many there must be hidden from sight. He figured there must be listening devices all over the room as well. This bothered him as it was just another reason to split his focus even more. Elizabeth announced that a nine minute introductory film was about to begin and then the doors to the left would open automatically upon its completion.

The room lights slowly dimmed and the video began with the Presidential Seal on the screen. Tony couldn't shake this feeling of doom being exuded from Mr. Twenty-two. He stood and weighed his options. The one most attractive to him was to feign not feeling well and just get the heck out of there. However, his conscious wouldn't allow it.

After his eyes adjusted to the limited light he scanned the room and noticed movement off to his right. Tony found what he was searching for. He began to shuffle to his right, quietly whispering "Excuse me" numerous times along the way.

His destination is the large man who, at first glance, appears to be listening to a ballgame through a very small earpiece. Based on his uniform this was very unlikely. Tony assumed correctly, this was a Secret Service agent, and that earpiece was his lifeline to everyone on duty.

Once again Tony said, "Excuse me" in a very hushed tone.

Agent Scott Goodman had seen Tony making his way toward him so he was prepared to casually greet him.

"How may I help you sir?" the big man asked in a deep, but hushed voice.

"I'm with this group for the 3:00 P.M. tour."

Agent Goodman asked, "Are you feeling okay sir?"

"Yes, I'm fine"

305

"You appear somewhat anxious sir," said Agent Goodman in an almost accusatory tone.

Tony was used to this kind of remark because of his facial tics. He disregarded the comment then said, "What I'm about to say will sound ridiculous, but please hear me out."

Agent Goodman turned his body to face Tony making his six foot five inch frame even more imposing. His intense glare made Tony start to re-think what he was about to tell him.

"Go on," said the agent.

Tony could feel himself holding his breath. Then he declared bravely, "I believe there's a man on this tour that may mean harm to those either in this room or elsewhere in the White House."

"Excuse me sir? Would you please repeat that?" Goodman said in a perplexed, yet alert tone.

Tony complied, but this time with a little more confidence since he was breathing properly once again. He figured he was in this deep so why not swing for the fences. Tony had Agent Goodman's complete attention.

Following his training and years of experience, Agent Goodman pressed a small button that provided just enough illumination for him to see. He began writing down the details of this unusual conversation on a small notepad.

Lord knows you don't have to write anything as the video and audio surveillance systems will record everything. But, I guess this is procedure, Tony thought.

"What did you say your name is?" asked Goodman with an all business look.

"I didn't."

"Well, then, what is your name?"

Tony complied without hesitation and said, "Tony James." He didn't think it would be a good idea to try and get by with just his last name this time.

"Are you a D.C. area resident?"

"No, I'm here on business"

"Where are you staying?"

"The JW Marriott."

Tony answered each question as it was asked. Goodman made his notes.

"First, Mr. James, which man are you talking about?"

Without pointing Tony said, "He's the man wearing the long raincoat standing in the second row."

Looking over Tony's head he said, "Okay, I see him. Second, why do you think he's a danger?"

This is where everything could get very sticky for Tony. He had no physical evidence to provide other than his intense flash of *impending doom*. All he had was a history of being dead-on with the accuracy of his threat assessments. Tony knew the information he was about to tell a Secret Service agent for the United States Government would likely only be proven out after the fact. He was about to sound like he just escaped the loony bin.

Fortunately, Tony's quick thinking enabled him to turn the tables and asked Goodman, "Have you been outside this afternoon?"

Goodman looked at him with a "Here's a nut job" look. Yet he was professional and polite enough to answer Tony's question. "Yes, I had lunch on the Mall," Goodman said with a quizzical scowl.

Tony quickly pounced before Goodman could jump in. "Then you know what type of weather we are having today," Tony said as if he were an attorney leading a witness. "Let me ask you, Agent Goodman, how many people were either carrying umbrellas or wearing *long raincoats* on this beautiful warm sunny day?"

Somewhat embarrassed, Agent Goodman quickly realized where this nut job's questions were taking him. Then, Goodman's eyes grew so wide Tony could see the images from the video screen bouncing off them. Agent Goodman was trained to spot a man such as this, but somehow missed him.

He looked back at Tony and thought, *This James fellow's no nut job. He did a better assessment than me. That man in the long raincoat does stick out like a sore thumb*, he wanted to bellow.

SOP, Standard Operating Procedure, demanded all agents on duty report any person that fit a particular defined profile. A man wearing a long raincoat in the White House on a warm sunny day definitely should raise red flags! This man should've been pulled out of the group for a thorough "investigation". In keeping with his training, and to save face, Goodman decided to take back control of the conversation.

"I can see he's not dressed appropriately for today's weather. But, why do *you* think that makes him a danger?" asked Goodman. He quickly followed up with "Do you know him?"

Tony decided he wasn't going down this trail of questioning because he knew it would just lead him into an unpleasant situation. He knew Agent Goodman was just doing his job and attempting to extract information and hold Tony.

Hey, I've got this unique talent and I can tell you he's here and up to no good, Tony thought.

He knew Jacquelyn is the only person who knows about his ability, but this time he wasn't so sure he should keep it that way. Tony felt so strongly about Mr. Twenty-two that he was seriously considering telling the agent. Tony swiftly wiped the thought away. There was just no way of him coming across as a reasonable, normal human being divulging such personal information.

"No, I've never met the man in my life," Tony calmly answered.

To Tony it now seemed Goodman became just as interested in Tony as in Mr. Twenty-two. Tony turned his head and noticed Elizabeth, miss actress, seemingly a little off or out of place somehow. She seemed to be splitting her attention between another man on the tour besides Agent Goodman, Mr. Twenty-two and Tony.

"Why don't you come with me Mr. James so we can have a more private and in depth conversation?"

"What if there's not enough time.   He could have an undetected, improvised weapon under that coat," proclaimed Tony.

Goodman eyed Tony closely and decided he really could be just a private citizen doing what he thinks is right. Logic won over and Goodman realized he needed to act.

"Stay right here Mr. James," Goodman ordered.

To Tony's relief Goodman quietly, yet sternly, spoke into his wrist radio giving Mr. twenty-two's position and description as he walked toward Elizabeth.

"Require all eyes on male wearing long trench. Acquire and confine with L-One procedure, repeat L-One," ordered Goodman.

As if appearing out of thin air the silhouettes moved without sound. Before the video was over, Elizabeth, with agent Goodman at her side, asked the group to move through the doors to the left. A dark haired athletically built agent stepped in and muscled Mr. Twenty-two through a door which wasn't noticeable unless you knew it was there. Four other agents turned their weapons on him from different angles. Mr. Twenty-two couldn't make a move or he'd be history. Elizabeth was no longer leading the tour. As Tony turned he saw her staring back at him while Mr. Twenty-two was escorted through the hidden door.

Before anyone could reach him Tony made a quick exit to the right and double-timed it back to his hotel room. So as not to draw attention he didn't run, but rather walked at a very brisk pace. He pretended to be late by looking at his watch every now and then. As he did this he allowed arm and shoulder tics to blend in with his natural body movements. When Tony got to the hotel room he quickly dead bolted the door, wiped the sweat from his forehead and let his tics come pouring out. When they subsided he sat down on the bed, his face cupped in his hands, and thought about what just happened.

This is crazy, he thought. "What did I just get myself into?" he said in frustration.

It was similar to the man with the scar at the airport, but this was somehow different. Tony tried to connect the dots. His memory flashed back to Elizabeth, the tour guide.

She didn't just see me leave. She watched me leave. She let me leave! Why'd she do that? Besides, the tour group began exiting in the opposite direction. Why wasn't she leading them? Maybe "actress" means she was simply just not in her usual role. Whatever THAT means, he thought. *Something was definitely off kilter in there. Then he made a decision. I'm not sticking around. I'm heading home...NOW!*

Miles away Director Don Williams had been viewing the live audio and video feed from his office. He picked up the phone and called the White House Secret Service. He needed to know just who this guy is that Tony went out on a limb to tell Agent Goodman about. He then placed another call to Agent Clark. This time it was to his agent's cell phone.

"Agent Clark," he flatly answered.

"What went on in there?" Williams asked emphatically.

Williams continued, "You were our plant. Why didn't he have any suspicions about you?"

"Sir, as you likely saw, Mr. James never paid any attention to me at all and I thought I played it up just as instructed," said Clark.

Williams heard a single, short, low-toned beep indicating a call coming in. He looked at the caller ID. "I'll have to call you later. I have the White House Secret Service calling me back."

Williams pressed the flash button on his phone to connect the call. This time it was a woman's voice on the other end.

"Sir, this is Agent Wolf."

"Elizabeth, what in God's name is going on!" he demanded.

"I can confirm that this man is on our ITWL."

"How did this man, who's on our International Terrorist Watch List get so close as to be on a White House tour?" Williams shouted.

Elizabeth continued unfazed, "His disguise is flawless sir. Plastic explosives were found in his MP3 player."

"My God," Williams said, barely audible.

Elizabeth continued, "He's being transported to The Station as we speak."

The Station is the code name for a secret detention facility located in a neighborhood that connects five government houses by underground tunnels. It requires no exposure to the public to transport Mr. Twenty-two.

"Thank you, Elizabeth. I'll expect your complete report by 6:00 P.M."

Williams, standing as he ended the call, walked over to his office window. As he stared out to no place in particular he said out loud to himself, "I don't know how he did it, but as far as test results go, Mr. Tony James just passed with red, white and blue flying colors!"

Williams picked up his phone and called Senior Special Agent Dennis Forman.

Back at the hotel Tony phoned Jacquelyn as soon as he had his new flight information. He let her know he was coming home later that evening simply saying he was done with the convention. There was no need to worry her. Tony would fill her in with all the details when he got home.

Jacquelyn offered to pick him up at the airport then remembered he left his car in the parking structure. Tony's next call was going to be to Audrey. He decided to send a carefully worded email instead. Tony wasn't up to explaining anything to her at the moment.

She's not going to be happy with me, he thought.

313

Chapter 37

Tony arrived safely back in Portland. He was especially surprised nobody from the government or law enforcement met him as he deplaned.

"Thank you," he whispered as he looked to the heavens.

He arrived home after the kids were already asleep. Jacquelyn was up waiting for him. Tony filled her in on the events of his shortened trip leaving out no details. Her reaction was that of complete concern for him. Not that he was in any kind of trouble, but she thought he could be in danger from this Mr. Twenty-two.

"All I care about is that you're safe and home where you belong," Jacquelyn said as she finally blinked.

She wasn't surprised by Tony's actions. He was no stranger to inserting himself into situations that required action. Just recently he and Jacquelyn were driving on Burnside Street, which is known as the busiest street in Portland.

Without notice to Jacquelyn, Tony quickly pulled the car into a bank parking lot, jumped out to single-handedly push a woman's disabled car out of harms-way.

Another time he happened to be driving by the lake near his home when he saw a dog fall through the early winter's new ice. He stopped and risked his own health by saving the dog just as it began to go under for what would have been the last time. The water was much deeper, and colder, than he expected.

Tony, more than a few times, helped the elderly when they were in trouble. On one occasion he saw an older woman fall and hit her head on the street curb. Again, he quickly pulled his car over, stopped, and in the end personally took her to the hospital.

Another time he came upon a terrible car accident just a few miles from home. He didn't witness the accident, but he was the only one who pulled over to make sure everyone was okay. Tony went so far as to place his fingers on the neck of both driver and passenger to see if either one had a pulse. The driver was dead and the passenger barely alive.

The man who apparently hit them was kneeling on the grass hysterically crying and repeating over and over "I killed them...I killed them!"

Tony knew one of them was dead, but he chose to ease the man's burden by telling him "I can hear breathing." He was of course splitting hairs, as "breathing" would not include both people in the vehicle.

Given his background Jacquelyn knew Tony would always step up when required. However, she knew this was different, because in this situation he used his ability putting himself at risk emotionally and quite possibly legally. Exhausted, they held hands, quickly kissed and called it a day.

The next morning Tony was awake by 5:00 A.M. His body clock was running about a half hour early. As usual, he was welcomed to the new day with an immediate eye blinking episode. He got up out of bed, but not yet ready for breakfast, therefore avoiding any and all sugar or caffeinated products for awhile. He fired up his work computer to check his email.

I need to make this look like a normal day to Audrey, he thought.

He knew full well this wasn't necessarily his primary reason to logon to the internet. Tony looked for a reply from Audrey, but thankfully didn't find one, yet. He quickly deleted the messages that required no action on his part and hurriedly replied back to the people he needed to get back to so he could get down to real business. The real business was to check if there was any news of a problem at the White House yesterday. He used his personal laptop for this. Tony made the logical decision to check the Washington news websites first. He specifically wanted to find out if there was any word of an arrest made at the White House.

No mention of it was found as he breezed through each news website. Tony didn't really think he'd find anything, due for the most part, because he thought the White House would never let this kind of information out to the public. It would just frighten most people. After all, the other tour guests were on their way through the tour doors as Mr.

Twenty-two was swiftly and quietly seized. There were no witnesses, so as a result, no reason to release a report.

But, I'm a loose end, he thought.

Tony knew deep down that information about Mr. Twenty-two wouldn't likely be reported. But, of course, he wasn't completely sure. He wondered if he did the right thing. After all, this man did absolutely nothing, but quietly stand in line for a tour of the White House.

Just as important to Tony, he pondered if he was right or wrong about Mr. Twenty-two. After quick deliberation Tony chalked it up to knowing and trusting his instincts. Tony James is nothing if not confident in his unique talent, but he does like to have confirmation when given the chance.

If Mr. Twenty-two did have evil plans, and followed through on them, it would have been big news. Just the fact that a man was detained for questioning at the White House then released, would have been breaking news. It seemed like everything on TV deserved the obligatory breaking news scroll or flashing banner these days.

"BREAKING NEWS…The sun came up this morning," Tony joked to himself.

Tony held the opinion that most journalists were under tremendous pressure, but some had also become lazy, in the world of the fiercely competitive 24 hour news cycle. Journalism had crossed the line into entertainment by sensationalizing the ordinary.

As Tony saw it, the newspaper and broadcast companies were competing for the attention of every person who had a television, and those who connected to the internet. Their need was to keep as many eyeballs on them to keep ad revenues up. After feeling much better about the results of his research Tony felt the rumble in his stomach as breakfast was calling. Just as Tony took a bite of a banana the home phone rang.

Caller ID showed it to be an unknown caller so Tony, as was his usual practice, let it go to the answering machine for screening. It seemed most of these calls were computer generated anyway. Tony hated these kinds of calls. Whoever was the first one to answer usually found them to be on the receiving end of a pushy sales pitch. To Tony's surprise the caller began to leave a message. He didn't recognize the voice and figured it to be just another annoying unwanted call that he or Jacquelyn would delete later when they got around to it.

Tony suddenly froze. He couldn't believe what he was hearing. Once the caller was finished he replayed the message again to make sure he understood who'd just called him. Tony pressed the blinking play button on the answering machine and listened intently.

"Mr. James, my name is Dennis Forman, calling from the Department of Homeland Security in Washington, D.C. When you get this message please contact me at your earliest convenience at 222-555-4551. You can reach me day or night. Thank you Mr. James and I look forward to speaking with you."

After replaying the message one more time Tony realized he'd stopped chewing. He snapped out of his stare and finished the piece of fruit in his mouth then set his breakfast down. He could feel the dark clouds of a personal storm approaching.

Tony was leaning forward as if ready to bolt from his own home. He wasn't sure what to do. He had to calm down and think clearly. Tony paced back and forth to run the message through his mind. There was just no way of getting around it. He knew why this call was placed to him. Tony thought he might get away with not calling back and everything would blow over. Unfortunately he also knew this was just a fantasy. This was the United States government calling.

Of course I have to return the call...or do I? After all, Tony figured, the government worked for him. He paid his taxes and, therefore, paid this man's salary.

"That's a load of crap", he groaned.

As Tony sat down he wondered how they knew to call him at his home number. He never told agent Goodman anything. Then his memory of their conversation came flooding back. He did provide him his full name and more. But, there had to be so many people named Tony James's in the United States. He turned to his computer, and the internet, then searched his name. There were 18,200,000 results for Tony James!

"How'd they zero in on me so quickly?"

319

Duh, this is the government of the United States, he reminded himself.

Then he remembered telling Agent Goodman not only his name, but exactly where he was staying.

A chimp could figure this one out, he thought.

This left all his delusional doubts behind about this call. He knew it was one which had to be returned. Tony decided to hold off on calling right back. It could look like he was screening his calls if he did so immediately. He, of course, was call screening, but never imagined this particular message. He'd wait until just before lunch. Eat lunch? There was no way he could eat anything until he returned this man's call. His stomach was doing more flips than a dolphin at Sea World. Tony decided to make the call just a few minutes before noon.

Just maybe I'll get voicemail and be able to put this off a little longer, he hoped.

At 11:58 A.M. Tony stared at the name and phone number he'd written on the paper he was holding. It was time. Prior to doing so he reasoned through all scenarios of how to begin the conversation. He settled on one that was very direct and business-like, yet what he considered coy. Tony truly hoped he'd get voice mail so he could possibly avoid the whole thing at the moment. He also decided to block his cell phone number by pressing star six-seven. On the third ring a robust voice on the other end of the line quickly said in a slightly escalating tone, "DHS."

Tony knocked the palm of his hand on his forehead and thought, *Oh Crap! I forgot I was calling into the Eastern Time zone. Lunch is already over for them!* DHS was obviously short for Department of Homeland Security, but Tony kept his wits and was going to stick with his plan.

Tony had rehearsed his opening often enough to spit it out clearly and in a confidant and direct tone, "Dennis Forman, please."

He'd decided not to say he was returning Mr. Forman's call as this could raise the percentage of him being put right through to him. He also expected the obligatory question of, "Who's calling please?"

Tony couldn't believe his own ears, but the man on the other end said, "This is Dennis Forman."

Tony froze for just the briefest of moments as Forman inquired in a sharp tone, "Hello?"

He quickly snapped out of it and said, "Hi, Dennis. My name is Tony James. I'm returning your call."

Tony was now extremely thankful that he was never one for Mr. or Mrs. He wanted to set the tone as a phone call that would be as casual as possible.

"Well Mr. James, thank you for returning my call," said Forman politely.

It wasn't lost on Tony that he didn't return the convention of using Tony's first name.

"Please, call me Tony."

"All right, *Tony,* thank you for calling back." Forman had dropped an octave when repeating Tony's first name.

Tony knew this call was potentially one of the most important conversations he might ever have. Agent Forman got right to the point.

"Tony do you know why I called you?"

Trap question, Tony thought.

Police officers ask this when they pull people over. Tony had contemplated these types of questions may be asked and wished to stay away from them. He completely ignored the fact that Dennis Forman had already said he was with the Department of Homeland Security in his message.

"I presume your company, DHS, wants to either sell or buy something. I'm hoping the latter," said Tony.

Forman laughed and then apologized for using an abbreviation. "I'm sorry Mr. James, I mean Tony. DHS is short for the Department of Homeland Security. Not that it matters, but I'm the Senior Special Agent assigned to you," he said coldly.

Tony could tell Forman let this linger just a little too long as an intimidation factor. Most people would've given into the urge to respond, but Tony was tuned in and decided to allow Forman to fill the void. Tony knew all too well there were many areas in life when people felt awkward, and silence on the other end of the phone ranked near the top of the list.

"Are you still there Tony?"

"Yes, I'm still here," Tony said cheerfully.

"I thought I may have lost you if you were traveling between cell towers."

Tony thought, *How the heck did he know I called him from my cell phone?*

The call was blocked so it couldn't be known if he was calling from a cell phone or a land line. The signal was at full strength and the line crystal clear. Tony concluded Forman just took a guess.

Forman was very surprised that Tony didn't seem at all uneasy talking with him. He was also impressed that he had the discipline not to have diarrhea of the mouth. After all, this wasn't just any agency from the government calling.

I'm intrigued, Forman thought.

Most people avoided returning his calls, but when they did, every single one of them would ramble then stumble. This wasn't the case with Tony.

Dennis Forman is known in Washington as a straight shooter, a guy you'd like to befriend and have a drink with, if you were on his side. However, he's a real bull dog on the job. He just never let go when he started something, but today he chose a path of the kind-hearted. He cut his teeth in the military then recruited by the CIA. Dennis Forman possessed many skills, but none better than making the right decision as to how to handle diverse personalities. Hence the reason Director Williams chose him.

Most insiders knew just how defined the lines were between the agencies dedicated to the safety and preservation of the United States and its citizens. All agencies had their own chess piece on the board when it came to the security game. Each piece moved in very specific ways without deviation. If one piece went rogue then it put others in harm's way.

Dennis Forman had been used as almost every piece on the board. He was under the umbrella of Homeland Security at all times. He was one of the few, however, that had the freedom to use his credentials and choose whatever letters of the alphabet would fit the success of the mission. Forman holds the highest rank of "Senior Special Agent," but preferred not to highlight the senior aspect of his title unless he deemed it helpful. Interestingly enough, few politicians in Washington actually really know him. That's because Forman is a human chameleon. In the case of Tony James his first instinct was to use the FBI title, but decided to use the umbrella agency based on the information provided in his file.

"Tony, I represent the government of the United States and the Department of Homeland Security," said Forman.

Tony remained silent. *I heard you the first time*, thought Tony.

Forman continued, "I'd like to meet with you regarding the incident at the White house that took place yesterday."

Hanging on every word, Tony zeroed in on two on them: *Meet* and *Incident*. This definitely meant something went on with Mr. Twenty-two. Not wanting to acknowledge that he even heard the word "incident" Tony once again, thinking quickly, asked, "When will you be in my area?" Hoping to prolong the process he thought it had the chance to become less of a priority and, in due course, blow over.

"You misunderstand, Tony. I'm asking that you come back to D.C."

"I'm really very sorry Dennis, but I've got obligations here, and can't just pick up and leave. Besides, the cost of travel, hotel and food would set me back a few bucks. Please don't hesitate to give me a call when you're in this area," Tony deflected, trying to end the conversation.

Forman said flatly, yet politely, "I don't plan on being in your area Tony."

Well, the brush-off didn't work so Tony bit the bullet and said, "How about right now over the phone?"

"That's not how we operate, Tony." At any point Forman was prepared to get tough with him, but experience told him to hold back from that tactic, for now.

Tony tried once again to ignore the negative response and took the reins of the conversation.

"When we meet what's the first question you'd like to ask me Dennis?"

Oh, this guy's very smooth, thought Forman. *I wonder where he was trained. He must have a great story to tell. Forman decided to play along.*

"My first question is why you rushed out of the White House so quickly after turning in an international terrorist?"

After a moment Tony realized that he'd stopped breathing. He moved the phone away from his mouth, then after a good exhale, he said, "Excuse me?"

"I think you heard me Tony. You stopped a wanted terrorist then fled. Why?"

Forman's real question was, *How did you know about this guy?* But, he didn't want to tip his hand just yet.

"I have no idea what you're talking about. I didn't turn anyone in. All I did was talk to the White House agent on duty about a man wearing clothing that seemed out of place."

"But why were you thinking this unless you had prior knowledge of him?" asked Forman. "Nobody turns somebody in just for wearing a raincoat. Where were you trained?" he added. This was fun for Forman. He knew Director Williams really wouldn't appreciate it, but he couldn't help himself.

Tony could feel he was being cornered. He thought it might be a better idea to meet him in person after all, but on neutral ground.

"Dennis, I can see this is going to take you some time clarifying the circumstances of yesterday and I want to cooperate fully. Will you cut me some slack? Can you think about meeting half way?"

Forman felt very good about this. *Now he's moving*, he thought. "I most definitely can."

This was a huge relief to Tony. It was certainly not his first choice, but better to meet face to face and get a real good read on Senior Special Agent Dennis Forman so he could take advantage of his ability and bring this to a quick and successful conclusion. Almost as important, it wouldn't take place on Forman's home field in D.C.

"Great, how about Chicago?" Tony asked earnestly.

Forman started with enthusiasm as he said, "I love Chicago...but that won't do. How 'bout D.C.?"

Tony could almost hear Forman's grin over the phone.

"You have no plan on meeting me anywhere but D.C., do you Dennis?"

"No Tony, I don't. Please don't take this the wrong way, but its standard operating procedure."

Tony light-heartedly asked, "Is there any circumstance with which you people in Washington don't have a standard operating procedure?"

Forman laughed. "There is, but when we have something important it's necessary to play within the rules. You have to remember, Tony, you asked if I can *think* about meeting you half way. I said I could."

"Let me guess, you thought about it for a millisecond and decided against."

In a playful tone Forman said, "That's right." Then he added, "Besides, I wanted to get to know you just a little before we meet since you seem to have an advantage in this area," Forman said to provoke a response.

Tony didn't bite.

"Will the government reimburse me for my expenses?" asked Tony.

"We've done one better. This is on us, up front. Your flight agenda will be arriving via email within minutes of this call. You've been set up at the same hotel and room…number 1002. It's been a pleasure talking with you Tony. My associate and I look forward to seeing you."

Two on one…A fair fight I guess, Tony thought. Still trying to wiggle out of going by lengthening the conversation he politely asked, "Who's your associate?"

"I think you two have met. Well, maybe not formally met, but have seen each other. Her name is Agent Wolf…Agent *Elizabeth* Wolf."

Tony's memory flashed to the White House tour guide and remained silent. This time his silence wasn't on purpose. He was utterly dumbstruck. Forman didn't give Tony a chance to ask where to meet him or even say goodbye. Silence never sounded so loud. Forman had hung up.

Still holding the phone Tony heard a chime from his office computer announcing the arrival of a new email. Before Tony went to open the email he needed to review the important content of this conversation he just had with Senior Special Agent Dennis Forman of Homeland Security.

Tony focused first on the big picture. *Something happened at the White House and it was because of my ability. No, Tony corrected himself, that's not why. It's because I acted upon the knowledge from my ability. I've done nothing wrong, but these days of terrorism anyone can get caught up in something by mistake.*

On a small positive note Tony did get his validation regarding Mr. Twenty-two. This was a small victory. Tony then realized Forman used certain words very precisely. The first that concerned him was "important." *He's playing by the rules because this is important.* The next word that stuck out was "done." Flight and hotel arrangements were used in past tense. This indicated Tony had absolutely no choice in this matter from the start.

What the heck did he mean by Mr. Twenty-two being a wanted international terrorist? That's a heavy duty title to be throwing around.

Tony automatically began peering around the corners of their conversation. He surmised Agent Forman called for two reasons. The first was to size him up. The second was to put the fear of God in him.

He succeeded on the latter, that's for sure, he thought.

Tony lingered on the most important word from the conversation last. Forman said that he would have an "advantage" over him when they met. He's never heard of Dennis Forman much less had a close encounter with him.

How could he possibly know that I'd have an advantage when we meet? Why wouldn't Agent Forman take care of this over the phone if he knew he'd be at a disadvantage? What advantage is he talking about? Does he know about my ability? How does this agent Wolf fit into this whole thing? Too many questions and not enough answers.

Tony had nothing to lose on the legal side of things. He'd done absolutely nothing wrong. In a post 9/11 world many people were speaking up about their suspicions. However, he's very protective and secretive of his capability that had been formulated and refined since childhood. He was still uncomfortable with it mainly because of his own foggy theory of how and why it came into being. This was the reason he didn't want anything to do with Agent Forman. The government knew something, exactly what he wasn't sure. Tony was just going to have to pull it together with an extremely focused effort and then move on with the life he's built with Jacquelyn and the kids.

Tony went to his work computer and saw the new email which had no information in the subject line. He opened it and surprisingly found it only had two attachments. There wasn't one single word in the body of the email. Even the attachments were so ordinary that he had no idea what they would be if not for just having had the phone conversation with Agent Dennis Forman.

The first attachment was simply entitled "1.pdf" and the second "2.pdf." He let his cursor hover over the first attachment with a concern that "Big Brother", especially the Department of Homeland Security, could be sending a key-stroke tracking program without his knowledge. Tony shook this surge of paranoia and reminded himself that he's an upstanding citizen with nothing to hide. Besides, if they tried, he was one individual with the knowledge and skill that could locate and remove a tracking program immediately.

A quick double-click and the first attachment began to open. To his surprise it wasn't the itinerary for his flight or hotel which he anticipated. He couldn't believe his eyes as he gazed upon twelve dated and time-stamped thumbnail sized photographs from the second he rushed out the door at the White House to the time he pressed the garage door to close at his home!

"Son of a —," he paused. "I've been under surveillance!" Tony blurted out loud.

They were on to him so quickly without his knowledge. They followed him and knew exactly where to find him. Since Tony led a very quiet and unassuming life this was a huge awakening. Alarms went off inside his head. Once again he felt the need to bolt, but remained, though unsteady. His stress level went up and very moderate tics kicked into overdrive. He reminded himself to breathe deeply.

Then he scanned the photos and saw himself leaving the hotel and getting into a cab. The one that topped them all was a photo while he was on the plane. Someone, for all he knew, could have been sitting next to him at some point, had actually been on the plane with him. This was something Tony thought he'd only see in the movies. But, it was actually happening to him. It was staring him right in the face.

Time to open attachment number two. He closed the first one and with great hesitation he double-clicked "2.pdf." From the second he clicked it to the moment it opened time stood still for Tony. There was no telling what might be next.

Do they have pictures of me releasing my tics? To his relief it was the flight and hotel itinerary. Three weeks from now. *At least they seem to have some heart by giving me a chance to provide enough notice to Audrey. Or, maybe they're preparing some kind of case against me,* he thought.

Tony wiped the bead of sweat off his forehead then printed everything that was sent. He decided to print the pictures so he could eliminate them from his CIT computer. Senior Special Agent Dennis Forman had some explaining to do when they meet. Tony released multiple violent *punching* tics accidently knocking over a few items on his desk.

An hour later, Audrey called. Tony let it go to voicemail. He was too preoccupied and hadn't had enough time to think through what he'd say to her. About thirty minutes later Tony finally decided to call and just tell Audrey the truth. Well, not everything.

I'm sticking to my code. No other person but Jacquelyn will ever know, he reminded himself.

"So did you get everything we needed out of the conference?" asked Audrey.

"I think it was important that we had a presence. There wasn't any cutting edge technology on display," replied Tony.

"Well, that's what I always thought about that conference. Unfortunately, if CIT isn't present others question why," she said.

He was happy to hear they were on the same page. Tony then swallowed hard and filled her in on the White House tour situation. To his surprise she had a similar reaction to Jacquelyn's and was more interested in his well being than anything else.

"Tony, usually I like to receive a written report, but let's forget about it this time," said Audrey.

"I will abide by your command," Tony said sarcastically.

"Yes, I'm sure you're very disappointed," she retorted. Audrey was guilt ridden as it was she who sent Tony to D.C. in the first place. She felt responsible because the real reason he wound up at the White House was, in part, due to her actions.

Tony reminded himself that he had only one thing he needed to hide. Everything else was open to government scrutiny. *If they want to follow me around...so be it*, he decided. He had to live his life as normally as possible.

So, with that mindset, he turned his attention to contacting Dr. Dillon to let her know he'd taken one tablet of Klonopin at bedtime for the last few nights without any change. She reminded him he is to take one at bedtime and one in the morning. Dr. Dillon considered the past few days of taking it only at bedtime as irrelevant.

"Start it right, Tony, doctor's orders."

Tony saved Agent Forman's message on the answering machine to play for Jacquelyn once the kids were sound asleep. As she listened intently she didn't realize the vice-like grip she had on the kitchen counter. Tony then took her through his entire conversation with Agent Forman.

"There must be something big with this terrorist guy or they wouldn't be flying you back to D.C.," she said.

With calm in his voice he said, "I need you to sit down Jacquelyn."

She looked at him with confusion in her eyes. He pulled out the surveillance photos from a large tan envelope and gave them to her. She looked at each one of them. As she moved to the last one of Tony pressing the button to close the garage door she looked up at him with her big brown eyes as wide as ever. She remained silent. Tony filled the communication void.

"Yes, I was followed by the government from the time I left the White House all the way home."

"This is unbelievable!" she finally exclaimed.

After they talked it through, in detail, they agreed he did nothing wrong and if going back to D.C. was required then that's what needs to happen.

Chapter 38

It was late and Tony finally took his bedtime dose of Dr. Dillon's newly prescribed medication. The next morning he took his second dose as pre-arranged. Tony continued to do his everyday normal activities for the next three days. He purposely didn't look over his shoulder so as not to give Agent Forman the satisfaction of appearing to affect his life. He waited the required three days to call Dr. Dillon with his results.

"Doctor, I don't think I feel any different."

"Have you felt any side effects?"

"None at all."

"Okay then, for the next three days I'd like you to take an additional tablet around 2:00 P.M. Call me in three days with your feedback."

Tony did as he was told. As a matter of keeping to a schedule he began to set his watch alarm as a reminder. He set the times for 8:00 A.M., 2:00 P.M. and 10:00 P.M. and followed this schedule to a tee. Thursday rolled around and he called Dr. Dillon to give his feedback.

"I think my tics are beginning to be reduced," he said excitedly. Tony explained exactly when he's taking each dose.

"That's wonderful news. What about side effects?" she asked.

"Zilch," said Tony.

"Okay, I'd like you to stay on this schedule for the following week. Let's see where you're at then. Call me late next week."

"Will do, Doctor, and thanks."

He asked Jacquelyn if she had noticed a reduction in his tics.

"I was waiting for you to ask me," she said with a big smile. "I know you can focus and try to hold them off for awhile, but I've never seen you like this," she said.

"Like what?" Tony asked gingerly.

"Like you don't need to tic anymore!" she exclaimed.

"Well, I still do, but you're right. They're less and I can hold out much longer than before even under the current circumstances."

"What about when you hold out longer? Do they come back as hard as usual?"

This was something he hadn't even considered. He paused then said, "No, as a matter of fact that's been reduced as well. I think I finally have the right doctor and the right medication."

"I'm so happy for you Tony."

She gently grabbed his face with both hands and gave him a big kiss on the lips. "You want to go out and celebrate?" she asked.

He said, "If you don't mind I think I'll wait. I don't think I'm quite there yet."

"What do you mean?" asked Jacquelyn.

"I mean I think it can still be better."

After their hug they held hands. Tony gave her fingers three quick little squeezes. She replied with four.

Three weeks were approaching and it was almost time for him to travel back to D.C. on Monday. He knew his medication was working well, but thought maybe another dose could make it even better. So, he called Dr. Dillon. When she returned his call they went through their normal routine. It was agreed upon that Tony was to take four tablets daily. His schedule would now be to take a one milligram tablet at 8:00 A.M., 1:00 P.M., 6:00 P.M. and bedtime.

As soon as Tony completed his first day of this new schedule for his medication he was beside himself. Tony sat still for what seemed to be an eternity. *This is amazing! I haven't sat still for this long since I was a little kid!* He just had to call Jacquelyn.

"Are you still up for going out to celebrate?" asked Tony excitedly.

"Is it for the reason that I think?"

"I can't read your mind," he quipped.

You could have fooled me, she thought.

As Jacquelyn hung up the phone she pictured Tony sitting in quiet peace without the urge to tic. A single tear of joy appeared in the corner of her right eye. *I'm so happy for you Tony,* she thought.

Travel day back to D.C. was finally upon him. Tony's direct flight was scheduled for takeoff at 6:20 A.M. This of course meant arriving at the airport two hours ahead due to security measures.

He packed the evening before and had his clothes ready to go so he wouldn't disturb Jacquelyn. As she slept he gave her a light kiss on her forehead before heading to the kids' rooms. Both Sam and Nick were sound asleep. He entered Sam's room and couldn't help but notice her favorite stuffed animal leaning a bit sideways on her shelf. The memories came flooding back to him when he used to lie on the floor next to her bed and pretend Le'Mutt spoke to her. She could only see her little stuffed dog and seemed to forget her dad was controlling his words, movements and high voice.

He started to adjust Le'Mutt then decided to pick him up and let him give her a peck on the cheek. He then tucked Le'Mutt into bed with her.

Ah, to be at such peace with the world, he marveled.

Little Nick was uncovered and curled up in a ball sideways on his bed. He probably was playing and then just drifted off into the world of dreams. Tony then noticed two toy dinosaurs next to Nick.

Sure enough, he played to the last second, and fell asleep. That's Nick, Tony thought.

Tony knew there was no way Nick would awaken so he picked up his little man and laid his head on the pillow, then covered him with his favorite blanket.

He gave Nick a kiss on the top of his head and said quietly, "Take care of Mom and your sister while I'm gone."

Tony left the driveway and couldn't help but think somebody might be following him, if not right away, then certainly at the airport. He checked one bag and took one carry-on. He then went through security without any issues. He gave some thought about going to the executive lounge. Audrey provided him with proper access for his travels. He didn't feel like going back there so soon.

As he sat waiting to board his flight he flipped through the four sections of the newspaper. He came across the crossword puzzle. As he stared at it his mind began to drift. He couldn't help but think back to the incident with the man with the scar. *I'm starting to build a track record with these guys,* he calmly thought. Logical Tony began to connect the dots. Then it hit him like a ton of bricks.

I wonder if they know about that as well! After all, I made contact with the Air Marshall. He'd certainly have to file a report. I'd likely be in that report, he quickly thought.

He then heard someone sit down behind him. Tony decided to allow this thought process to take its course on its own time frame. He wasn't going to push. Tony went back to reading his newspaper thinking, *Could that be a person who might be following me?*

Once on the plane he looked everyone in the eyes. If he was being tailed he wanted to know by whom. Of course he was such an amateur at this cloak and dagger stuff. Nevertheless, he had to at least try to figure out who the professional might be, but knew it was next to impossible. He figured whoever it was is sitting behind him for obvious reasons.

Maybe there isn't anyone following me right now, he reminded himself. Try to relax Tony, he prodded.

Tony changed his watch to reflect the time zone change. At the appropriate time the chime from his watch alarm told him he needed to take his 8:00 A.M. medication. He very quickly pressed the button to turn the sound off. Even while taking his medication he tried to be secretive.

I'm staying with what I promised myself all those years ago. Stick to the code. Tell no one, he affirmed to himself.

He even came up with a back-up story if anyone were to ask why he was taking a pill. He figured epilepsy was as good a reason as any. Tony found a way to wiggle one of four small tablets from his front left pants pocket. He then bent down pretending to re-adjust his briefcase he stored under the seat in front of him. As he did this he easily slipped the tablet into his mouth. Tony had built up enough saliva to wash it down as he looked up to adjust the airflow from the small nozzle in the ceiling of the plane. Gravity did the rest.

As he deplaned he casually looked back, then all around as he walked to get his suitcase at baggage claim. He was tired of feeling paranoid. He was more disappointed that he wasn't able to detect anyone following him.

Then he had a thought. *I forgot, this is "Big Brother" we're talking about here. For all I know they're watching me from cameras. I'm sure it wouldn't be the first time they electronically kept an eye on their target.*

Tony actually felt a little relief. His medication was doing a great job. His tics had become almost undetectable. All without side effects to this point. He still had the urge to tic, but at such a very low level. He was thrilled.

Thank you Dr. Dillon, he thought.

After picking up his luggage at baggage claim carousal number four, he proceeded to the car rental area. Here he was pleasantly surprised he wasn't going to have to wait in line. His vehicle had already been pre-paid. Tony figured it was by CIT, but the man behind the counter said he wasn't at liberty to tell him who paid. Tony found this odd.

Agent Forman I presume, he deduced.

Tony located his assigned vehicle and began to get into it. He stopped short from sitting on an envelope that was laying on the driver's seat. Tony turned it over and it read "Pick you up in front of your hotel at 11:50 A.M." Tony took note that the GPS was already on and programmed to take him to the JW Marriot.

I could get used to having stuff done for me like this, but then again, this could be creepy, he thought.

As he checked in, he was told his room had been taken care of so payment wasn't required. The only mandatory ID was to show his driver's license. He didn't even have to provide a credit card for incidentals.

Dennis, you're spoiling me, he kiddingly thought.

Once in his room Tony removed the few items he'd packed and decided that if his room was bugged it didn't matter. No way was he wasn't going to say or do anything stupid.

I've done nothing wrong, so bite me, Big Brother, he thought.

Tony decided to place an additional eight tablets of his new medication in his left front pants pocket just in case. He wasn't sure why, but it somehow made him feel better.

Tony called Jacquelyn and left her a voice message that he arrived safe and sound and in his hotel room. He really wanted to leave more details than that, but kept it short and sweet. From his Smartphone Tony answered a few emails for work that required his attention. He looked at his watch and realized it was already 11:30 A.M.

Tony took the elevator down and strolled into the lobby scanning as he walked. He felt like he was in a movie. There were at least a dozen people sitting reading newspapers as they sipped coffee. Telling the locals from the out of town guests was easy. Tony had noticed that most people in large cities on the East Coast read their newspapers folded into thirds. He supposed this was a space saver, as well as a way to free up a hand while riding on the subway systems. It's just another nuance of life that he seemed to have a knack for noticing. Tony looked for a person who held the paper fully open with both hands, like he'd done, indicating possible suspicious behavior that someone was perhaps tailing him. He cared, but knew he couldn't do anything about it, so out the front doors he went.

Tony was prepared to talk about almost everything. He was intent on keeping to his code. A light breeze washed over him as he stepped outside to survey the vehicles that were parked in the pick-up zone. Tony then located a bench and sat down to await his ride. As he sat, Tony gave some thought about how he was going to take his medication without notice at 2:00 P.M.

I'll deal with it when the moment comes, he thought.

At exactly 11:50 A.M. he heard a vaguely familiar voice coming from behind him. "Good morning Mr. James. Will you please come with me?" she asked holding out her credentials.

Tony didn't want to appear as startled as he really was, so he hesitated, and then turned slowly, finding the leather bound flip style Department of Homeland Security ID at eye level.

In a surprised, questioning tone he looked up and said, "You?" *Actress*, he quickly reminded himself. As he focused on Agent Elizabeth Wolf he received the exact same feeling as the first time from the White House.

So as not to show his nervousness he said, "You've moved up in the world. No longer giving tours at the White House?"

343

It appeared she wasn't much for small talk. The red-headed agent turned sideways waiting for Tony to get up and walk beside her.

"My vehicle is in the back," she said as if talking to no one in particular.

Agent Elizabeth Wolf had been given strict orders not to engage in any personal or excessive communication with this Person of Interest. She understood why the order had been given. During preparation for the job at the White House she was privy to *almost* every piece of information regarding their POI, Mr. Tony James. She knew he wasn't a creep or dangerous like some of the other candidates had been who'd made it this far.

This guy seems really normal, she thought.

Her opinion of her boss, Director Don Williams, was that he first looks out for the defense of his country. In second place came himself and then finally any agent in his charge.

I wish he'd have let me in one hundred percent on what this guy is about, she thought.

Tony followed the red-headed Homeland Security Agent to the obvious dark tinted window SUV. *A real spook mobile*, Tony excitedly thought. They both got in.

I pray he's not better than his file indicates, Agent Wolf thought anxiously.

Tony didn't know what he was in for and had so many questions at the ready. He didn't' want to come off as too eager for information so he figured he'd get to know his escort on the ride to their destination.

"So, Elizabeth, how long you been with the Department of Homeland Security?"

"It's Agent Wolf, and my job is to pick you up and make sure you get to where you're going on time," she said impassively.

"I'm sorry. I didn't mean to offend you...bad day?" Tony asked sincerely.

She remained silent. Tony looked around inside the SUV. He took note that this was the cleanest vehicle, other than his own, that he'd been in for quite some time.

"Tidy ride. Have you gotten the bugs worked out yet?" he said knowing the obvious double meaning.

Her eyes stayed trained on the road ahead and she remained speechless. Tony figured the SUV was either bugged or Agent Wolf was just not going to engage in conversation. He thought he might be able to figure which one it was. Tony began to poke in an uncharacteristic fashion for him. He started with a stereotypical social premise.

"So, why were you pretending to lead a White House tour?" Tony blurted.

Once again silence. Not even a flinch. "Were you the one they picked, because you're the Miss Congeniality of Homeland Security?"

She tried not to show it, but Tony could sense her displeasure at the question.

"I doubt they had to take a chisel to your skin and completely make you over." He continued, "But, if they did, I think they did an outstanding job. I have to tell you that I don't think any woman should be placed in that type of situation just because they're attractive." He noticed an easing of her grip on the steering wheel.

"Take my bride for instance. She is the most beautiful woman on earth, but taken seriously because of her brains and guts to stand up for herself. I've always believed a person should have the opportunity based on merit rather than physical attributes," he continued verbally jabbing her. "Women get the short end of the stick, don't they?"

Still silence, but her body language told him she agreed.

"So, I know you were chosen to pretend to be a tour guide and now you're a cab driver. Obviously someone must not see you have the brains to go with your obvious good looks…pardon my saying."

Before he knew it, the SUV shifted and forced his body to the left as Agent Wolf abruptly pulled over to the right side of the road.

"Look, I know what you're trying to do and you hit your mark…HAPPY? To be perfectly honest I am tired of not being utilized to my fullest potential! But, my orders are very clear. I'm to pick you up and drop you off on time. You seem like a really good person and I'd love to have a nice conversation with you, but I can't."

346

"Why not?" asked Tony.

"Because my orders also include that I'm not to engage you in any conversation. Do you understand?"

Now Tony was getting somewhere. They were conversing.

In a quieter tone he asked, "Are you asking if I understand your orders or that they don't completely believe in you?"

Tony knew he went too far. Agent Wolf checked her blind spot and put the pedal to the metal. *Well I don't think this SUV is bugged*, he smiled inwardly looking out the passenger window. Tony didn't say another word.

Upon arrival, and after the security checks, Agent Wolf was about to open the door to the same building Audrey just visited with Don Williams recently.

She put her hand on the one of the main entry doors and turned to Tony saying in a very hushed tone, "Thanks for understanding and I'm sorry I couldn't be more up-front with you. Try to relax in there. Remember, nothing is really as it seems." Perplexed, Tony apologized for being brash and forcing the issue.

Tony was delivered to a sparse twelve-by-twelve foot room by a security guard the size of an NFL linebacker. This man's eyes reminded him of Mike Singletary when he played for the Super Bowl Champion Chicago Bears...incredibly intense.

As the door closed behind him he heard a double click as if the lock had been engaged. Tony checked and sure enough it was locked. He tried the door on the opposite side of the room with the same result.

Alarmingly he thought, *Am I a prisoner?* He sat down. *What a drab room compared to the rest of this place. It must be set up like this on purpose.*

The only items in the room were an old institutional style table bolted to the floor with a chair on each side facing one another. *This looks like an interrogation room from an old TV show,* he thought. Tony decided to sit in one of the chairs. *No sense just standing here.*

He saw the mirror window run the entire length of the right wall. *Oh no, I am in an interrogation room!* He then looked up and saw cameras in each of the corners of the room. Tony remembered what Agent Elizabeth Wolf said just before they entered the building. *Nothing is really as it seems.*

Chapter 39

Glancing at his watch, Tony saw it was 12:30 P.M. No one seemed too eager to come for him. With plenty of time to think he decided to take what agent Wolf had said to heart. Tony had a very early start to the day and was now awfully tired. He folded his arms on the table then rested his head on top. A soft alarm off in the distance nudged him awake. It was his watch. 2:00 P.M., time for his medication. Even under these circumstances he didn't want to allow anyone to see him taking his next dose.

He got up and paced. Tony realized that every inch of the room likely could be seen by either the cameras or through, what he presumed to be, a two-way mirrored glass window. He put both hands in his pockets and snagged a tablet with his middle finger from his left pocket. Pretending to cough he placed his hand over his mouth. By doing so Tony had successfully taken his medication and knew he needed it.

Tony then meandered over to the mirror and cupped his hands to try and see through, but without success. As he was sitting at the table at 2:15 P.M. he felt a presence. It was one of his feelings. To his surprise someone nearby was giving off the vibe of...*calculating!* Tony slowly looked up to the mirror. He flashed back to the meeting in Audrey's office. He pictured her long wall mirror. Next he was remembering the executive lounge at the airport.

The chances of this happening again are staggering, he thought.

Behind the surveillance mirror one man had just entered to observe Tony. Both rooms were sound proof and the man behind the mirror said into his wrist transmitter, "Did you see that? As soon as I entered he looked directly at me."

Director Williams had finished his conference call in his office and was watching on the big screen TV for only a minute when he heard Agent Bobby Starks' words.

"Bobby will you please repeat your last statement?" Williams asked talking into the speaker on his coffee table.

Starks obliged. Williams turned the sound up on the TV monitor.

"What was he doing all this time?" Williams asked.

"Before what appeared to be an initial surprised reaction he was just sitting, sleeping and then pacing, sir."

"Were you and Ted monitoring the surveillance camera's the entire time he's been in there?"

"Yes sir. Are you sure the glass isn't defective?"

"Of course it's not defective," derided Director Williams. "Why?"

Agent Starks explained what just occurred.

"You're telling me as soon as you walked in behind the mirror he looked directly at you?"

"That's correct sir. Just like at CIT," he added.

"Okay, Bobby, let's get him a little more comfortable. Send in Dr. Zander's assistant to apologize for the delay. Let's ease Mr. James' apprehension and get him to the edge of being slightly open to conversation. Then we'll move him to see Dr. Zander upstairs."

Tony wasn't certain if he had pin-pointed the exact location of where the vibe *calculating* was emanating from, but as Agent Stark began to walk out of the room Tony's eyes were compelled to follow. Agent Stark watched Tony's eyes follow him as he walked the length of the soundproof viewing room behind the glass.

"Now that's just freaky," Starks said softly.

Finally Tony heard a knock at what he considered the back door, since it wasn't the way he came in. A man in a white lab jacket walked in smiling.

"We are so sorry for keeping you waiting this long, Mr. James."

Tony was angry, but decided to play nice. What he really wanted to do was to rip into this guy, but figured this wasn't the person in power. He certainly knew it wasn't Senior Agent Dennis Forman's voice.

After sitting at the table across from each other asking and answering inane questions Tony was finally on the move once again. The linebacker was summoned to escort Tony.

Tony entered and saw a very plush office. *Now this is more like it*, he thought.

"I'm Dr. Zander, Mr. James. Please have a seat anywhere," said the pudgy balding man in the white lab coat.

Tony could have chosen any chair as they were all very inviting.

"May I get you anything?"

"Yes, actually, I'd like to eat lunch."

"Oh my goodness, you haven't been fed yet? Let's rectify that immediately," he said in a nasally tone.

The doctor pressed the speaker button and connected to a female voice.

"Yes doctor?"

He turned to Tony and asked if a tuna salad sandwich, chips and a cold beverage would suffice.

Tony said, "Yes, but just water to drink, thanks."

Dr. Zander pressed the button and repeated the meal order. "It will only be a few minutes and you'll be functioning on a full stomach," he said light-heartedly.

Tony consumed his meal in short order. He felt so much better and his mind seemed to clear as well.

Dr. Zander now sitting across from Tony asked, "May I call you Tony?"

"That's my name," Tony said as he gave an affirmative nod.

"I'm sure you're wondering why you're in my office."

No, I just stopped by for a bite to eat, thought Tony.

"Actually doctor, I'm wondering why I was being held in an interrogation room like a criminal."

The doctor didn't know anything about that and said he'd look into it for him.

Sure you will, Tony thought.

Then Tony asked, "What kind of doctor are you?"

"My specialty is the brain, in particular, individual and collective intelligences. Not mine of course," he said with a chuckle.

Tony imagined he'd told that one hundreds of times before without anyone getting the joke.

"Tony, you are in my office today basically so I can ascertain your level of IQ."

Taken totally off-guard Tony responded with a simple, "What?"

Dr. Zander continued, "You see Tony, you were involved in something at the federal level and I have been asked to provide a report of your intelligence."

Tony was confused. *What does taking an IQ test have to do with the incident at the White House?* Agent Wolf's message replayed once again in his mind. *Nothing is really as it seems*, he reminded himself.

Tony thought about telling him to take his test and shove it, but decided he'd play along just to put this whole thing behind him. Dr. Zander explained how the test is given and Tony began.

The first two pages had the usual questions on an IQ test. When he got to the third page however, there were questions that had nothing to do with IQ. Questions such as, "Have you ever had an out of body experience?"

"Can you now or in the past see people who have passed away? If so, are you still interacting with them?"

"Can you read minds?"

"Do you have a sixth sense?"

"If you answered yes, how does it manifest itself?"

These types of questions were interspersed throughout the test. Tony now thought he was beginning to catch on to at least part of the bigger picture.

Nothing is really as it seems. Tony asked Dr. Zander if he could take a break and go to the bathroom.

"I'm sorry Tony this is a timed test and must be completed without interruption."

Tony completed the test making sure he didn't answer any of the non-IQ questions in the affirmative. Dr. Zander collected the test from Tony and called an escort so he could go to the men's room. Tony's medication was working very well, but he thought he still needed to release a few tics in the bathroom. To his surprise it was nothing severe like he usually experienced before.

As a matter of fact Tony stood realizing, *I really don't need to do this at all. Old habits die hard*, he thought.

While in the stall he had to think about what the heck was going on. *Based on those odd questions I definitely suspect they think I have some kind of sixth sense or something. The problem is they're kind of right! So how do I play this?*

No answers came to him at the moment. Tony thought he'd be escorted back to Dr. Zander's office, but he was wrong. Instead the linebacker walked him to the elevator and both rode it down in silence.

He was taken to another doctor. This time it was for a physical. Complete blood work and all. Tony wasn't up for it, but knew he really had no choice in the matter. If he wanted to put this episode of his life behind him cooperation was the name of the game at this point.

Once there he was given athletic clothing and told to change into them in the small private locker room. He was then hooked up with more gel suction-cups stuck to his body than an Olympic athlete ready for testing. After wetting his head they placed what looked to Tony to be a clear rubber swimming cap on him and secured it tightly. It had hundreds of different colored wires within a pliable gel. Out of the top, all of them ultimately converged into a two-inch high wire encased in solid plastic. Tony was told this was new wireless technology to monitor certain brain function during physical activity.

Upon hearing this he complained, "Wow, this is uncomfortably tight," in hopes that he could avoid any probing of his brain.

"It's either this or we shave your head for more gel cups," the technician said forcefully.

Tony realized he shouldn't push it. "Never mind, I don't think my family would recognize me if I came home bald as a cue ball."

He was instructed to step onto the treadmill. They pushed him to his physical exhaustion point. Little did they know that they were doing him a BIG favor! Tony didn't know it at first, but they weren't just looking for his level of fitness. They also wanted to know his levels of competitiveness and mental toughness.

Tony pushed himself harder than ever knowing it would reduce his urge to tic. After completing this he was given a sports drink and allowed to shower. While alone, he poured the drink down the drain knowing it was full of sugar. He filled it with water and quenched his thirst. Just as he was getting dressed and back into his own clothes his watch alarm rang out. It was already 6:00 P.M. and time again for his medication. He reached into his pocket and located a tablet. Tony then re-set the alarm for his 10:00 P.M. dose. This would be his last reminder for the day.

At least this time they didn't forget to feed him dinner. Another linebacker escorted him to one of the many cafeterias within the complex. To his surprise he was taken to a table where he saw, from a distance, the red hair of Agent Wolf. He sat down without saying a word.

She gave the linebacker a nod and he left.

"So, how was your day at the spa?" she asked.

In typical Tony deflection fashion he asked, "What are you doing here?"

"A girl's gotta eat."

"So *now* you can talk to me?" asked Tony.

"If you recall I spoke to you on the way over here," she said without looking at him.

"You and I both know you lost it and made a mistake. But, I want to thank you for the heads up you gave me just before entering the building. What did that mean exactly?" he asked.

"What are you talking about?"

"You remember, '*Nothing is really as it seems*', " he said in a hushed voice.

"Have you figured it out yet?" she asked quietly leaning forward.

"I have no idea what the heck is going on."

"Well, think about your day. Can you come to any conclusions based on connecting the dots?" she asked just a little too eagerly.

Tony wasn't born yesterday, and knowing she was sent to obtain as much information about him and his reaction to the day. Through the rest of the conversation he came across as a man who really had no idea what was going on. Agent Wolf completed her meal and was then on her way.

As she got into the SUV she placed a phone call to Senior Special Agent Dennis Forman. She provided him with her report stating that Mr. Tony James has absolutely no idea what's going on. She, of course, didn't mention that she just as much tipped him off before entering the building.

Forman asked, "So, what's your take on this guy?"

"Sir, not knowing one hundred percent of his file puts me at a disadvantage to answer that."

"Then give me your take on what you *do* know," he said in a blistering tone.

"Personally, I think we're wasting our time again. As I said this guy doesn't have a clue", she said flatly. "If it's supposed to have anything to do with any extra-sensory activity on his part I think this is a misuse of assets," she lied.

Forman was pleased. He knew much more than Agent Wolf based on his higher security level. She hadn't seen any of the videos to this point. Forman wanted Tony to be unencumbered during this testing phase.

"Thanks Elizabeth, I'll give Director Williams a call to see how he wants to proceed."

After she had driven a few miles Elizabeth parked the SUV on a side street. She first turned her pen light on then opened a map and placed it on the dashboard as a diversion just in case. Once she had on her skin colored disposable latex gloves, she reached under her own driver side seat and pulled a small thin battery from the tape that was holding it in place. Leaning over to the passenger side she did exactly the same, except this time, extracting a disposable cell phone. She had purchased the phone while on vacation in Florida the previous winter and paid cash. This would be the first and only time the phone would be used. She placed the battery in the phone. Once it was on and fully functional, Elizabeth wrote a very short cryptic text then sent it to the designated number. When she saw it was confirmed to be a successful transmission she quickly powered the phone down and took the battery out. Replacing the cover to the battery compartment she drove off to dispose of each item in separate locations never to be found.

Tony was taken to a very nice room that was much like a hotel suite. The door was locked from the outside so he couldn't leave. After his initial panic he settled down repeating to himself that this was part of their procedure.

This has to be some kind of stress test, he decided.

This helped him settle down a little. As he surveyed the room he saw it didn't have a phone, radio or television.

No outside interference, he thought.

Exhausted, he flopped backward on the bed to review the events of the day. Then he realized, *I really need to call Jacquelyn*. As he lay there thinking of his little family his eyelids got heavy and he slowly dosed off.

"Don, I'd like to come over and begin talking with Mr. James about the White House incident," said Forman.

"We should have his complete test results within an hour," Williams declared. "Did Agent Wolf glean any pertinent information?" he asked as a follow-up.

"According to her he has no clue what's really going on."

"By the tone of your voice it doesn't sound like you agree."

"You know I don't need those test results. What I need is to be face-to-face with him. This guy has proven himself too smart to make many mistakes. Remember, I spoke to him on the phone and I believe the sooner we get down to it the better."

"I disagree with you Dennis, but you've earned the right to override me on this. I personally think a little more stress will prove to be very helpful, so I booked him a room here at 'Hotel Security'," said Williams. "And, just for the record, I think you'll find the Surveillance Room Report an interesting read. Come directly to my office when you arrive."

Within the hour Forman identified himself with his thumbprint then knocked on Don's door.

After Williams checked the video screen he said, "Come on in."

Director Williams pressed a button that looked much like a remote control for a car. As Forman walked in he was a little surprised to find the team that had tested Tony earlier in the day present and prepared to be part of the discussion.

"I thought it to be prudent we should assemble the team to get a full picture of Mr. James," Williams said to Forman while proudly looking at his extended SSD team.

Still standing Forman said, "No thanks, Don. I just need two things."

"And those are?"

"Very succinctly tell me what the results of his tests are and second I'd like to read the report you mentioned on the phone earlier."

"Yes sir," Williams said sarcastically while locking eyes with the bulldog of Washington.

Everyone in the room knew Forman was the only person that could get away with talking to Director Don Williams like that. The history those two shared seemed to create a bond as if they were brothers. The team assembled remained silent as Director Williams summarized the results of each stage of Tony's testing.

"A few things stick out. All indications point to the fact that he is very intelligent, but not in the genius category. His tests show that he has the heart close to that of a Navy SEAL. His brain structure and activity did have some anomalies, but nothing unexpected. His quickness of mind is outstanding, as you know."

He handed Forman the full report he requested.

"Thanks. I'll be across the hall. When I'm done I'll bring it back." Forman never acknowledged the other people in the office.

Williams turned and said to his team, "Thank you for staying late. Good work today. You're all dismissed."

Forman was surprised at the remark that the guy he spoke to just weeks ago showed initial test results of having what it takes to be a Navy SEAL.

Never judge a book by its cover, he thought.

In the vacant office across the hall, Forman read the report with his feet up on the desk.

"Blah, blah, blah," he said with his eyes fixed on the pages in one hand and a cup of coffee in the other.

Then his eyes opened just a little wider. He took his feet off the desk, set his coffee mug down and closely examined the next page twice over.

Forman put the report down for a moment and said to himself, "This guy, for the second time, pinpointed our operative without having to actually see him? That's incredible!"

He read the rest of the report then sat back and wondered just what capabilities Tony James actually possesses.

I have no idea to what depths his capability goes. The others were so easy compared to this, he thought.

Forman checked his watch and decided he didn't want to begin talking with Tony since it was so late. He went back to Williams and they agreed to hold Tony overnight and begin in the morning. Forman also agreed this would allow them to see Tony under added duress.

As Forman began to leave he snapped his fingers, turned and reminded Don he wanted to discuss Agent Wolf's performance as of late. Her review was coming up and he wanted to give Don some important input before he met with her.

At 10:00 P.M. Tony awoke to his watch alarm. He got up, took his medication as inconspicuously as possible and waited. About ten minutes later he finally heard a solid knock at the door. Tony had been sitting patiently in a chair and sprang to life as another linebacker-sized man opened the door. He was hoping he was free to go back to his hotel. Unfortunately, Tony consumed the words that were typed on a card saying he was staying the night as their guest. Without speaking, the big man gave Tony pajamas and then turned the card over. It let Tony know they would be knocking on his door at 8:30 A.M. tomorrow for breakfast and then his final meeting.

"And after the meeting I can go home?" Tony asked pleadingly.

Without speaking, the man gestured shrugging his shoulders with palms up, giving Tony a definite *I don't' know...I just work here* look. As the door clicked shut Tony yelled, "I need to call my wife and kids!"

"I'm actually being held against my will," Tony said to himself in complete frustration. "This is illegal! I don't deserve this! I did nothing wrong."

What do I do now, he wondered. The answer came to him immediately. *Try to relax and deal with the MAN when he arrives. So far I have yet to see Senior Special Agent Dennis Forman.* From a built up rage he thought about trashing the place in a show of defiance. Logic quickly took control. *I'm in no position to cause such problems*, he thought. Tony desperately wanted to call Jacquelyn. He promised to call her and the kids. He always did so anytime he spent the night away from home.

"What am I going to do?" he asked in an almost silent voice.

He just knew Jacquelyn would read to Sam and Nick extra long awaiting his call. The image of her worrying churned in Tony's stomach. *I promised to call*, he thought dejectedly. That promise wouldn't be kept.

As he stood in the middle of the room, conceding he couldn't speak to Jacquelyn or the kids this evening, he began to tic slightly more than he had since being on his new medicine schedule. However, these tics were so very minor in comparison to his pre-Klonopin days.

I'm sure Jacquelyn's been trying to reach me. I wish I could at least request that they call and let her know I'm okay. Suddenly the question popped into his head. *Am I okay?*

He saw his reflection in the mirror. Tony's face slowly began to take on the characteristics of a man resolute in his purpose. *All right, focus on what I CAN do, not what's out of my control*, he demanded of himself.

Unknown to Tony, Jacquelyn had already received a call. It was from Ryan O'Connor. Earlier in the evening Jacquelyn had tried to contact Tony via email, texting his cell phone and calling the hotel. She verified with the JW Marriot that he was still checked in. She didn't want to upset the kids so she went through their normal evening routine. One thing she did differently, however, was to have the home phone within arm's length and her cell phone in her pocket just in case Tony called during the lengthened bedtime stories. The home phone rang out.

Without waiting for caller ID to appear Jacquelyn quickly picked up on the first ring "Tony?" she answered frantically.

"Jacquelyn, this is Ryan O'Connor with CIT. I hope I'm not disturbing you," he said in a very relaxed yet upbeat tone.

Jacquelyn handed the book to Sam indicating her to continue with Nick.

"I'm sorry, but who am I speaking with?"

"This is Ryan O'Connor, I'm Vice President at CIT and work closely with Audrey Shelton and Tony."

She stepped out into the hallway then made her way downstairs. *What's wrong?*, she thought.

"I'm in D.C and just calling to let you know Tony is involved in a very important meeting and it may be awhile until he's available. I'm calling on Audrey Shelton's behalf so you needn't worry," he said.

"Is Audrey in D.C. too?" Jacquelyn asked.

"No, she was just here recently," he said confidently.

Why are you calling instead of Audrey. I know of you, but I don't really know you. This doesn't make much sense, she thought. So, she asked him point-blank why Audrey Shelton didn't make the call.

"She gave me strict orders, since I'd be out here visiting family that it was up to me to keep you informed if his schedule might interfere with contacting you."

"How did you know that Tony was going to be there? This situation has nothing to do with CIT," stated Jacquelyn.

O'Connor delicately reminded her Tony was in D.C. while on CIT's time when this state of affairs occurred.

"I'm here quite often. You might say I've almost become a beltway native. Since Tony had to clear his trip with Audrey she told me to look after him. As soon as he can, he'll call, but in the meantime please know that I'm looking after him. Get some sleep. I'm sure he'll check in with you tomorrow."

Ryan O'Connor's words rang hallow. For some nagging reason Jacquelyn didn't trust him. She would certainly have preferred to hear from Tony himself. At this point even Audrey's voice would have been better than Ryan O'Connor's. She really only knew Audrey through Tony's stories and quick greetings at occasional company gatherings. But, Ryan O'Connor calling her somehow made her feel uncomfortable. She knew him even less. Tony never spoke much of him that she could recall.

"He sounded very nice and caring," she uttered.

Jacquelyn tried picturing Ryan O'Connor, but couldn't conger up the slightest idea of connecting the voice to his face. She knew his name from Tony, but that was all she could remember at the moment. Right now the only thing she could think to do was to call Audrey. She thought being the CEO of a major corporation that maybe she could possibly pull some strings.

Jacquelyn looked at the time then decided she definitely would only be satisfied to hear Tony's voice. *I'm not going to call the CEO of Tony's company just because he hasn't called yet,* she thought.

She went back upstairs and wrapped it up with Sam and Nick then properly tucked them into their beds with a kiss on each of their foreheads.

Staying up much longer than usual she tried one more time to reach Tony by phone, text, and email. Jacquelyn left a voice message attempting to put Tony at ease saying that she and the kids love him and she can understand how busy he must be. She expressed that she hoped everything was going well. She pressed the numbers two, three then one at the end of her message before completing the call. It was her way of ending the message with a digital tone of *I Love You*. After completing the call she held the phone in her hand imagining Tony's four digit response...*I Love You Too*.

Like a song she couldn't get out of her head, Jacquelyn kept mentally replaying Tony's outgoing cell phone message. Just hearing his voice made her feel that much more secure in this troubled world. However, she desperately wanted to hear his voice live and right now. Her mind was made up. She at least had to try or she'd never forgive herself if something was wrong.

Jacquelyn decided to make the call to Audrey.

"I don't care if she were the Queen of England. I want to know that Tony's okay," she quietly said to herself.

She sat at the family computer and looked up Audrey's home phone number. Jacquelyn pressed the digits on the phone and held her breath hoping that Audrey would pick up.

"Do I call her Audrey or Ms. Shelton? Tony always uses her first name."

In an upbeat extended two-syllable tone Audrey said, "Hello."

"Hi Audrey, this is Tony James's wife, Jacquelyn," she said nervously.

"What a nice surprise to hear from you, Jacquelyn. How are you dear?" she asked politely.

"Not too well actually."

"What's wrong?" Audrey asked in a darkening tone.

"Um, first let me tell you I'm really sorry to call you at home, but I'm concerned about Tony." Jacquelyn started shaky, but then caught her stride. "I appreciate you asking Ryan O'Connor to look out for Tony, but —" Audrey cut her off in a gentle manner.

"Hold on dear. Please slow down. I'm not quite sure what you're talking about," Audrey implored.

Once they were on the same page Audrey decided to lend an ear more than talk. She did tell Jacquelyn that O'Connor was in D.C. She didn't go so far as to confirm or deny that she asked O'Connor to look after Tony. However, given Jacquelyn's urgent tone she knew what she had to do.

"Let me make a few calls Jacquelyn. When I have information I'll call you right back. Are you okay with that?"

"I'm grateful Audrey. It's just not like Tony not to call. I feel like something's wrong."

After ending the call with Jacquelyn, Audrey sat back pondering her options. She had to make a quick decision. Call Ryan O'Connor or Don Williams. After quickly weighing the pros and cons of each she picked up her personal cell phone and placed the call.

Williams was working very late and still at his desk. He let his office phone ring a few times then finally looked at the caller ID name on the display and then picked up.

"Audrey, to what do I owe the pleasure?" he asked robustly.

"This is not a pleasure call Don," she said forcefully.

"What's this about?" he asked in a concerned tone.

"I think you know exactly what this is about."

Audrey didn't get to where she was by not believing that every call Don took on his office phone was recorded.

"Do me a favor and call me back on your personal cell phone immediately," she demanded. "We need to have a private conversation." Audrey ended the call.

Don really wasn't sure why Audrey was calling. He grabbed his personal cell phone, quickly found her name in his encrypted contacts list, and then pressed send. Audrey answered swiftly knowing it was Don.

"What do you think you're doing!?" exclaimed Audrey.

"Will you kindly fill me in on what you're talking about?" Don asked calmly.

"You know exactly why I'm calling!"

"Honestly, Audrey, I have no idea," Don pleaded.

"You mean to tell me that you've had nothing to do with keeping Tony James, my employee, from calling his wife and children?"

Just the fact Don paused briefly gave Audrey her answer. "Remember who you're talking to before you put your foot in that big mouth of yours. I want an honest answer," Audrey demanded.

Don asked meekly, "How did you know about this?"

"It was real hard," she said sarcastically. "Tony's wife just called me worried sick because she hadn't heard from him."

"I can explain," Don said.

Audrey listened to what she considered to be a deficiency of detailed preparation on his part. "You should have known better, Don. Isn't lack of communication what got you into trouble with your first wife," she blistered.

"Hey, let's keep this on a professional level," he scolded.

370

She continued, "Tony and Jacquelyn have a great relationship. They actually think of how each other might feel if they're running late. They do things like call after their plane lands so unnecessary worry doesn't take place."

Don purposely paused to make sure Audrey had gotten most of it out of her system.

Audrey thought the connection had been dropped, "Are you still there Don?"

"As I said, I can explain."

He paused once again to allow Audrey to feel she was in control of the conversation.

"Well, go ahead and do a better job of it this time," Audrey demanded.

"The truth is that isolating him aids us in cultivating the proper atmosphere to obtain information from him."

"So, this is on purpose," Audrey said in a tone more fitting of an adult chastising a child.

"That's correct Audrey," Don said boldly.

"I understand you need to take certain measures to complete your process, but don't you think I should have been the one to call Jacquelyn instead of Ryan O'Connor?"

Don wasn't sure if he had heard her right. He asked her to repeat her question. Once confirmed that he had in fact heard her correctly he said, "What does Ryan O'Connor have to do with this?"

"You tell me, Don," Audrey demanded.

After a healthy give and take they both came to similar uncomfortable conclusions. They weren't on the same chapter or page, but seemingly, reading from the same book. Unfortunately they could only assume all of the possibilities without further evidence. They agreed to tread lightly and pursue this later as a team. Audrey told Don she was uncomfortable with him holding Tony, but she would call Jacquelyn back and put her mind at ease. Unfortunately, for both Don and Audrey, neither one of them were at ease when it came to the subject of Ryan O'Connor's involvement.

Chapter 40

After doing deep breathing exercises Tony changed into the pajamas provided for him then opened the bedside drawer. To his surprise he found a Bible.

Aside from not being able to leave, it really is just like a hotel room, he thought.

Tony bunched the pillows so he was sitting up in bed. He closed his eyes to say a prayer. He knew he must lay his troubles with God. Tony was so tired of trying to be in control. Tony needed to relinquish that to Him. He then opened the Bible to the book of Job. After about forty-five minutes of reading Tony drifted off to sleep. He tossed and turned most of the night and wound up in a deep sleep for only a few hours.

In the morning Tony got up, showered and was ready for the impending knock at the door. His watch alarm went off at 8:00 A.M. reminding him to take his medication.

I'm glad I set that or I would've forgotten, he thought.

He then realized the serendipity of placing extra medication in his pocket at the JW Marriot Hotel.

How did I know I'd need it?

Then at precisely 8:30 A.M. the triple knock on the door arrived. Though he was expecting it, Tony almost jumped out of his skin at the sound. He really didn't think the man meant *exactly* 8:30 A.M. Tony quickly clasped his hands behind his head and sat in the chair, feet up on the table, looking as if he hadn't a care in the world.

"Come on in," shouted Tony.

Of course the new linebacker on duty had already begun to open the door. Reality hit Tony once again that this is certainly not a real hotel.

At breakfast Tony ate alone. He paid close attention to stay away from sugar and caffeinated products. He opted for water rather than take the chance the orange juice wasn't natural and contained lots of sugar. Plain oatmeal was always a safe bet. Bread without sugary jelly would also suffice. Fresh fruit had become a staple in his diet so he filled a small plate. Tony really wasn't hungry due to nerves, but knew it was important to fuel his body to try and keep his sleep-deprived mind sharp. Not surprisingly, as soon as he was finished his escort appeared to take him to his next destination within the cavernous building.

The linebacker-sized man led him to what Tony thought of as a large and very beautifully decorated boardroom. Tony figured the huge mahogany oval table was approximately fifteen feet long. He gauged this on the fact that a racquetball court is twenty feet wide. All the leather chairs looked cushy and were a subdued red color. Then he found what must be the head of the table. That particular chair had a larger back with satin black and red upholstery. Once again, almost without notice, he heard the door click behind him. He knew it had just been locked and didn't even bother to check this time. He looked around some more and noticed the large flat screen television on the wall at what would be the foot end of the table. The American flag stood proudly in one corner along with POW and an MIA flags. Next to them was a picture of the President of the United States.

He figured he was being watched by several cameras that he could never identify. *This room has got to be wired for sound too*, he decided. He reviewed how he'd been treated since arriving back in Washington D.C.

I've been treated like a suspected criminal. My rights as a citizen have been trampled on. The only acts of kindness I can think of have come from Dr. Zander and Agent Wolf. And what do I know about her? My sense tells me she's a little actress...whatever that means, he thought.

In an act of child-like defiance, which came naturally to him, Tony decided to choose the chair where he would sit for his expected meeting. He eased himself into the one at the head of the table.

This ought to tick someone off, he inwardly grinned.

He was so thankful his medication was working so well. However, being under this amount of stress he couldn't help but have an elevated urge to tic. Tony began to employ his cover techniques. Believing this room was under surveillance he hid his tics the best he could. Thanks to his new medication, diet and exercise this seemed to be an easier task than ever.

He figured whoever was making him wait was doing so on purpose. On the outside Tony purposely looked as if he hadn't a care in the world. His insides were that of an industrial washing machine set on the highest agitation cycle. Tony once again clasped his hands behind his head, leaned back and crossed his feet up on the expensive boardroom table. He began to run through his options and decided upon numerous strategies based on need at the time.

"Look at this guy," Forman said to Williams incredulously.

Williams was at his desk and couldn't see the large screen monitor. "What's he up to?"

"He's relaxing, with his feet up, sitting at the head of the table like he owns the joint."

Williams got up and looked at the screen and smiled. "I was wondering how he was going to react to all this. My best guess, and based on his evaluation, is at this point he knows he's being watched and is sending a message," said Williams.

"Oh, and what message would that be?"

"Simple, you've got nothing on me and I'm not afraid of you," Williams said calmly.

"I would think that the way we treated him so far he'd be scared out of his mind!" Forman said loudly.

"Maybe he is and this is just a cover. We've both seen it before," said Williams.

"Yeah, but not to this degree," added Forman.

Director Williams looked at his watch and said, "I think we should get this thing started don't you?"

"Well, it's about time," said Forman in an exasperated tone.

"Are we clear on the plan?" Williams asked Forman staring directly into his eyes.

"Crystal clear," Forman replied ready to go.

"Do you have everyone in place?" Williams asked.

"You know this isn't my first rodeo, Don. By the time we're done we'll know if we have a true patriot with Savant Syndrome or a just a guy that's done the right things under coincidental circumstances."

Dennis Forman, the bulldog of D.C., then turned away from Don and headed for the door. He turned back and asked, "Are you ready to do your part?"

Director Williams kept his feelings about Forman hidden from him and answered, "You know I am."

Chapter 41

As Agent Forman walked to the boardroom where Tony was waiting he placed a few calls. Unknowingly to Forman, Williams also made his own calls. Forman's first was to his surveillance team.

"Dot your "I"s and cross your "T"s. I want everything nailed down to the last detail," Forman directed.

His next call was to Agent Bobby Stark. "You ready?" he asked.

"Yes sir."

Lastly he placed a call to Agent Elizabeth Wolf. "I need you with the surveillance team now," he said in a gruff voice. "You remember the signal if you're needed?"

"Yes," said Agent Wolf.

Satisfied everyone was ready he called Don and verified it was a go.

Tony heard a noise behind him and was surprised to see a graying, yet somehow youthful man, carrying a thick red folder enter through a disguised door he didn't see before.

"Hello Mr. James...I mean Tony," said the friendly voice.

Startled, Tony turned and realized he was finally going to be face-to-face with the person he was here to see. He recognized the voice of Senior Special Agent Dennis Forman. How could he forget? This time he was in no mood to ask him to call him Tony. The sudden impact of the situation created a spike in his urge to tic. Tony tried not to move and didn't say a word. He was beyond angry and having a very tough time holding back from taking a swing at the man. Tony thought the emotion he'd feel would be fear, but after being treated like a criminal he was absolutely furious.

Forman walked over to Tony, who remained seated with legs crossed and feet still on the boardroom table. Holding his right hand out, expecting reciprocation from Tony, he found himself withdrawing it without the obligatory handshake.

"So, not in such a good mood are we?" said Forman in a playful tone.

We?, thought Tony. Tony remained silent. He tried to focus on the agent and got the strange feeling delivered to him...*mercury. What the heck does that mean? Maybe I'm too ticked off and tired that my sensors are on the blink to be able to read this guy properly*, he thought.

"Would you mind taking your feet off the table, please?" Forman asked politely.

Tony thought about it and obliged without a peep since he asked nicely. Forman sat down on the chair to Tony's left. Along with the red folder, he had with him an ancient looking light tan leather briefcase with buckled straps on the front. It appeared to be ready to burst at the seams if not for those straps.

Is all that information about me?, Tony questioned silently.

Tony knew he was being held against his will and knew he had rights. He expected to exercise those rights, but before he did he wanted to hear what Dennis Forman would reveal to him. He decided he wasn't about to say a word without an attorney present.

I did nothing wrong but try to help at the White House, he reminded himself.

"Well Tony, I want to thank you for being a man of your word and coming to the D.C. area to meet with me," said Forman.

Tony wanted to say, *Are you kidding me? You've held me against my will and you'll pay for that!* Instead Tony put on his best poker face and just stared back.

For most of Dennis Forman's adult life he'd been in the bloodiest of combats, infiltrated terrorist groups, negotiated the minefields of the political machine in Washington D.C under the radar and has yet to be intimidated by any person on the planet. Most of all he learned the skills to be a chameleon to survive. He certainly wasn't about to let this untrained civilian try to push his buttons unless he decided that's what the situation called for.

"You can drop the silent treatment Tony. This isn't second grade," Forman said unenthusiastically. He quickly followed up with, "Your bride was called last night. It was explained to her you were in meetings and will call her from the airport later today."

Tony forced himself to remain stoic, but an eye tic slipped out. Forman was pleased to see this. He hit his mark.

Tony felt relief on two fronts. The first was Jacquelyn likely wasn't worrying and secondly he'd be able to call her as a free man later today.

This actually can be over after this meeting, Tony thought.

The effect of knowing this eased Tony's attitude, and thus his stress level considerably. He quickly decided to change tactics with Forman.

"Why all the cloak and dagger stuff?" asked Tony.

"What do you mean?

"You've held me against my will and put me through tests which have nothing to do what-so-ever with the White House tour situation!"

Forman, seeing that Tony needed to get some aggression out said, "This is just standard operating procedure when it comes to the safety of the United States of America."

"Give me a break! First I'm put through an IQ test with completely unrelated bogus questions. Then I'm given a physical exhaustion test as part of a routine physical to see how much I can take. You locked me up for the night. What was that all about!? Not allowing me to speak to my family. All this is standard operating procedure? Give me more credit than that Agent Forman! Oh, and let's not forget the surveillance photos sent to me!"

Forman knew that as long as he let Tony express himself in a quick emotional outburst it would be much easier to get down to business. He looked at it like letting air out of a balloon. Sooner or later there wouldn't be any more air. He expected Tony would shrivel very soon.

"Tony, I don't make the rules, but I do follow them," Forman said leaning back in his chair.

That statement jogged Tony's memory of their phone conversation the day after he'd gotten home from his trip to the convention in D.C. Somewhere in the shadows a memory was trying to climb to the surface. Then it hit him.

He clearly remembered during that call Forman saying, "When we have something important it's necessary to play within the rules."

Tony paused. He stared at Forman, leaned in resting his clasped hands on his thighs and calmly said "I just realized something." This time he paused for effect. "You're not in charge."

Forman just stared back. Tony detected an almost imperceptible shift in Forman's demeanor. Most people wouldn't have noticed, but when Tony's *instincts* were on high alert nothing escaped him. It was as if a bell had rung and the boxing match began with a right hook.

Oh, he didn't like that, thought Tony.

Forman fired back at Tony in a threatening tone. "Son, if you don't cooperate with me there's nowhere else for you to go."

This was exactly what Tony was looking for. In a nanosecond Forman's adjustment went from a bob and weave jab artist to joining the heavyweight division in a boxing match.

Gotcha! Tony exclaimed silently.

On one level Tony was of course controlling his tics. His new medication was working great. On the other hand, he was trying to absorb information about the strange situation he found himself in. At the same time he was trying to figure out Dennis Forman. Finally, he realized the meaning behind what his ability delivered to him regarding Senior Special Agent Dennis Forman...*mercury*. At first he'd been confused and had no time to really clarify that it wasn't the planet.

He's like mercury...the element! I can try to put my thumb on him, but he just squirts out the other side! He'll change his spots in an instant. This is such valuable information. Now that I know the rules I can cope much better. He really should have dealt with me over the phone, thought Tony confidently. Tony sat back with an almost imperceptible subtle grin on his face.

"What's with the smirk?" asked Forman.

Tony wasn't about to reveal what he just found out about Agent Forman so he just slightly shook his head and said, "Nothing."

Forman, now in tune with how Tony's mind works, got the impression that he'd just been made. Given the information in Tony's file Forman knew this was a very good possibility. In his view Tony seemed to relax a little too much. Changing his tone he asked Tony if he'd like some coffee. Tony declined. Forman got up and pressed the speaker button on the space age looking phone in the middle of the conference table and ordered himself a cup. Little did Tony know that this was a signal Forman had pre-arranged. Forman sat back down and the waiter came in to deliver his coffee. Three of the multiple cameras were focused closely on Tony's facial expression. The audio was tuned to pick up any sound that came from him.

Without speaking, the waiter set Forman's coffee in front of him. He stood next to Forman, turned to Tony, then asked, "Nothing for you sir?"

Tony couldn't believe it was happening again! His eyes opened wide and his mouth began to form the beginning of a word. Two of the digital surveillance cameras had already zoomed in on each of Tony's eyes. The cameras were connected to a CIA computer software program ironically built, once again, off a CIT design.

In the surveillance booth one of the technicians spoke into the microphone in a quiet monotone voice telling Agent Stark that Tony's pupils had dilated which indicated surprise and, most importantly, recognition. Tony barely shook his head no, but never took his eyes off of him. As Tony sat looking at the man delivering coffee, he couldn't help but question the odds of this coincidence happening once again...*calculating*. Without knowing it he let out a quiet sound that couldn't be heard by the human ear. He uttered the syllable "cal—" then apparently cleared his throat in the manner of trying to free a tiny popcorn kernel that was stuck.

Forman didn't want to wear an earpiece because he thought it would disrupt his process with Tony. Set up in advance, Agent Stark placed cream and sugar on the table to convey messages to Forman. Cream provided Forman the signal that the optics software confirms Tony's reaction to Agent Stark. It also picked up audio, but wasn't discernible. The sugar represented a verbal hit.

The waiter, Agent Stark said, "I wasn't sure if you wanted sugar this time sir." This informed Forman they weren't sure what they had picked up verbally.

"No, thank you," said Forman without looking up.

The waiter left the conference room the same way he came in. Tony's eyes followed him until he was out of sight.

"You look like you saw a ghost Tony," said Forman in an almost playful tone.

I didn't see one, but I think I've been revisited by one, Tony thought. Realizing his stare he then snapped his head back to Forman.

"Something on your mind Tony?" asked Forman.

Without missing a beat Tony replied, "No, why?"

"It just seemed like you were somewhere else, that's all."

Tony engaged in conversation while trying to figure out what was happening to him. *Is it possible I'm under so much stress that I'm misreading this?* Now that Forman confirmed an important piece of information he was ready for his next step.

Director Don Williams, sitting on his cushy chair directly across from the large flat screen, watched this play out from his office. "I'll be…he did it again!"

He contacted the lead surveillance technician. "What are the optics and verbal results?" The technician confirmed what Williams already suspected.

Back in the conference room Forman opened the red folder and pulled out numerous photos of different men and dealt them to Tony as if they were playing cards.

"Tell me how you know these men," Forman quietly demanded.

Tony looked at each photo and said, "I don't recall ever seeing any of these guys in my entire life."

Tony made sure he didn't create an absolute out of his answer. He called upon a memory from a college pre-law course he had taken. Tony remembered that using the word "recall" provided a legal reprieve to reverse his answer if needed later. Tony also knew he wasn't on trial, but he wasn't taking any chances. He really hadn't seen any of the men, but he was going to make sure that the recorded transcript didn't box him in just in case.

"You've never seen any of these men before that day at the White House?"

"Not that I can recall."

"You're not in a courtroom Tony. We're just talking here," said Forman a little too nicely.

I may not be on trial, but for all I know this entire recording could be used against me, Tony thought.

"Look Agent Forman, I'm cooperating without the benefit of an attorney present. I don't need to do this. But, I believe you and I want the same thing."

"Oh, and what would that be?" Forman asked in a cocky tone.

"A free and safe nation," Tony said with a dart.

Forman didn't expect that answer, but recovered quickly. "Good, because as you know that's exactly why we're here today," Forman answered in a cold manner.

He spun one more picture toward Tony. "Do you recognize this person?"

That's Mr. Twenty-two at the White House. Finally we're moving along, Tony thought. "Yes, I believe I might recognize him," replied Tony.

"And, where do you know him from?"

"I don't know him. I answered your question that I think I recognize him," said Tony staring directly at Forman.

After what he's been through this kid really does keep his wits about him, thought Forman.

Next Forman spun another picture toward Tony. It was of the man with the scar in the airport before the trip to Punta Cana. Again, Forman had the same questions. Tony was taken by surprise, but again Tony had the same answers.

Stepping up the pressure Forman decided to escalate the process. The next picture was the inside of Audrey Shelton's office. Forman hadn't slipped it over to him just yet.

"Now don't freak out, but I need you to identify the two people in this picture," Forman said slowly.

He gently set the picture down directly in front of Tony this time. Tony knew that when someone told you not to do something that it's usually what they want from you. In this case he had to hide his feelings like never before.

Holy crap! That's Audrey and me in her office, he screamed silently in his head. However, his answer came out as calm as can be.

"It appears to be Audrey Shelton and myself."

"And?" prompted Forman.

"Are you just using a conjunction as a question or do you have some specificity to go along with it," Tony said in a habit to deflect questions.

"What do you think about this picture?" Forman said losing patience and tapping his right index finger on the photo.

That's another stupid wide open question. Does he not get the message? "The color is much better than my printer at home. I like the way the sunlight provides unique elongated shadow shapes. It must be late in the day. It also —" Forman cut him off.

"Stop, stop, stop, what are you doing?" asked Forman intolerantly.

"Ask a stupid question and get a stupid answer," Tony said trying to pierce the tough skin of Senior Special Agent Dennis Forman.

Tony knew better than to poke a hornet's nest, but he wasn't going to deviate from answering anything that wasn't a specific question.

"All I'm looking for is your reaction to this photo," Forman said slowly and deliberately.

Staying within his playbook Tony said flatly, "My reaction is this appears to be a photo of Audrey Shelton and me in her office."

In frustration Forman dealt four more sequential pictures of Tony looking directly at the mirror from which the photos had been taken off the digital video recording.

"Listen to me closely Tony. Why are you looking directly into the lens of the camera in these photos?"

Finally a question I can answer! But I'm not going to. "I don't recall doing any such thing. I never saw a camera lens," he quipped.

Forman sat back in his chair and placed his hand on his chin then rubbed his stubble with the back of his fingernails. Tony thought, *Who does this guy think he is, The Godfather?* What Tony didn't know was that this was another silent signal.

I suppose he's now going to make me an offer I can't refuse, thought Tony not so amusingly. Tony didn't realize the "Godfather" scratch was the signal for Forman's departure and Agent Wolf's entrance.

Director Williams, still sitting by himself in his office, actually began to laugh at that last exchange. He felt the urge to call someone in to watch it with him. Williams was enjoying seeing someone hold his own with The Bulldog. He can't remember the last time that happened. Don's demeanor then quickly changed. Director Williams began to realize that if Tony James can hold his own with the most senior and experienced agent then he could become more than an extraordinarily successful asset. That meant more funding for SSD. A lot more.

Before Forman got to his next question the door to the conference room began to open. They both looked and the distinct red hair of Agent Wolf appeared in the doorway.

That's my luggage she's wheeling behind her, Tony shouted silently.

She quietly walked over to place the luggage against the wall then strolled toward them and whispered into Agent Forman's right ear. Forman's face quickly changed to a surprised look.

He turned back to Tony and said, "I have to attend to a pressing matter so Agent Wolf will keep you company in my absence." He directed his agent to take his seat. She did so while placing her briefcase on the floor next to her.

Tony found it unlikely that Agent Forman was the type of individual to leave his file and briefcase open if it weren't on purpose. However, Tony was completely happy to see his luggage. It represented the finish line for him. It's also a classic way to make Tony a little more receptive.

The old good cop bad cop routine with a twist. Nice touch, he thought.

Forman exited the door in which Agent Wolf had entered. She smiled and said hello. Tony wasn't sure he was completely happy with this situation. On the one hand he preferred to speak with Agent Wolf than Agent Forman. After all, she did give him a heads up prior entering this building. He still wasn't sure what she meant, but it was appreciated none-the-less. On the other hand Tony knew he was no longer dealing with the decision maker. His emotions were mixed.

"So, Agent Wolf, are you here to just have a seat or are you going to ask me more stupid questions like your boss?" Tony bluntly asked.

"Neither, and please call me Elizabeth."

"Then you must be here to ask the smart questions, right?"

"We can't pull a fast one on you can we," she said dripping with sarcasm.

I like this much better...for now, thought Tony.

"So, what have you been looking at?" Elizabeth asked craning her neck to see the pictures.

"Just some photos," said Tony.

"Who's that?"

"That's the CEO of the company that I work for. Why do you ask?"

"Just curious I guess."

As instructed she said, "I won't ask any more questions if you don't want me to Tony. Sorry."

Director Williams held his breathe as he watched and waited to see if Agent Wolf would be allowed to proceed.

Tony strongly believed Elizabeth was a good little actress, but if she was acting there's no way she would lay that out there if she didn't mean it. *Would she really let me just sit until Forman returned?*

After considerable thought Tony replied, "No, that's okay. I don't mind. It's just that I'm tired and want to go home. Thanks for bringing my luggage."

Williams exhaled.

Elizabeth turned her head to the luggage then back to Tony. "It's the least I could do," she said in a sincere tone.

Forman's original plan was to monitor Agent Wolf and Tony from the surveillance room, but changed his mind at the last moment. He wouldn't admit it, but Forman felt he just might begin to tell Elizabeth what to ask rather than trusting her. That's if she even got that far. He had his doubts about her experience. There was something else about her that just didn't sit well with him. So, instead he went directly to Don's office.

After placing his thumb on the pad he knocked on the door and announced himself. Williams looked at the video monitor on the side of the door then opened it with the small remote. No surprise to Forman, the large screen TV showed multiple views of Agent Wolf and Tony James in the conference room.

"What are you doing here? The plan was to have you positioned in the surveillance room if you tagged out," Williams declared.

"I want to view it with you," said Forman. "If we have to make some quick changes we should be eyeball-to-eyeball with each other," said Forman. As he sat down he asked, "Did I miss anything?"

"You mean other than your lunch being handed to you?" Williams said with a smile. "Agent Wolf is over the first hurdle," he added.

They both sat with their eyes glued to the TV. Williams decided to wait for another time to needle him further regarding his bout with an untrained civilian closing to a draw.

Back in the conference room Agent Wolf continued, "So, what are all the rest of these photos?"

"These are of some guy I have no clue about." Tony had uncharacteristically dropped his guard without knowing.

"And this guy I think we both recognize", Elizabeth said picking up the White House tour photo of Mr. Twenty-two. "Tony, have you taken a real close look at these photos?"

"Not really. Why?"

"Because, it looks to me, there's something familiar between these two," she said tapping on them.

Tony laid the photos of the two men on the table in front of him and cleared away the others. After looking at them like this there seemed to be a similarity between them.

"You know Elizabeth, you're right. They could be distant cousins or something now that I look at them side by side."

Agent Wolf sat back once again, changing the subject on purpose, appearing to keep Tony off balance. She chose her words carefully knowing full well every move and sound made was not only being recorded, but evaluated instantaneously.

Seemingly to imply that she was speaking of the similarities of the photos she said, "Don't you hate it when things aren't what they seem?"

Now it was Tony's turn to sit back. *She's not stupid. Is she part of this or is she trying to send me a message? I have to find out. If she stops me then I'll know*, he thought. He leaned forward looking intensely at the photos in front of him.

As he did this he said, "That's the second time you've said that to me," he blurted, slowly tuning his head to look at her reaction.

Skilled in deception, Agent Wolf casually said, "You must have me mistaken with someone else."

"No, I distinctly remember as we arrived at this building —" she cut him off.

"Let's not quibble over something like this Tony. I'm sure you want to get home so the more time we waste over what someone else said to you would just be a time sink-hole," she said peering directly through his eyes into the back of his head.

Well, I got an answer. She's on the inside, outside or both sides of whatever this whole thing is about. She might be one of the good guys, but I just can't take the chance and completely trust her. This is clear as mud, he decided. My watch alarm went off ten minutes ago and my next medication dose was due. I'm in need of a little tic relief, he thought.

"I'm hungry Elizabeth. What's the chance of getting something to eat?" he asked.

"No problem. I'll have some lunch brought in."

"That'd be great, thanks," said Tony.

She got up to use the same phone Dennis Forman had used on the conference room table. As she did this Tony picked up a photo with his left hand and held it up closer to his face. He had already secured his tablet from his pocket hoping it was without notice. He figured the chance of that was slim, but he was going to stick to his code. With a cough he slipped the tic reducing pill into his mouth. After he picked up another photo he raised them up as if to get another look from a higher angle. As he did this he was able to swallow without the small tablet getting stuck in his throat.

Even if this room is as wired as I think, not taking my medication is worse than them seeing me take it.

"Food's on its way," she declared.

"Thanks Elizabeth," said Tony as he got up to stretch his legs and disguise a few tics.

"Find anything interesting?"

"About what," he asked.

"With the photos you were looking at," she nodded.

"Only that when you put them side-by-side it's just as you said, they look similar."

"I think *you* said that Tony," she corrected.

Good, now we can get tied up in knots about who said what, Tony smiled on the inside.

After about fifteen minutes of Tony turning each subject on its head, Agent Wolf was ready to burst, but kept a calm exterior. She had read enough of Tony's file to know his quick wit was a great asset to him. As a Federal Agent trained in this area she'd never gotten to the point of such high frustration. Fortunately, the food arrived. This time it wasn't delivered by Agent Stark. Only one lunch was brought in and Agent Wolf stayed seated in her chair.

Before she could say anything Tony said, "I want to ask you a question Elizabeth."

"Ask away, but how about we make this a little more interesting. You ask a question then I ask a question," she added using a reciprocating motion with her arms. "We'll take turns. Is that fair Tony?"

Of course it's not fair because you guys are holding me against my will, he thought. Tony then jumped right in.

"Sure, why were you pretending to be a tour guide at the White House?"

"Great start. I was deployed on assignment to be a part of an assessment operation."

"What was it you were —", she cut him off.

"My turn, remember?"

In Director Williams' office Don turned to Dennis Forman and said, "Well I'll be."

"What?" Forman asked.

"Looks like you may have just been replaced. She's doing great! Let's see where she takes this before we go to the next step. It may not be needed. *You* may not be needed," Williams needled.

"Yeah, yeah," said Forman in a sardonic tone. "I'm ordering a late lunch. You want anything?"

"Not right now," answered Williams.

Back in the boardroom Elizabeth asked, "How did you know to turn this guy in?" as she pointed to the picture of Mr. Twenty-two.

"I'm sure the answer's in the thick file in front of you," Tony said with a head nod. He continued, "It was an absolutely beautiful day and he was wearing a long raincoat."

Agent Wolf began to ask a follow-up question and this time Tony cut her off. "What were you assessing during your assignment?"

She paused and thought about the ramifications of telling Tony the truth. Elizabeth could easily just lie and move on, but that might create problems with her plan well down the road. On the other hand she could cut right to the meat of what she wanted to know. After a pause she decided to ride the fence.

"I was asked to play the part of tour guide in an effort to flush out a POI."

"A what?" he asked.

"Sorry, that's short for a Person of Interest." She wasn't lying, but she also didn't tell him that he was the POI.

"So, he was wearing a nice London Fog overcoat. Why be paranoid about it?" she asked.

"It wasn't just the raincoat. There was something about him that just didn't feel right so I reported it like we've been told by the government since the 9/11 attacks. Was I wrong in doing that or did they change the policy?"

"Hey, that was an extra question," she said with a smile. "Rules are rules. "My answer to both of those questions is *no*. Now I get two questions in a row", she declared with an effortless smile.

Tony had become even more at ease. He was actually enjoying this back and forth game-like banter especially since his medication was working so well.

"What do you mean that there was something about him that just didn't feel right?"

Oh no, I can't believe I said it like that, thought Tony.

He recovered quickly. "You saw the picture. He looks kind of creepy. I for one was *not* going to take any chances just in case he meant anyone harm. As the saying goes, better safe than sorry."

"Was there anyone else in there that didn't feel right to you?"

I guess that's a logical question, but a wasted one. "I don't understand the question. I'd ask you to clarify, but I wouldn't want to break the rules," he said with eyebrows raised.

Elizabeth replied, "Of all the people on the tour you pinpointed the only real threat. There was another person in there that, let's just say…was a major part of the assessment."

"I didn't hear a question yet," said Tony.

"Why just him?" she point-blank asked.

Tony thought, *Because I seem to have this capability to pick something up from people like this. Then I just can't seem to help myself from doing something about it.*

He calmly answered, "He just seemed…out of place."

It didn't take Tony long to think he'd finally pieced things together. He was so concerned about keeping his ability a secret that he never thought he might be looked upon as a co-conspirator.

They're trying to figure out if I just got lucky or did I know something that no one else could possibly have information about unless involved. That must be why I'm tagged as a person of interest, he realized.

"Elizabeth, I can assure you that I had no previous knowledge about this man's intentions. I'd never set eyes on him before. I'd never communicated with him that day or any day prior, or since. As I've said before I'm just a husband, dad and a computer geek. I was in D.C. that day for the convention. Terrorism is not on my resume."

"Tony, we know you don't have ties to any terrorist group. Why do you think we didn't pick you up immediately?"

No longer was Tony thinking about the back-and-forth question game. He jumped in and asked, "Are you serious?"

"When it comes to national security I'm always serious." We've had our eyes on you for some time now," Elizabeth said in an authoritative tone.

Tony was almost dumbstruck. With his jaw just about on the floor he asked, "Say that again?"

Back in Director Williams' office, "Please tell me I didn't hear what I think she just said," Forman implored elevating his voice. They both looked at each other with complete surprise.

"Where'd that come from? Stop her before we lose him!" Williams shouted to Forman. Agent Forman raised his left arm and spoke into his wrist transmitter.

"Agent Wolf, back off NOW!" Forman said.

Tony frowned and asked, "What do you mean…had your eyes on me for some time?"

She paused before answering. Tony didn't know if it was for effect or she was searching for the proper words. He looked at Agent Wolf and repeated his question in a more demanding tone. It appeared to him that she wasn't even listening to him.

Earlier, using Tony's lunch delivery as a distraction, Agent Wolf had removed an exact White House tour duplicate photo of Mr. Twenty-two from her briefcase. She had previously creased the bottom right corner of the photo for ease of recognition. Agent Wolf effortlessly slid it under the other pictures and documents making sure the bent corner was in her sight. It hadn't moved since.

As she handed it to Tony, straightening the corner with her index finger and thumb without notice, she said, "We keep tabs on a lot of people Tony. Even quiet upstanding citizens just like you."

Tony's mind was focused on getting an answer. Then, recognition in Tony's eyes signaled to Elizabeth that he saw her note. In very small font it read:

Your ability is known. I'm here to help you. Say out loud that you have already seen this photo and hand it back to me face down.

Tony stared at the note then flipped it over and slid it back to her following the instructions. As he sat frozen in his seat, completely puzzled, the door to the conference room began to open. Agent Wolf quickly removed and hid the self-adhesive note in one swift move as all eyes were on the door.

Chapter 42

Forman had just positioned himself in the surveillance room waiting for Director Williams to make his entrance. What he was seeing alarmed him. He spoke into his wrist transmitter "Don, what in God's name is going on?"

Williams was slowly strolling, taking his time pacing, in the hallway out of sight from the conference room when he heard Forman barking in his ear.

He stopped and calmly asked, "What are you talking about?"

"That VP from CIT, Ryan O'Connor, just walked into the room!"

Williams continued his leisurely stroll. "What's he's doing here?"

Forman was about to take action and bark orders into the microphone when Williams said, "Wait, let's see what this is all about."

Forman, in disbelief, could only muster a simple, "It's your hide, not mine. How well do you know this guy?"

Williams didn't reply.

"Ryan! Am I glad to see you!" said Tony as he stood up. Tony couldn't believe his eyes.

"Hi Tony, is everything going okay?" O'Connor asked in a concerned tone.

"Is everything okay?" Tony repeated in disbelief. "What's going on here," Tony demanded looking back to Elizabeth.

Agent Wolf was totally taken by surprise. Ryan O'Connor was the last person she thought she'd see, especially in this building.

"Excuse me sir, but this is for authorized personnel only," she said extending her credentials as she popped up out of her chair. Agent Wolf stepped in front of Tony as if she were protecting him from harm forcing Tony to fall back into his seat.

With his arms and palms motioning in a calming manner O'Connor said, "No need to be alarmed."

He began to reach into his left inside blazer pocket, but was startled at the flood of visual and verbal warnings from Agent Wolf.

As quick as a cat Elizabeth trained her weapon on O'Connor as she shouted, "Freeze!"

O'Connor froze.

"Very slowly place both hands and forehead on the table surface!"

"But I was just —" she cut him off.

As quickly as Tony has seen anyone move she had Ryan O'Connor's hands zip-tied behind him as he lay bent over on the conference room table, feet still flat on the floor.

"But I was just getting —" Agent wolf silenced O'Connor.

Tony saw Ryan O'Connor as the only possible sign of anyone knowing where he was. On the one hand he was excited about this. But, on the other, he couldn't quite process how he knew or even gained entrance to this secure building. And then again there was agent Wolf's reaction. Tony sat frozen in his chair digging his fingers into the fine leather. He knew he couldn't do anything. The shear intense overload of the situation created a vacuum with, to his surprise, not the slightest urge to tic.

"Don! Get in there now!" He's an intruder!" Forman demanded.

As he entered the conference room, Williams evaluated the situation. He kept to his training and said nothing to O'Connor.

"Agent Wolf, detain him in 1R. We'll deal with him later," he ordered.

Tony turned his attention to this new person in the room. The feeling he got from him was *angler*.

"Agent Wolf, I want you, and only you, to secure him properly."

"Yes sir," she replied quickly.

Yes sir? She obliged without as much as a peep. This must be the MAN, Tony thought.

Once Agent Wolf and Ryan O'Connor exited the conference room Williams turned to Tony.

"Mr. James my name is Don Williams. I'm the Director of a division of Homeland Security and the reason you're here. Each person you've met during your time spent with us ultimately reports to me."

They cordially shook hands as Williams was now the third person to sit next to Tony. *That's a pretty vague title*, Tony thought.

"I'm very sorry you've been put through this ordeal," Williams said.

Tony quipped, "Do you mean what just happened or that fact that I'm being held captive?"

"I'd say both actually," replied Williams.

Tony didn't expect an honest answer from this guy. *I wonder what "angler" means*, thought Tony.

Out in the hallway Elizabeth, standing behind her zip-cuffed prisoner, had her weapon trained on his head. The door clicked shut behind them and she pointed her gun to the floor sliding her right index finger along-side and above the trigger.

"What are you doing here!?" she exclaimed in a hushed tone.

O'Connor turned around and said, "I received a call from Don to make that entrance. He knew I was in town." O'Connor then added "You did a great job in there."

"But, I don't understand," said Agent Wolf.

"This was unexpected for me as well. He said he would explain at another time. I told him it wasn't necessary. That's all I know."

She quietly said into O'Connor's ear, "Do you think he suspects?"

Returning the favor he said, "Not a chance. Even with all his resources no one has a clue that you're my daughter. Director Williams told me to give you something. Cut me loose will you?"

"I can't do that. To be safe, not until you're out of the building."

"Then reach into my front jacket pocket and take the envelope"

Elizabeth read the written instructions to personally walk Ryan O'Connor out the front door. Acting like a typical parent he said, "You better confirm that with him."

She tucked the envelope into her back pocket and did so immediately.

Chapter 43

In more of a statement than a question Williams said to Tony, "How about you and I get down to business?"

"That'd be a nice change of pace."

Williams was up-front about wearing a communication device. He held up his right index finger to Tony, turned his head slightly and spoke into his wrist microphone. "Confirmed," he said to Agent Wolf.

"I'm sorry Tony, but I don't have the luxury of taking this thing off since I run the show."

Tony looked at him with surprise and said, "I understand."

Holding up the photo of Mr. Twenty-two Williams asked, "Please tell me how you pegged this man to be a threat."

"I already covered that with Agents Forman and Wolf."

"Yes, but you didn't cover it with me," replied Williams. Then he followed up with, "Do you really expect me to let you sit there and tell me you made a hunch based on a raincoat?"

"Yes."

Williams pulled out a remote control and brought the large screen television to life. The video began with an odd upward angle of Dr. Dillon explaining what Tourette Syndrome is in a calm and very straight forward manner. Tony sat straight up and glanced at this mystery man sitting next to him then back to the screen. Williams paused the recording showing Dr. Dillon frozen in mid-sentence.

Forman, running the surveillance room, previously thought this was the perfect way to get Tony to talk. He took delight in the fact that Williams completely turned the tables and Tony was unquestionably taken by surprise. He sat back and gave a chuckle.

"That'll teach you to play games," he said mumbling. "You have no idea who you're dealing with kid."

"I can see you're a little unsettled Tony," said Williams giving him an opening.

Tony didn't bite and remained silent. Williams didn't wait long. He nonchalantly lifted his right arm while looking at Tony, pointed the remote at the screen and once again pressed play. Dr. Dillon completed her statement and then the venue changed. Although now, viewing from a ceiling angle, Tony recognized the airport gate area in Portland immediately. A slow motion montage of him pegging the man with the scar ran over and over. Once again Don paused the recording.

"Have you anything to say now Tony?"

Again he remained silent. Next up was the airport executive lounge. After that it was Tony in the interrogation room from behind the two-way mirror within this very building. This showed, in slow motion no less, Tony following Agent Stark's precise position as he walked across the room behind the mirrored glass. Tony put his head into his hands not wanting to see anymore.

I didn't know I could do that, he thought.

"Are you ready to talk to me?"

Tony slowly rubbed his eyes covering a few tics then decided to look straight at the TV screen. Williams didn't hesitate. Next up was the video taken from the White House surveillance cameras as Tony waited for the tour. It clearly showed him keeping an eye on Mr. Twenty-two while pretending to be looking around. There was a close up of Tony inside while the introductory video began playing. The surveillance camera picked up a compound facial tic and very clear audio of him clearing of his throat three times. He watched his eyes dart back and forth from Mr. Twenty-two and the tour video screen. Multiple facial tics were visible and repeated in succession. The audio had been enhanced for the throat clearing tics. It seemed as if the sound was coming from everywhere in the room. This, of course, was by design.

Williams pressed pause once again. "Do I really need to go any further Tony? These are just a few of the highlights. We have so much audio and video on you we should really order popcorn."

Tony hesitated.

"Here, let me skip to the next one we have in slow motion." He began to raise his arm and Tony finally stopped him.

"Enough already," Tony said in a descending submissive tone.

Williams put the remote down on the conference room table in front of Tony as a goodwill gesture. Tony picked it up and pressed stop. The screen turned bright blue. He couldn't bear to watch or hear anymore. The last thing he wanted to see was the possibility of them having video of him releasing major tics in a bathroom somewhere.

"I know I'm in no position to ask, but I'm going to just in case you have a heart."

Williams was intrigued, "Ask away Tony."

"We'll have an in depth conversation and I'll answer everything to the best of my knowledge on one condition."

"Let me guess. You want to make a phone call," surmised Williams.

"That's right."

Forman, still sitting and watching from the surveillance room said, "Oh, give me a break. You're in no position to be laying down conditions."

Williams replied, "Tony, in all my years in this business I've never allowed a person of interest, especially in your position, to have contact with anyone on the outside until I'm done with my investigation."

Tony dropped his head into his hands for dual purposes. He then looked up at this person who said he's the big shot around here.

"Well then I guess we have nothing to talk about," Tony said defiantly and without hesitation.

He was bluffing of course. He couldn't stand this much longer. In the forefront of his thoughts was the fact that his luggage was sitting just a few feet from him. More importantly his medication was in his briefcase if they kept him one more day.

"Tony, believe it or not, I'm not the bad guy here. You don't have the total picture," Williams said emphatically.

Tony looked at him in utter disbelief.

"I know you haven't been able to contact your family and I want to rectify that," said Williams. "If you answer just one question with a simple yes or no then you may call your bride."

Bride...these people know way too much about me to continue to sidestep this whole thing, Tony realized. "May I ask you two questions before you do?" asked Tony.

"Sure, go right ahead," said Williams.

"Are you really part of the government?"

"Yes," Williams emphatically replied.

"Specifically, which part? Homeland Security, FBI, CIA?"

"That's really three questions, but the answer is yes on all counts," Williams said very forthrightly.

Williams could see Tony's eyes widen. Forman began to laugh while he watched this unfold in front of him as he sat in the surveillance room.

"Don, may I ask you a favor?" Tony asked politely.

"That depends on the favor," he replied.

He leaned in and said, "Will you tell that jerk, Agent Forman, to leave while we have our conversation?"

"But he's not even here," Williams said in a slightly surprised tone as he looked around the conference room.

"Oh, he's here all right. I can feel his presence," declared Tony.

This time Williams' eyes widened. This was the first small confirmation Tony had allowed. Williams couldn't help the slight upward curve to his mouth.

"How does he do that!?" shouted Forman. He then pressed his transmitter and told Don to put the hammer down. He had enough of Mr. Tony James.

Williams looked directly into Tony's eyes and thought, *No need to ask my question. It's been answered.* Then he said, "Agent Forman, I'm taking Mr. James to my office to continue our conversation in private so he can make a phone call."

Williams turned to Tony and said, "Grab your luggage and you can call from my office. We'll continue our conversation from there."

Chapter 44

Once in Williams' office he said, "Please make the call to your wife a quick one and put it on speaker."

Tony was thankful and used his own cell phone to call Jacquelyn. She answered by saying, "Tony! Oh thank God!"

"Jacquelyn, I'm sorry I didn't call you earlier, but these meetings are real boogers," he said hoping she'd catch his terminology.

Tony knew he couldn't use that word twice in one conversation. As a matter of fact, it probably sounded pretty juvenile to hear a grown man describe a meeting in Washington, D.C. this way. Tony didn't care. He hoped Jacquelyn would pick up on the SOS code.

"When are you going to be home?" Jacquelyn quickly asked.

Tony thought she had missed his message based on her reaction. "Jacquelyn, either my phone or yours broke up a little bit. Did you hear what I said?"

Williams was sitting across from Tony and lifted his right hand and used his index finger in a rotating manner telling him to wrap it up.

"I'll call you when I'm free. I love you."

"I love you too, but —" said Jacquelyn.

Tony had ended the call. Jacquelyn, taken by the sheer speed of the abrupt conversation, just looked at her phone in disbelief.

Tony turned his phone off as instructed and handed it to Williams. After checking that it was indeed off, Williams handed it back to Tony and watched him place it back into his briefcase. As Tony did so all he could think was, *Did Jacquelyn get the message?*

Williams and Tony settled in sitting across from one another in the conference area of his office.

"Before we begin, Tony, I need you to look this over and place your signature at the bottom, then date it right here."

It was the same form Audrey had signed when she met with Williams recently. Tony had the usual questions and reasons for not signing anything without an attorney approving it first.

Williams said, "Just read it. Then determine if you'll sign it."

Upon Tony's review it appeared to be a very straightforward and simple document. "This is just a basic non-disclosure agreement," said Tony.

"That's all it is...an NDA. If you don't sign it I can't provide you with information that's deemed classified," said Williams.

Against his logic, but incredibly intrigued, Tony signed and dated the one page document and handed it back to him.

"Tony —" Williams began before being cut off.

"Aren't you forgetting something Don?"

He gave Tony a quizzical look.

"Do you have another blank one of those forms?"

"Of course I do," replied Don not knowing where this was going.

"May I have one please?" Tony asked.

Williams handed it to him. Tony used the pen and scratched out two words on it, wrote something and turned it back to Williams.

"Please initial here and here, then sign and date it at the bottom," demanded Tony.

"Are you kidding me?" Williams said in an astonished tone.

"Why should you and the government be the only ones protected by an NDA? I think it's only fair we're on a level playing field," said Tony.

"It's the same document just in reverse," he said.

Williams had never run across this before in all his years working for Uncle Sam. He knew he would give up the ability to use his recording of this meeting and more. However he deduced that bringing Tony up to speed was the right step. Williams decided to comply to move things along. Tony reviewed it, folded it and placed it in his back pocket.

415

"Do you always think ahead like this, Tony?" Williams inquired.

"Only when I'm awake," he quipped.

"You and I are going to get along just fine," Williams said with a genuine smile.

"So what's so classified that we need a document to allow us to talk?" asked Tony.

At this point Williams usually got up and gave his grand speech about patriotism and the opportunity to serve. His own instincts told him to forgo the norm and get to the heart of the matter.

"Tony, we know you have a special capability," Williams said plainly. "However, we're not one hundred percent sure to what extent." Out of habit he got up and began to walk and talk. "Tony, I'm the Director of the Savant Syndrome Division, or SSD, for the CIA."

After listening to Director Williams talk and explain for twenty minutes straight Tony finally decided to pipe up. "So, in a nutshell, you recruit people who you think have special talents and use them to protect the interests of our country."

"No, Tony, but you're close. My division doesn't deal strictly in talent, although that's a bonus. We deal with special abilities. On paper there's not a big difference. I'll give you that it's a fine line. However, in real world application there's a tremendous differentiation," said Williams. "The wash-out rate is incredibly high."

"Well, no wonder. If you treat every potential candidate like you've treated me then why would anyone want to associate, much less work with you," Tony said emphatically.

"We put a lot of thought into how we proceed with each individual. In your case we tested and re-tested what we think is a person who has a special ability to automatically, and to a high degree of accuracy, do a threat assessment without the need for any external prompting."

Tony was surprised, but not stunned. "So you basically kidnapped me?"

"All those tests you took in this building provided us the needed feedback on how best to react to what you do instinctively. Without it we'd be at such a disadvantage. We had to push you out of your comfort zone," explained Williams.

"So, are you saying you were trying to find my weak spot to deal with me?"

"Exactly, and it worked. You're here aren't you?"

Tony didn't have to think about this very long. He asked, "Why not just be up front about it. It didn't take a brain surgeon to know what each test was about."

"Tony, we didn't know until all the tests were complete and evaluated how best to deal with you."

"And what, may I ask, is the best way to deal with me in this situation?"

"Please keep in mind we've never come across anyone like you before. The answer to your question is to deprive you of your normal personal security system and replace it with a fragile default. Someone with whom you think you can trust. Enter Agent Wolf. We know she could never take the place of your wife's support, but removing the possibility of talking with her allowed you to, in a most fragile and artificial way, hang on to the thought that she was in your corner fighting for you."

"Are you telling me that what she said to me before we entered this building was planned to give me some sort of confidence in her?"

Williams' face contorted slightly. In a somewhat puzzled tone he asked, "What did she say to you?"

Tony's radar was still on high alert. *He doesn't know,* Tony thought. "You tell me, Mr. CIA," replied Tony. "You seem to have all the answers when it comes to dealing with me."

"I have no idea what she said to you, but it's irrelevant. You, on a very fragile level, thought you had one person you could count on, if only by a thread," said Williams.

Tony thought about it and decided he was basically right. He never really trusted Agent Wolf, but she was the best choice out of all bad ones. *There's something still unsettling about her though,* he thought.

"We knew from our intelligence reports we couldn't walk onto your turf and just talk with you. We also knew we had to come at you from various directions by way of home field advantage. Ultimately we knew we had to rig the rules just to get to the point of conversing freely, as we are right now," explained Williams.

Tony thought about this and once again decided Williams was most likely correct. "Okay, let's say you're right on all counts. How on earth do you plan on treating the next candidate?"

Tony had finally touched the edges of what Williams' vision is for this clandestine division of extraordinary misfits. "You're the key to that, Tony," he declared.

"How could I possibly be the key to a world I know nothing about?"

Without answering his question Williams required one more test result. "Tony, do you mind if I bring two individuals in here? These people won't say a word and would only stay for a minute or so then leave," said Williams.

"Why?" asked Tony.

"I just need to confirm a final point. You don't have to say anything if you don't want to," Williams added.

"I've come this far," Tony said in an exhausted tone. He gave the go ahead.

Williams pressed the intercom on his desk phone and said, "Send them in at the same time."

Williams walked over to the door then began opening it after checking the small video screen. He asked Tony to change seats so he was now facing the door. Tony was more nervous than ever and let out a couple of small tics. Rolling through the doorway was the first of two large cylindrical metal tubes. Each tube was identical to the other. To Tony they both looked like shiny adult-sized torpedo coffins. There was no way to see or hear anything that may or may not be inside. Williams confirmed they were soundproof. He moved them so they were side-by-side.

Very quickly, after the initial visual stimulation wore off, Tony focused on the cylinder to his left. He couldn't believe what was uniquely delivered to him. Tony then focused on the one to the right. He actually stood up and quickly sat back down. This certainly didn't go unnoticed by Williams. Already satisfied, Williams maneuvered the objects back into a single file and moved them out through the doorway. He shut the door and the flat screen TV came on showing the tubes just outside the door.

Williams went over to his phone and said, "Thank you." There was no return voice as he turned his gaze upon Tony.

"Tony, will you please write down whatever you wish regarding the contents of the cylinders on the paper in front of you?" asked Williams.

Tony did so.

"Will you please reveal to me what you wrote?"

Tony held up the paper without looking at him.

Williams sat down across from him. "You wrote *mercury* and *double-edged sword*. Is that right?"

"Yes," Tony replied in a soft tone.

Williams only asked this so the audio equipment being used recorded the verification. He knew full well what he had signed, but went about his business as usual.

"If you would, Tony, come and sit over here so you can see the TV screen. "Are you willing to tell me who you believe to have been in those cylinders?" asked Williams.

Tony hesitated. Looking at his feet he began to realize the CIA knew exactly what they were doing. *This is no time to mess around,* thought Tony.

Reading what Tony wrote Williams asked, "Are these codes of some sort?"

I guess they don't know everything. They don't know about "my" code, thought Tony.

"I'm willing to bet you can associate a name with each," Williams challenged.

Tony said, "I'm not just going to say it out loud to be tricked. I'll write down the names, but how are you going to prove to me if I'm right or wrong?"

"We have a camera on them just outside the door."

Tony wasn't going to play by Williams' rules. "I'll write as you asked, but pardon me for saying that I don't trust you as far as I can throw you. How about you bring those tubes back in here and open them in front of me so I know you haven't played any video tricks," Tony proposed.

"That's excellent," said Williams as if he were a proud father.

"First you write what each code name means then we'll get the tubes back in here in exact order and we'll have a look. Again, you don't have to say a word if you don't want to," added Williams.

He pressed the speaker phone and, as ordered, in came the silver shiny tubes one more time.

"Hand me your paper," Williams said.

Tony folded it and gave it to him.

Once again Williams set the tubes up side-by-side just as before. Tony knew they were in exactly the same order because of a small scratch mark on the stainless steel that he noticed on the left one from before.

Both Tony and Williams stood over the first tube. "Would you mind if I took a look at what you wrote before we open them?" asked Williams.

"I don't care," said Tony.

Williams took a step back and unfolded the paper. He quietly took in a deep breath then looked at what Tony had written. Suddenly, it was as if someone let the air out of a Macy's Day Parade balloon.

"What's wrong with you?" asked Tony.

"Uh…I just had such high hopes. Well, let's get to it," Williams said dejectedly. Tony stared at him not understanding his change in mood.

Williams pressed a button at the top of the cylinder. As he was busy Tony took the opportunity to quietly release a couple quick tics. The overlapping cover slowly began to rotate into itself revealing Senior Special Agent Dennis Forman.

"Hello, Director Williams. Hello Mr. James," said Forman in a playful tone. "How'd he do?" Forman quietly followed up.

"He's one for one," said Williams.

Forman sat up and awaited the next cylinder to be opened. Don then told Forman to remain silent.

"Tony, can you tell me why you first wrote *mercury* for the contents of this cylinder?"

"Yes I can."

Williams waited and Forman did the same. "Well, what's the answer?" asked Williams.

"I'll tell you privately," Tony said turning to look straight at Forman.

"Okay. I have no problem with that," Williams said slowly. "All right, let's get to the other cylinder," said Williams.

"Wait," said Tony.

Williams turned to him and said in a hopeful tone, "You want to change what you wrote for this one, don't you?"

"No. I want you to get him out of here before you open the other one," said Tony tilting his head at Forman.

Williams agreed and off went Forman with the greatest dumbstruck expression that Tony will never forget. The door was then secured shut behind him. Tony turned to look at the TV and he saw an irritated Agent Forman. Tony smiled.

"Are you ready now, Tony?"

"I am."

Williams asked Tony to do the honors. He pressed the button and then noticed Williams had turned and taken a few steps back.

"Where are you going?" asked Tony.

The cylinder door began to move. "I'm just disappointed that's all."

"Why?"

"I really thought you had the ability which is the key to —", he stopped mid-sentence with his eyes as big as saucers and mouth hanging open.

"Tony!"

"Audrey!"

"I thought nobody was ever going to open this thing! What's wrong with him?" Audrey asked now sitting up looking at Don.

Williams was flush up against his desk bracing himself so as not to fall.

"I have no idea," said Tony.

"Are you okay Don?" asked Audrey.

Tony's head whipped around so fast toward Audrey they both could hear his neck crack.

"You know him?" asked Tony.

Realizing her mistake she said, "I do know him. Don, you look like you've seen a ghost," said Audrey.

"Yeah, what gives?" Tony asked Williams.

Williams looked at Tony, Audrey, then the paper in his shaking hand. He turned to Tony and asked, "How...how did you know? Agent Stark was supposed to be in there. I set that up personally," he said perplexed.

"Don't look at me. I just wrote down what I was supposed to," said Tony.

"Were you tipped off or something?" Williams asked.

"Oh, you didn't get the memo? My boss is coming by today in a coffin-like stainless steel tube," Tony said sarcastically. "How could I possibly have known since you've had me under surveillance since I got here?" declared Tony.

"Is that true Don?" Audrey said forcefully.

The look of Don's confusion began to change as a slight grin appeared while looking at Tony. Both Tony and Audrey were looking at Don's fragmentation of emotions spilling out. They looked at each other with equally confused looks on their faces.

Audrey then asked Tony to help her out of the cylinder. As she planted her feet on the floor she brushed her navy blue pant suit as if getting ready to make a proper entrance to a high profile meeting. She straightened up and looked directly at Tony.

"Have you been treated all right?" she asked Tony in a motherly tone.

"I'm fine," said Tony.

Audrey leaned in and gave Tony a big hug which he returned in kind.

As they embraced she very quietly whispered into his ear furthest from Williams, "Jacquelyn got your code."

Tony's eyes opened wide. He was so relieved and could feel his body relax for the first time all day. As they pulled away from their embrace they both looked at each other. They each had questions for one another, but knew the time for that was later.

Chapter 45

Williams began to compose himself then said, "All right you two. Let's sit down."

Once again back in the conference area of his office Don handed Audrey a pen with a document they both recognized. Tony could see how many pages of signatures there were with Audrey's name in a red folder that was stamped confidential. Confused, Tony looked from the NDA to Audrey then to Williams. Audrey averted her eyes.

Knowing from Audrey's reaction toward Williams when appearing from the cylinder, Tony couldn't help but see there was some kind of history between the two. Williams put the signed form into the red folder and placed it on his desk.

Tony wanted to get the jump on the conversation so he asked, "How do the two of you know each other?"

They both began at the same time stumbling over each other's words.

Don politely acquiesced to Audrey and said, "Be my guest."

Audrey explained how CIT, through Ryan O'Connor's efforts, began to form a relationship with the government for contract work many years ago.

Maybe that explains O'Connor's appearance today, thought Tony.

Taking the cue from Audrey, Don interjected that before this assignment he used to work on the information technology side for "The Company".

"You worked for CIT?"

"No, Tony, that's just a nickname for what we call the CIA," said Don.

"So the two of you have known each other for how long?" asked Tony.

Don and Audrey looked at each other and once again trampled on each other's words.

Different answers. Why the different answers, he wondered.

Audrey began answering much more quickly than Williams. However, they both still talked over one another again.

"Okay. Tony we need to start from the beginning," said Williams. "I want to remind you that you signed a non-disclosure agreement. You can't tell anyone what I'm about to tell you."

Tony nodded in agreement thinking, *You signed one too*.

"Don, don't you think it would be more prudent to explain to Tony exactly why he's here? I think you owe him, as well as me, an explanation of your actions," said Audrey choosing her words carefully.

"I suppose you're right," he said. Audrey became a spectator at this point. She'd jump in if she felt it necessary.

428

"Are you okay with that Tony?" asked Don.

Since the idea came from Audrey he said, "Sure."

"I think you know why I set up the cylinder test," Williams said leading Tony.

"Of course, you had to verify for yourself what you based your hypothesis upon. But why were you so surprised when your agent wasn't in the cylinder?"

"That's a good question," Williams said striking a look at Audrey.

He continued, "I had Agent Stark set up to be in the second cylinder so when I saw that you had written Audrey's name I then believed you failed. At that point I thought you to be of little use to my program. Up until then you showed more promise than any candidate to date," he said. "Then…well you know the rest," explained Williams.

"Tony, as you well know, we live in a world full of technology. Keeping our country safe is at the top of the list for most public servants within the Department of Homeland Security."

"You said most, not all," commented Tony.

"Thanks for picking up on that", Williams replied glancing at Audrey.

Once again he continued, "There are some who are in this business for the wrong reasons. I don't pretend to understand their line of thinking." In an impassioned tone Williams said, "Prior to 1990 our government put more emphasis and money into the development of what we refer to as "boots on the ground." These are real people doing the job of keeping the citizens of America safe. After 1990 we all fell in love with technology. The "techies" began to be promoted into positions of power. This resulted in the replacement of good solid agents in the field who'd built relationships and could communicate and think as only a human being can. As mentioned already we know technology really is wonderful. However, nothing can beat the human brain. Right after 9/11 we were all given a challenge by The Secretary of Defense to bring something new to the table. The world had changed on one historic day. I felt we had a mandate to get back to the powerful intelligence gathering, not just by means of technology, but also by putting boots back on the ground. Our task was to become a blended intelligence gathering product."

Audrey's experience aided her in seeing that Don was heading down the track of too much detail.

She piped up and asked, "Specifically how does that impact Tony?"

Don looked at Audrey with a blank face. The message was clear that Audrey wants to appear to be a background player in this.

Williams continued, "We already have a team of assets that are working on various aspects within SSD."

"When you say assets you mean people with so-called special talents or abilities?" asked Tony.

"That's right. I'm not at liberty to divulge information regarding any of them or what field of expertise in which they're involved. I hope you can appreciate that Tony," Williams said as an additional follow up.

"Yes, actually it puts my mind at ease a little. At this point the less I know the better," he said.

"To date I've placed each asset into the best possible situations to utilize and take full advantage of their talents and abilities on an individual basis. My vision is to create mix and match teams to work together building off each other's specialization. The problem has been finding someone who has the unique ability and characteristics that could take the lead role once in the field."

"Is that what you meant by me being the key?" asked Tony.

"Exactly," Williams said pointing at Tony.

Tony ran this through in his mind and wasn't sure how he could be considered the key, so he let Williams continue.

"You see, Tony, you have a very unique ability to see into the core of individuals with whom you meet. Your actualized ability is that you can't be fooled. To you, people are who they truly are. There's something within you that detects the very heart of a person's most dominant characteristic. It seems as though your ability requires no time to develop. It's instantaneous. We don't have technology that can come close to what you do automatically in a matter of seconds," he added.

"So how does that make me the key for you and your team?" asked Tony.

"First, you could cut through almost all the steps you had to go through. Second, you have a natural instinct to lead. Third, you not only want to do the right thing, but you act upon it."

"How could I possibly take the place of what you have right now?" asked Tony.

"Think about it Tony. You just have to meet the person of interest and you could give a thumbs-up or a thumbs-down based on your instantaneous assessment. It would save time, money and speed up one of the slowest processes that we have in recruiting the right assets to protect American lives," Williams said emphatically. "And that would just be the beginning. Your leadership on our teams in the field would give us an advantage that no one could equal."

"Are you telling me after further recruitment you want me to play a part in actual spy games?"

"We don't call it that, but absolutely," Williams said insistently.

Tony thought about this for a few moments. It didn't go unnoticed to Tony that Audrey has remained silent. *Where's your protective instincts for me now*, he wondered.

"Okay, let's say you're right. We just met. How do you know I have what it takes to lead in an arena such as this?" asked Tony.

Don and Audrey looked at each other. It was time for her to jump in.

"Tony, in all my years I have never seen a young man with the aptitude to be in the right place at the right time as you. Furthermore, you manage to always take a clever and correct line of action," she said.

"No offense Audrey, but we've really only known each other for a short period of time," said Tony.

"Maybe it's been short for you."

What does that mean? Tony wondered.

"Director Williams isn't the only one who knows how to do a background check. Well before being hired you were tagged as a person of interest even before you applied for your job at CIT."

It wasn't lost on Tony the verbiage Audrey had just used. "There is an area of our business in which we look for people who think differently than most. In your case this goes back a number of years to your professional racquetball days."

Tony's eyebrows rose upward as he heard this.

"What're you talking about Audrey?"

"Well, Tony, what would you say was the difference between you and the rest of the players you competed against?"

"What does that have to do with —" he was cut off.

"It has everything to do with it. Now, come on and think," she prodded.

I pray to God she's not talking about Tourette's, he thought.

433

"I'd have to say my preparation," Tony said playing along.

"Yes, that would be part of it. However, it was the skill you possessed in how you thought your way around your opponents, Tony," she proclaimed.

"How would you know?" he asked in a slightly demanding tone.

"My husband, God rest his soul, was an avid player back then. Most CEOs would golf or have other activities when they traveled. Andrew loved to play racquetball. He played for his health and by no means was he even close to your level of a tournament player. But, Andrew was a very good student of the game. Anytime he had the opportunity he would schedule his travels around the pro tournaments. Since we built a small presence in all fifty states he of course traveled to each one of them. Andrew almost always came home with a racquetball story. Since you were a local player he watched you play in the US Open. He couldn't stop talking about how you would adjust your style of play just as your opponents began to understand your strategy. Andrew said you seemed to know exactly when to change tactics at precisely the perfect time and your mind was your most lethal weapon. He said something to the effect of while your opponents were playing checkers you seemed to be playing chess. At this point he began to make sure he watched you play as much as possible. Andrew marveled at your physical skills, but was truly in awe of your mental abilities to surgically dismantle your opponents. I remember him talking about you and how uniquely you defeated your opponents. He said you did it in a different manner almost every match. You became a person of interest to my husband and therefore of course CIT," she finished.

"Are you saying I was pre-destined to work at CIT?" Tony asked incredulously.

"No, I'm not saying that at all. However, we do keep records of people we've run across that are…of interest," she said.

"So when I applied my name was flagged as being one of the many people of interest?"

"That's exactly right Tony."

"So the job was mine when I filed my application?"

"It's a little more involved than that," she said in a slight condescending tone.

"You said something about an area of CIT's business that you look for people who think differently. What'd you mean by that?" asked Tony.

Audrey turned to Don to confirm, "He signed, right?"

"We wouldn't be having this conversation if he hadn't. You know that Audrey," he said.

Audrey turned to Tony and began to explain the relationship between the US government and CIT. She left out quite a few details, but Tony got the idea that they worked hand-in-hand, and needed certain types of personnel to work on that side of the business.

"Okay, now I get why some employees are top notch and others are, let's just say…average," said Tony delicately.

He was thinking of his original boss who didn't even know he went floor hopping.

"I wish that were the case Tony, but that's just corporate America. As you know there's a full range of skill levels," she replied. Then she added one more piece of the puzzle. "Tony, do you think it was a coincidence we were in the same coffee shop that Sunday morning when we met? I'll fill you in another time about that," she said.

Holy crap! How deep does this rabbit hole go?!, he wondered.

Tony had been convinced Director Williams was onto something when it came to people who had special abilities. Tony was stunned to find out that CIT knew more about him than he ever imagined. So he decided that in order for him to move forward and get home he needed to press the issue further.

"Don, what are you asking of me?" Tony leaned forward asking.

He looked at Tony, crossed his left leg on top of his right and said, "Come work for me."

Tony looked at Audrey and was shocked to see her so calm. *This guy is trying to steal one of your employees and you just sit there?*, he thought.

"But I work for Audrey at CIT," exclaimed Tony.

"I don't mean you would be leaving CIT. You would be…on call…as needed," he said adding the last part to make it sound a little better.

"You're offering me a job with the CIA?" Tony asked bluntly.

"I am," said Williams.

"And you're okay with this Audrey?"

She chose her words carefully. "We all have a duty Tony," she answered. Then she followed up with, "You'll still be working for me at CIT."

"I have one last thing I need cleared up," said Williams.

"Why did you write *mercury* regarding Senior Special Agent Forman?"

"*Mercury* indicates to me that he's hard to put your finger on. You know…slippery," said Tony.

Don gave a knowing smile. "And what's the meaning of *double-edged-sword?*"

"No offense Audrey, but it just meant to me there are two very different sides to you."

"Amazing," Don and Audrey said, almost in unison.

"You pegged me the minute I walked into that coffee shop, but just didn't know the context yet," she said.

After many questions from Tony to Don he was satisfied with how everything would work. He'd continue in the same capacity at CIT, but also work for the government of the

United States, specifically the CIA in SSD. Tony's head was swimming. He didn't think he was up for the task.

Director Williams finally said the words Tony was longing to hear. "Go home and think about it. That's all I ask. If you have any questions give me a call and we'll discuss it."

Tony said, "I don't think Jacquelyn's going to like this too much."

Don jumped in quickly, looking as if he were going to pounce, and said, "Nobody can know about this Tony, not even your wife."

"I have to tell her," Tony said defiantly.

"Do you remember the non-disclosure agreement you signed?"

Tony remained silent.

"The United States Government severely punishes those who choose to ignore them."

"What do you mean by severe?" asked Tony.

"In a nutshell you'll be hurting the very person you will tell because you'll be in prison," Don said bluntly.

Tony looked at Audrey and she sheepishly nodded her head in confirmation. He looked back at Don then moved to Audrey once again. His eyes were pleading with Audrey to speak up regarding this. She didn't disappoint him.

"Tony, at some time in all our lives we must think of the greater good. You have the potential and opportunity to do a lot of good for our country. I believe Jacquelyn would understand you protecting her, Sam and Nick. I promise you that in time you will come to embrace the fact you could change history in a positive way. You'd only be trying to do what's right."

Tony looked at her and let the words sink in.

"I think you need to fly home with me and give this some deep consideration," she said in a comforting voice.

Chapter 46

Tony and Audrey, the only passengers on the private jet, sat on the tarmac in silence. Audrey broke in and asked, "Did you get in touch with Jacquelyn?"

Tony, looking out the window of the jet had a delayed and distant reaction to Audrey's question. "What? Oh, yeah I did."

Tony's watch alarm rang out telling him it was time for his medication.

A little embarrassed, he looked at Audrey. She said, "As far as I'm concerned Tony, it's one of the many things that make you even more interesting. When you don't have so much on your mind I'd like to learn more about Tourette's than what I read in your file," she said.

Which file would that be? The Government's or CIT's, he wondered.

Tony downed his medication, buckled back up and went back to staring out the window as the jet began to pick up speed. *I never told anyone outside of Jacquelyn about my diagnosis. What doesn't she know?*

As they were in the air they could speak even more freely over the jet engine noise. Tony had a few things he needed to clear up with her. He looked at Audrey sitting directly across from him and asked, "Before I ask how you became involved in today's events, can you tell me why Ryan O'Connor was there?"

"As I said Tony, some people work in different areas of CIT."

"So you weren't surprised?" She didn't have time to answer as Tony fired off another question. "Was he really detained or was that all a show?"

"I don't really know," she said with a slightly confused look on her face. "I just don't know why or how he got into that building in the first place," she said as her voice trailed off.

"How'd you wind up in one of the cylinders?" Tony asked bluntly.

Audrey knew this question was coming and didn't hesitate. "I received a phone call last night and hopped on this private jet to get here as quickly as possible. It was Jacquelyn. She called very concerned that something was wrong because she couldn't reach you and you hadn't contacted her. I know Don's boss pretty well and let's just say he owed me one. It was in his best interests as well. He thought throwing a monkey wrench into that last test would bring some added validity to it."

Tony wasn't surprised Jacquelyn called her. *But that was last night. I just spoke with her a few hours ago using our code for Sam and Nick. The timing doesn't add up*, thought Tony. He decided that could wait.

After a short time looking out the window Tony's peripheral vision caught Audrey glancing at him every now and then. He decided to confront her with a few things that had been nagging him.

"Audrey, were you part of the thing at the executive lounge at Portland International?"

Keeping this from him was weighing on her. She thought if he wound up working at CIT and with the CIA that transparency was crucial. Her answer came quickly.

"I was part of it, but not proud of it," she said.

This stunned Tony for just a few seconds. He remembered the double-edged sword aspect she brought to the table.

"What about Ryan O'Connor? Did you send him into the conference room?"

"I had nothing to do with that."

Audrey indeed had nothing to do with that. She was kept in the dark. The fact was that Ryan O'Connor was one of the calls Don Williams made before he would appear in front of Tony in the conference room. He asked O'Connor to come by. Don properly set up his secure entry to the building and allowed him access to the conference room. He didn't tell him the real reason why. Ryan, so eager to please the hand that feeds CIT bolted over at the speed of light to continue to build his relationship with Don Williams.

Don's reasoning was to show Tony that someone he knows from his own world knew he was there. A single

442

solitary lifeline if you will. Don thought it would tip the scales in his favor. It did. Prior to that, he had contacted Ryan to call Jacquelyn and told him what to say to her.

Don Williams had become one of the most powerful contacts Ryan O'Connor developed over the many years he represented CIT in Washington, D.C. Quite a lot of business came his way courtesy of Don Williams. Of course Ryan thought he had cultivated a close relationship with Don for the purposes of obtaining favor for CIT. In fact, it was the other way around. All along Don was playing Ryan like a fiddle. He saw no harm. In the end both parties would benefit. Williams didn't tell Audrey about the role Ryan O'Connor unwittingly played. He made sure O'Connor wouldn't say a word to Audrey if he wanted more business thrown his way.

Audrey then told Tony of her conversations she had with Jacquelyn.

"Ryan O'Connor showing up just didn't add up Tony. This was something that was to play out with no interference from external forces. There was to be no outside interfering from anyone. As you know this is a serious matter that either is right or not. There's no gray in-between. In this case Ryan interfered for some reason of which I have no details." Her eyes seemed to fade into another dimension.

"Tony, you don't have to answer this, but when you met Ryan for the first time, did you get a feeling about him?"

Tony paused for a brief moment.

"I understand if you don't want to tell me", said Audrey.

"That's not it," said Tony. "I just don't think you'd believe me if I told you."

"After watching you in action and with your track record...I'd believe you," she said resolutely.

"The first time I met him was at corporate headquarters. I'd just started floor hopping. I entered the elevator on the fifth floor and he was the only other passenger. It hit me like a ton of bricks, but I didn't think much of it."

"Why not"?

"Because at the time I didn't know who he was. I'd never seen him before. He was very upbeat and happy to talk. I figured I'd just stay out of his way."

"That's Ryan O'Connor alright. As you know by now he talks to everyone," said Audrey.

Tony began to tell her then stopped, because he thought she'd think he was making it up. He wasn't. Tony could remember that moment clearly.

"Tony, I trust you and I hope you know that you can trust me. Jacquelyn did last night when she turned to me for help."

She sealed the deal with that.

"What I felt was...*traitor,* Tony said awkwardly. He knows she and O'Connor are very close. "I didn't understand what it meant then and I still don't," he said quickly as if apologizing. "But, then again, I haven't thought much about it either."

Audrey just stared at Tony.

444

She broke the silence and said, "Just so you know I didn't trust him as far as I could throw him when we were first introduced. Obviously that changed over the years."

It was Tony's turn to reflect and look out the window.

The private corporate jet touched down at Portland Hillsboro Airport without the usual hassles of its larger counterpart. Tony reminded Audrey that he flew commercial out of Portland International. Audrey offered a ride. This gave her a chance to talk a little more to him.

"Let the offer from Don marinate. Settle back in and try to get this whole thing out of your mind if you can and try to enjoy time with your family."

She ordered him to take the next week off. Tony didn't hesitate to obey his boss.

"However, I'd like to meet sometime mid-week and discuss it." Audrey added, "Tony, remember that Director Williams does not kid around about prosecuting anyone who violates the government's non-disclosure agreement, especially when it comes to his very own case files."

Tony and Audrey then said their goodbyes at street level in front of the Portland International parking structure elevators. As he walked through his parking level Tony noticed a man to his left smoking a cigarette next to the blue level painted concrete pillar. Further ahead, about forty yards, he saw the burning embers of another cigarette. This one to his right. Slowly Tony felt himself give into the feeling that they were here for him. He began to perspire, but continued to look straight ahead. His urge to tic was beginning to get the best of him however not as intense as before. His new medication continuing to work very well.

Deliberately dropping his car keys, Tony bent down to pick them up looking back inconspicuously to locate the first smoker and was filled with relief.

Not coming for me yet, he thought.

The person was still there. He looked ahead and saw the other person stamp out the small cigarette butt. Pretending to tie his shoe Tony pressed his car alarm on his keychain. The blaring sound of his still vehicle caught the attention of both of them. At almost the exact same time they started walking toward him. Tony was frozen with fear. Then the two turned ninety degrees and began to walk toward the Hertz car rental stationed on this parking level. He pressed the alarm button once again to shut it off and waited to catch a better view of them as they turned to look back. Both were wearing the uniform of Hertz employees. It was just his imagination shoved into overdrive.

Welcome to my new world, he thought.

Once in his car he could only think of the scene in the movie "Pelican Brief" where once the key in the ignition is turned the car blows up. Tony took a deep breath, turned the key and...the engine started. *I don't know if I'm cut out for this stuff,* he thought. He drove out of the concrete structure and began his trip home.

As he was driving he had to think what he was going to tell Jacquelyn. Audrey's voice and words of caution kept creeping in.

I don't think I should keep this from her. On the other hand I can't allow myself to be prosecuted for violating an agreement with the US government, he thought.

The dialog inside his head continued until he finally reached his street and he could see his home. *I'll be honest and answer any question she has without violating the agreement. Jacquelyn and the kids come first. I'm going to protect and defend my family. I just can't put them in a precarious situation over this. But, I've literally got something in my back pocket to work with*, he decided.

Chapter 47

He pulled into the driveway and pressed the remote button to open the garage door. To his surprise Jacquelyn, along with Sam and Nick wearing their pajamas ran out to greet him. Sam got to him first with Nick right behind.

"Daddy!" they shouted and jumped up into his waiting arms.

"Did you bring me anything?" asked Sam excitedly.

Nick took the cue from his big sister. "Yeah, what'd I get?" he shouted.

Tony was so glad to see, and not surprisingly, that Jacquelyn had insulated the kids from the last two days events. With Tony's hands full Jacquelyn reached hers to Tony's face and gave him a great big kiss. The kids made noises as if they were being tortured.

"I missed you," said Jacquelyn.

"I love you too," Tony said with a smile.

Later, Tony and Jacquelyn sat on the couch in the living room next to each other holding hands. Jacquelyn began to ask what seemed to be a million questions about Tony's trip back to D.C. He focused on the idea that the government thought he was in on the terrorist activities that day at the White House.

"What? Are they nuts?"

"Just covering all their bases I guess."

Jacquelyn, ever so sensitive to Tony's needs, then asked about how his new medication worked out in this extra stressful situation. This was something Tony could latch onto and avoid more sensitive questions, at least for now.

"There's no way I could have gotten through without it. I can't believe what a difference it's made in my life," Tony said excitedly. "I almost feel normal," he added. "I'm so sorry I didn't call. They wouldn't let me communicate with anyone except them."

"Why was that anyway?" asked Jacquelyn.

"I guess that's how seriously they take defending the good old US of A."

"I suppose it's better than the alternative," she said in an almost defeated tone.

"Maybe it's because the guy I turned in is a wanted terrorist," he said.

"What? He's a real terrorist?" she exclaimed. Jacquelyn now completely understood why Tony wasn't allowed to contact anyone until they were satisfied he had nothing to do with this man's terrorist activities.

Tony's week off was now at its halfway point. Normally he'd begin feeling as if he were going back to the grind. However, this evening he was looking forward to his new day…his new adventures.

Jacquelyn took the kids to school the next day so Tony could leave early for his quick meeting with Audrey at CIT.

Audrey met Tony as soon as he got off the elevator. She offered him a cup of coffee as part of their tradition. As he followed her he couldn't help but look at the white framed full length mirror and wonder. They sat at the circular table with comfortable chairs and exchanged pleasantries. Tony felt somewhat of a new kindred spirit with Audrey. He wondered how many large company CEOs worked with the various government agencies in the way she does.

"Tony let's get down to business if you don't mind," she said in a sincere tone as if she really did want to know if he minded. "I've been asked to be your handler here in Portland," she said flatly.

"What does a handler do?" asked Tony.

"It's a fancy word for the go-between."

"Between what?" he asked.

"Basically I'll know exactly what you're doing for the government and help facilitate any of your needs. I'll also be your sounding board here."

Tony was pleased that this would be the case.

"You said here. I take it a handler's been designated in our nation's capital then?" he asked.

He was thinking of turning it down if he had to deal with Senior Special Agent Dennis Forman.

"Yes, Agent Forman has accepted the role for now," she said excitedly.

Audrey could see in Tony's eyes he was not happy with this news. "Tony, I've known Dennis for quite some time. He's excellent. I don't know what went on out there between the two of you, but I can assure you he is the best."

Somehow her conviction softened Tony's view for the moment.

"Why are you talking as if I've decided to do it?" he asked.

"Tony you know your ability has saved lives before and you're not afraid to act upon your natural impulse," she said seriously.

"You almost sound as if I don't have a choice," he said.

"Of course you have a choice, Tony. I'm sorry, but I assumed —" she didn't finish.

"Well, you know what happens when we assume," Tony said stone-faced. He gave her a few seconds to catch up with his sarcasm.

She slowly smiled and said, "You, Mr. James, keep me young."

After explaining he was only placing one test toe in the water at the moment, Tony had some things he wanted cleared up for his sake.

"What happened with Ryan O'Connor?" he asked.

"All I can tell you is nothing has changed. He's still CIT's Vice President in charge of sales."

Audrey's phrasing wasn't lost on Tony.

"You can't or won't tell me more?"

"I can't," she said with a knowing look.

Little did Tony know, but Audrey really didn't have any idea about the truth just yet. At that moment Tony figured she'd been muzzled by the pen stroke of her initials and signature. Tony doesn't trust O'Connor, but let it go for now.

Where there's smoke there's fire, he thought.

"So how did you clear your conscience by not telling Jacquelyn everything?"

"Who's to say I didn't," Tony answered flatly.

Audrey looked at his poker face trying to figure out if he was being sarcastic once again. "No, really, how'd it work out?" she followed up.

"Audrey, that's something you'll have to just trust me on. You have your secrets and I have mine," he said. He could see that Audrey was not comfortable with the uncertainty of this.

Tony added, "I work for CIT. I now also work for SSD, the CIA or is it XYZ? Well, something from the alphabet soup anyway. I answer to my employers regarding *work*. My home life is private and off limits", he said with intensity. Then he added "Besides, how do I know who's listening in on our conversation right now?" He motioned toward the mirror.

452

"Please tell Don I'm going to give it a try and if it doesn't feel right I'm out."

"Consider it done," she agreed.

"Also, just so you're aware I've made arrangements with two separate attorneys regarding the NDA Director Williams signed. It's my insurance policy."

"That was a brilliant move," said Audrey.

She wasn't' there when I had him sign it and I never told her. Only one other person could have told her. They talk to each other more than she let's on, he decided.

Audrey looked at him and said enthusiastically, "Good for you Tony. I wouldn't have it any other way."

She knew Tony well enough to know he'll find great personal satisfaction just as she has over these many years. They talked for a while longer on many subjects then Audrey looked at her watch and said, "I'm sorry Tony, but I have a conference call in fifteen minutes and I need to prepare."

Tony didn't know if this was CIA, FBI, SSD or CIT business. He really didn't care. He still had a few more days off.

"Before you go Tony, Director Williams asked me to give this to you."

Audrey walked behind her desk and picked up the plain, brown sealed box. She walked back with a smile and presented it to him.

"It's probably not best that you open it here. I'll see you Monday," she said.

As Tony was riding the second elevator down to go to his car it hit him that his life had changed considerably from the time he was diagnosed with Tourette's to accepting a secret job with the government. Tony quickly punched number two on the elevator panel. He stopped on the second floor to pick up some needed supplies for his home office. Tony entered the supply room and found it to be unoccupied.

His thoughts reflected back in time to when a six year old little boy had been tagged by a tormentor that seemed to try to crush him. Then, for some inexplicable reason, he thought of how diamonds were made. They're under continuous constant pressure resulting in one of the most coveted items on earth. They don't look like much at first, but after being highly polished, they're almost priceless. He wished he could go back in time and tell that little guy that one day he'll sparkle like a diamond. Then a dreadful thought entered his mind. Tony realized he was still going to have to continue to cover up at a whole new level.

"My lot in life is that of a diamond still in the rough. No polishing for me," he said aloud in a melancholy tone.

Tony felt a surge of gratitude towards Dr. Dillon. Then he felt a deep sadness filling his heart. Tony stood in the middle of the room and realized he's one of the lucky ones. He certainly still had verbal and physical tics, though so greatly reduced, through his efforts and the wonders of the medical community.

So many people with this disorder just don't stand a chance.

He didn't feel particularly talented. Tony knew he wasn't the smartest guy around. He felt so very average looking. His sense of himself is that of a survivor, nothing more. And there he stood with the need to release just a few very minor tics. Nothing he couldn't cover up if required. Tony stood quietly in a room that used to give him relief and began to realize the extraordinary journey he's been on.

Right then and there Tony declared he would do everything in his power to help his fellow Tourette's sufferers and others.

I now have access and leverage to people at the very top of the money ladder for research. I can help, he thought.

The image of him and Jacquelyn star gazing while on their glider rocker came flooding back. He remembered her question like it was yesterday.

When did you first realize you had this unique ability at your disposal?

At the time he thought that question was a big deal. Now, given his current circumstance, he realized he was just at the base of the mountain ready to ascend to the unknown.

Tony got into his car after placing the office products in his back seat. He did a double-take and decided to put the box from Don on the front passenger seat. Tony started the car and began to put the shift into reverse then paused and changed his mind. His curiosity of the box got the best of him.

He opened it to reveal a Smartphone. It looks exactly like the one he currently has. To his surprise the phone was almost fully charged and already on. He noticed the display showed one voice message and one text waiting. Tony put the phone on speaker and listened. He recognized the voice immediately. It was that of Director Don Williams.

"Welcome to the team. This will be the only voice message you will receive on this part of your phone. Please review the special operating instructions enclosed and destroy them once memorized. If you have questions you know who to ask. Erase this message now that you've heard it."

That was it. *What does he mean this part of the phone?* He glanced at the box and saw the instruction manual, but decided to review it sometime later. Tony deleted the message as instructed.

Next Tony read the text message. He couldn't believe his eyes. His face went ashen. The words burned themselves into his memory. Tony knew the phone number from where it came would be untraceable.

It read, "REMEMBER, NOTHING IS REALLY AS IT SEEMS."

— The End —